Praise for *Catch a Falling Star*

★ ★ ★ ★ ★

"Anytime a novel makes me tear up, laugh out loud, or put my hand against my chest because the romance is just *that* good, I tend to give it a big thumbs-up. *Catch a Falling Star* had me doing all three! It pulled me in, kept me reading well past my bedtime, and left me eager for more from this talented author. Beth Vogt knocked this one out of the park!"

—Katie Ganshert, author of
Wildflowers from Winter and *Wishing on Willows*

"Beth Vogt has once again captured my complete attention. With a slightly different feel from her debut, *Wish You Were Here,* Vogt's latest, *Catch a Falling Star,* is rich with true-to-life characters who sit down beside you and invite you into their lives. The story unfolds with humor, tenderness, and a few poignant moments that will have you savoring each well-written word. Vogt points the way toward grace, healing, and hope without preaching, but presents an honest portrayal of real lived-out faith and how it can impact lives. Another wonderful offering by this very talented author!"

—Catherine West, award-winning author of
Yesterday's Tomorrow and *Hidden in the Heart*

"*Catch a Falling Star* is one of those books you keep thinking about after the end. Poignant characters, crackling dialogue, and a central theme we can all connect with: What happens when things don't go according to plan? Beth K. Vogt writes from the heart with such an engaging voice . . . and she definitely has a permanent place on my must-read shelf!"

—Melissa Tagg, author of *Made to Last*

"Beth K. Vogt has accomplished what all debut authors aspire to do—write a great second book. *Catch a Falling Star* is fun, quirky, and filled with Vogt's well-crafted prose and signature voice. What a great thing—to discover a new author for my favorites list."

—Rachel Hauck, award-winning author of
The Wedding Dress and *Once Upon a Prince*

"This is one of *those* kinds of books: the kind you open thinking you'll just read a chapter or two, and then before you know it, you're turning the last page with a smile and sigh. I don't know how she does it, but Beth's characters seem to live and breathe. I closed the cover after reading the last page and found myself a little bit sad, wondering where all my new friends had gone."

—Siri Mitchell, author of *The Cubicle Next Door* and *Unrivaled*

"After reading Beth Vogt's debut novel, *Wish You Were Here*, I knew her books would have a permanent place on my bookshelf. *Catch a Falling Star* is laced with Beth's signature humor, well-developed characters, and spiritual truth, but her writing maturity shines. Her stellar ability to craft soul-stirring happily-ever-after romances leaves me craving more of her books. She does what every author desires—keeps readers turning pages way past their bedtimes."

—Lisa Jordan, award-winning author of
Lakeside Reunion and *Lakeside Family*

"*Catch a Falling Star,* Beth Vogt's sophomore novel, delights with an intriguing cast of characters, a page-turning plot, unexpected twists, and sharp writing. I loved this tender story framed in second chances and heartfelt dreams that proves fairy-tale lives come in all shapes and sizes."

—Megan DiMaria, author of
Searching for Spice and *Out of Her Hands*

"Beth Vogt is a rising romance star with this amazing second novel. Delightful, sparkling romance and a story that is sure to keep you up all night. Bravo!"

—Susan May Warren, bestselling and
award-winning author of *Take a Chance on Me*

ALSO BY BETH K. VOGT

Wish You Were Here

catch a falling star

★★★★★★ A NOVEL ★★★★★★

BETH K. VOGT

HOWARD BOOKS
A DIVISION OF SIMON & SCHUSTER, INC.

NEW YORK NASHVILLE LONDON TORONTO SYDNEY NEW DELHI

Howard Books
A Division of Simon & Schuster, Inc.
1230 Avenue of the Americas
New York, NY 10020

Scripture quotations marked NIV are taken from The Holy Bible, New International Version® (NIV®). Copyright © 1973, 1978, 1984 by Biblica US, Inc.® Used by permission. All other Scripture quotations are taken from the New American Standard Bible. Copyright © 1960, 1962, 1963, 1968, 1971, 1972, 1975, 1977, 1995 by the Lockman Foundation, La Habra, California. All rights reserved. http://www.lockman.org.

First Howard Books trade paperback edition May 2013

HOWARD and colophon are trademarks of Simon & Schuster, Inc.

For information about special discounts for bulk purchases, please contact Simon & Schuster Special Sales at 1-866-506-1949 or business@simonandschuster.com.

The Simon & Schuster Speakers Bureau can bring authors to your live event. For more information or to book an event, contact the Simon & Schuster Speakers Bureau at 1-866-248-3049 or visit our website at www.simonspeakers.com.

Designed by Jaime Putorti

Manufactured in the United States of America

10 9 8 7 6 5 4 3 2 1

Library of Congress Cataloging-in-Publication Data
Vogt, Beth K.
    Catch a falling star : a novel / Beth K Vogt.
        p. cm.
    1. Women physicians—Fiction. I. Title.
PS3622.O362C38 2013
813'.6—dc23
            2012029693

ISBN 978-1-4516-6027-2
ISBN 978-1-4516-6029-6 (ebook)

catch a falling star

CHAPTER ONE

★ ★ ★ ★

*W*hat exactly was she celebrating?

The question haunted Kendall all day long. It was her birthday—she ought to be able to answer it.

She pulled into a parking space outside her favorite Mexican restaurant. Shifting into neutral, Kendall turned off the Jeep and deposited her keys into her purse, exchanging them for a tattered makeup bag and her ever-handy GorillaTorch.

Just once, she'd like to put her makeup on in front of the bathroom mirror like a normal person.

Attaching the twistable hands-free flashlight to her steering wheel so her face was illuminated in her rearview mirror, Kendall twisted her body to the left so she could trace a hint of brown eyeliner. *Sheesh.* Most women used a makeup mirror. Tossing the pencil into the bag lying open on the passenger seat of her Jeep, Kendall sorted through the containers of eye shadow and lip gloss, looking for her mascara. A quick peek at her phone lying on her dash told her that she had five minutes before she was officially late to her birthday dinner. Yep. Enough time for mascara and a little blush. She assessed her short brown hair—all it required was a quick comb-through with her fingers.

Her closest friends waited inside On the Border, eager to celebrate. Nineteen hours into her birthday and she wanted to label it RETURN TO SENDER. Kendall couldn't help comparing today with her thirteenth birthday, when her mom decided to deluge her with pink frilly clothes. *Pink.* She looked like an overdose of cotton candy on a too-short stick. She returned all her gifts—except for the oversized stuffed pink bear her then-three-year-old-sister Bekah refused to release—and pocketed the cash.

Kendall swept blush across her cheeks. It wasn't that she didn't have a satisfying life—an exciting life, even. It's just that at thirty-six years old, she'd hoped for . . . more.

The buzz of her phone mocked her attempts to be on time. Why did she think she'd ever be in control of her time and be the first to arrive? She abandoned that ideal the day she entered medical school. Besides, all the other partygoers tonight were physicians like her. They'd understand when Kendall walked in late. Half made up. As usual.

She switched from blush to mascara as she turned her phone to speaker. "Dr. Haynes."

"Kendall, it's Mom."

Kendall's eyes closed as she mentally and physically sat straighter, as if her mother could see her. "Hey, Mom. How are you?"

"I'm fine. Are you having a good birthday?"

"Just finished clinic. Going to dinner with friends."

"Oh, how nice. I'm so glad you've found some friends there in Colorado."

Of course she'd found friends in Colorado. She wasn't in high school anymore. She had a thriving solo family practice, friends, even a dog to round out the picture of a satisfying life.

"Look, Mom, I'm running late—"

"Well, this is rather important . . ."

Kendall stared out the window of her Jeep, watching people walk into the restaurant. Rachel had just walked by her with a friendly see-you-inside wave. Most likely Melissa and Sonia were already seated, having ordered their usual Guac Live. Would there be any left by the time her mother finished talking?

"I've got about five minutes. Is that enough time?"

"I'll get straight to the point. Bekah's boyfriend, Ryan, is going to propose. I'd like to give him Mina's ring so he can give it to her."

Kendall dropped the tube of gloss she'd pulled from the makeup bag. "B-but Mina bequeathed the ring to me—"

"Because she assumed you'd get married first, since you're ten years older than Bekah. You know the ring traditionally goes to the first daughter who gets married. If she'd left the ring to your father, I wouldn't be put in this awkward position of having to explain all this." Her mother's sigh echoed over the phone. "The reality is, Bekah is the one getting married. Not you."

"Yet."

"Excuse me?"

"I said 'yet.' I'm not getting married *yet*." Kendall reached for the necklace she'd slung over her rearview mirror—a strand of silver ovals that matched her earrings—and transferred it to her neck.

"You're thirty-six years old, dear. A professional woman. And in today's world, it's perfectly fine to focus on your career and stay single. No one's blaming you. But—" With a slight pause, her mother lunged with her closing argument. "—Bekah will be married in the next year. Your sister loves that ruby ring as much as you do. You know how much fun she has mixing vintage clothes with modern styles."

Had her sister coached her mother on what to say? *Make sure you remind Kendall I'm all about mixing vintage and modern, Mom. That will get her to say yes.*

Her mother's next words broke into Kendall's thoughts. "You don't want the ring to go to waste, do you?"

Of course she didn't want the ring to go to waste. But it wasn't *going to waste* . . . She was waiting to use it, that's all.

"Mom, I've gotta go. I saw Rachel walk into the restaurant, which officially makes me the last one to arrive. Again."

True statement, even if Rachel had waved at her ten minutes ago.

"But we haven't finished talking about this—"

"I'll think about it, 'k? And thanks for the birthday call."

Disconnecting, Kendall slid her feet into her four-inch platforms. Good thing tonight was all about sitting or her feet would ache within an hour. But every once in a while she enjoyed being eye-to-eye with other people. Well, almost eye-to-eye.

The warmth of the Mexican restaurant shoved away the cool night air and tucked the remnants of the phone conversation into the corner of Kendall's mind. Voices swirled around her, the scent of fresh tortillas teasing her nose and causing her stomach to rumble. The Greek yogurt she'd wolfed down mid-morning in between patients had worn off hours ago.

Thanks to a bouquet of brilliant Mylar balloons, Kendall spotted her three friends in a back corner booth. She nodded at the hostess and wove her way past tables crowded with families, couples, and several groups of college-aged kids. The steady hum of voices muted all the should-have-said-this-to-Mom responses scrolling across her mind. Words like *possession is nine-tenths of the law* shouldn't be used between a mother and daughter.

She slid into the booth next to Rachel, who gave her a quick hug and then motioned toward a black stone bowl of guacamole and a paper-lined bowl of chips. "Catch up with us. Drinks are on the way. We ordered you an iced tea. Are you on allergy call for the ER tonight?"

Kendall dipped a chip through the chunky mix of avocado, chilies, and spices. "No. Just a quick chat with my mom. You know, the required birthday call." Ignoring the rectangular envelope stamped with the name of a local salon and her name scrawled across the middle, Kendall tapped a pile of papers on the table. "What's this?"

Sonia fanned the printouts, an eager smile lighting her face. "I know it's your birthday celebration—happy birthday, by the way—but we also need to finalize our decision for this summer's trip. I've been watching the airfares and the vacation spots and narrowed it down to a couple of places."

"You don't think we should wait until we get closer to our departure date—maybe snag a last-minute deal?" Kendall squeezed lemon into her tea and then savored a long sip.

"That was easy to do when we were all single." Sonia rested her elbows on the table, soft blond curls framing her face as she seemed to hesitate for half a second. "But now that Melissa and I are both married, it's better to plan things out. Kevin still wants to find time for some sort of vacation for the two of us."

Melissa nodded, her long brown hair tucked underneath a stylish black beret. "And I need to make sure that I've got the twins covered for that week. I can't leave that until the last minute."

Made sense.

Rachel shifted in the seat next to her, twisting her hands in her lap. Her cornflower-blue eyes darted from friend to friend and she chewed on her bottom lip.

Melissa leaned forward. "Something on your mind, Rach? You're not backing out, are you?"

"No . . . I wouldn't think of missing this trip. Especially now."

"Especially now?" Kendall turned to stare at her friend. "What's that supposed to mean?"

"I'm engaged!"

Kendall reared back as Rachel flung her left arm out across the table, nearly tipping over her margarita.

Melissa and Sonia erupted in a cacophony of "What?" and "When?" causing other people in the restaurant to turn toward them. How had Kendall missed the diamond on Rachel's hand? Of course, her friend had kept her hands in her lap—not even indulging in the chips and guacamole, and taking almost-timid sips of her margarita.

"Tony proposed this past weekend. Can you believe it?" Rachel paused to admire her engagement ring, which she'd set off by indulging in a French manicure. "We've only been dating three months!"

Three months—and the man proposed? No, Kendall most definitely couldn't believe it. Their foursome had started out as a group of single female physicians, focused on establishing themselves in Colorado Springs. Now married, Melissa stayed home with her twins full-time, and Sonia worked part-time. Now Rachel was headed for "I do" while Kendall remained an "I haven't"—a status she probably wouldn't change anytime soon.

She forced herself to look at her friend's dazzling pear-shaped diamond ring. She was happy for Rachel—truly. Tony seemed like a good guy, someone who didn't mind Rachel's long hours as an ER doctor.

"Tony thinks a December wedding is perfect, so I don't see any problem with still having our girls' vacation in June." Rachel bounced on the blue vinyl-covered seat, threatening to unseat Kendall in her excitement. "Maybe we can make it a weeklong bachelorette party! I want you all to be in my wedding, you know that, right?"

Perfect. Another wear-it-once dress to add to her closet. It seemed as though she'd never break the tradition she started way back in high school. Of course, she didn't even get to wear her homecoming dress for the entire evening.

Whoa. Rachel was engaged and she was wandering the wrong way down memory lane. Where was the waiter? She needed a refill.

"Melissa, I was hoping you'd be my matron of honor." Rachel reached across the table and clasped Melissa's hand even as her smile encompassed each friend. "And I want Kendall and Sonia to be my bridesmaids."

Oh.

Kendall hoped her face didn't reveal any surprise or disappointment. Of course, Rachel could arrange her bridal party any way she wanted. Kendall shouldn't assume she'd be the maid of honor.

A lanky teen boy wearing a faded T-shirt and baggy jeans crossed her line of vision. What was wrong with him? Exiting the restroom area to a table in the center of the room, he seemed unsteady on his feet, almost disoriented. Was he . . . high? He slumped into a wooden chair, a series of raspy coughs shaking his shoulders. Maybe he was coming down with the flu. A broad-shouldered man with short-cropped hair sprinkled with gray—probably his father—leaned toward him, as if asking a question. Kendall watched as the coughing grew worse and the boy tugged on the collar of his maroon T-shirt. Maybe he was choking . . . But why wasn't the kid's father doing anything?

"Kendall. Kendall." Sonia waved a hand in front of her face. "Hey, the party's in this booth!"

"Excuse me for a minute." Kendall slid out of her seat, tossing the words over her shoulder. "Something's wrong with that kid."

By the time she crossed the floor to the table where the man and his son sat, she sensed the other customers' surveillance as she watched the teen cough. And cough. She knelt beside him. Touched his arm.

"Are you choking?" Even as she asked, she knew he wasn't. His lips were swollen, his face blotchy with hives. The boy's eyes flamed with panic as they darted between her and his father. "What are you allergic to?"

"He's not allergic—" The man stood and towered over her.

"A-avocado."

"Your son is allergic to avocado and *you didn't even know it?*" Some parents had no right to have kids. Kendall got to her feet, the swift movement causing her to rock back on her platforms. "Where is your EpiPen?"

"He doesn't have an EpiPen—"

"With this severe an allergy, your son needs to carry an EpiPen at all times."

"He's not my son—"

Kendall turned to the teen. "Do you have an EpiPen?" When he shook his head no, she shouted for Rachel to bring her purse. "Somebody call nine-one-one."

The man pulled an iPhone from the pocket of his wool jacket hanging on the back of the chair. "I'll call nine-one-one."

"Fine. Do something." She didn't mean to sound so abrupt,

but she didn't have time to apologize. The teen was her concern—not whether she'd offended his dad. His son needed help—fast.

Rachel appeared beside her, already digging in Kendall's purse for the EpiPen. "What can I do?"

"Call nine-one-one."

"I'm already dialing—" The man waved his phone in her face.

"Okay, then. I'm stepping back." Rachel retrieved Kendall's purse from where she'd dropped it on the floor. "But remember, I'm right over there."

"Right." Kendall focused on the teen, talking to him as she popped the cap off the plastic device. "You know how this works. It doesn't hurt that bad. Here goes. One, two, three . . ."

★ ★ ★ ★ ★

Griffin wanted to turn away—maybe even walk out the door and escape what was happening. But he hadn't done that, not once in the last four months, no matter how many times the thought crossed his mind. Standing here, watching his brother gasp for breath, only confirmed once again that Griffin was the last person who should take responsibility for Ian.

"Have you reached nine-one-one?" His brother's rescuer barely glanced at him.

Her question jerked him back to reality. He punched the numbers before answering her and then stayed on the line with the dispatcher and watched the woman work with his brother. Ian's teeth clenched, lips tinted a pale blue, as silent tears streamed down his face. Ian hadn't shed a single tear during their parents' funeral. Did he even realize he sat in the middle of a restaurant, crying? Probably not. He was too busy struggling to breathe, despite the woman kneeling next to him and at-tempting to keep him calm.

While the dispatcher talked with the ambulance driver, Grif-fin paced closer, tilting the phone away from his mouth. "Who are you?"

She flicked her eyes up at him for the briefest of moments, a look of irritation storming across their gray depths before she focused on Ian again. "I'm a physician. I'll take care of your son until the EMTs get here."

"Ian's my brother, not my son."

"Look, I can't really have a conversation with you and con-centrate." The woman brushed the long strands of Ian's dark hair away from his eyes, her tone softening. "Feeling any better? Y'know, if you were gonna do something like this, you picked a good place. All my friends over there? They're doctors, too."

The hint of a smile crossed Ian's face, despite the fact his breath still wheezed in and out as if his lungs were a pair of worn-out accordions.

"Sir, can you hear the sirens yet?" The dispatcher's dispas-sionate voice broke in on his thoughts. "They should be almost there by now."

With everyone in the restaurant silently watching the drama at their table, Griffin could easily hear the strident wail of the approaching medical truck. "Yes, I hear them."

"How's he doing now, sir? You said he's your brother, right?"

"He's better." Griffin watched for flickers of emergency lights outside the restaurant's front window. "There's a doctor here. She had an EpiPen."

"Good. If he was having a severe allergic reaction, she did the right thing."

Griffin scanned Ian's face, noticing that, while he was still pale, the blotchiness was fading. The doctor had gotten Ian to sit up straight rather than slump forward in his chair. She'd kicked off a ridiculous pair of shoes and looked barely more than a teenager herself—a female Doogie Howser. Had he risked Ian's life letting this unknown woman take over?

The red-haired hostess pushed open the restaurant's wooden front doors, stepping aside to let the EMTs pass through, trundling a metal gurney across the black tile floors. Griffin could almost feel everyone in the building exhale. The manager followed the medical team over to their table. One of the EMTs nodded to the woman kneeling beside Ian.

"Hey, Doc!"

"Hey, Andrew." After a quick nod at the EMT, the woman refocused on Ian. "Good to see you again."

"You've got everything under control, I see." The man snapped on a pair of purple vinyl gloves. "Mind if I take it from here?"

"Be my guest." The woman stood. Leaned over and whispered something to Ian before patting him on the shoulder. "I'll get back to my dinner."

"Sorry for the interruption, Doc."

She winked at the EMT. "It happens."

As she bent to pick up her shoes, Griffin stepped forward. "I want to thank you for helping my brother."

Shoes dangling from her fingertips, the woman stepped back, tilting her head so she could make eye contact with him. "Ian's your brother?" She looked at Griffin, then at Ian. "You don't know him very well, do you?"

"Let's just say I haven't been my brother's keeper."

"Too bad for him." She waved aside Griffin's attempt to interrupt. "You're risking Ian's life by not knowing about his allergies. By not carrying an EpiPen *all the time*. Forget the thanks. Just be the guy Ian needs you to be."

And with that verbal slap in his face, she walked back to where her friends waited.

Not that he didn't deserve it.

Griffin positioned a chair next to his brother, watching the young man check Ian's vitals and jot notes on a clipboard. The manager talked with another EMT.

"We're recommending that Ian go to the hospital, sir." Andrew began putting the medical equipment away.

"Is that really necessary?" Griffin watched his brother, thankful he didn't have to turn his head to the left and deal with the ongoing threat of dizziness.

"Your . . . brother, is it? He had an anaphylactic reaction to eating avocado—guacamole, right? His throat started to close up on him, cutting off his airway. It's best to get him checked out more thoroughly. They might decide to keep him overnight. Or they might send him home with you. Depends."

Great. Why couldn't they just grab a quick dinner, go home, deal with homework and the pile of dirty laundry that mocked him every time he walked through the door? Nope. Nothing came easy lately. And tonight was going to be topped off with a run to the ER. If Ian was allergic to avocado, why'd he agree to Griffin ordering the chips and guac? How was Griffin supposed to know details like that? Had their mother ever mentioned allergies?

"Whatever needs to be done is fine." He watched the medical personnel settle Ian onto the gurney and then walked over to the manager. "I've already paid for my dinner. Do me a favor— the woman who helped my brother? Add her dinner to my bill."

"She's with a group, sir. It's her birthday."

"Well, since we managed to interrupt her celebration, go ahead and charge the whole thing. But don't tell her I paid for it, okay?"

★ ★ ★ ★ ★

After the night she had, Kendall was not up to Sully's attitude.

And since she'd abandoned him all evening, he would most definitely have an attitude.

Her satchel handbag slung over her shoulders, hanging on to the bunch of birthday balloons in one hand, Kendall clomped up the stairs to her loft. She inserted a key in the door's lock and pushed. The door moved an inch—and no farther.

Sully.

"This is no way to act." Kendall rested her forehead against the door. "Get out of the way of the door and let me come in."

She pushed on the door again. Nothing.

"Come on, Sully. I'm tired." She stomped her foot, balloons dancing around her face. "I'm the one paying the mortgage on this place. Let me in already!"

Another shove. Another inch.

"Let me in and I'll give you a treat . . ."

At the word *treat,* Kendall heard the welcome sound of four big paws scraping on the floors. She'd forgive the big hairy goldendoodle for scratching her custom cement floor if he'd stop stretching out in front of the door, blocking the entrance. As she stepped inside, she braced herself for Sully's frontal attack. A basso profundo "Woof!" and then two large paws landed on her shoulders.

"Off, you stupid dog. Off!" Kendall staggered back, trying to keep the balloons out of Sully's way. "Don't you even remember going to obedience school?"

Apparently not.

Sully's furry chocolate-brown face came nose-to-nose with hers, his mouth parted in a welcoming doggy grin.

"Thank you. I missed you, too. Yes, I had a nice birthday.

Somebody even paid for dinner. The girls all say hi." She shoved him down to the ground. "Now sit. Stay."

As she headed toward the kitchen, Sully bounded in front of her. "Fine. Lead."

She tossed her purse on top of the red granite countertop stretching across the front of the kitchen, separating it from her dining room/living room area. Sully nudged at her elbow until she opened a silver tin of doggie snacks and tossed him two. After tying the balloons to the back of a chair and leaving Sully lounging on the floor, she went off in search of more comfortable clothes.

Her phone went into its waiting charger. Her shoes went in the ever-growing shoe pile at the bottom of her closet. She tugged off her wide-leg black slacks and plum-colored cashmere sweater and slipped into a pair of checked pajama bottoms and a waffle-weave long-sleeved top. Rubbing her eyes, she wanted nothing more than to crawl into bed. But she was a stickler for hygiene, and her bedtime routine awaited. And before that, Sully needed a quick walk outside.

Half an hour later, Kendall sat on her bed, a faded, black-velvet jeweler's box cradled in her hands. She probably should keep this in a bank box of some sort rather than in a fire safe in the back of her closet. But she liked keeping her most treasured possession nearby.

Flicking back the lid, she traced the outline of Mina's ring.

How many times had she stared at the ring as a little girl, watching its delicate white-gold filigree glint in the sunlight as her Mina embroidered or made bread or stirred a pot of soup on the stove? How many times had she asked to wear the ring? She would slip it on her finger as she lay in bed, waiting for the tightness to ease in her lungs, while Mina read her fairy tales of princesses hidden away in towers waiting to be rescued. How many times had Mina patted her hand, whispering that one day the ring would be *hers*?

She'd lost count.

But she never lost sight of the dream hidden in the jewel's red depth. One day, she'd have it all: Romance. Love. Marriage. A husband. A family. And yes, a career, too. Because she was going to be a doctor. With all the time she spent in the hospital during her elementary and middle school years, she had at least part of a medical education just by osmosis. She would put all those hours, days, weeks, months spent in a hospital room or a doctor's office to good use and grow up and help kids like her whose lives were affected by asthma and allergies.

And she had.

She was living her dreams.

Almost.

She closed the box, the soft click a whisper of a rebuke. But it took two to make happily ever after come true—and lately no one pursued her. Well, not anyone who she wanted to be "caught" by. Kendall shook her head, catching her reflection in the mirror, the corner of her mouth twisting in the parody of a smile. Her last few dates hadn't been worth a let's-try-again to see if things would go anywhere. Both guys were hoping to get her one place: in bed. Her sister might laugh at her old-fashioned ideals, but Kendall had managed to resist temptation this far. More like fight it off.

Of course, at this rate, she might die a virgin and an old maid, clutching Mina's ring in her gnarled hands.

If that was God's will, then she was content with that.

Right?

Yes, yes, she was.

She had to be.

CHAPTER TWO

★ ★ ★ ★

*N*o matter how you tricked it out, Griffin considered a doctor's waiting room a little corner of hell.

Dr. Haynes's office wasn't bad—especially compared with the military, one-size-fits-all medical offices he tried to avoid. Maybe the civilian doc hired a professional interior designer to put everything together. Muted, earth-tone walls. Comfortable chairs that weren't so close together you needed to hold your breath to prevent inhaling your neighbor's germs. Several watercolor paintings with words woven through them. Were those Scripture verses? Since the events of the last eighteen months had stopped him from stiff-arming God, the thought intrigued him. But Griffin wasn't wandering around a doctor's office. Stroll through enemy territory? No, thank you.

Griffin shut his eyes to block out the view of his surroundings, but it only served to increase the volume of the mental soundtrack he'd tried to ignore for months.

"We'll review your health again in May, Colonel Walker, and decide then if you can return to active flying status."

These months in limbo were a tortuous wait-and-see marathon. Never fly again? That was his whole life—the only thing he cared about.

Ian shifted in the seat next to him, pulling Griffin back to reality. He needed to focus. Compartmentalize. Today's medical visit was about Ian—not him.

"Does any doctor ever see you on time?"

Griffin's thoughts exactly. "What? You're so eager to get back to school?"

"I'm missing a math test." His brother's long fingers drummed on his jeans-clad thigh. "Gonna be a hassle to make up."

"Well, I'm missing work—"

"Sorry I'm always a pain in your butt." Ian picked up a magazine, flipped it open, and began reading.

Griffin wanted to laugh out loud. Would his mom let Ian get away with that kind of talk? If he'd said that to their mom when he was sixteen, she'd have given him a liberal dose of liquid soap accompanied with a lecture. His mother wasn't . . . *hadn't been* a prude, but she demanded Griffin keep his mouth clean. If he didn't, she did it for him. He assumed she raised Ian the same way. But he left home long before his parents adopted Ian, so how could he know?

Laughter threatened again when he realized Ian was reading *Good Housekeeping*. Since when did Ian care about menu planning and coordinating his spring wardrobe? Anything to shut Griffin out. And what was his problem? Ian could complain all he wanted about being inconvenienced by the appointment, but Griffin couldn't? His brother twisted everything Griffin did into some sort of personal insult.

The muffled wail of a young child threaded through the

tension and tiredness pervading the waiting room. Or maybe Griffin was the tense and tired one. Across from Griffin, a young girl snuggled in her mom's lap, eyes large, lower lip trembling. "I don't wanna go see Dr. Kendall, Mommy . . ."

The mother brushed back the girl's curls. "Honey, you know Dr. Kendall is just going to listen to your lungs today . . ."

Another toddler bolted for the front door but his mother snagged the back of his jeans, halting his escape.

Yeah, Griffin knew just how the little kiddos felt. This Dr. Kendall must be worse than Dr. Haynes.

He looked up when a receptionist wearing purple scrubs adorned with some sort of multicolored flowers called his brother's name. He lagged behind when Ian approached the counter.

"I'm sorry for the delay." The slender Latina woman offered a smile that asked for patience. "Dr. Haynes had several emergencies this morning and is behind. Renee, one of the medical assistants, can take you back to an exam room now."

And they'd probably sit there for another twenty minutes. Griffin wiped his hands down the sides of his blue uniform pants. *Relax, Walker.* This was Ian's appointment, not his. And if he was the one with a cold stethoscope planted on his chest, he'd tell the doc he was fine. No dizziness. Well, none worth mentioning.

Ian settled onto the rolling stool placed to one side of the exam table, his legs spread wide, feet planted on the floor. Griffin chose a stationary chair.

Since they probably had a wait ahead of them, it was time to clear up a few things.

"So, why didn't you tell me about your food allergy?"

Ian shrugged, eyes hidden behind his long brown bangs as he stared at the carpet. As his guardian, Griffin should probably make his brother get a haircut.

"You didn't ask."

"Right. Out of the blue I'm supposed to ask *Can you eat avocado?* What else are you allergic to?"

"Nothing much." Ian pushed the stool back and forth, his tennis shoes unlaced. How did he keep them on his feet? And what did he mean by "nothing much"? For now, Griffin would focus on the basics and let the doctor handle the rest.

"You're going to start carrying an EpiPen."

"You're not the boss of me."

At last, his brother looked him in the eye. "Yeah, I am, Ian. We may not like it, but this is where we are."

Ian stood, his movements so fast that the stool slammed against the wall behind him. "I didn't ask you to bring me here—living in a stupid townhome filled with boxes you haven't even unpacked. Eating fast food—"

"Hey! I'm doing the best I can—"

His brother shoved past him, yanking the door open. "I get it, Griffin. And I hate this setup as much as you do."

"Ian, get back here—"

He took several steps to follow his brother, hoping to corral him back in the exam room, but was brought up short by the appearance of the petite version of Patton who rescued Ian last night. Was she the only doctor in town?

"You seem to be batting a thousand."

She was garbed in a white medical coat with the requisite stethoscope slung around her neck. And judging by the look on her face, she wasn't any more impressed with him this morning than she had been last night. Not that it mattered.

"What are you doing here?"

He sounded like a grouch. She might as well be a new student pilot who'd botched a takeoff for all the friendliness in his voice.

The woman stopped, a clipboard held against her chest. "I'm Dr. Kendall Haynes. This is my office and, hence, my exam room. I assume this is a follow-up appointment for your son."

Not again.

"Ian is my brother."

His words caused a faint blush to stain her face as she glanced at the paperwork on the clipboard. "Right. I forgot. I'm sorry."

"Let me go get Ian."

He slipped past her, exiting the office and looking to the right and left before spotting Ian standing near a workstation of some sort.

"Come on, Ian. Let's not waste any more of the doctor's time."

"Forget it. Let's just go home."

"Look. You were the one who decided to eat something you were allergic to." Griffin lowered his voice, aware that the young woman seated at the computer—was she a nurse? a technician of some sort?—could hear everything he and Ian said. "The ER doc insisted you have a follow-up appointment and recommended this doctor. Stop arguing with me and come on."

He waited while Ian walked past him and reentered the exam room. A row of framed diplomas lined the wall across from him. A University of North Carolina–Chapel Hill medical school diploma stating Dr. Kendall Haynes graduated with the highest honors. Another diploma announcing her graduation from a family medicine residency program at Loma Linda University. The final certificate declared her completion of a two-year fellowship in allergy and immunology at the prestigious National Jewish Health respiratory hospital in Denver. The woman had impressive credentials.

Ian stuck his head back out of the room. "Are you coming?"

"Yes."

Time to stop reading about Dr. Haynes and get this appointment over with.

As he walked into the room, Dr. Haynes offered her hand to his brother. "I'm Dr. Haynes, Ian. You look like you're feeling a lot better than you did last night."

Griffin watched as Ian stood straighter, tugged at his T-shirt, and then shook the doctor's hand. So, the kid had manners. Who knew? Score one for Mom.

"I'm doing okay."

"Breathing all right?"

"Yes. They gave me some sort of treatment at the ER last night."

"Mmm-hmmmm. Not surprised." She motioned for Ian to sit on the exam table. "Mind if I check you out?"

Ian's ears turned bright pink. "Well . . . um . . ."

"Just a standard exam, Ian. Lungs. Heart. That kind of thing. If you want your—" She turned to Griffin. "—brother, right?"

Griffin found himself standing taller, parodying his brother's action. Was he invisible? He needed every advantage he had with this woman, and being a good foot taller than her was most definitely an advantage.

"I'm Ian's *brother*—and his legal guardian."

An awkward silence filled the exam room. Ian sat on the exam table. He and the doctor watched each other.

Dr. Haynes tilted her head. "I was going to ask if Ian wanted you to stay in the room during his examination. And your name is . . . ?"

Right. At this point, his sixteen-year-old brother had more manners than he did.

"I'm Lieutenant Colonel Griffin Walker."

Griffin couldn't tell if a small smile curved her lips because she picked up the clipboard and flipped through the papers.

Probably mentioning his rank was a bit over the top, but he kept feeling as if he was scrabbling for equal footing with the woman. "This information is fairly sketchy. I'd like to request that Ian's medical records be transferred to our office."

Dr. Haynes assumed a bit much.

"I didn't say Ian was going to be your patient."

She closed the chart. "Why don't you tell me why you're here."

"After his allergic reaction, the EMTs took Ian to the ER and the doc recommended that he have a follow-up with a primary care physician. He recommended Dr. Haynes. You." Griffin paused, not sure if he should admit his mistake. "To be frank, I thought you were a guy."

"Excuse me?"

"That came out wrong. I mean, I know you're not a guy—"

"Thank you for the compliment."

Out of the corner of his eye, Griffin saw Ian's shoulders shaking with barely contained laughter. "Look, I know you're a woman. I just didn't know your name—and that you were Dr. Haynes. So I assumed you were a guy—"

The quirk of her eyebrow alerted Griffin to the fact that he'd insulted her. Again.

The she-doctor surprised him by coming to his rescue. "You're saying this is a onetime follow-up appointment."

Griffin nodded. Better to keep his mouth shut at this point.

Dr. Haynes eased the conversation back on course, her soft-spoken words precise. "Let me clarify something for you, Colonel Walker. Your brother didn't just have an allergic reaction last night. Anaphylaxis is a *life-threatening* allergic reaction. If I hadn't been there, Ian could have died."

And thank you, Dr. Haynes, for pointing that out. Griffin had tossed and turned most of the night, replaying the image of Ian's blotchy face, blue lips, his frantic efforts to breathe.

"I'm concerned why you, as his legal guardian, didn't know about Ian's allergy. Why didn't you know that he needs to carry an EpiPen at all times?"

The woman hadn't moved, but he felt as if she'd backed him up against the wall. He didn't need this woman pointing out his failures.

"I'm new at this, Dr. Haynes." He held up his hand, warding off her interruption. "It's no excuse, I know. Our parents died four months ago—and that's when Ian moved from Florida to come live with me. I had no idea he was allergic to anything."

He heard his brother clear his throat. "That's my fault."

Dr. Haynes leaned against the counter. "You didn't tell your brother you were allergic to anything?"

"I forgot."

"I see." She settled the stethoscope so that it was positioned to fit in her ears and moved closer to Ian. "I suppose there's been a lot on your mind since you moved here."

"Yeah."

"New school."

"Yeah."

"Making new friends."

"Yeah."

Griffin watched Dr. Haynes chat with his brother, at the same time performing a basic exam—lungs, heart, eyes, nose, throat. Her hands were slender, the nails trimmed short, but her touch seemed to exude both confidence and gentleness. The walls held a few medical implements and a photograph of a high mountain meadow filled with brilliant red, yellow, and purple wildflowers. After the exam, she sat at a small desk that held a laptop and small printer and typed, the soft click of her fingers on the keyboard the only sound in the room. A few moments later she turned back to face them.

"I understand that you may or may not decide to have me be Ian's physician. If nothing else, I'd like to prescribe several EpiPens for him. And I'd like him to watch a brief video about how to use them—you, too, Colonel Walker."

She stood, crossing the room and opening the door, forestalling any comment from Griffin.

"Ian, if you go down the hall to the medical assistants' station, you can ask for Renee. Tell her that I'd like her to set up the instructional video on EpiPens. Your brother will be with you in just a moment."

Dr. Haynes certainly knew how to control a situation.

After Ian left, she faced him again.

"Colonel Walker, we got off to a bad start, I'm afraid." She tucked her hands into the pockets of her lab coat. "Besides your thinking I'm a man, I mean."

"I wanted to apologize for that but figured it was wiser to be quiet."

"Probably."

Did the woman have to agree with him?

"For some reason, Ian didn't tell you that he was allergic to avocados. I doubt he forgot. It's important he be seen by a physician who can establish a baseline of care here in Colorado. There's a possibility that he's allergic to more than avocados." She paused before she spoke again. "I can give you the name of another allergy specialist. Ian also needs a good family physician here in town. I happen to be both, but given our rocky start, I realize you may want to choose another family doctor."

Dr. Haynes was only stating the truth, but her words amplified the guilt that lurked at the edges of his mind every hour of the day. He was Ian's guardian. His parents would expect him to take care of Ian—not kill him. But how was he supposed to do that when his brother barely talked to him?

"I'll take any recommendations."

Was that a small flicker of disappointment in Dr. Haynes's eyes?

"Ask Evie, my receptionist, for the contact information on your way out. Anything else I can do for you?"

"Not that I can think of."

"Well then, an exciting movie awaits you, Colonel Walker."

"Lead the way, Dr. Haynes."

★ ★ ★ ★

For once, Evie would walk through the back door without carrying a gift of some sort.

Presents did not solve anything. She'd been the mom bearing gifts for weeks now and all she got from Javan was a six-year-old version of a mini iceberg. She thought Javan would be thrilled when he found out they wanted to adopt him. Instead, he'd withdrawn from her.

She'd heeded the advice of her counselor—and the virtual red warning light in the online bank account—and resisted a quick stop at Target for something, *anything*, to entice a smile out of Javan. Tonight it would be her and Javan. And Logan, of course. Javan's favorite person in the whole wide world—her husband, Logan.

Her phone played the opening notes of "Hay Otro En Mi Vida." *Nice timing, Logan.*

"You pulled into the carport ten minutes ago. Did you get lost?" Logan's deep baritone used to be enough to lure Evie into the house each evening—and into his arms. "Javan's excited to see you."

No he wasn't. Evie knew that. Logan knew that. Did her husband have to resort to a lie to make her come home at night? Had it come to that?

She pushed open the van door and stepped out into the darkness, finally noticing Logan standing at the back door, warm light from inside the kitchen illuminating him. No little boy in sight.

"Liar."

"He was at the door a minute ago . . ."

"On my way. Hold the door open. I picked up dinner." Evie snagged her purse and the large extra-cheese pizza off the passenger seat. She only snitched one piece on the ride home from work. No need to feel guilty stopping to pick up Papa John's pizza. This was dinner, not a gift, even if it was Javan's favorite food.

As she stepped inside, Logan wrapped one arm around her, taking the pizza from her with his other hand. "Honey, I told you I started dinner . . ."

She did a quick survey of the kitchen. No Javan, though his Legos littered the linoleum floor around the table in the breakfast nook. Peace offerings from days past.

"You did?" The scent of Parmesan chicken filled the kitchen. "I forgot."

Now who was lying?

She shrugged out of her tailored teal coat, draping it across the back of one of the white ladder-back chairs, knowing Logan would follow behind her and hang it in the foyer closet. "Javan, Mama's home."

Footsteps pounded down the hallway—away from her.

What had the counselor said? "He's the child, Evie, you're the adult. He's angry with his birth mom for abandoning him, not you. Remember that she's not here and you are."

And so Evie got all the rejection. All the tears. And Logan was Superdad. Well, Super-Almost-Dad. All the man needed was a cape.

Before she realized what he was doing, Logan stood behind her, wrapping his strong arms around her and pulling her close. He nuzzled her neck, his breath warm against her skin. "Missed you today, babe."

She leaned against him, inhaling the scent of peppermint from the gum he chewed nonstop all day as he worked on clients' websites. "Miss you every day, babe."

"How's the good doctor doing?"

"It was a busy day—a couple of emergencies." Evie closed her eyes, acknowledging the ache in the small of her back, the base of her neck. "Nothing I couldn't handle."

Her husband's whisper sent another tingle of warmth across her neck. "He's watching you."

Evie opened her eyes halfway to see Javan peering at them from the end of the hallway. "Hey, sweetie. Mama's home."

His head, topped with a mass of black curls, disappeared.

"I've got pizza."

Javan's eyes and nose came into view again.

"Don't bribe him, Evie." Logan followed his whispered words with a soft kiss on her neck. "Let him come to you."

"If I wait for him to come to me because he wants to, he'll never come."

"Yes, he will."

"No, he won't." She pushed away from the security of Logan's arms. "We go through this every night for—how long? The past six months?"

"Give it time."

"*I have.*" She pulled her hair out of the rubber band securing it in a low ponytail, running her fingers through the strands. Ah, relief. "I will. I'm just . . . tired. Long day."

She watched Javan scoot on his bottom down the wooden floor toward the kitchen, inch by inch. What happened to the days when he used to run to the door when she came home? What was she doing wrong? Maybe the truth was she deserved to be treated like this.

Evie shoved the thought to the darkest corner of her mind. It couldn't be the truth. "Come on and get dinner, niñito."

"I'm not a baby." Javan stopped. "I'm six."

"Yes, you're my muchacho grande." Evie walked to the pantry and searched for paper plates.

"I'm not your muchacha grandie."

She gripped the edge of the shelf. *Let it go, girl. Let it go.* He wasn't being mean on purpose. He was just working things out—and she was his target.

"Okay, you can be Daddy's big boy tonight. How's that?"

She slid open the pizza box, the aroma of basil and oregano simmered in tomato sauce and then slathered with melted cheese urging her to indulge in another piece even before they sat around the table. "How many slices do you want, Javan?"

"Don't want any. Daddy made chicken." He stood behind her, his tone a foreshadowing of future teenage rebellion—if they survived that far into the future.

Evie pulled out a single slice of pizza, placing it on a plate and carrying it to the table nestled in the breakfast nook. "That's fine. You and Daddy can have chicken while Mamá has pizza."

As Logan cut bits of baked chicken coated with Parmesan and Italian dressing, Evie removed the top layer of cheese from her pizza and nibbled on it. She watched her husband place a kiss on Javan's cheek as he set his plate in front of him, imagining the softness of his skin. She closed her eyes when Logan snuck in a quick tickle, relishing the giggles that erupted from the little boy. If only she could tuck each one into her heart, save each one as an antidote to the sulky glances he gave her.

She needed to snap out of it. She was the adult here, not another six-year-old who could stomp off in a huff because Javan didn't want to play with her. Javan clung to her when they first took him in as a foster child. Surely his negative attitude would change if she loved him enough.

When Logan began to clear off the table, Evie stood, too. "Why don't I give Javan his bath tonight?"

She couldn't blame her husband for the way his hazel eyes widened in surprise, his eyebrows skyrocketing. "Really?"

"Yes, really." She took a deep breath and straightened her shoulders. "It'll be fun."

Logan set Javan on the floor. "Hear that, buddy? Mom's gonna give you a bath tonight."

"No! You do it, Daddy!" With those words, Javan ran down the hallway, his footsteps pounding up the stairs.

Let the fun begin.

By the time she got upstairs, Javan had tossed his tennis shoes, jeans, Elmo shirt, and underwear all over the bathroom, and dumped his plastic toys into the empty tub. She ran the water, testing the temperature.

"Ready to get in, Javan?"

"I want Daddy to help me."

"But I thought it would be fun to help you with your bath tonight." She picked up one of the bright-colored musical dolphins floating in the water. "Want to play dolphins?"

"Nuh-uh."

She tapped the dolphin on its head so that it played a note. Really, Javan was too old for these now, but he loved them.

"Well, let me get you in the tub."

Javan held himself stiff as she picked him up. What happened to the little boy who used to love to cuddle? Would she ever find him again?

Once in the tub, he found a blue measuring cup and filled it up with water. Dumped it out. Filled it up. Dumped it out.

All the while ignoring her.

She picked up his clothes and tossed them in the wicker hamper, keeping an eye on the little boy who seemed oblivious to the fact she was even in the room. Sitting back down, she wet the washcloth and added a liberal dose of body wash.

"Okay, time to get clean."

"I want Daddy to do it!"

She was beginning to hate those six words.

"Javan, Mamá is doing the bath tonight. Let's wash your neck." She tried to make a game of it. "You know that's where the dirt likes to hide. Tilt your head back."

"I want Daddy!"

"Javan!" Her voice seemed to bounce off the bathroom tiles. "Let. Me. Do. This. Now."

She hadn't yelled. Not really. But still, Javan's eyes widened, filling with tears in the same instant. Within seconds, his wail drowned the echo of her harsh words.

Logan appeared in the doorway. "What happened?"

"Nothing." Evie stood. "Why don't you finish his bath to-night?"

"Evie, come on. He needs time with you—"

"Not when I make him cry, Logan. I'll try again tomorrow."

She knew her husband wouldn't follow her to their bed-room—he couldn't, not with Javan in the tub. Evie shut the door, locking it. She walked past the wall that held the framed photo from their wedding day, back when all the promises seemed so ready to come true, and into their small bathroom and sat on the side of the tub. As she twisted the hot-water handle, she ignored the pressure of tears building in her throat, demanding release as a sob.

What a waste. She'd cried buckets of tears, gallons of tears, in her life and they hadn't changed a thing. Not her past mistakes, not her present situation.

She uncapped the bottle of her favorite bubble bath and dumped a stream of it into the tub, the scent of coconut and lime flowing into the room. Evie watched bubbles froth on the surface of the water. She was too tired to go all 'round the be-a-good-mommy mulberry bush. Maybe tomorrow.

Or maybe not.

This adoption had seemed so right after months—years—of infertility. But maybe she wasn't meant to be a mother. Maybe that was her penance for one long, long-ago mistake. It seemed too high a penalty . . . but apparently, she didn't get to choose.

CHAPTER THREE

★ ★ ★ ★

"*M*rs. Jamison, this is Griffin. Griffin Walker—Ian's brother."

Griffin tucked his iPhone underneath his chin, anchoring it to his shoulder so he could unwrap the grilled chicken pita he'd bought for dinner a couple of nights ago. It would do for breakfast. The aroma of butter, onions, garlic, and roasted chicken drifted up, causing his stomach to rumble. At least it wasn't drive-through food. He'd made Ian get out of the car and walk into Pita Pit with him to order dinner.

"Griffin." Something in the woman's warm greeting tugged at Griffin's heart. Reminded him of coming home to an afternoon snack. And his mom. "Mac talked about Ian last night during dinner. I'm so glad they keep in touch through Skype and texting."

Griffin leaned against the Sandstone Corian kitchen counter, the pita in one hand, his phone in the other. Since his parents' death, had he eaten a meal sitting down? He swallowed a too-large bite of pita, dropping the food to grab his THE SKY IS NOT MY LIMIT. IT IS MY PLAYGROUND mug and wash it down with a gulp of coffee. *Hot.* He forced himself to swallow the liquid even as it scalded his tongue and throat. "Yeah. I just have to make sure my brother gets offline and does his homework."

"Ian is a good student. Your mom and dad were always so proud . . ." She paused. "I'm so sorry. I know thinking about them must be painful."

Well, yes. And no. Because when thoughts of his parents flared in his mind, Griffin doused them with a dose of harsh reality. His parents were dead. He couldn't change that fact. He had to stay focused. Take care of Ian. Try to get his career back on course.

"So how is Ian?"

"He's better today, but the other night . . . Mrs. Jamison, did you know about Ian's allergies?" Griffin leaned against the breakfast bar. Sitting down, standing up—these days it was easier to avoid basic moves like that.

"Of course. Ian's had serious allergies and asthma ever since he came to live with your parents. We always had a medical power of attorney when Ian stayed with us. I'm sure it's all documented in the medical papers in your parents' files."

His parents' files. Sure. Those would be a big help. Except after the funeral he put his parents' stuff in storage, closing up their house and pocketing the key. He stuck any of the papers the lawyer labeled IMPORTANT in a corner in his den—one of the rooms still unpacked. The only thing Ian brought with him besides his clothes was his bedroom furniture.

"You did read through the files, didn't you?"

"Not exactly. I've been . . . busy." Griffin rewrapped the half-eaten pita and laid it on the countertop. Maybe he'd have more of an appetite after this phone call.

"And Ian didn't mention anything?"

"Not until yesterday morning—after a pretty scary episode at a restaurant when he ate some guacamole and had an allergic reaction."

The woman gasped. "Is he all right?"

"As far as I can tell." Griffin noticed the white cereal bowls and mismatched spoons piled in the stainless-steel sink, along with all of his glasses. A total of six of them. "We spent the rest of the evening in the ER. Now I need to get him a doctor here in the Springs."

"Maybe a friend could recommend one?"

He hadn't thought of that. Kendall Haynes's receptionist handed him a list of potential doctors for Ian—as if Griffin could sit around and spend his days on hold waiting for a doctor to talk to him. Maybe his friend Doug could recommend someone local. And did Ian really need to see a specialist? Couldn't he see a regular doc? Or a pediatrician? Wait . . . did teenagers even go to the pediatrician? There was so much he didn't know.

"Do you want the name of Ian's doctor here? I'm sure he can talk with you about Ian's history."

"That might be a good idea." Hot water splashed across his hands as he rinsed off the dirty dishes and piled them in the dishwasher. It wouldn't be full, but he'd run it anyway.

"Let me get his number. We use the same doctor your parents do. Did."

He heard Mrs. Jamison opening and closing several drawers, mumbling, "Now where did I put that card?"

"Wait. Mrs. Jamison, that's not really the reason why I called . . ."

"Is there something else you need?"

He needed to not blow this next part. "Ian is having a hard time adjusting. To school. To Colorado Springs. He misses, well, everyone. The move, on top of our parents' deaths, is harder for him than he expected."

"I had no idea." Mrs. Jamison clucked sympathetically. "I mean, Mac mentioned once or twice . . . but I assumed living in Colorado would get easier as time went on."

"I think Ian needs to get back to Florida." Griffin dropped six spoons into the silverware container.

"That's a wonderful idea. Maybe he could come spend a few weeks with us this summer?"

"I called to see if you would consider being Ian's guardians— in my place."

The silence that followed this statement couldn't be a good sign. Not that he expected an immediate yes. But he had expected some sort of reaction.

"Mrs. Jamison?"

"It never occurred to me that you wouldn't want Ian with you after your parents' deaths. I mean, you're brothers."

Shutting the dishwasher, Griffin paced through his almost vacant living room. He only had to dodge the overstuffed extra-long couch and the worn-out lounge chair that he needed to replace. The flat-screen TV was anchored to the wall. He and Ian weren't brothers—not really. And the age difference was too much to try to overcome at this late date. "Even though we're . . . family, I'm not sure my parents made the wisest decision when they made me Ian's guardian."

"But surely you can see why they would want Ian to be with his brother."

"Quite honestly, I don't think my parents ever expected to die in a plane crash on the way home from celebrating their fortieth anniversary." Griffin dragged in a breath. "And twenty-two years' difference—Ian and I don't have a lot of things in common."

"Except your parents."

Mrs. Jamison was not as open to the idea as he'd hoped. "All I'm asking is that you consider the idea. Maybe talk about it with your husband? Pray about it."

"Have you prayed about it, Griffin?"

"Sure. I mean, yes, I have." Griffin came to a halt at the base of the stairs that led up to his brother's room. Ian's door was shut—locking him out, as usual. But any minute now, his brother would come downstairs, ready to leave for school. Griffin needed to speed up this phone call. "Obviously, I'd want Ian to finish out the school year here, so I was thinking, if we agreed to this, that we could make the change in the summer."

A minute later, Griffin headed down the hall toward his bedroom. He almost paused at his brother's room. Almost knocked on the door. But Ian made it clear he wasn't in the mood to talk. Ever. He knew moving back to Panama City and living with the Jamison family would be the best thing for his brother. He'd talk to Ian once everything was settled.

He hadn't expected Mrs. Jamison to go online and print out a ticket for Ian to fly back to Florida tomorrow. But why couldn't she be more open to the idea, see the benefit to Ian? Why didn't her mom-heart kick in and feel sorry for a homesick teenage boy? Maybe he'd follow up with an email, detail how much Ian missed his school, his friends.

If Griffin was honest, he wasn't much different from Ian. Uprooted. Forced to move, thanks to vertigo plaguing him for over eighteen months. And his own stupidity for downplaying the seriousness of his condition.

God, I want to be in the Springs about as much as Ian does. Help me figure out a way to get him back home. It's challenging enough trying to get my life on track. I don't want to be responsible for Ian's, too. I'm not the best choice for Ian's guardian. We both know that.

★ ★ ★ ★ ★

Time to face the day.

Kendall kicked through the water a few more times, slowing the rhythm of her arms and legs. The welcome feeling of buoyancy succumbed to gravity, and she sank so her feet touched the bottom of the pool. Warm water splashed into her face and she sputtered, wiping moisture away from her eyes.

From his perch along the edge, Sully barked.

"Stay, dog." Kendall held up a dripping hand. "The day you jump into my pool is the day I give you away. Got it?"

The dog whined and paced back and forth but—wonder of wonders—stayed high and dry. Not that she'd do anything more drastic than fuss if Sully decided to go for a swim with her. He'd endured residency with her, adapting to her long hours spent in the hospital. She'd pretended not to notice that he'd slept in her bed, not his. Somebody might as well—she certainly wasn't. Their relationship worked—in a dysfunctional owner–dog sort of way, because, well, she loved the hairy beast.

The water slowing her steps, Kendall walked to the side of the compact pool and tugged off the neon green swimming cap. It clashed with her red one-piece bathing suit, but protected her short hair. Sully came and sat beside her. "Do not—I repeat—do not lick me, dog. There's a reason why you have a water bowl over in the corner."

She rested for a few moments, considering the somber view out the back of her office windows. A mist shrouded the Front Range Mountains, hinting at snow. This early in April, snow was just as likely as sunshine. But who knew? The sun might trump all the forecasters' predictions and break through the clouds by midmorning. But by then she'd be preoccupied with patients, tracking between one exam room and another.

Chlorine-scented water evaporated from her shoulders, causing a chill to work its way across her skin. Pulling herself up onto the edge of the pool, Kendall walked over and turned off the endless-current machine before wrapping herself in an oversized yellow towel. Sully followed behind and took a hesitant swipe at her ankle with his rough tongue.

"No, Sully! Go drink out of your bowl." Kendall pointed to the other side of the room. "Use. Your. Bowl."

The dog took two steps away from her, then flopped on the floor with a weary sigh.

"You're not a dog, you're a slug." A low whine elicited a chuckle from Kendall. "My apologies. I'm cranky this morning. You know I love you."

His ears perked up when her iPhone rang. She grabbed it from the small table in the corner of the room, hoping it wasn't an emergency. Her schedule would be wrecked before the day even started.

"Dr. Haynes."

"Kendall, it's Bekah."

An emergency indeed, in the form of her little sister, Hurricane Bekah.

"Morning, Bekah. A little early for you to be up, isn't it?"

"I've got Zumba class today, so I'm out of the house early before school."

Bekah, the professional college student. She'd been taking classes for eight years and switched career options so many times Kendall struggled to remember her revolving majors. Art? Philosophy? Business? Kendall wove her fingers through her hair, twisting the short locks and then letting them go in an effort to release tension. How'd that build up so quickly?

"So, Beks, what can I do for you today?"

"Well, it's more like what can you give me."

Uh-oh. Round two about Mina's ruby ring was about to begin. Ding, ding, ding!

"Give you? And that would be?"

"Kendall, I know Mom talked to you about Ryan proposing."

"She did. Congratulations."

"Mom said you're being stubborn about Mina's ring."

Inhaling a gulp of the warm, moist air surrounding her, Kendall wrapped the towel tighter, fending off a chill threatening to seep into her body. "Technically, it's my ring, since Mina bequeathed it to me."

"Traditionally, the ring should go to me because I'm the first one to get married. Mina should have never given that ring to you."

"But she did." Why did Kendall feel as if she were playing keep-away with her sister?

"You're not using it. It's just sitting there in a box, gathering dust."

"Come on, Bekah, I'm single—not dead!"

Her sister's snort was anything but feminine. The girl needed to be careful or one day she'd jiggle loose her crystal nose piercing. "Let's just keep it simple. You're thirty-six. Somebody might call you an old maid, but I'm not that kind of person."

Sure she wasn't.

"Come on, you're more likely to be killed by a terrorist—"

"Bekah, have you been watching *Sleepless in Seattle* again?"

"Fine. Ignore statistics. All I'm saying is look at who's getting engaged—and look at who's not. Do you really want to mess up family tradition?"

Kendall slid her feet into a pair of faded green flip-flops, grabbing the inhaler she'd used before her morning swim, and heading for the back staircase that led upstairs to her loft. Combining her office and her home was one of her smartest decisions ever. Sully trailed behind her, nipping at the towel draped over her shoulder.

"No, I don't."

"What?"

Kendall could hear the faint ring of victory in her sister's voice. "I don't want to mess up family tradition. But I am not going to give you the ring that Mina gave me. She wanted me to have it."

"Ooooooh!" Her sister's high-pitched squeal almost caused Kendall to laugh. Almost. But she wasn't interested in going another round with Bekah. "You're being unreasonable, just like Dad."

Kendall stopped her ascent, her hand clenching the railing. "Don't. Don't bring Dad into this."

"Mom said—"

"You heard me, Bekah. Don't bring Dad into this. Sic Mom on me if you want. Call me morning, noon, and night. Leave me voice mails. Send me snarky texts. But don't talk badly about Dad. Got it?"

"Are you going to send Mom the ring?"

"No. Final answer."

"Why not?"

"Because it's mine, plain and simple. Mina gave it to me. And I plan on using it."

"As if—"

Kendall disconnected the call.

And wished she could do another half hour in the pool to drown the internal echo of the conversation with her sister. But now she was an adult—the doctor, not the patient. And despite what other people thought, she did her best not to keep patients waiting. She needed to shake it off. Her Friday could only get better from here, right?

Were all families like hers? Even now, eighteen years later, memories of her father were still tender. She spoke to her mother and sister on an as-needed basis. And her younger brother Tanner had left home for college—and never looked back.

As she entered the interior back door of her loft, her flip-flops slapped against the cold cement floor. Not for the first time she wondered if she should have opted for something warmer, like wood. Or thick carpeting. Nah. She loved the look of her one-of-a-kind floor, with its broad red marbled strips.

Sully abandoned her in the large open living area, choosing to flop onto his well-worn dog bed positioned by the black Clark Sofa. One day she'd upgrade to a real couch, but she loved the utilitarian lines of the sleeper sofa she purchased during medical school. Paired with two no-frill gray chairs from IKEA and a long, rectangular black coffee table, the furniture gave the room an open feeling—and put the focus where she wanted it: on the floor-to-ceiling windows showcasing a twenty-four-hour view of Pikes Peak.

Kendall couldn't resist stopping to appreciate the ever-changing masterpiece. Yes, the low-hanging clouds obscured the Peak this morning, but she knew the imposing mountain was there, lurking behind the blur of gray. And by the time she came home tonight, she might view a charcoal sketching of a ridge of mountains against a dark blue sky.

Enough window-gazing. It was a workday.

A quick glance at the clock on her bedside table revealed she had time for a fast five-minute shower, thanks to this morning's verbal sparring with her sister. Kendall ignored the aqua-and-green comforter left in a mound on her bed. She just needed to remember to close her door when she left so that Sully would not assume he was welcome to take an afternoon nap in her unmade bed. Once in the bathroom, she stored the inhaler away before turning on the shower full blast and peeled off the still-damp bathing suit, hanging it on a hook on the back of the door. Pulling back the shower curtain covered with huge pink, purple, orange, and green flowers, Kendall stepped into the shower and adapted one of her favorite show tunes to her mood.

"I'm gonna wash that girl right outta my hair. I'm gonna wash that girl right outta my hair . . ."

By the time she walked downstairs to her office, Kendall determined to forget the conversation with her sister. Bekah asked for the ring. She said no. Done. Now she needed to focus on work. She was the boss. She set the tone for the office. Arriving with a frown on her face would affect everyone from her receptionist to her medical assistants to her nurse practitioner.

She slipped into her office, thankful to see that Evie had left a copy of the day's schedule on her cherrywood roll-top desk. She covered her dress pants and red silk blouse with a starched white lab coat emblazoned with the words ROCKY MOUNTAIN FAMILY PRACTICE in deep maroon, scanning her appointments. She was booked, as usual. A few older patients, but mostly children, many with allergies and asthma. Barring any emergencies, she'd be on schedule.

Not that she ever stayed on schedule.

A quick rap on the door and Evie poked her head in. "You ready to get started?"

"Is everyone at the MAs' station?" She followed the receptionist out into the hallway.

"Yes. Paul is half full, but I'm sure he'll be booked solid before the day's over." Evie joined the trio of waiting MAs and the lone male, Paul, the practical joker but oh-so-proficient nurse practitioner.

"Good morning, everyone." Kendall took a moment to make eye contact with each of her staff. "Ready for another day taking care of the most important people in the world?"

As everyone nodded and murmured agreement, Kendall held out her hands. "Let's pray, then."

She bowed her head, not bothering to watch and see what anyone else did. She knew everyone in her practice was at a different place in his or her faith walk. Some were believers like she was; some were questioning. And then there was Evie. The best receptionist she could ever hope for. Kind. Considerate. One step ahead of Kendall most of the time. But when it came to God—nothing.

Still, anyone she hired knew her practice was faith-based—and one of the things she always did was start the day with prayer. Her practice, her privilege.

And today, after her early-morning standoff with Bekah, she needed a few minutes to refocus on God before turning her attention to her patients.

"God, we ask you to bless our interaction with each patient today. Give us wisdom and discernment to meet their needs—physical, emotional, and spiritual. May what we do and say bring people one step closer to Jesus. Amen."

Kendall stepped back, watching her team move toward their stations.

"All right then. Let's get this day started."

★ ★ ★ ★ ★

If only there was a way to package these moments of peace and quiet and parcel them out during the weeks she missed church.

Kendall sat in the back of the auditorium, savoring the echo of praise and worship music lingering in the room following the morning service. She counted the cost of being a physician before entering medical school—and all along the way. But there were times when she resented how it shoved so many other things out of her life. Relationships. Hobbies. Involvement in her church.

People stood in scattered small groups—couples, families. Making plans for later in the day, later in the week. Truth was, being thirty-six and single—*Yes, Bekah, I heard you*—made her a misfit in her church in a way that her job didn't. Most people her age were married. Were moms. And in the medium-sized church she attended, the so-called college and career group catered to young twenty-somethings.

Still, she loved the worship. The teaching. And today she'd been surprised to see another physician, Heath Parker, walk on stage to share his vision for a ministry to support the health needs of families in Africa. She'd met Heath several times when they'd attended the same medical conferences throughout the years. Not that he'd remember her. Usually he was one of the speakers at a regional or national medical conference, thanks to his work overseas in infectious diseases.

Kendall gathered her brown leather satchel that worked as both a purse and a briefcase and her wool car-length coat. She'd stop by the hospital and check on the toddler who was admitted last night after a bad asthma attack. Then she'd take Sully for a walk so they could both enjoy the warm weather before the snow predicted for midweek rolled in over Pikes Peak.

As she exited the double doors of the high school where her "out of the box" church met each week, Kendall heard the sound of fast-paced footsteps. She muffled the sigh building in her chest. Most likely someone with an If-you-have-a-minute-I-have-this-funny-rash question. Such requests came with the medical degree.

"Dr. Haynes. Kendall!"

Now, that sounded like . . .

The next moment, Heath Parker jogged past her, turned around, and slowed to a walk, staying a few paces in front of her. The wind riffled through his receding hairline, tossing the dark brown curls into an appealing tangle. Brilliant blue eyes locked with hers.

"Kendall. Hey. I was afraid I wouldn't catch you."

Kendall stopped walking. He'd noticed her, sitting all the way in the last row? She held out her hand. "Dr. Parker. Good to see you again. I enjoyed your talk—"

"Heath. Call me Heath, please." He wrapped her in an exuberant hug. "And can the I-enjoyed-your-talk spiel. Old friends like us don't need to do stuff like that."

Old friends . . . like them? Well, maybe in a very general manner of speaking. Kendall did a mental headshake even as she enjoyed a tantalizing whiff of Heath Parker's musky cologne. Made her want to duck in for another hug.

Heath stepped back, tucking his hands into the pockets of his khaki slacks. "I talked with your pastor before church. He mentioned you attended. I looked for you, but didn't see you until just now."

Ah. That explained it. The pastor had given him a heads-up. But still, Heath looked for her. Nice thought.

"So, do you have time for lunch? I'm told Thai Basil is good. I'm still learning my way around the restaurants in town."

The unexpected invitation stalled Kendall's response. She'd planned on heating a sweet potato in the microwave before walking Sully. "Lunch? Sure. Sounds great."

"Terrific! Let me walk you to your car and then we'll caravan there." Heath fell into step beside her.

Despite the fact that she was all of five feet tall—five three, if you counted her leather boots—she found it easy to keep up with Heath. Average height, he ambled alongside her, asking general what-have-you-been-up-to questions about the church and where she lived. At her Jeep, he opened the door, waiting while she buckled herself in, and then leaned on the door frame.

"A Jeep, huh? Somehow I imagined you'd drive something fancier."

"I rebuilt this car with my dad. Nothing fancy for me. I'm a Jeep girl."

Heath patted her hand where it rested on the steering wheel. "Okay, Jeep girl. I'll see you at Thai Basil. Looking forward to learning more about you."

Kendall watched him walk across the parking lot to a black Hummer H3. To each his own off-road assault vehicle. But from the shine on his custom wheel rims, Kendall doubted Heath Parker went into anything more remote than a gravel parking lot. Oh, well. She wouldn't judge the man by his car.

As Heath followed her out of the parking lot, she made a mental note to stop by the hospital later that evening and check on her patient. Today was not going the way she planned. Not at all.

★ ★ ★ ★ ★

"This is one well-thought-out setup, Kendall." Heath turned a circle in her apartment, stopping to face the bank of windows revealing a view of the mountains. Sunshine streamed through the clouds, casting them into varying aspects of shadow and light. "And all you have to do is walk downstairs to go to work each day."

The satisfaction that lit inside Kendall like a slow-burning Fourth of July sparkler whenever she contemplated her combo work/home environment glowed brighter. "I'd say I'm happy here, but I'm not."

Heath shot her a startled glance, the afternoon sunlight glinting off his Colorado-sky-blue eyes.

A little-girl giggle escaped. "I'm over-the-moon happy here."

Heath nudged her shoulder, his chuckle joining hers. "So, when do I get to meet Sully?"

"Ah, Sully. I'm warning you, Heath, the dog has no social graces whatsoever. This, despite repeated attempts at training him."

"Some dogs aren't meant to be tamed. Like some men." He waggled his eyebrows at her. "I'm not afraid of your dog."

Kendall let Sully out from the bedroom, where he sat whining as if she'd ignored him for hours. Which she basically had, thanks to lunch with Heath. The dog bounded out in a flurry of paws and legs and "woofs," skidding to a stop in front of Heath, who knelt to meet him.

Please don't let the dog-who-never-met-a-person-he-didn't-love scare him off.

Not like she expected Heath Parker to be around much. Or again, for that matter. No sense getting her hopes up.

She watched Heath bury his hands deep in Sully's brown, curly fur, turning his head away from Sully's kisses. Going to the kitchen, she gathered the dog's leash and other walking supplies.

"You sure you want to come along for this?"

Heath gestured to the outdoors. "It's a beautiful day in Colorado. I've been invited to go on a walk with a lovely woman and her very friendly dog. Why would I say no to that offer?"

Right, then.

"It's just that you're a little overdressed for the occasion . . ." Kendall motioned to his navy blue blazer, white dress shirt, and yellow tie.

"Next time I'll make sure I'm appropriately attired." He shucked off his tie, tucking it in his pocket. "And this is easily dealt with."

Next time.

"If you want to hook this on his collar, I'll just grab my flats and my windbreaker and we'll go."

"Perfect." Heath took the brown leather strap from her.

If this had been a romance novel, this was where the author would insert the line: His hand seemed to linger on hers.

All right, girl. This is not a romance novel. Real life. Your life, remember? Romance for you never leads to happily ever after.

A few minutes later, she and Heath walked behind Sully, who acted as if he'd never heard the command "heel!" She would enjoy the sunshine, the just-right warmth of the April afternoon as they walked to a nearby park—except Sully yanked her arm first to the right and then to the left as he investigated unseen scents along the sidewalk.

"Let me try." Heath slipped the leash from her hand, then positioned her hand in the crook of his arm.

Very smooth, Dr. Parker.

"So why a goldendoodle?"

"Well, I had asthma as a child." *Oh, good grief, am I really starting with my childhood?* "Some people believe goldendoodles are hypoallergenic. My goal was to let Sully come into the office sometimes, cheer up the patients, that kind of thing. I liked the idea that he wouldn't aggravate patients' allergies or asthma."

"But?"

"You're walking him. Sully's a big galoot. Friendly as all

get-out—but uncontrollable. Until he behaves, there's no way I'd let him in my office."

"And you named him Sully because . . . ?"

Of course he'd ask that. Her innate honesty compelled a truthful answer. "Um, *Dr. Quinn, Medicine Woman.*"

"Clarification, if you please, Dr. Haynes."

"In the TV show *Dr. Quinn, Medicine Woman,* Jane Seymour plays Dr. Mike, a female frontier doctor. Sully is the love interest." She kept her eyes trained on her dog. "I decided every female doctor needed a Sully."

Heath's deep chuckle teased a responding laugh from Kendall. "Only your Sully has four feet."

"Exactly."

"Kendall, you are delightful." He threw an arm around her shoulders, pulling her to his side in a brief half-hug. "I didn't think one of the advantages of moving to Colorado was seeing you again."

"R-really?"

"I knew it was time to leave the mission field, to come back to the States. I knew God was leading me back here. I'm not sure what's next—"

"But what about your medical goodwill organization?"

"There is that. I'm still in the early brainstorming stages. Colorado Springs has so many faith-based organizations—and I see this as something a little different." Heath turned onto the path leading into the park.

"How so?"

"Well, broader-based."

"Nondenominational?"

"More than that. I don't even want to label it as a faith-based organization. If I do that, I lose out the opportunity for federal funding."

Kendall sidestepped a couple of toddlers chasing after a stream of iridescent bubbles blown by their mother. "Is that so bad?"

"No, not necessarily. But I feel like it's an option I'm supposed to pursue—at least initially. My goal is to get as many people as possible excited about improving the health of people in third-world countries. And I believe I know just how to do that."

"How?"

Heath shook his head. "Ah, today is not a day to talk medicine. Although I can't think of anyone else I'd rather have listen to my ideas and give me feedback. According to your pastor, you're quite well respected in town."

"You mean, I work long hours."

"No. He told me about your practice. A solo practitioner in this day and age? Almost unheard of." Heath tightened his grip on the leather leash when Sully tried to run after a boy who biked past. "And your monthly asthma clinic at Front Range Mission Outreach? Methinks you have a generous, caring heart, Kendall."

"The same could be said of you."

"But we weren't talking about me, were we?" He walked in silence for a few minutes, eyes trained on several children swinging, legs pumping hard and fast, propelling them high into the air. "Let's talk about something more important."

"Such as?"

"Such as when we're going to go out again. Dinner later this week?"

CHAPTER FOUR

★ ★ ★ ★

"I'm glad you were free this afternoon, Kendall." Rachel unbuckled her seat belt, tugging her straw cowboy hat off her head and releasing her long hair. "This way we have some one-on-one time before we meet up with everyone else tonight and go looking for my wedding dress."

"Me, too. This was a great idea."

"Thanks for leaving the top off the Jeep today."

"No problem. This is crazy-warm weather for April." Kendall tucked her keys in her hip pouch and climbed out of the CJ5. "I'm starving. You?"

"That's why we're here." Rachel led the way into the rustic restaurant tucked into the mountainside along Highway 24. The vivid mural painted on the outside was a colorful hint that one side of the building was dedicated to Colorado wines. But today they were focused on the restaurant. "Is a table outside good for you?"

"Absolutely." Kendall already knew what she was ordering—the Buffalo Wine Burger. Her mouth watered at the thought of char-grilled meat flavored with just a dash of red wine topped with grilled onions, roasted green chilies, and sautéed mushrooms. She always topped it off with a slice of Swiss cheese.

Rachel placed her order for a portobello mushroom sandwich and the waitress brought their drinks, leaving the two women to relax at their creekside table. The faint sound of water tripping over rocks gentled Kendall's spirit, wiping away the last remnants of work stress. Sunlight through bare tree limbs and evergreen branches and a whisper of a breeze tickled the back of her neck.

"This is a great way to spend my afternoon off." Kendall closed her eyes, inhaling the hint of springtime in the Rockies.

"And this is the perfect place to eat." Rachel leaned back in her wrought-iron chair, legs stretched out in front of her. "Sometimes I forget it's up here."

"I know. And then I eat here again and I think, *Why don't I come here more often?*"

"Exactly. I'll have to mention this place to Tony. We should bring his family here when they come out for the wedding."

Kendall scrunched her nose, tempted to peek at her phone. But even without checking, she would bet it had been less than ten minutes since Rachel last mentioned Tony. Or the wedding. It was all right. Rachel was in love. Engaged. Tony and the wedding were top priority.

"Speaking of the wedding—" Rachel turned her head so she could look at Kendall. "—I wanted to check something with you."

"Sure. Is there something I can do?"

Even as she asked the question, Kendall doubted Rachel needed anyone besides Melissa-the-über-organized to keep track of all the wedding to-dos.

"I wanted to make sure I didn't hurt your feelings."

"Hurt my feelings? How?"

"When I asked Melissa to be my matron of honor, instead of asking you　did I hurt your feelings?"

Kendall made certain she didn't look away from Rachel when she answered. "I'm fine, Rachel. Really."

"You didn't answer the question." Rachel sat up, twisting around to face her. "I did, didn't I?"

Now would be a good time for the waitress to come back with their food, but of course Kendall ordered her burger medium well, not rare. "Rachel, the four of us are all friends. You're free to arrange the wedding party however you want. The important thing is that we all are going to be a part of your wedding."

"Still evading the question, Dr. Haynes." Rachel reached over and clasped her hand, her diamond glinting in the sunlight. "And I have my answer. I'm sorry I hurt your feelings."

"It's fine. Really. I'm happy for you." Kendall squeezed her friend's fingers. Once. Twice. Let go. "It's your day. You plan it the way you want it to go."

"I wasn't *not* picking you, Kendall. It's just that I thought it would be easier for you if you weren't the maid of honor, you know?"

"No . . . I don't know."

"We've been friends how many years now? Five? How many weddings have we attended together?"

"Probably an even dozen."

"And we both dreaded them." Rachel shook her head as if replaying scenes from weddings past, her long, dark hair swishing around her shoulders. "Watching another single gal walk down the aisle while we either wore a dress she picked out for us or sat in the pew and wished it was us."

Kendall sat with her chin resting in the palm of her hand. "Wow, you make us sound like two sorry single women."

"Well, I know there were days we felt sorry for ourselves." Rachel stopped talking as the waitress delivered their food.

For a few moments, Kendall focused on her late lunch. The ciabatta bun was as fresh as always, the lettuce crisp when she bit into her burger. She'd swim an extra ten minutes tomorrow to pay for this indulgence.

Rachel swallowed a bite of her sandwich, wiping the corner of her mouth with a napkin. "I remember watching another thirty-something woman like me get married about a year ago. Deanna Jensen—I met her through work. As she walked down the aisle, this thought skipped across my mind: *Now her life begins.*"

Kendall watched her friend take another bite of her lunch. Swallow. Take a sip of her Diet Coke. Then Rachel looked at her, her sparkling blue eyes dimmed.

"Wasn't that a terrible thing to think? *Now her life begins?* Like nothing before the wedding ring counts." Rachel's voice sharpened. "This woman is a successful physical therapist with her own practice in Denver. That doesn't count for anything?"

"You're not saying anything I haven't thought myself." Kendall forced herself to swallow a piece of her burger lodged in her throat.

"Why would we think something like that? We've worked hard and accomplished a lot for being in our mid-thirties."

"Did you think *Now life begins* when Tony proposed?"

"A little tiny voice in my head started to whisper it, but I stuffed a sock in it." Rachel stabbed a fork in her coleslaw.

"Good for you."

"I remember when my sister had her first child. She told me the ob-gyn talked about prodromal labor and how nothing before four centimeters counted as real labor. Can you imagine? You can be having contractions—but somebody decided it doesn't count." Rachel crumbled her napkin. "If I think my life begins because I'm finally engaged, then it's like everything before this is a prodromal life."

This was one of the reasons Kendall valued Rachel's friendship: because she spoke her mind, even when it made others—and herself—uncomfortable. She wasn't outspoken just to be outspoken. Rachel wrestled with life out loud and invited others to join her in wrestling with doubts and truth.

"Were you content with your life before Tony proposed?"

"Yes. And no." Rachel shoved her plate away, shifting in her seat and staring out across the deck. "God and I went nose-to-nose on the topic of the desires of my heart more than once. I'd been engaged once before—"

"You had? When?" And why didn't Kendall know this?

Rachel ran her hands through her hair, shaking it away from her face. "During college. Senior year. Oh, my. I was sooo in love with Gary. We were the perfect couple. Everyone told us so."

"What happened?"

"He proposed. I said yes. And then he expected me to give up my plans to go to medical school."

"But didn't he know that was your goal all along?"

"Yep."

"What happened?"

"Oh, I cried. Prayed. We were both believers, so we talked with our pastor. There was just no common ground. Somehow it became all or nothing for Gary." Rachel lifted her hands and then let them fall back into her lap. "If I loved him, I would not go to medical school. Period. And I felt like if he loved me, he wouldn't ask me *not* to go to medical school."

"And—?"

"And so I gave him back the ring. Went to medical school. Cried myself to sleep for weeks when I heard he proposed to another girl a year later. They got married. Had a passel of little Garys—five boys. Could you see me as the mother of five boys?"

"So he broke your heart." Kendall watched her friend and could see that even as she joked about what she'd lost, her eyes glistened.

"I think we broke each other's hearts. I don't think I was completely myself with Gary. Back then, I was more about letting a relationship define me than knowing who I was." Rachel sat up straighter, stiffening her shoulders. "Look at me, like I'm the Answer Woman. I started off wanting to apologize for hurting you. Then I confessed my doubts. Now I'm talking about my past life."

"It's what friends do on a beautiful April day in Colorado." Kendall paused as the waitress refilled their drinks. "We talk about life. The questions that have answers—and the ones that don't."

"Speaking of questions, whatever happened with the kid who had the allergic reaction at On the Border? Did you ever hear anything?"

"Believe it or not, he and his brother showed up in my office the next morning." Kendall wiped her fingers on her napkin. "The ER doc recommended me for a follow-up and we had an opening. Let's just say I don't expect Ian Walker to become a regular patient."

"Really? Why not?"

"His older brother—his name's Griffin—well, he and I didn't hit it off. Oil and water. Tomato, tomahto. Bert and Ernie. Wait, they get along."

"You saved his brother's life."

"I'm a doctor. It's what I do." Kendall couldn't hold back a gurgle of laughter. "Sorry. That sounded way too egotistical. I gave the elder Mr. Colonel Walker the name of another doctor. End of story."

The two women paid their bill and walked back out to Kendall's Jeep. As they buckled up, Kendall couldn't resist sharing what had happened on Sunday. "There is one guy who might be interested in me."

"What are you talking about?" Rachel pulled her hair back in a ponytail and then anchored her cowboy hat on her head.

"Heath Parker, a doctor I've met before at some medical conferences, was at church. He invited me to lunch."

"And?"

"And . . . who knows? He mentioned dinner later this week. We'll see what happens."

"Aren't you excited?"

"Rachel, I'm thirty-six. Could I get excited? Sure. Am I going to let myself get excited? No. I've learned the hard way to assume nothing, absolutely nothing, when it comes to men."

★ ★ ★ ★ ★

After dropping off Rachel at her apartment, Kendall drove home and quick-changed into a pair of dark gray jeggings, a light, fitted fuchsia sweater, and a wide leather belt. Then she slipped on a pair of black wedge shoes before reapplying her makeup and gelling her hair.

"Here's the deal, Sully." She held his don't-leave-me-home-alone sad face between her hands and scratched behind his ears as she forced him to look her in the eyes. "I'm going dress shopping. I'll be back later. When I come back, I expect you to let me in. Got it?"

Not above backing up her request with a bribe and the promise of a long walk, Kendall tossed Sully two dog treats and headed to her least favorite place: the local bridal salon. She had nothing against bridal shops in theory. Over the years, she invested in several dresses for friends' weddings. Not enough to compete with the fictional character in the movie *27 Dresses,* and none of the dresses was as outlandish as a kimono. Still, she couldn't help but wonder when she'd have the opportunity to say "Me" when the saleswoman asked, "Who's the bride-to-be?"

Rachel, Sonia, and Melissa were already browsing the racks of dresses when Kendall arrived. Rachel's mom, who was thrilled that her only daughter was getting married at last, stood off to one side. Seeing Kendall, Rachel rushed over and wrapped her arms around her neck in a move that was half choke hold, half hug, as if they hadn't just spent half the day together. Rachel had changed too, discarding the cowgirl look in favor of a slim-fitting midnight-blue faux-wrap dress paired with black heels.

"Now we can finally get started." Rachel grabbed both of Kendall's hands and pulled her farther into the wedding frenzy. A quick count revealed five other women trying on different styles of gowns, and all of them looked much younger than Kendall. Why was she not surprised?

"You shouldn't have waited for me, Rach." Kendall followed her friend to where the other women arranged chairs in front of a mirrored dressing room with a pink heart-shaped card taped on it. When Kendall looked closer, she realized Rachel's name was scrawled across the heart.

How . . . cute.

"The attendant is already selecting different styles for me." Rachel pointed to a chair on the end. "But I didn't want to try anything on until everyone was here."

As Rachel hugged her again, a flash of light exploded in Kendall's eyes. "Wha—what was that?"

With a giggle, Melissa stepped back and waved a camera that hung from a strap around her neck. "Just doing matron-of honor duty. I promised Rachel to take a gazillion photos of everything: her finding her dress, us trying on our dresses, the bridal showers—everything!"

"Great. Now I just need to find my way to the chair." Kendall felt for the padded chair arms and sat back.

The attendant, who looked as if she'd barely edged over into her twenties, directed Rachel into a dressing room while everyone claimed chairs and got ready for the fashion show.

Melissa stood in front of the group, holding a stack of bright pink index cards. "Before we see the potential dresses, we need our cards."

Our what?

"I've numbered each card one through five. One is 'No way' and five is 'It's absolutely Rachel.'" As she talked, Melissa handed Sonia and Kendall their packs of cards. When she tried to give a set to Rachel's mom, the woman waved her away.

"I'll know the dress when I see it. I don't need any silly pink cards."

"Are you sure?" Melissa hesitated.

"Just sit down so we can get started."

Kendall patted the seat next to her. "Come on, Melissa. The attendant's peeked out three times already. The rest of us will use the cards."

Rachel walked out of the dressing room, looking from one friend to the next, and then finally to her mother. Her fingers touched the delicate lace lining the V-neckline, then fluttered across the bodice. The same lace formed three-quarter-length sleeves that fit snug against Rachel's toned arms. Her friend's Pilates workouts paid off. The dress was full—tiers of lace that reflected an old-fashioned beauty perfect for Rachel.

Kendall didn't hesitate. She raised the "It's absolutely Rachel" card, not surprised when Sonia and Melissa followed. Rachel's mom requested that her daughter turn and then said, "Well, we'll see. It's the first dress, after all."

For the next hour, it seemed as if Rachel was determined to try on every dress style—if not every dress—in the shop. Princess gowns. Fitted gowns. Mermaid dresses. Lace dresses. Gowns that seemed more appropriate for the bedroom. One gown that required a hoop and harkened back to *Gone with the Wind.*

Despite all the silliness of the numbered cards, despite the niggling disappointment of not being the maid of honor—and really she didn't have the time or the creativity to do it properly anyway—Kendall enjoyed seeing her friend flushed with excitement as she tried on wedding dresses. Even when the dress was less than perfect, Rachel's vivid blue eyes glowed whenever she gazed at herself in the long row of mirrors, turning this way and that, examining the what-ifs.

As Rachel changed into yet another dress, Kendall watched an attendant hand a twenty-something young woman in a wedding dress a small brass bell. The bride-to-be listened to the saleswoman whisper something, closed her eyes for a few seconds, and then rang the bell as a triumphant smile lit her face.

"Another bride has found her gown!" The saleswoman hugged the girl as her friends surrounded her in a group hug.

Even with the gown held closed with oversized white clips, Kendall could see why the girl selected it. It was a wisp of a white sheath cut on the bias. Simple, yet elegant. Kendall forced herself to refocus on Rachel. She was here to help her friend find a gown—not to daydream.

One by one, the gowns were returned to their hangers, until

only one design remained—the very first one Rachel tried on. Kendall watched Rachel slip into the lace gown a second time. The style accentuated her slender neck, the ivory tones warming her skin and setting off the highlights in her brown hair as she held it up in a casual bun on top of her head. Tony's diamond glinted in the salon lights as she turned first one way, then the other.

Staring at her reflection in the mirror, Rachel bounced on her toes. "This is it."

Kendall had to agree. And so did Melissa and Sonia.

"I don't like it." Rachel's mother, who had sat silent for the evening, spoke up.

"What, Momma?" Rachel looked over her shoulder, still facing the mirror.

"I don't like it."

Kendall watched Rachel smooth the skirt of the dress, her eyes moving from her mother's face, back to her own reflection.

Her friend's response was a whisper. "This is the dress I've always imagined wearing on my wedding day."

"That style makes you look old. Frumpy." Her mother shook her head. Sniffed. "Do you want to look old on your wedding day?"

Kendall managed to hold back a gasp, crumpling the number five in her lap. Had Rachel's mother really said that?

"Of course not. But I think this dress is perfect. Tony will love it."

"Hmmph. I've known you a lot longer than Tony." Rachel's mother wrinkled her nose. "I think I know what looks best on you. And I said I'd pay for your dress—but not that one."

Kendall waited. Rachel was a physician. She could afford to buy her own wedding gown. She needed to say she wanted the dress and be done with it.

"All right, Momma. If you don't like it, we'll keep looking."
As she walked toward the dressing room, Rachel motioned for
the attendant hovering off to the side. "We've got lots of time to
find a dress."

What had just happened? Why didn't Rachel buy the dress
she wanted?

★ ★ ★ ★ ★

While Rachel changed back into her regular clothes, Melissa
gathered up the pink index cards and tossed them into a wastebasket. Rachel's mother bundled herself into her brown tweed
coat and went to stand by the door.

"Well, I guess that's it." Kendall turned to Sonia and Melissa.
"Although I don't know why she doesn't buy the dress herself."

"Rachel's waited a long time for this day." Sonia wrapped a
teal scarf around her neck. "She wants everything to be perfect."

"I don't know of anyone who's had a perfect wedding."

Melissa put the lens cover on her camera. "Well, she's entitled
to try."

When Kendall suggested dinner, the other women all had
reasons they couldn't make it. Rachel had to get her mom home
and then wanted to call Tony. And Melissa and Sonia both had
families waiting.

Kendall watched them go before climbing into her CJ5.
Driving home, the dream and reality of having it all swirled
around in her head like the snowflakes dancing in front of the
car headlights. No form, no pattern, and by tomorrow, they'd
all be an icy mess, sure to create a risk of slipping and falling.

Was there any way to have it all—and be happy?

Mina always said there was. She promised her that every time
she read a fairy tale, finishing with "and they lived happily ever

after." Mina lived it out, married for more than sixty years to her husband, the man she called her "prince." And bequeathing the ring to her—breaking the family tradition that the ring would be given to whichever granddaughter got married first—seemed like her grandmother's way of saying *I believe in you. I believe in your dreams. Don't give up.*

Her friends had found happiness—or some form of it. "All" looked like less of some things and more of others. Letting go of one thing to embrace another. Melissa seemed happy as a full-time, stay-at-home mom, occasionally backfilling for a day or two in her former dermatology practice when a colleague took vacation. As anesthesiologists, Sonia and her husband both juggled their schedules for the same group at Penrose Main Hospital.

Was Kendall going to ever have it all? Or was her future going to be more of the same—work and friends, and learning to accept that it was enough?

Once home, Kendall dropped her coat and satchel onto the couch, giving Sully an absentminded greeting and promising to take him outside soon. First things first. She crouched in front of the bookshelves lining her bedroom wall, her fingers grazing the books she salvaged from Mina's belongings after her funeral ten years ago. While others discussed who got the china, who got the antique mantel clock, who got the carnival glass collection, Kendall requested Mina's collection of fairy tales. Kendall could close her eyes and see each book—from an odd assortment of individual stories and collections—in her grandmother's hands. Hear her grandmother's voice begin, "Once upon a time there was a man and a woman who had long, but to no avail, wished for a child . . ."

She understood those fictional characters—their longtime wishing for an ever-elusive something. And yet, even in the darkest version of Rapunzel or any other fairy tale, "happily ever after" came. Sometime. And always, always, Mina reminded her that a life grounded in faith had so much more than anything written about in a fairy tale.

"Fairy tales . . . all they have is the made-up magic of fairy godmothers and elves and, yes, evil sorceresses. But you, Kendall, you have faith in a real, powerful God. And nothing can stop the happily ever after he has planned for you."

Sometimes, though, she felt like Rapunzel, locked away in a tower of unfulfilled dreams. Waiting. Still waiting.

CHAPTER FIVE

"*A*w, come on!" Griffin slammed his fist on the fender of his Jeep. A sharp pain radiated up his wrist. "That was stupid. Last thing I need is to start making weekly trips to the ER."

What a way to start the week. Stranded on the side of I-25 during the tail end of rush hour. Traffic rushed by, car lights reaching through the dusk as commuters focused on getting home—not stopping to offer him assistance. Griffin couldn't blame them. If his Jeep was working, he would be all about where he was going, too.

But right now, he was going nowhere. It's not as if he carried a spare fuel pump in the back of his CJ7. From the way the Jeep sputtered and jerked to a stop, Griffin figured that was the problem. Repeated calls to his buddy Doug went to voice mail, which meant Doug wasn't available to come tow the Jeep back to his house.

So, he was walking. But first he needed to call Ian and let him know to sit tight with his friends until Griffin got to Jeff's house. Exactly how he was going to get to his little brother was a mystery. Jeff lived a couple of miles away. He needed to think. But first, he needed to start walking.

Griffin wiped his hands together to dust off the grime from sniffing around the engine, keeping an eye on the cars and trucks speeding by him on I-25 as he walked to the driver's side of his Jeep. In the beams of the headlights, he could just catch a glimpse of a few snowflakes floating to the ground.

Great, just great. It was snowing and he'd be walking to the next exit.

Sliding behind the steering wheel, Griffin speed-dialed Ian. At least he'd been smart enough to put the kid on his cell phone plan. It rang several times before switching over to voice mail.

"Ian, what's the good of having a cell phone if you don't ever answer it?" Griffin checked himself. "Sorry. My Jeep broke down. I'm gonna be late picking you up. Hang tight at Jeff's. If that's going to be a problem, call me. Better yet, just call me when you get this."

He stared out the windshield, watching a steady line of tail-lights stream north. Wouldn't hurt to try again. Maybe the Jeep would surprise him and start. But a quick turn of the key produced nothing more than a pathetic sputter. Yep, he was still walking. He twisted off the cap of the SoBe bottle that lay in the passenger seat, grimacing at the lukewarm liquid as it slid down his parched throat. He'd get something to eat and drink once he got to Ian—whenever that was.

As he tugged on his gloves and pulled the collar of his blue uniform jacket up around his neck, Griffin watched a red Jeep pass him on the highway, then ease over to the shoulder and back up. Offering a quick prayer of thanks that "real Jeeps never leave another Jeep stranded," Griffin stepped back out into the cold night air and moved toward the Good Samaritan.

The door to the Jeep CJ5 opened and a diminutive form bundled in a long coat stepped onto the silver nerf bar and then onto the gravel shoulder. A woman—but still a Jeep person. When Griffin recognized Dr. Kendall Haynes in the glare of the passing headlights, he almost turned around, sprinted back to his Jeep, climbed inside, and locked the door.

"Hi. I'm Kendall. Can I—*you!*"

The look on the woman's face was so comical—her mouth forming a perfect O, her eyes widening as if Griffin pulled a gun on her—that Griffin burst out laughing.

"Good evening, Dr. Haynes."

"Colonel Walker."

They stood on the side of the highway, snow swirling between them. If she knew that he'd assumed she was a man coming to his aid, she would never forgive him.

"Well, this is awkward." Dr. Haynes moved toward him again. "But I stopped because I figured someone needed help."

"That I do." Griffin trudged beside her back to his disabled Jeep, the hood raised like a dented surrender flag.

She stopped at the front, turned, and waited until he stood beside her. "Do you want me to take a look?"

"What?"

She motioned toward the engine. "Do you think you know what's wrong or do you want me to take a look?"

"It's the fuel pump. And this is a Jeep, Dr. Haynes, not a body."

"Oh, good grief." Kendall Haynes closed her eyes, her mouth twisting in frustration. "Are you really that chauvinistic?" The woman stomped her foot, crunching gravel with her heel. Again with the heels.

"I'm just saying, there's quite a difference between the human body and an engine—"

"Have you checked your fuel filter? If it's clogged, then it's a quicker fix than a new fuel pump, which could also cause problems." She pointed into the engine. "That's the in-line filter right there, for your information."

Griffin did not like this woman. But she knew her Jeep engines. "Well done. You didn't learn that in med school."

She waved a hand toward her CJ5. "I rebuilt my Jeep with my dad when I was in high school. He said if I was gonna own it, I was gonna know it."

"Sounds like a great guy."

"He was. The best." Her smile wavered. "So, now that I've convinced you that I know something about engines, do you know what's wrong?"

"As I said, fuel pump."

"Do you want a tow or a ride home?"

The woman was offering to tow his Jeep?

"I have a friend who can help tow this thing tomorrow. And I'd accept the offer of a ride, but it's not quite that simple." Yeah, he'd accept the offer if he had to, not because he wanted to. But he doubted the woman wanted to play surrogate mom and go pick up Ian, too.

"Look, Colonel Walker, I realize you've decided not to like me. But that shouldn't stop you from accepting common courtesy from me." She pulled a pair of gloves out of her pocket and slipped them on. "We're both Jeep lovers. You can trust me. I promise to get you home safely."

"It's not that." Although the idea of being with Dr. Kendall Haynes for any length of time had as much appeal as his annual medical exam. "I have to pick up Ian at a friend's house a couple of miles from here. So maybe you could take me to the nearest gas station and I'll call a taxi?"

Snowflakes had settled in Kendall Haynes's short brown hair and along the shoulders of her coat. She ran her fingers through her hair, causing it to stand in short spikes, before pulling the hood of her coat over her head. "My offer stands. I'm not on call, so I'm free."

Letting her help him made sense. He didn't like it, but it was the fastest way to get to Ian.

"Deal. Let me just secure things."

"Okay." She started back to her Jeep. "I'll let Sully know you're coming."

Wait—what? Sully? She had a guy with her? Or a kid? What had he agreed to?

His decision to insist on calling for a taxi disappeared the moment he opened the passenger door to be greeted by an oversized, overly friendly dog.

"Sully!" Kendall Haynes tugged on the dog's collar. "I told you to get in the back. We have a guest. "

"You have a dog?"

"Yes." She stopped trying to shove Sully into the back. "What? I'm not the type of person you expect to have a dog?"

He waited to slide into the front seat until the dog lumbered to sit behind him. Actually, she wasn't. Poor dog. "I hadn't thought about it, one way or the other."

"Uh-huh." She adjusted her seat belt, waited for a break in the traffic, and then moved back onto the highway. "So, you said Ian's at a friend's?"

"Yeah." Griffin gave her the address, which she told him to punch into her GPS. "Let me give him a call and tell him I'm on the way."

As he left yet another message for his brother, Griffin watched Kendall Haynes. She'd lowered the hood of her jacket, and the soft fur surrounded her face. Within seconds, Sully leaned forward, squeezing the upper half of his body between the two front seats and resting his head on her shoulder. She reached up and scratched behind his ear, whispering to the dog. Silence filled the car once he finished his calls.

"So, you're military?" Dr. Haynes's question appeared to be asked out of politeness, an attempt to start a conversation.

"Air force."

"Are you at the Academy?"

"No, I'm down at Schriever."

"What do you do?"

"I'm a pilot." Griffin shifted in the seat, realizing that his statement probably required an explanation since there was no airfield at Schriever Air Force Base. "I'm flying a desk right now."

"Excuse me?"

"I'm grounded. Flying a desk."

"Oh. Funny. Flying a desk."

Hysterical. Take a pilot out of a plane—the reason he was in the military to begin with—and stick him in a cubicle. He laughed all the way to work. But he had no one to blame but himself. For convincing himself the dizziness was no big deal. No need to mention it to anybody, least of all a doctor.

Sully's wet nose snuffling at his neck pulled Griffin from his thoughts. "Hey, guy." He scratched underneath the dog's neck. "How ya doing?"

"Just tell him to leave you alone."

"He doesn't bother me. I like dogs."

"Probably easier to talk to him than to me."

Griffin turned in the seat, catching her quick glance his way. "You're pretty direct, aren't you?"

"Well, all I've been getting is one- and two-syllable words out of you. You're either the strong, silent type or extremely uncomfortable."

"Guilty as charged."

"Or more likely, both." She slowed the Jeep as they headed onto an off-ramp. The snow was falling harder, beginning to cover the ground. "So, how's Ian doing?"

"He's okay."

"Did you get him in to see another allergist?"

"When I called to make an appointment, the receptionist told me that he's booked until May."

"Figures. I'm booked until about then, too."

"Then how did we get into see you?"

"I had a cancellation that day. You got lucky." A soft giggle followed her statement. "Although I realize you may not see it that way."

Griffin cleared his throat. "Maybe it would help if I explained my situation with Ian . . ."

"No need."

"I'll keep it brief. You can see there are a lot of years between Ian and me—twenty-two, to be exact."

"Wow, your mom must have been shocked to find out she was pregnant."

"My parents adopted Ian when he was six. He'd been in foster care before that."

"Ah."

"About four months ago now, my parents were killed in a plane crash—my dad was the pilot. Bad weather. They were . . . coming back from a cruise after celebrating their fortieth anniversary." He paused, waiting for the tightness in his throat to

ease. He cleared his throat again. "Anyway, they appointed me
to be Ian's guardian. I don't think they ever thought it would
actually happen—"

Griffin's words trailed off. What else was there to say?

"I'm so sorry, Griffin."

Kendall Haynes's words filled the silence with an unexpected
moment of comfort. Up until then, he'd been Colonel Walker.
But his name slipped naturally from her lips. At work, he was
Colonel Walker, too. At home, more silence flowed between
him and Ian than words. It was nice to be recognized. To be
listened to—even if it was by Kendall Haynes.

★ ★ ★ ★ ★

And that was the end of that conversation.

Kendall waited for Griffin Walker to say something, but the
only sound was Sully's heavy breathing as he sat between them.
Griffin's jaw was clenched so tight, she would be taking him to
an emergency dentist for a busted molar if he didn't relax.

A few moments later, Mr. Strong and Silent, with an emphasis
on Silent, pointed to the left. "I think you turn at this light—"

"I know, the GPS is a great invention. Turn at this light." She
downshifted and turned left. Within five minutes, she pulled up
in front of a stucco home at the center of a cul-de-sac.

The man had the door open before she came to a complete
stop.

"I'll go get Ian."

"And I'll—" She watched him disappear up the sidewalk.
"—wait here. No, I don't want to come inside. Thanks. I'm
good."

Sully's please-let-me-get-in-the-front-seat whine broke the
silence.

"Don't you dare like that guy, dog. He's trouble with a capital *T,* as Professor Harold Hill would say. He's wound as tight as a tourniquet. Last thing I need is some uptight guy hanging around. Now, Heath Parker—you can like him all you want."

She had to admit Griffin Walker had a certain masculine magnetism Heath Parker lacked. But then, with his muscular build and brooding dark eyes, Griffin seemed to like to be in charge. She knew his type. Bossy to a fault.

She leaned forward when Griffin walked out of the house—alone. He stood facing the car, looking first right, then left. As he paced back to the Jeep, he pressed his phone to his ear, his brow furrowed.

Kendall waited until he'd ended the call before asking the obvious. "Where's Ian?"

"That's the question of the day. And I have no idea." He scratched at the scruff of dark whiskers lining his jaw. "Jeff's mom said the boys worked on their science project for a while and then went to get something to eat—almost three hours ago."

"Did she say where they went?"

"No. She thought they said Subway. Or maybe McDonald's. Or maybe Red Robin—"

"Yikes."

"She's calling Jeff now. I'll call Ian again, but he hasn't answered any of my calls so far." Griffin stared at the keypad of his iPhone as if trying to figure out who to call next—or waiting to see if somehow Ian would call him.

Just then, a Honda Civic came around the corner, the deep beat of the stereo's bass preceding it up the road. It pulled into the driveway. Laughter spilled out of the car along with five teenage boys.

"I assume one of those boys is Ian." Kendall tilted her head to see around Griffin.

"Yep. He's got some explaining to do." Griffin strode up the driveway toward the group. "Ian! Where were you?"

Kendall watched the teen's relaxed posture stiffen. He moved toward his brother, putting space between him and the other boys.

"Griffin. What are you doing here?"

"I'm your ride home, remember? I told you to wait here until I came to get you."

"Uh, yeah . . . I got that. The guys and me . . . we went out for dinner. No big deal."

"You said you were going to be at Jeff's working on your science project."

"I was. We did. Then we got hungry. Like I said, no big deal. I'm here now." Ian walked past his brother but stopped short of Kendall's Jeep. "Where's your Jeep?"

"It broke down, so obviously I'm not driving it. Dr. Haynes saw me on the side of the rode and offered me—us—a ride home."

"Dr. Kendall? Cool! Let me go get my stuff." A few minutes later, Ian clambered into the back next to Sully, shoving a gray backpack in the corner. "Great dog. What's his name?"

"Sully." Kendall started up the Jeep, ready to get some heat circulating again. "You buckled in, Ian?"

"Yeah, I'm good."

Kendall waited while Griffin settled into the front seat, twisting around to focus on his brother.

"Well, let's get you home." Kendall backed up, then stopped. "Um, directions?"

Griffin seemed oblivious to her presence, all of his attention on his brother. "So where were you, Ian?"

"I told you." Ian rubbed Sully's ears, causing the dog to settle half in his lap, half on the backseat. "We went to dinner."

"That's it?"

"Sure."

"Because you smell like cigarettes."

Glancing in the rearview mirror, Kendall saw Ian freeze. Caught.

"Um, yeah. That's because . . . because Jeff's dad smokes." Instead of looking at his older brother, Ian watched Sully. "And so his car smells like cigarette smoke."

"Jeff drives his dad's car?"

"No. I mean, yeah. And his house smells like cigarettes, too."

Was Griffin buying his brother's story? This was not the time for her Dr. Kendall act. Not the time for her to lecture him on the dangers of cigarette smoke, either firsthand or secondary, especially when she didn't know his full medical history. How else might Ian be compromising his health?

"Gentlemen, I'd love to sit here all night and listen to you two chat." Kendall tapped her gloved fingers on the steering column. "But then one of you will be taking Sully for a walk around this neighborhood. Which way is home?"

As she drove toward the east side of the Springs, Kendall chatted with Ian about his science project. Griffin resumed his silent act. The address he entered in the GPS had her pulling up in front of a fairly new townhome. So this was where the Walker men lived. Snow covered the front yard, as well as the driveway and the path to the door. No lights welcomed them home.

"Ya wanna come in, Dr. Kendall?" Ian sat with a snoozing Sully's head in his lap.

"Not tonight, Ian—" Griffin was already halfway out of the Jeep.

"It's not that late." His brother continued to sit in the back.

Kendall faced the teen. "I don't think your brother cares for doctors. Or maybe it's just me."

Ian's grin offered an apology. "It's a pilot thing."

Griffin peered back in the car. "Ian. Out of the Jeep. Now."

After his brother exited her Jeep, Griffin leaned back inside. "Thanks for your help tonight."

"From one Jeep lover to another, no problem." The next words spilled out of her mouth before she could stop them. "Let me know what happens with your CJ7. And maybe Ian could come over for dinner sometime soon. I'd be glad to help him with his science project. And you're welcome, too, of course."

He stepped back, his eyes hidden from view. "Sure. Maybe. I'll, um, get back to you on that. Thanks again. G'night."

She watched Griffin follow his brother into the house, barely noticing when Sully clambered into the front seat. Why had she suggested Ian come over for dinner sometime? Griffin Walker would rather starve than sit down at a table and share a meal with her.

"And those are the Walker brothers, Sully. I don't expect you'll be seeing them again."

She drove home, careful to keep a good distance from other cars as the road got more and more slippery with the increasing snowstorm. She needed to give Evie a call and see what the overnight forecast was and decide whether to rearrange the first appointments for tomorrow. Living right above her office, she'd have no problem getting to work, but oftentimes patients canceled due to weather.

While she allowed Sully a quick walk around the side yard, next to the combo office building/home sweet home, her phone pinged, signaling a text message. Heath Parker, perhaps? Probably not. They had dinner plans later in the week, so there was no reason for him to contact her. But you couldn't blame a girl for wishing.

As she walked upstairs to her loft, she glanced at the text. Tanner.

Hey Ken
Happy B day
Yes I'm late
Forgive your little brother, 'k?
Love you

Kendall tapped a quick reply. Only two people got away with calling her "Ken"—her brother and her dad. And since her father's death, only her brother used that nickname.

You did a good job, Ken-girl. I'm proud of you.

Even all these years later, the faint whisper of her father's voice still carried the tang of both sweet and bitter. In some ways, everything she did was so she could hear the echo of her father telling her that he was proud of her. Even though it reminded her that she couldn't see her dad, couldn't talk things out with him, ask for his guidance.

Sully's soft whine inviting her to snuggle with him on the bed pulled Kendall back to reality. Along with the most basic commands, the dog had never learned "Stay off my bed."

"Sorry. I don't feel sleepy anymore." Kendall slipped on her robe. "I think I'll wander downstairs and catch up on paperwork. Wanna join me?"

As she headed down the dimly lit hallway to her office, Sully trailing behind her, a prayer slipped past her lips. "Oh, God. I know even back then you had a plan." The words came swiftly. It was always the same. "And I trust you. But I don't understand why you took Dad from me. I just . . . don't."

CHAPTER SIX

★ ★ ★ ★

*I*f anyone told Griffin he'd be driving back to Kendall Haynes's office within two weeks of their first disastrous appointment, he'd have told them they were certifiable.

But here he was, pulling into a parking lot out front and stopping near the huge stone sign with the words THE ROCKY MOUNTAIN FAMILY PRACTICE CLINIC carved in it. As much as Griffin didn't care for the woman, Ian insisted it was Dr. Kendall or nobody. Griffin finally gave in, willing to concede this battle to his brother. He just wasn't sure if Ian wanted to see her because he liked going to Dr. Kendall or if he liked irritating his brother.

Ian didn't even wait for him to turn off the engine before climbing out of the passenger seat and heading down the sidewalk.

The lot looked fairly empty. A good sign. Now if only the waiting room was empty, too. Maybe they'd get in there, see the doctor, and get home. He could feel his heart rate elevating the closer he got to the front door, the name of the practice etched across the glass against the outline of a mountain range.

The same tall receptionist with the welcoming smile staffed the front desk. Today dancing thermometers adorned her scrub top.

"Colonel Walker, it's nice to see you and Ian again." She handed him a neon purple clipboard containing several pieces of paper. "I'm sorry Dr. Kendall didn't have a morning appointment. The good news is, she's running ahead of schedule today."

"Terrific. Excuse me, um—" He glanced at her name tag, adorned with the outline of Pikes Peak. "—Evie, didn't we fill this out the last time?"

"Yes." As the phone rang, she adjusted the mouthpiece of her headset. "Just double-check to make sure everything's correct and then have Ian give it back to me."

Griffin walked over to where Ian slouched in a chair, dropping the paperwork in his lap.

"Hey!" The teen looked up. "What's this?"

"Your medical paperwork. Make sure everything's right." Griffin settled himself in next to his brother, ready to check his emails on his iPhone.

"Why aren't you doing this?"

"Your information. Your responsibility."

"But Mom always did this kind of stuff."

Griffin held up his hand, blocking Ian's attempt to hand back the clipboard. "I'm not Mom."

"No kidding." Ian shifted away from him.

Enough already.

"Ian." He waited, staring at the back of his brother's head. "Look at me when I'm talking to you."

"Going all hard-core guardian on me?"

"Just asking for a little respect—and a little eye contact."

He pulled the boy's orange-and-blue Florida Gators cap off his head, ignoring the teen's protest and tossing it on the table beside him. "I understand it's hard for you without Mom and Dad."

"Sure you do."

"They're my parents, too."

"I get it. They're your real parents—not mine."

Griffin lowered his voice. "That is not what I said at all. We both miss them."

"As if."

Ian's hazel eyes glinted with unshed tears before he dashed them away with a balled-up fist. Where was all this emotion coming from?

"You never talk about them. Never. Forget about it." Ian stood and walked across the room, settling into another chair and training his eyes on the papers.

What was his brother doing, lobbing a verbal grenade like that? What did Ian want him to do, sit around and mope? His parents were dead. And he was Ian's guardian—and as far as he could tell, he was doing a lousy job at it. When it was just him, Griffin didn't care if the fridge was mostly empty. He'd swing by Whole Foods, stroll through the hot food section, and grab a quick dinner. Or drive through Chick-fil-A and order a value meal. Apparently that kind of lifestyle wasn't keeping Ian happy. Well, he was sorry about that, but he hadn't cooked a meal in . . . well, he didn't cook.

And laundry? If his mom were alive, he'd call her and thank her for every pair of socks, every pair of jeans, every single T-shirt she ever washed, folded, and put in his dresser drawers. He was lucky if he got Ian's clothes moved from the washer to the dryer.

He was flunking this whole guardian gig.

"Ian Walker?"

One of the medical assistants stood at the door that led to the exam rooms. Ian bolted from his chair, not looking at Griffin.

Should he follow? Stay in the waiting room?

Kendall Haynes's words came back to taunt him: *Just be the guy Ian needs you to be.*

Staying was not an option.

He followed the MA down the hall, standing outside the room while she took Ian's blood pressure and temperature. Once she left the room, he sat in a chair. Silence shrouded the room.

"Ian."

The teen stared at the wall. What was he doing, memorizing the words on one of Kendall Haynes's framed certificates?

"Ian, I'm . . . sorry."

He was rusty at saying those words. It felt as if he was coughing up boulders. Griffin swiped a hand across his face, stared up at the ceiling. What more should he say? "I miss them. Mom and Dad." He shook his head, the familiar sense of unreality filling his mind. "I still expect a phone call, you know?"

"Yeah." His brother's reply was choked. Guttural.

"I didn't get home often. But I always knew . . . they were there." He huffed out a breath.

A knock rapped against the door. As it opened a few seconds later, Griffin thanked God, knowing he was too much of a coward to continue the conversation.

★ ★ ★ ★

What had she walked into?

Kendall cast a covert glance at the Walkers as she took the clipboard from Ian. He sat on the exam table, the white paper bunched up beneath him, his eyes hidden by a ball cap. Griffin sat ramrod straight in the chair, watching his brother. He looked ready to walk out the door. If he was so unhappy about being here, why had he come back?

"Ian. Good to see you." She turned to his brother. "You too . . . Griffin."

After rescuing him from the side of I-25, Kendall figured she could risk going the informal route with him. Maybe put him at ease.

Griffin's lips thinned, his jaw clenching.

Then again, maybe not.

"So, Ian, let's focus on you today, shall we?" Maybe she could at least establish a good relationship with one of the Walkers. Besides, Ian was her main concern. All she wanted from Griffin Walker was for him to understand how serious food allergies could be.

"Sure."

"Thanks for filling out your medical history more completely. You confirm your allergy to avocados, as well as bananas and latex rubber, and seasonal allergies. And you were also diagnosed with asthma when you were six?" From the shift in Griffin's body language, she could tell this was new information to him.

"Yeah, but that's no big deal. I don't need to use an inhaler."

"Well, that may have been true at sea level, but it may change now that you're living in this climate." Kendall leaned against the counter, trying to ignore the tension radiating off the elder Walker. "I need to listen to your lungs again and ask a few questions. It's important you answer me honestly."

"Sure."

She positioned her stethoscope around her neck, warming it against her palm. Resting one hand on his shoulder, she stood beside Ian. "I can see you're going to be as tall as your brother."

"He's not my real brother."

Okay, then.

"Just because you were adopted doesn't stop you from being a real family, Ian." Kendall patted his back just above his shoulder blade. "I'm going to raise your T-shirt just a bit. As I recall, I didn't see any tattoos the last time."

Ian's snort of laughter diffused some of the tension. "No, but Griffin's got one."

"Really?" She listened to both of his lungs, and then dared to make eye contact with Griffin. Oops. Not laughing. "Well, seeing as I probably won't be your brother's physician, I doubt that I'll be seeing his tattoo anytime soon."

"It's on his—"

"Ian!" Griffin growled a warning.

"Why don't you just tell me what the tattoo is, Griffin?"

Griffin's growl was now directed at her. "Why don't you concern yourself with my brother, Dr. Haynes?"

Ian joined in the fun. "She likes to be called Dr. Kendall, Griffin. The MA told me."

"Whatever works for your brother is fine with me." She tucked her stethoscope in the pocket of her lab coat. "So how's school going?"

"Fine. I've got this stupid biology project."

"That was my favorite subject in high school."

"Really? Were you good at it?"

"Of course." She went to the door and looked for Renee, speaking to Ian over her shoulder. "I'm going to have my medical assistant administer a breathing test. I want to evaluate your lung function."

"His what?" Griffin's question jerked her attention back to him. If the guy ever smiled, he'd be quite handsome in a rough-around-the-edges kind of way. Not that she was noticing—not really.

"I'll explain it all after Ian takes the test. Suffice it to say, I want to see how well Ian's perception of his breathing matches up to reality. I'll be back in a few minutes to discuss Ian's results with you."

While Renee worked with Ian, Kendall checked with a radiologist about the results of an X-ray. As she talked on the phone, she could hear Renee chanting, "Blow, blow, blow, blow!" to encourage Ian to exhale as hard and as long as he could. About ten minutes later, she was back with Ian and Griffin.

Griffin stood leaning against a wall. "I've got to admit, I enjoyed watching someone yell at my brother."

"Very funny." Ian rolled his eyes.

Kendall motioned for Griffin to sit in a chair beside Ian, turning the computer screen full of numbers and a graph so they could easily see the information.

"Ian's breathing test scores weren't as good as I'd like." She pointed out the numbers marked on the chart. "Normally, you want a range of eighty to a hundred twenty percent of normal. Ian's hitting about seventy-one percent."

"So what does that mean?" Griffin moved closer, and Kendall repositioned the screen.

"We need to treat him more aggressively so his numbers come into a normal range. People get used to breathing at a less-than-optimal capacity—but they consider it normal. If we put Ian on a daily inhaler treatment, his lungs will improve over time. Then we'll establish what's called a 'personal best' peak flow by using a handheld meter at home every day for a while. Then later, he can check it at home if he thinks he's getting into problems." Kendall forced herself to stay focused. This was no time to wonder if the man across from her wore aftershave or stuck with good, old-fashioned soap.

Soap. She was betting on soap.

"And even though Ian says his asthma is no big deal, I recommend that we start him on a daily steroid inhaler."

"What does that do?"

"Hmmm? It helps decrease lung inflammation."

"But I'm fine." Ian twisted his cap around so that it sat on his head backward.

"I believe you *were* fine, most of the time, in the climate back in Florida." Kendall tapped the papers with her pen. "But these numbers indicate that you're not fine here. A lot of people who have no problems living in, say, North Carolina or Tennessee have breathing problems when they move to Colorado because of the drier, colder air. I also suggest having an inhaler on hand in emergency situations."

Ian nodded agreement. "You're the doc."

"Let's talk about your allergies." This was going to be the tricky part. "You know what you're allergic to, right?"

"Sure."

"Remind me how old you were when you were diagnosed with those allergies?"

"First grade. It was right around the time Mom and Dad adopted me."

She really needed to get his medical records. "With your latex allergy, have you dealt with skin rashes?" When he nodded, Kendall continued, "Do you know what type of medication your doctor prescribed to help?"

"I used to take a pill—but I don't remember what the name is."

"I'll contact your previous doctor for that information. So you know what you're supposed to eat and not eat, right?"

"Yeah. Mom taught me all about asking what was in stuff if I wasn't sure. And she made certain I had an EpiPen and my allergy pills with me, and that I knew what to do if I had a reaction."

Kendall wasn't certain, but she'd bet Ian hadn't told his brother any of this.

"So what's different now, Ian?"

"Whaddya mean?" The boy stopped making eye contact with her, playing with the hem of his gray Hurley T-shirt.

"You know what to do . . . but you're not doing it." Kendall positioned her body so she focused just on Ian. "You want to tell me what's going on?"

Silence reigned in the exam room for a few minutes. Thank God Ian was her last patient of the day. Kendall hadn't wanted Ian's appointment to be during the middle of the day so there was a clock ticking during this conversation.

"Ian?"

"I'm just . . . tired of it, y'know?"

She waited for the teen to explain himself, hoping and praying he felt safe enough to talk to her.

"All through school, I'm the different kid. The one who couldn't eat special snacks. Or was always checking labels. It got to be a joke."

"Lots of kids have allergies, Ian."

"I know." He ran his fingers through his long hair, and then repositioned his hat again. "Anyway, I ate some guacamole at a friend's house when I first moved here. Nothing happened. I thought maybe . . . I wasn't allergic anymore. It can happen. The next time, I got a little itchy, but no big deal. I was being careful."

"But not careful enough." She looked at Griffin, who followed the back-and-forth conversation as if he were watching a tennis match. "Your brother needed to know about your medical history, Ian. It wasn't fair to hide it from him. What if I hadn't been at the restaurant when you had that reaction? You could have died."

"But you were there . . . and I'm fine."

"Thank God." She moved over to the computer in the exam room. "I'm printing up a couple of prescriptions. One for the steroid inhaler and one for the rescue inhaler. Remember to rinse your mouth after you use the inhaler. You've already got the EpiPens. Keep one at home, one at school—maybe in your backpack. Just don't leave it in your car. Extreme changes in temperature affect the medication."

She paused, debating her next step. What she was considering was unusual. Not unethical, just crossing the lines of a normal physician–patient relationship. But Ian Walker needed a friend. And she understood what he was going through—not that he or Griffin knew that.

Did God want her to be Ian's friend? Before she could talk herself out of her decision, she stood, ramming her fists into her pockets. "It's the end of the day for me. Kinda quiet." She could ignore her notes for a while. "Ian, would you like to go upstairs to my loft and say hi to Sully? Maybe take him for a quick walk out back?"

The teen jumped up from his chair. "You live upstairs? How cool is that!"

Griffin stared at her as if she'd suggested suiting up and trying to fly a jet.

"Come on, Griff." Ian was already out the door and halfway down the hallway.

Kendall watched the older Walker brother, trying to decipher his unspoken thoughts. "Don't feel obligated to go. I'll run upstairs, get Sully's leash, and let Ian run the dog around for a few minutes."

"Why?"

"Why? Um, because he's been cooped up all day and—"

"No, I mean why are you doing this?"

Weren't men supposed to be the uncomplicated gender? "I thought it might be fun for Ian. No big deal. He could play with my dog for a few minutes. Look, if you want, when I get the leash, I'll grab a stopwatch, too, and keep the time at a strict ten minutes."

Well, look at that. The hint of a smile lurked on Griffin Walker's face. One day she might say something to get the guy to loosen up and laugh.

"I have no ulterior motive to complicate your life. Ian seemed to like Sully. And he also looks like he needs a friend." She paused. Just how honest did she want to get with Mr. Strong and Silent? "And I understand what Ian's going through because . . . well, because my dad died when I was eighteen."

And that was all she intended to say about that.

★ ★ ★ ★ ★

Griffin did not need Kendall Haynes to get personal.

Which is why he didn't respond to her disclosure that her father died when she was eighteen. Sure, he felt bad for her. Who wouldn't? But that was years ago. She was over it by now.

He waited just outside the two-story brick building surrounded by a neatly manicured area of green grass and a small parking lot mirroring the one in the front while she commandeered her mind-of-his-own dog and got both him and Ian downstairs. Griffin and Kendall stood side by side, watching as Ian took off running behind Sully, who seemed intent on chasing an invisible rabbit.

If it was all about location, location, location, Kendall Haynes made a wise choice purchasing this building. She had an incredible view of Pikes Peak. Griffin watched the setting sun turn the mountain range into a black backdrop rimmed in a golden glow. As far as he was concerned, Colorado's sunsets had no rival. Since moving to the Springs, he hadn't seen the same one twice.

Kendall's voice broke through his thoughts. "Did you get the fuel pump fixed?"

"Yep."

"So your Jeep's running smoothly again."

"Not exactly."

He wasn't surprised to hear her give a knowing chuckle. Since she was a Jeep girl, she understood how temperamental the things were.

"So what's the problem now?" She shifted, coming a bit closer. What perfume was she wearing? And why didn't she smell like a hospital or something . . . medicinal?

"Started hearing a clicking noise up front—driver's side."

"Hhhhm. Wheel bearing? Maybe the brake caliper?"

Whoa. A woman who talked mechanics. Not that it was cute. Or appealing. It was just different.

"Could be the universal joint."

He knew Jeeps, too.

"True. So, you investigating?"

"That's what Saturday is for."

They stood in silence, both staring at the Peak. She broke the silence flowing out into the cold night air first.

"So . . ."

"So?"

"If you need any help, I'm available." Kendall stuttered over her next words. "I-I mean, I love working on Jeeps. I've got a closet full of my dad's tools—always happy to put them to good use."

Was Kendall Haynes trying to take care of him, too? First his brother, now him. But then again, she admitted to being a Jeep girl. And she'd rebuilt her CJ5 with her dad—so she knew Jeeps inside and out, and probably backward and forward. Griffin shoved her offer aside. How difficult would fixing a universal joint be? Half an hour, max. He could handle it.

"I appreciate the offer, but I've got it covered."

"Well, good." She shrugged, pulling the collar of her lab coat up around her neck.

"Thanks anyway."

"Anytime."

He could almost feel the temperature dropping degree by degree as they stood in silence, waiting for Ian and Sully to return. Maybe that stopwatch wasn't such a bad idea. When he caught the faint sound of his brother's laughter intertwined with a dog's raucous barking, Griffin pulled his keys from his pant pocket.

"Sounds like it's time to go."

"Don't forget the prescriptions—"

He patted his wallet. "Got 'em."

"Good. And the peak flow meter—"

"Pocket."

"You're set, then." She stepped forward as Sully skidded to a stop in front of them, tail wagging and tongue lolling out of his doggy grin. "If you have any questions—"

"I'll call the office."

"Right." She took the leash from Ian. "Come on, dog. Time for dinner. Thanks for walking him, Ian."

Ian bent down and scratched behind Sully's ears. "Anytime. He's a great dog."

Walking backward, the woman dragged the goldendoodle toward the building. "He's sixty-five pounds of stubbornness."

As he followed Ian around to the front of the office to where his Jeep was parked, Griffin swallowed a laugh. Kendall probably didn't weigh a whole lot more than her dog. And they were both strong-willed.

Perfect match.

CHAPTER SEVEN

★ ★ ★ ★ ★

Griffin searched the Y's cardio room and found Doug already logging miles on one of the exercise bikes in the back. The man might be a good twenty years older than him and retired from the air force, but he worked out as if he still needed to pass an annual fitness test. Even in the gym, Doug carried himself with the attitude of someone in command—although he now indulged in a close-cropped beard, something his military career never permitted. Walking along the perimeter of the room, he made his way over to Doug and selected a cycle beside him, adjusted the seat, and climbed on. The sound of people exercising—the rhythmic thud of feet pounding on treadmills, the steady whir of the motorized stepper—melded together with the odor of sweat.

Working out. Nothing like it.

"Good to see you." Doug nodded in his direction, his legs pumping at a steady rate.

"You, too, sir."

"How many times do I have to tell you? Drop the 'sir.' I haven't been your Academy sponsor in, well, do we really want to say how long it's been?"

"Sometimes I can't believe it's been sixteen years." Griffin cranked up the tension on the bike.

"Time has a way of going a lot faster than we think—and things have a way of not going according to our plans."

"You got that right." Griffin's life proved that. The past was littered with choices he'd thought were the right ones that somehow went wrong.

"Pick up your pace and tell me what you're thinking, son." Doug took the white towel wrapped around his neck and swiped at a line of sweat trickling down his forehead into his full beard.

Griffin leaned forward and increased his rotations. "Same stuff—and then some."

"Ian still giving you problems?"

"Yes. First he loses Mom and Dad. Then, because I'm stationed here, I take him away from all his friends. Who can blame the kid?" Griffin gripped the handles as if the bike might careen off its stationary path and into the line of treadmills in front of him. "And then I find out he's been hiding the fact that he has asthma and is severely allergic to avocados and a bunch of other stuff. He almost died on me."

His words caused Doug to slow down. "What happened?"

Griffin related the events at On the Border, the image of Ian's blue lips, his body racked with coughs still rattling him like a bad altimeter reading. "I should have known."

"How? No one told you—"

"Really? My mom never mentioned Ian's allergies? Or did I just not listen? I never took the time to get to know my little brother . . . and now I'm his guardian." Griffin snorted. "Some guardian. I almost killed him."

His words caused the woman wearing a COLORADO: THE OTHER RECTANGLE STATE T-shirt on the cycle to his left to look at him with raised eyebrows.

"Griffin, wallowing in guilt will get you nowhere." Doug leaned over and grasped his shoulder, his gaze direct yet compassionate. "You've made mistakes. Learn from them and move on."

Easier said than done. He had enough consequences looming ahead of him for years to come. And he had two years to do right by Ian before the kid turned eighteen and walked out the door and never saw him again. He needed to call Mrs. Jamison again and see if she and her husband had made a decision about taking Ian.

Doug's voice intruded on his thoughts. "Don't believe everything you're thinking."

"What? Is that in the Bible somewhere?" Griffin respected how Doug, the man who guided him from confusion and hopelessness to God, always spoke truth grounded in Scripture.

"Yes and no. It's my updated way of saying something Paul said in Philippians. It boils down to 'Don't believe everything you're thinking.'"

"Ian barely speaks to me. The only time we had any sort of a decent time together was the night we hung out with Kendall Haynes and her dog—"

"Who?"

Griffin held up his hand to stall the *Are you dating?* question. "*Dr.* Kendall Haynes, the woman at the restaurant when Ian had the allergic reaction. She also helped me out one night when my Jeep broke down on the side of I-25. She let Ian walk her dog one night after his appointment. She feels sorry for him—that's it."

"You seem to have an awful lot of run-ins with this Dr. Haynes. Is she single or married?"

"Most definitely single—and I'm not surprised, or the least bit interested."

Doug's shout of laughter bracketed his eyes with lines and tugged a smile across Griffin's face.

"Not your type, eh?"

"She reminds me of Tracey. Opinionated. All about her career." Griffin sat up, rotating his shoulders to ease the tension from his back. "She may be five feet tall, but she has a Patton-sized personality. I'm not surprised she drives a Jeep—just surprised she doesn't have a driver."

"You sure she's not interested in you?"

Now it was Griffin's turn to laugh. "Unless you're talking about her being interested in verbal sparring, most definitely not. Believe me, her focus is Ian. She lost her dad when she was a teenager, too, so she understands how he feels."

The two biked sided by side for a few minutes. When the world began to tilt to the left, Griffin sat up straight. When would he have one day without vertigo pushing his brain off balance?

"Ian's not the only one who's missing your mom and dad, Griffin. You're grieving, too."

Griffin mulled over his friend's words, staring straight ahead, his hands resting on his thighs, his T-shirt damp against his back. "That doesn't make any sense. I mean, yes, I'm sad. I even admitted as much to Ian. How could I not be? I loved my parents. But I'm thirty-eight years old. I left home at eighteen to go to the Academy. Got married at twenty-two. I've been on my own for years. I'm handling this."

Griffin knew Doug watched him but refused to make eye contact with the older—and much wiser—man.

"All true. But you still lost your parents in an unexpected, tragic accident. It's normal to be sad about it. If you don't grieve, you're not allowing Ian to grieve."

Was that true? What had Kendall Haynes called him—Strong and Silent? There was nothing wrong with that . . . it was just who he was. Not a talker. But was his not talking hurting Ian?

"You want to help your brother?"

"Yes."

"Then you have to choose to have a relationship with him."

There was that word: *relationship*. Another thing he failed at. So long as *relationship* meant no expectations on either side, he was good.

"I'm not the best at relationships, Doug. You know that."

"What do you call this?"

"What do you mean?"

Doug motioned back and forth between the two of them. "You and me."

Huh? What kind of question is this?

"We get together. We talk. Work out. You listen. I talk. You give me advice. We pray together. Um . . . we're friends."

"Took you . . . long enough . . . to say it." Doug's words came out in between little huffs of breath as he upped the tension on his bike and stood up in the pedals. "Not gonna get . . . all 'bromance' on you. That's what they call it . . . right?"

"I have no idea."

"We're friends. We spend time together . . . we talk. That, son . . . is a relationship. Do the same thing with Ian."

"He barely says hello to me."

"You used to . . . call me 'sir.'"

"I still call you 'sir.'"

"Rarely. Takes time . . . but things change. Put the effort into it." Doug cycled in silence for a few moments before easing back on the tension and sitting again. "What's on the agenda tonight?"

"Ian's studying. I'm getting dinner on the way home."

"What are you getting?"

"It's Friday, so that means burgers and fries." Griffin ignored the burn in his legs, forcing himself to pedal faster.

"You eat . . . standing in the kitchen and Ian eats at the table while he studies."

"Pretty much, yeah."

"Change it up. Make dinner tonight."

Griffin glanced at the clock positioned on the front wall of the cardio room, above the bank of TV monitors. Almost seven. Then again, even if Ian snacked on a predinner bowl of cereal, he would be ready for something decent.

Griffin ran his fingers through his sweat-soaked hair. "I don't have a cookbook."

"Excuses, Colonel?" Doug snapped his towel at him. "You have a grill?"

"Top of the line."

"Put on a coat and grill some steaks. People grill year-round in Colorado. Make baked potatoes. Voilà! Dinner. Throw in some conversation and you, my friend, have the start of a relationship with your brother. Repeat as needed."

Grill, huh? He could do that. He might even enjoy doing that.

The gray hairs mingled in with Doug's brown hair must be a sign of wisdom, just like the Bible said. The two men biked in silence before Doug eased the tension on his bike.

With his next question, Doug brought up the topic always lurking in the back of Griffin's mind. "Have you heard anything from the medical board?"

"I'm due for my reassessment examination by a neurologist and a flight surgeon the end of May."

"How's the vertigo?"

"Fine."

"But you're still having episodes, right?"

"Nothing worth mentioning."

The two men cycled for another two laps on their virtual racetracks.

"So how did that whole 'not worth mentioning' approach work out for you the first time?" Doug's question came at him like a Stealth fighter—quiet, but lethal.

Bull's-eye.

"You know the answer to that question." Griffin slowed his pace, stretching his arms over his head.

"Yes, and so do you. Don't make the same mistake twice."

"That's always my plan—not to make the same mistake twice. But I also need to get my flying status back."

"Not if you're not healthy."

"I will be."

He had to be.

When he walked into the house forty-five minutes later, Ian was stretched out asleep on the couch, a textbook on his chest. Griffin remembered many a study session at the Academy that turned into a nap. He'd let Ian snooze while he prepped the steaks and baked potatoes, then wake his brother up right before he threw the steaks on the grill. Maybe by then he'd think of something to talk about.

★ ★ ★ ★ ★

"I apologize for being late again, Heath." Kendall faced away from him as he helped her slip on her paprika-colored wool coat. The man knew how to treat a woman with quiet respect.

"I'm a doctor, too. If anyone understands about a clinic running late, it's me." He stepped outside her back door, waiting while she locked up, and then walked beside her downstairs, his hand on the small of her back. "Besides, it gave me a chance to catch up on emails."

The touch of the cool night air began to ease some of the tension from Kendall's temples. She'd caught only glimpses of the outside while she sat in her office writing notes and then dashed to her loft to change for dinner. Sully sulked in his corner, not at all pleased at a quick walk around back.

"Let's look on the bright side." Kendall finished buttoning her coat. "We avoided the first rush of people for dinner at P. F. Chang's."

"If there's one thing I've learned about eating out in the Springs, there's always a wait on Friday nights." Heath guided her to his black Hummer.

Oh. Sounded like she wasn't the first woman going out on a date with Dr. Heath Parker. Which was fine. Absolutely fine.

"Or so I've been told." He used the keyless entry to unlock the car, once again opening the door for her and waiting while she settled herself in the passenger seat.

Kendall watched him walk around to the driver's side. In a casual pair of slacks and a dark brown leather jacket over a cream-colored turtleneck sweater, Heath looked confident yet relaxed. And who knew a guy with her dad's old-fashioned manners still existed? She waited while he settled into the driver's seat before resuming their conversation.

"How's house hunting going?"

"Nothing so far." Heath turned the car toward the Shops at Briargate. "Supposedly it's still a buyer's market, but my Realtor hasn't shown me anything I've fallen in love with. It's the Goldilocks syndrome: *This one's too big. This one's too small.* I know the saying, 'It only takes one,' but I haven't found my 'just right' one yet."

"It must get old, living out of your suitcase."

"I've traveled so much the last five years that I'm used to it. I think the real adjustment is going to be when I have more than a few shirts and a couple pairs of pants hanging in a closet, much less a house full of furniture."

"How long were you overseas?"

"Five years." Heath adjusted the heat and then turned the radio on low so that a soft melody underscored their conversation. "Before that I was finishing up my master's in public health and tropical medicine at Tulane."

"Do you like being stateside?"

"Yep. There are definite advantages to being here in the Springs." The allusion to a compliment, coupled with the way Heath tossed a grin her way, warmed Kendall. The man was easy to like.

Heath turned the conversation to small talk all the way to the restaurant, entertaining her with stories of life in Africa. The wait for a table was minimal, and before long they sat in a booth ladling bits of savory chicken into lettuce leaves and waiting for their main courses.

"I wonder—oh, never mind." Heath focused his attention on folding a lettuce leaf over the filling he'd scooped inside.

Kendall swallowed the bite of appetizer. "What is it, Heath?"

"I don't want to impose, but I could use your help with something."

"Well, ask. I'll let you know if I can't help you."

"I'm considering raising funds for the organization by selling some products from Kenya. Things made by women—mostly single moms. Jewelry. Baskets. That kind of thing." He motioned for her to help herself to some more shredded chicken. "I need to have several boxes of sample items shipped here. Three, maybe four boxes. I'm actively house hunting and I'm not certain how long I'll be at the hotel. I'm not sure when the boxes will arrive—you know what overseas mail can be like. I'd hate to have the boxes get lost because I'm moving around. Would you mind if I had them shipped to your office?"

Sounded simple enough. "That wouldn't be a problem at all."

"Really? Kendall, thank you so much."

She waved off his thanks. "It's no big deal. I'll let my receptionist know to expect them."

"It may take a few weeks. Just let me know when they arrive and I'll come over right away and get them out of your way."

"Where are you in putting your organization together? I mean, what's your plan of action, if you don't mind me asking?"

"I don't mind you asking at all." Heath paused as the waiter stopped beside their table with their entrées. She'd convinced him to try one of her favorite dishes—a chicken, melon, and walnut mixture in a sweet sauce—and she hoped to conquer his skepticism.

"I'm putting together my board now—mostly other medical professionals with overseas experience, but I've included a lawyer so that I properly walk through all the red tape. And my Realtor is also looking for an office space—nothing as nice as yours. I'm trying to keep costs down."

"I wouldn't have managed my building, except for an inheritance from my grandmother. I'd invested it for several years—and it paid off well." Kendall scooped brown rice onto her plate. "And doing the combo home and office means I'm only paying the one mortgage."

"If I was a smart man, I'd have you on my board, too." Heath paused with his chopsticks midway to his mouth. "Wait. I am a smart man. Why don't you come to the next board meeting?"

Kendall stared at him over the rim of her glass of Merlot. "Just because I agreed to let you ship a few boxes to my office doesn't mean you have to invite me to a board meeting, Heath."

"That's not it at all. Look, I know you're busy with your practice, so I'm not asking for a long-term commitment—yet." Heath paused to finish off a bit of melon. "But I'd love for you to sit in on the next meeting, get a better understanding of my vision. Tell me what you think. And then, if it's something you'd be interested in getting involved with, let me know."

"I have to admit, that's an intriguing proposition."

"The next meeting is in a couple of weeks. I'll call you with the time. We're meeting at the Craftwood Inn over in Manitou."

"Ve-ery nice. That's reason enough to say yes."

"Ah, I can see you're not above being bribed, Dr. Haynes." Heath's chuckle disappeared as his face turned serious. "No, really, one of the reasons I would love to have you involved is because your reputation precedes you."

"There's no need for flattery, Heath. I've already said yes."

"This is not about flattery. You're well respected in the medical community here, Kendall, by other medical practitioners. And by your patients. That's admirable."

"Thank you. I've worked hard to build my practice. I hope it has a good reputation."

"One of the best." He motioned to the entrées sitting in front of them. "This is just as good as you said. Catch up with me before I eat the rest."

"I'm glad I didn't steer you wrong."

"Not at all. Lead on, Kendall. I'll follow you wherever you suggest."

Yeah, the guy was a bit on the corny side. But she liked it.

She sighed when the ping of her iPhone pulled her attention away from the man seated across from her.

"Excuse me, Heath. I'm on call. I need to get this."

"Sure thing. Go ahead."

Kendall walked to the front of the restaurant, slipping past the crowd of people waiting to be seated to go outside to better hear the caller. The night air wrapped her in a chilly hug, reminding her how quickly temperatures in Colorado dropped once the sun disappeared behind Pikes Peak.

"Dr. Haynes, this is Nurses on Call. I have a Griffin Walker asking to speak with you."

Kendall paused just outside the restaurant's entrance. "Griffin Walker? Did he say what the problem was?"

"Not specifically. He said you were aware of the situation."

Odd.

"Dr. Haynes?"

"I'm sorry. Go ahead and patch Colonel Walker through."

Within seconds, Griffin Walker's frustration-tinged voice came over the line. "Kendall?"

"Hello, Griffin. Is Ian all right?"

"Yes, he's fine. That's not why I'm calling."

Kendall paced in front of the restaurant, the heels of her shoes clicking on the sidewalk. Why had she left her coat inside?

"Are *you* sick?"

"No, no. I'm fine." There was a moment's pause. "Is your offer to help with my Jeep still open?"

"Excuse me?"

"My Jeep—you offered to help me work on it."

Kendall stopped walking, facing the restaurant. Inside—back where it was warm—sat Heath Parker. And here—outside where it was so cold her teeth were chattering—she stood talking to a man who didn't even like her.

"You called the emergency line to talk to me about your Jeep?"

"I didn't know how else to reach you. Look, I've spent the last four hours fighting with a universal joint. Right now, the universal joint is winning."

Kendall tried to contain the laughter that burst past her lips, but she couldn't.

"Fine. Laugh at a man when he's down. I'm desperate. You said you had an arsenal full of tools. You wouldn't happen to have a disc grinder, would you?"

"You realize this does not constitute a medical emergency, Griffin."

"If you spent the last four hours working on your Jeep with nothing to show for it but some bloody knuckles and a head full of words you're struggling not to say, you'd be more sympathetic. What happened to your loyalty to another Jeep comrade?"

She decided not to make the man grovel. Besides, she was freezing. "It just so happens I have a disc grinder. And I'd be happy to bring it over tomorrow. Is that soon enough?"

"Yes. I concede the battle with the beast tonight." The man sounded worn down, his voice ragged. "I stripped one of the bolts and now I've got to cut it off with a grinder—which I don't have."

"It's no problem. I think my dad owned every tool ever made."

"I'm so frustrated right now, I could almost sell this thing. But hey, it's—"

"It's a Jeep. I know."

Their laughter mingled together over the phone.

"I'm abandoning my garage and getting a shower—and then I'm going to order a Meat Lover's pizza and watch a movie. Something where we win the war."

"Sounds like your best option. I'll be over around eight tomorrow to rescue you. Sound good?"

"Make it nine. No need to get up early."

"I don't have a choice about that, Griffin. Sully's the early riser in the family. G'night."

"Good night, Kendall. And thanks."

She double-stepped it back into the restaurant, her fitted skirt hindering her attempts to get back inside and thaw off.

Imagine that. She had a mostly friendly conversation with Griffin Walker. And he asked for her help.

Huh. Miracles still happened.

★ ★ ★ ★ ★

"I should have called you sooner."

Griffin looked across the garage to where Kendall sat on the middle step that led back into the house. She wore a pair of scuffed blue cowboy boots, faded jeans, and a long-sleeved red henley top. All in all, the woman looked about sixteen years old—and cute, even with a streak of grease across her chin. As she took a sip of water from the bottle he'd gotten for her, he noticed her hands were also marred with grease.

At his admission, Kendall raised the water bottle in a mock salute. "True."

"Now, was that nice?" He wiped his hands on a piece of old towel, being careful not to displace the Band-Aids on his knuckles, and then tossed it into a white plastic bucket in the corner of the garage near the snow shovel.

"I just agreed with you."

Griffin walked over to the spare fridge he kept in the garage, searching among the assorted sodas and bottled waters and selecting a Mountain Dew. It wasn't as if he needed an extra fridge. The one inside the house was never more the one-third full. Milk. Eggs. Bread. Lunch meat. Lettuce and tomatoes that spoiled. Oranges that usually shriveled up. And after Ian's near-death episode, he stopped buying avocados and bananas. Some days it was easier to skip the produce section of the grocery store altogether.

He sat on the cement floor in front of Kendall, unable to prevent a groan from slipping out. "Thanks for the help."

"It wasn't me. It was the grinder. And maybe the coffee I brought along."

Griffin twisted off the bottle cap, holding the cold bottle up to his forehead. "That, too. But don't downplay your part. You do know Jeeps."

"I thought we settled that on the side of I-25."

When she tossed him a wink, he chuckled. "So, didn't you say your dad and you rebuilt your CJ5?"

He waited as she took a gulp of water. Swallowed. Stared at the mostly empty wooden tool bench on the opposite wall of the garage.

"Yeah, yeah, we did." She tilted the water bottle to her lips again for another long drink. "I spent most of my weekends during high school rebuilding that Jeep with my dad. Good times."

Griffin watched Kendall's profile. He could guess what life had been like for a girl like Kendall Haynes back in high school. Someone who was smart and cute and wasn't afraid of an engine. He bet her phone rang nonstop. She probably worked on the Jeep during the day, cleaned up, and then went out on dates every Friday and Saturday night. But then she must have decided she wanted a career more than family.

Just like Tracey.

Kendall's soft voice pulled him away from his thoughts.

"My dad was a mechanic." Warmth lit the gray of her eyes. "First in the army. Then he opened his own shop. He loved working on cars. Trucks. Jeeps. My mom used to say he would have slept in the shop if she hadn't called and reminded him to come home every night."

As she talked, she tore bits of the label from the water bottle, letting the pieces fall to the cement at her feet.

"He died when I was eighteen. It was two months before I graduated from high school." She stared past him, seeming to focus on the red Jeep parked along the curb. "We'd just finished rebuilding the CJ5."

She bit her bottom lip, her eyes closed for one second. Two. Three. What was she remembering?

"He asked me to go get him a glass of water . . . he was, um, thirsty, you know? I didn't rush. It was such a beautiful day. Sun shining. Breezy. I'd been in the garage since early that morning and I thought, *Take your time.*" She sniffed. Rubbed the bridge of her nose with her index finger. "I always thought maybe if I had been quicker . . ."

Griffin kept himself still. He didn't know what to say, was afraid to interrupt such a fragile memory.

"When I got back to the garage I couldn't see my dad . . . he'd fallen down . . . nothing I said, nothing I did helped. I ran back to the house, yelling for my mom. For my brother and sister." She inhaled a breath that shook her shoulders. "He died while I was in the kitchen getting him a glass of water. I still remember walking across the stage to get my high school diploma. Looking out at the crowd, expecting to see him smiling at me. Cheering me on. Calling me 'Ken-girl.'"

When she stopped talking, the silence between them grew. What could he say? "Sorry" seemed so . . . useless. The woman shared something personal with him and he sat there like an idiot. What would Doug say?

Kendall saved him from having to figure out what to do or not do by rising to her feet and tossing the empty water bottle into the blue recycling bin by the stairs.

"Well. I apologize for that."

"No need—"

She waved off his comment. "Griffin, it's okay. I can't help thinking about my dad when I work on a Jeep. Occupational hazard."

She held out her hand, offering to help him up. "If there's one thing my dad taught me, it's to take care of your tools. Come on, Walker."

He clasped her hand and allowed her to pretend to haul him to his feet. Doing so only served to emphasize how much taller he was than Kendall Haynes. Her head only came up to the middle of his chest.

"Mutt and Jeff." Kendall tilted her head back and squinted up at him as if he were a long, long way above her.

"What was that?"

"We look like Mutt and Jeff. Which is why I never like dating guys a lot taller than me. We look like a cartoon couple."

Really? That's not what he'd been thinking at all.

Not that he'd ever allow himself to date a career woman like Kendall Haynes.

Once had been enough. And the first time he was stupid enough to marry the woman.

CHAPTER EIGHT

★ ★ ★ ★ ★

"You two finished yet, Griffin? I'm ready to go look for cars."

Ian Walker hurtled into the garage pulling a black sweatshirt over his head and slamming the door behind him.

"Did you even shower?" Griffin walked toward his brother as he gave him a once-over, providing Kendall a chance to refocus. Despite her offhanded comment to Griffin Walker, he'd been anything but a cartoon character the last few minutes.

"Yep." Ian shook his head in a motion reminiscent of Sully after a bath. Drops of water from his hair dampened Griffin's face. "Even used soap. Didn't have time to shave, though."

"Right." Griffin wiped his hand across his jaw. The man had an attractive profile. Rugged. And she was noticing this because . . . ?

"Hey—" Ian swung a playful punch at his brother.

"Save it." Griffin caught Ian in a headlock, reminding Kendall of the times Tanner and her dad used to wrestle in the living room—until her mom yelled at them to stop.

"So is Dr. Kendall going with us?"

"I think I've monopolized enough of Kendall's time today." Griffin half turned toward her again. "She doesn't want to go car shopping with us."

"Didja even ask?"

Kendall couldn't resist the urge to tease Griffin. "Yeah. Didja even ask?"

A smirk twisted Griffin's full mouth. "What? You want to go look at a Jeep with me and Ian?"

Did she? It was that, or go back home and pay bills. "Sure. I'll never turn down the opportunity to go check out a Jeep."

Ian whooped as if his favorite NFL team just won a play-off game. Griffin paused mid-stride.

"Right. Now you're going to want to go home and 'freshen up,' right? Trade in your cowboy boots for another pair of ridiculous high heels—"

"Hey! What do you have against high heels, Walker?" Kendall surveyed her outfit, dusting off the seat of her pants and straightening the hem of her top. "There, ready to go."

"No shower? No freshening up your makeup?"

"We're going to look at a Jeep, not meet royalty. I'm fine. What about you?" She inspected Griffin's outfit of a worn pair of jeans topped with a faded gray flannel shirt that fit his broad shoulders well. Whoever decided flannel shouldn't be limited to women's winter pajamas was a wise person, indeed.

"Let me grab my car keys—"

"Leave your Big Boy at home, Walker. I'll drive. Where are we heading? If we've got time, I'd like to run by and do a quick check on Sully."

Griffin seemed to consider her offer. "Monument Motors just up I-25 north. Heard of it?"

"Actually, I have. And my house is on the way. My nurse practitioner and his wife bought their last car from there. But I thought they handled Subaru."

"Mostly—but they get the odd car or Jeep as trade-ins." Griffin stood half inside his house, half inside the garage. "Let me go get my wallet and coat."

Ian followed Kendall to her Jeep. What was she thinking, hanging out with the Walkers? Whatever it was, this wasn't about Griffin. She wasn't attracted to the handsome, brooding man with the secretive past—and a teenage brother. That guy had never figured in any of the fairy tales Mina read to her. This was about building a friendship with Ian. She knew all about being a teenager and losing a parent.

After checking on Sully—and cleaning the grease streaks off her face and hands—they drove through Starbucks and grabbed drinks and finally headed to Monument.

Griffin surveyed her Jeep. "Not bad for a CJ5."

"What do you mean, not bad?" Kendall patted the slate-colored dashboard. "My father and I put a lot of time and effort into this Jeep. He wanted to put on thirty-three-inch wheels, but with the short wheelbase it sounded like the perfect setup for rollovers. So I stick with thirties."

"I prefer my CJ7."

"The one that keeps leaving you on the side of the road? The one that we just spent the morning working on?"

"I haven't been able to keep up with working on my Jeep. Been busy."

Ian leaned forward so that half his body was wedged between the two front seats. "Hey, don't blame your Jeep problems on me."

"I didn't blame it on you, Ian. I was busy before you got here."

"Uh-huh." His brother slumped back, arms crossed over his chest.

Kendall and Griffin made brief eye contact as Griffin gave a slight shrug. Maybe Kendall could help reestablish a better relationship between the brothers by the time they got to the car dealership.

"So . . . tell me about this Jeep you're considering buying."

"It's a Cherokee—an 'indoor.' Got some new parts. Decent mileage. I think it would make a good first one for Ian. Of course, he'll need to drive it, see how he likes it."

Silence from the backseat.

"Sounds good." Kendall raised her voice, trying to include Ian in the conversation. "Have you looked anywhere else?"

"Ian and I looked at the want ads. There are some options there, too, but one of the guys at the office said this place is trustworthy."

Kendall looked at Ian through the rearview mirror. The teen sat and looked out the window. "So, Ian, you interested in a Jeep?"

"I guess."

Maybe a change of topic would help.

"How's the science project coming?"

"Pretty good."

"If you need any help, let me know. I'm available."

Kendall didn't miss the moment's hesitation before Ian replied. "Sure."

By the time they got to the car dealership, she managed to get Ian laughing over some ridiculous YouTube videos of stunts gone wrong. Griffin sat in silence. What, he didn't like YouTube?

The wind whipped around them as the trio walked toward the office building, offering a hint of impending snow. Kendall looked toward the mountains to the west. Gray-tinged clouds hovered over Pikes Peak, a sure sign that a storm was on the way. They'd likely have snow by nightfall. Or not. This close to the foothills, you never knew where the forecasted snow would actually show up.

Within minutes, they were looking at the rust-colored Jeep. It looked clean, and Kendall caught the whiff of the just-washed and -vacuumed smell as Griffin opened the door and sat in the passenger seat. He motioned to his brother. "Ian, you get behind the wheel."

"Me?"

"Sure. If we decide to buy it, it'll be your car, not mine."

Kendall stood off to the side, watching the brothers interact. When Griffin made eye contact with her, she gave him a thumbs-up. A saleswoman wearing a vivid yellow down vest handed Ian the keys. "Do you want to drive it, check it out?"

"Can I?"

"I need a license and then I'll put a dealer tag on the Jeep. You're good to go."

"Sweet."

"You do have to bring it back." The saleswoman tugged on the key, a playful smile on her face.

"Sure."

Griffin motioned Kendall over. "You brave enough to come along? You could wait in the office, enjoy a cup of coffee instead of risking your life."

"I never miss the opportunity to ride in a Jeep. Besides, I taught my brother to drive." She climbed into the backseat, memories of instructing Tanner in the finer points of a stick shift washing over her.

"You're a good sport." Griffin buckled his seat belt after handing over his license, waiting while the woman checked Ian's license, too.

"I'm sure Ian's a reliable driver. I'm good."

She settled back and watched Griffin and Ian prepare for the test drive.

Griffin insisted that Ian look over the dashboard, checking out the basic controls. "You do know how to drive a stick, right?"

"Kinda."

"Kind of?"

"Well, yeah. Dad had taught me, but I usually drove Mom's automatic, so I'm probably gonna be rusty."

Kendall bit back a grin. This was going to be fun.

She knew it took all of Griffin's willpower not to grab hold of the dash as Ian pulled out of the parking lot, the Jeep lurching as if it were having convulsions. Her own fingers gripped the edge of the seat, her eyes locking with Griffin's in the rearview mirror.

"So, where to?"

For a moment, everything was blessedly still as Ian waited for instructions.

"Let's stay off the highway for now. Turn left and let's go up Highway 105 toward Palmer Lake. Take it easy on the curves. You're just seeing how the car handles, not racing."

"Sure thing."

While Ian drove, Griffin checked the radio, the wipers, the heater and AC—or at least tried to. After bumping his head on the dash when the Jeep sputtered to a stop at a red light, Griffin settled back in his seat. Kendall had to give him credit for not throwing instructions at Ian about how to handle the Jeep. She kept a tight rein on her own words. Ian was Griffin's brother, not hers.

As Ian concentrated on operating the clutch, Griffin shifted in the seat so he could look at her. "So your brother is younger than you?"

Kendall answered his unspoken questions. "His name's Tanner. He's five years younger than me. And then there's my sister, Bekah. She's ten years younger than me."

"Do they live in Colorado, too?"

"No. Bekah lives back east—still lives at home. Tanner's the adventurer in the family. He's overseas right now teaching English."

The conversation ceased as Ian approached railroad tracks.

"What now?" Ian sounded as if he wanted to trade places with Griffin.

"What do you mean, 'What now?' Slow down and cross the tracks."

Griffin's advice to slow down came a moment too late and they endured a jolting five-second ride that had Kendall grabbing for the edge of the seat so she didn't bounce all over the back of the Cherokee.

After five more minutes of lurching around Palmer Lake, Griffin instructed Ian to pull over. "Let me drive back."

"I'm doing okay, aren't I?" Ian focused on the road, looking for a safe spot to pull over.

"You're doing fine." Griffin stretched his neck right, then left. "But if we're buying this thing, I want to check out how she handles."

Within seconds of arriving back at the dealership, Ian was ready to buy the Cherokee.

"Calm down." Griffin rested a hand on his brother's shoulder. "I think we're getting the Jeep, but I'm not ready to say yes yet. Let's see if the price is negotiable at all. Then we'll go have lunch and think about it."

"But you'll tell 'em we're interested, right?" Ian still stood beside the driver's-side door of the Jeep. "I don't want anyone buying it while we're at lunch."

"Yes. I'll make certain they know we're interested."

Leaving the Walkers to negotiate, Kendall walked back to her Jeep. Try as she might, she couldn't think of a single restaurant in town that offered neck massages with a side of Motrin.

★ ★ ★ ★ ★

On the drive to California Pizza Kitchen back in the Springs, Kendall and Ian discussed the merits of the Jeep, even debating whether Ian wanted to lift it or not because it made it harder to climb into the Jeep. Griffin tried to ignore the ache nagging at his temples, not even up to the effort of teasing Kendall that she'd need a footstool to get into the Jeep if they did too drastic a lift. Decisions. It was less complicated to watch the scenery pass by. The Academy football stadium came into view, the words AIR FORCE written across the western stand of seats in towering white letters. How many Saturdays had he marched out on the field before a game, then run back down into the Falcons' end zone to do push-ups near the goalpost whenever Air Force scored a touchdown?

He had his life all planned out back then: Graduate. Get married. Fly. And here he was sixteen years later. His life looked nothing like he'd envisioned when he was twenty-two. How did he get so off course?

The lunch crowd was heavy at CPK, but they settled into a booth in the back after a short wait. Griffin inhaled the crusty aroma of fresh-baked pizza. At least letting Ian commandeer the driver's seat hadn't ruined his appetite. Griffin watched Ian and

Kendall as the black-clothed waiter handed them each a menu and explained the specials. His brother radiated adolescent energy, while Kendall looked as if she could lean back in the booth and doze off.

"Tired?" Kendall's question implied she'd noticed the grooves lining his forehead.

"Yeah."

"Anything on your mind—besides Jeep problems, I mean?"

"No. Nothing more than everything that goes with having a teen boy in the house." Griffin looked over at Ian, thankful his brother was so busy trying to figure out what he wanted to eat that he'd missed that offhand comment. So far they'd had a good day no need to knock Ian back into an attitude.

"Hey, Griffin, you okay if I order a whole pizza?" Ian shoved half a slice of bread into his mouth. "I was thinking I'd get the Meat Cravers."

"Sure." Maybe there'd be leftovers. Or maybe not. "What about you, Kendall? I'm paying. You provided manual labor this morning and you drove this afternoon."

"I love the fish tacos here. It's my go-to order every time."

"Sounds like we're ready, then." Deciding on the tostado pizza, with its blend of black beans and cheese, Griffin closed the menu, looking up when someone stopped by the table, expecting to see the waiter with their drinks.

"Griffin Walker. I thought that was you."

The red-haired woman wearing a casual pair of khaki pants and a white scoop-neck top stood directly beside him, a hint of a seductive smile curving her lips. Or maybe that was more of a taunting look. He could never tell with his wife.

Make that his ex-wife.

"Tracey." Griffin slid from the booth. Stood. Cleared his throat. "I didn't know you were in the Springs."

"I—we're house hunting. Considering a move back here. You know how Academy grads love Colorado Springs. Funny that we'd both end up back here."

Was there a laugh track playing somewhere? His ex-wife and her family in the Springs. Great.

"Mom, let's go."

"Yeah, Mom, let's go."

Two girls, both wearing jean jackets and frilly skirts, stood next to Tracey. How had Griffin missed them? With their red curly hair and matching coats and Uggs, they had to be Tracey's daughters. His ex-wife must still spend her off hours at the mall—and now she had two more reasons to shop. He'd heard she had kids, but the sight of her two daughters still made him feel as if he was in a plane that had lost altitude too quickly. Tracey swore she never wanted children—and here she stood with two.

"Just a minute." She clasped the girls by their hands and pulled them forward. "Girls, this is Griffin Walker, a friend of Mommy's from the Academy. Griffin, this is Claire and Sarah."

The girls chimed hello, revealing gaps in their smiles. How did they manage to both be missing the same teeth?

Tracey's green eyes scanned the booth behind him. Griffin froze, realizing Ian and Kendall were watching the exchange between him and his ex. Any minute now, Tracey's husband would walk up and the whole happy reunion would be complete.

Tracey motioned to Ian and Kendall. "Is this your family, Griffin? I thought you couldn't—"

"No. No family." Griffin shoved the words out.

Kendall's voice broke through the silence. "I'm Kendall Haynes, a friend of Griffin's. And this is his brother, Ian."

"Ian. I never had the chance to meet you." Tracey shook their hands. "How nice."

"Hey." Ian settled back into the booth, grabbing another piece of bread, acting as if they ran into his brother's ex on a regular basis.

But Tracey had never met Ian. They'd spent two years together, two years apart, and then one year back together, fighting their way to a divorce. There was no time to go visit his little brother.

Tracey refocused on him. "So you're stationed here now, Griffin?"

"Yes." Griffin shifted his weight from one foot to the other, wishing he could sit back down.

"Not flying?"

Obviously, since there wasn't an A-10 base in Colorado. "No."

"That's too bad. You were all about flying back in the day." Tracey gave him a slow once-over. He remembered that calculating look. "Still single?"

"Yes." Not that it was any of her business.

Her daughters tugged on her hands again, causing her oversized charm bracelet to jangle. "Let's go, Mommy. Daddy's waiting for us at the door."

Griffin saw a husky guy with a crew cut standing by the front of the restaurant. In his arms he carried a toddler. A boy. Tracey had *three* kids. And a new husband to pay off her credit card bill. Maybe this guy didn't mind a wife who never said no to a sale.

Tracey answered his unspoken question. "Yes, three. Me, of all people. I never imagined how much I would love being a mom." She caressed the tops of her daughters' heads. "Well, this was such a surprise. I'm sure we'll run into each other again, if we move here."

Oh, he hoped not.

Griffin refused to watch Tracey walk away—into the life she'd sworn she never wanted. At least, not with him. Marriage. Kids. And Griffin agreed with her—at least the "no kids" part. And eventually they both argued their way out of the marriage, too.

The arrival of the actual waiter stalled Griffin's explanation of his interaction with Tracey. He appreciated Kendall's nonchalant act and Ian, being sixteen and a boy, was already thinking about the could-be-his-Jeep again.

"Sorry I didn't introduce you." Griffin considered ordering a beer. Not that drinking a beer would help. It was probably best to say it straight up, not that it was any of Kendall's business. "That was my ex-wife."

Kendall played with her straw, stirring the ice in her glass of tea. "I kinda figured you and she had some kind of past."

Ian leaned forward, craning his neck to look at the front of the restaurant and catch another look at Tracey. "That's Tracey? The way Mom talked about her, I always thought she was taller."

His mom talked about his ex? She only met her a couple of times, once at the wedding. What could she have to say about Tracey?

"Yeah, she went on and on about how bossy she was . . . didn't like her at all."

Kendall swatted his brother's arm. "Ian, stop. You're talking about Griffin's ex."

"Exactly. He must not have liked her much, either."

Griffin didn't need his brother hypothesizing about his failed marriage. "Tracey and I realized getting married was a mistake."

"That's what everybody says." Ian reached for his third piece of bread.

Griffin pulled the bread out of his hand and deposited it back on the plate. "Ian, go to the bathroom and wash up."

"What? I'm not six, Griffin."

"Just go."

As his brother walked away, Griffin tugged on the chain resting around his neck. Why did it seem to weigh so heavily all of a sudden? "Sorry. I didn't handle that well."

"Understandable. Your ex shows up while you're having lunch. You're gonna be rattled."

"I haven't seen Tracey since the divorce. Hard to believe, huh? I knew she got married. Knew she had kids." The image of identical twin girls scrolled across his mind. "Still . . . the woman I knew was all about her career. And swore she'd never, ever have kids."

"A lot of us make plans, Griffin. And then life changes."

"I get that. And I even see some good that came out of the whole mess that we—that I made."

Kendall rested her chin on the palm of her upturned hand. "What's that?"

"I'm good with being single. I'm satisfied with the way life turned out."

"Come on, Griffin. Just because things didn't work out with you and Tracey doesn't mean—"

"This really isn't something I want to talk about." Griffin leaned away from the table, looking to the left, which caused the world to tilt. *Ignore it.* Where was Ian? Or the waiter? He didn't want to get personal with Kendall Haynes.

When he looked back at the woman sitting across from him, her gray eyes were the hue of the storm clouds looming over the Peak.

"If you recall, Griffin, I didn't start this conversation. You did." She bit her lip, as if attempting to stall herself from saying anything else.

There was the Kendall Haynes he knew. The one who spoke her mind—and who reminded him of his ex. The funny thing was, Tracey looked angry only when she was backing him into a corner, determined to make a point. Kendall's feistiness was woven through with a sense of humor that made her appealing. Almost alluring. He liked the way she went nose-to-nose with him—at least when she was sitting down. The thought caused him to chuckle.

Wrong response.

"For the life of me, I can't figure out what's so funny right now." Kendall shifted her position away from him. Was she walking out? Now, that would be a direct repeat of his ex-wife's behavior, although he doubted Kendall could slam the restaurant's door the way Tracey did when she exited a room mid-argument. "You are . . . infuriating."

He could say the same about her—if he dared.

"Look. You're happy being single? Great. You don't want to talk about it? Great." Her lips thinned into an overstretched smile as Ian rejoined them. "I'm just here for the food."

CHAPTER NINE

★ ★ ★ ★

After the weekend at home, Evie looked forward to a Monday at the office.

She glanced at the small clock display at the base of her computer screen. Ten more minutes before the answering service turned the phones back over after covering them during the weekend. The deluge of requests for same-day appointments would begin. Between the phones and patients, she wouldn't have a moment to think until lunchtime.

Next to going another round with Javan, who alternated between hiding from her or screaming at her, dealing with demanding patients would be easy. She knew how to prioritize, empathize, and postpone—whatever was the proper response.

Evie bit into the breakfast burrito Logan made her that morning. Another advantage of his working from home: She rarely drove through to pick up something to eat on her way to work. Too bad the spicy combination of egg, sausage, cheese, and salsa grew cold while she heated up a cup of Earl Grey tea in the break room and then settled into her workstation.

She studied the schedule displayed on the computer screen. Both Kendall and Paul had almost-full days. Kendall had two same-day appointments available, and Paul had three. All five would go to the highest bidders—or rather the first callers. Five minutes to go.

Evie pick up a framed photo of Javan and Logan positioned on her desk. Should she call and apologize to Logan for slipping out of the house while he was wrestling Javan into a pair of jeans and a Broncos sweatshirt, readying him for kindergarten? No. Why disrupt her husband's schedule? She'd done them all a favor by leaving for work early. Javan didn't play dodge-a-parent if she wasn't around. And she left Logan a note on the counter to counteract her sudden disappearance. Besides, her husband witnessed Javan's nonstop "Go away! Don't want you!" from Friday to last night until he fell asleep. Did she have to explain anything? Leaving was easier.

Less painful.

"Morning, Evie!" Renee followed up her greeting with a quick pat on the back.

"Good morning." Evie pinned a smile on her face—her work face. "Did you have a good weekend?"

"Saw the new Reese Witherspoon movie. Yep. Great weekend." The MA set her usual Starbucks venti Cinnamon Dolce Frappuccino on her desk. The woman had a serious addiction. "You?"

"Fine."

"Don't forget, a pharmaceutical rep is bringing in lunch today."

"Got it."

Evie heard Renee power up her computer.

"How's the day look?"

"Busy as usual." Evie motioned down the hall. "Liz is stocking the exam rooms. I'm going to check in with the answering service."

By eight thirty, Renee had roomed two patients, several sat in the waiting room, and Evie needed to refresh her tea. Just as she was about to ask Liz to watch the front desk, a woman in a pair of frayed sweatpants and a pullover came in carrying a little boy.

Mrs. Peterson and her son, Sean. They had a nine thirty appointment. She was way early.

The woman shifted her son in her arms, adjusting the flannel Scooby-Doo blanket so it was snug around his shoulders.

"Hello, Evie."

"Mrs. Peterson. Good morning. I have you down for a nine thirty appointment for Sean—a routine checkup. You're a bit early."

"I know. I tried to call, honestly I did." Her son rested his head on her shoulder, eyes closed, his blond hair matted against his forehead. "I've been up all night with him. I think he has the flu. Fever. Throwing up. Every time I called, the line was busy—and then Sean would get sick again."

Evie reached across the counter and felt the back of the little boy's neck. He most definitely had a fever.

"I'm so sorry. But Dr. Kendall is booked until your appointment—she's even running a little behind . . ."

"That's fine. I don't mind waiting. It just felt smarter to bring him here than to keep him at home. And I thought maybe if Dr. Kendall could see him earlier, somehow . . . if we were here . . ."

"Momma, I don't feel good . . ." The little boy's words bobbled.

"Ssh, ssh, baby. I know. I've got you. You're going to see Dr. Kendall, remember?"

"I don't feel good . . ."

Oh, this might go bad. Fast. Evie couldn't let Sean get sick all over the waiting room. And his mother. Time to ignore the phones. "Mrs. Peterson, why don't you come with me."

She pressed the button on the wall to the right so the woman had access to the back, holding the door open for her. As she walked past the MA station, she motioned to Renee to follow.

Caught between the two women—Mrs. Peterson a few steps ahead of her, Renee double-timing to catch up—Evie evaluated her options. "Is the procedure room available?"

Renee nodded yes, stepping past them to open the door. "What do you need?"

"Grab a basin. Quick. I think Sean's going to be sick. We'll figure out what else we need after that."

Within minutes, Evie's premonition proved true. "Renee, let Dr. Kendall know the Petersons are here—and that Sean is sick. They understand they're going to have to wait unless something changes in her schedule."

Evie could hear the phones ringing. She knew Renee and the other MAs would handle things, but she needed to get back to her desk. Still, she found herself standing in the doorway of the procedure room, watching mother and son.

Mrs. Peterson sat on the exam table, which was positioned so it partially reclined, cradling Sean close against her body. Even feeling as sick as he did, Sean seemed content with his mom, snug beneath his aqua-blue blanket. One little hand held on to hers, refusing to let go. The whole time he'd been sick, Mrs. Peterson whispered, "I'm so sorry, sweetie. Mom loves you. I'm so sorry. Mom's here." He'd taken only a few sips of water from the paper cup Evie offered him, and then turned back to his mother's waiting arms.

"I love you, Sean."

"Love you, too, Mommy . . ."

The words pummeled Evie's bruised heart. The last time Javan had been sick, he wanted only Logan. She made up a special tray of chicken noodle soup and crackers, but Javan rolled away from her when she entered the room. No matter how she coaxed him, he refused to come out from underneath the blankets. She returned the tray to the kitchen, admitting defeat. Again.

In so many ways, Evie was failing as a mother. Why did she ever think she could be a mom? If she believed in God, she'd figure this was punishment for her mistakes. But what kind of God would allow one mistake to haunt her for all the days of her life? Wasn't there some sort of expiration date on consequences? She had so much love to give Javan. And at first he'd been receptive. She could love him enough to convince him that she would be good enough to be his mamá . . . couldn't she?

She watched Sean's mom's fingers, stroking the damp hair from her son's forehead. Her lips pressed a kiss . . . just there . . . on the soft curve of his cheek, where she so often wished to kiss Javan. Evie bit down on her bottom lip to keep it from trembling. In her arms, that woman held everything Evie craved. The chance to be a mom. To love. To hold. To comfort. Javan was so close—in her home. Tucked in bed every night by Logan. But he was so far away. And it seemed like every day put more distance between them.

"Evie?" Renee touched her shoulder.

"Yes?" She stepped back into the hallway, shutting the door on the tender scene.

"Dr. Kendall needs me in the exam room. You able to get back to the desk now?"

"Yes. Just making sure Sean and his mom didn't need anything."

"All right, then."

Walking back to her desk, Evie squared her shoulders, taking a deep breath. With a quick shake of her head, as if she could dispel the image of mother and son, she repositioned the headset and focused on the here and now. Not her past. Not the future.

All she could do right now was the next thing.

Just the next thing—and nothing more.

★ ★ ★ ★ ★

"Hi . . . Evie, right? Dr. Haynes called and said some boxes came for me?"

Evie turned from faxing some papers over to Penrose Hospital admissions office. Whom had Dr. Kendall said those boxes were for? Parker . . . Dr. Heath Parker. And he was probably the cute guy leaning on the front counter. He gave her an open smile that reached all the way to his blue eyes. Okay. She needed to be professional. Besides that, she was married. But she wasn't dead. Dr. Parker had the casual appeal of Jude Law, combined with that inexplicable mixture of friendliness and just a touch of charisma. One of those guys.

"Yes, they came this morning." Evie pushed her bangs out of her face. Midafternoon, and she was a frazzled mess. That's what the Monday rush did. "I've got them in the break room."

"Terrific. I'm thrilled they came so quickly."

"If you'll give me a minute, I'll go get them for you." Evie started the fax, and then moved back to the desk, smoothing the wrinkles out of the front of her cotton scrub top.

"No need. Just buzz me into the back and I'll go get them."

She considered the option. There was no reason Heath Parker couldn't go in the back. "Dr. Kendall's seeing patients, so she won't be able to talk to you. I'm sorry—I'll let her know you came by."

"Understood. Wouldn't want to bother Kendall while she's working." He bent down, disappearing from view, and then reappeared to place a tall rectangular glass vase overflowing with brilliant pink roses on the counter. "Would you put these on her desk for me?"

Evie touched one of the soft petals, inhaling the delicate aroma. "These are stunning."

"Your boss deserves a bit of beauty to start the week, don't you think?" His raised eyebrow and roguish grinned pulled her into his conspiracy. "If you make sure she gets these, I'll collect my boxes and get out of your way."

Evie pressed the button that released the lock, allowing Dr. Parker into the back. Once inside, she took a few moments to introduce him to Liz, the medical assistant who was updating Kendall's nurse practitioner on a patient's labs. Then she picked up the floral arrangement and led him down the hall, directing him to the break room before slipping into Kendall's office. As usual, reports, phone messages, and medical journals cluttered Kendall's roll-top desk. Her leather satchel sat on the floor, stuffed with even more paperwork needing her attention.

Setting the vase on the top of the desk, Evie took a few moments to straighten the piles, knowing her boss would appreciate the semblance of order when she returned later in the day. Then Evie rearranged the flowers, straightening stems and pinching off a few errant leaves. She checked the water level, making a mental note to refresh it midweek. Kendall's roses deserved special attention. The only time the last guy Kendall dated ever showed up at her office was to ask for free medical advice.

Evie walked back down the hallway that was painted a warm cocoa color past the procedure room and several exam rooms before noticing Dr. Parker standing near the exit to the waiting room. Two boxes sat at his feet. He was talking to the Harringtons, who'd brought their eleven-year-old son, Peter, in because his asthma had flared up.

Why is he still here?

She slowed her pace, even pausing at the end of the MAs' station to look over some papers that lay on the counter, trying to catch what he was saying. She wasn't eavesdropping, not really. But why would Heath Parker need to talk to the Harringtons?

"—you might be interested in this new supplement, Mrs. Harrington. I've seen Kupu do wonders in building immunity in young children."

"Really?" Mrs. Harrington examined a small white bottle, turning it around to read the label.

"Absolutely. It would be perfect for someone like your son."

"Is it available over the counter?"

"Here's my card. Why don't you call me and I can answer other questions."

As Evie watched the doctor hand Mrs. Harrington a slim piece of paper, she stepped up beside the trio. "Is there anything I can help you with?"

Mrs. Harrington turned to include her in the conversation. "Dr. Parker told me about something to help Peter—"

"Vitamins. Supplements. That sort of thing. Dr. Haynes and I both believe it's essential to encourage good nutrition and overall health in patients." Heath picked up the boxes and stepped toward the door leading to the waiting room. "It was wonderful to talk with you both. I know how important Dr.

Kendall's patients are to her. Would you get the door for me, please?"

Dr. Parker waited as the Harringtons walked out ahead of him, thanking the man for holding the door open. Evie watched as the three exited the office, chatting again. There was no reason for Dr. Parker to talk with patients. But then, there was no reason for him *not* to talk with patients. He was a doctor, too. It was what he did—help patients.

The front-desk phone chimed in her ear and Evie clicked the headset button.

"This is the Rocky Mountain Family Practice. Evie speaking. How may I help you?"

"Mrs. Gardner?"

Evie stilled. "Yes?"

"This is Carolyn, down at Javan's school. I tried to reach you on your cell but I didn't get an answer."

"I'm sorry. I don't answer my cell while I'm at work. Is Javan okay?"

"There's been a problem at school. I need you to come in as soon as possible."

"Is he hurt?" Evie moved away from her desk, waving her hand to catch Renee's attention. "Is he sick? Have you called my husband?"

"No, ma'am. Javan isn't sick or hurt. And, yes, I tried to call your husband, but he didn't answer his cell phone, either. When do you think you can get to the school?"

"I'll be right there. Can you tell me what happened?"

"Javan got into a fight with another boy in his class."

"He what?" Evie held up her hand, preventing Renee from mouthing questions at her. "What happened?"

"Why don't you come down to the school and we'll talk about it then. Javan's waiting in the principal's office."

"All right." When the phone disconnected, Evie tugged the headset from her ear.

"I need to leave."

"What?" Renee looked at the clock. "It's only two. Dr. Kendall has a full clinic—and so does Paul. You can't leave now."

"I have to. Javan got into a fight a school. He's in the principal's office." She fast-walked down the hallway to get her purse from the staff lockers, sidestepping a patient who exited an exam room. *Why didn't Logan answer his phone?* Then she remembered. "Logan's in Denver today, working on-site with a client. I have to go."

Evie unlocked the cabinet, grabbing both her purse and her windbreaker, and headed for the back parking lot. "Do me a favor and punch my time card for me, please."

★ ★ ★ ★ ★

Evie stormed into the school office as if she were rescuing her son from a swarm of pint-sized ninjas. "I'm here for Javan—" She paused. She couldn't call him by her last name yet. The adoption wasn't final. "Javan."

She knew Carolyn casually from parents' nights and other school events she managed to attend. "Hello, Mrs. Gardner. Javan's in with Mr. Edwards. Let me take you back."

Evie stopped to study Javan through the small rectangular piece of glass inset in the principal's office door. Slumped shoulders. Eyes downcast. Bottom lip thrust out. She knew that expression so well. The principal stood as she came into the room. Javan didn't budge.

"Good afternoon, Mrs. Gardner." Mr. Edwards shook her hand, his eyes compassionate behind his wire-rim glasses, and motioned for her to sit beside Javan.

"Good afternoon." Evie tucked a piece of hair behind her ear, letting her purse slip to the carpeted floor beside her feet. "Javan, are you all right?"

Silence.

Evie focused her attention on the principal, willing her heartbeat to settle back into its normal pace. "What happened?"

"I'd prefer Javan tell us. But he's not feeling very talkative right now." The principal leaned against his desk. "Do you want to tell your mom what happened, Javan?"

Nothing.

Maybe she should try to start the conversation. "I was told there was a fight . . ."

Mr. Edwards nodded. "One of the teachers' assistants said Javan punched one of his classmates—"

"Did not!" The little boy spat the words out as if he tasted some kind of bitter medicine and refused to swallow it.

"Javan!" Evie touched his arm, but he shrugged away from her.

"He punched me."

The principal kept his voice low, calm. "Javan, the teacher saw you and Trevor—"

"He punched me!" Javan bellowed the words, this time looking at her with tears filling his brown eyes.

"Don't yell, Javan. We just want to find out what happened."

"I told you. You don't believe me. The other kid punched me." Javan crossed his arms over his chest. "I told 'em to call Daddy. He would believe me."

Javan's accusation was a verbal punch to Evie's gut. What was she supposed to do? Let Javan get away with hitting another kindergartner just so he knew she loved him?

"I'm not saying I don't believe you." She touched Javan's knee, trying to connect with him again. "I'm trying to find out the whole story. If you hit someone, you need to say you're sorry."

"He didn't say he was sorry to me!" Javan jerked his leg, pushing her hand away. "Where's Daddy? I want Daddy!"

"Daddy's at work. I'm here. Let Mamá help."

"You're not my mamá!"

Evie's breath hissed through her clenched teeth. She refused to look at the principal. She pressed trembling fingers against her lips, searching for something to say.

"You're right, Javan. I'm not your mamá." Evie inhaled. Exhaled. "But I want to be. Daddy and me . . . we want all three of us to be a family. And that's why I'm here. Because mamás come get their niñitos when they're upset about something."

Javan looked up at her, his chubby cheeks streaked with tears. "My momma doesn't."

Evie lowered her voice to a whisper. "Your momma doesn't what?"

"My momma isn't coming to get me. She left me."

Oh, what could she say to heal this little boy's hurt? "I know. I know, Javan. But I'm here. Can I help you . . . just today?"

Evie watched Javan's lower lip tremble. Heard him hiccup back a sob. "'K. Today."

Today. She'd take today. And hope for tomorrow.

Mr. Edwards's voice interrupted the brittle quietness resting between them. "Javan, why don't you go to your classroom and get your things?"

The little boy slipped off the couch and exited the office.

"Mrs. Gardner, you handled that well. I understand what's going on between you and Javan."

"Yes."

"I've seen other adopted children act out this way. Truthfully, I've seen children act this way with their biological parents."

"Believe me, some days are much, much harder than others." Evie stood, turning to face the principal. "I know Javan's angry at his birth mom, not me. I just never realized I would be fighting her for my son."

"It's almost the end of the school day. Go ahead and take Javan home. Let him settle down. Talk to him about what he did, about needing to apologize to Trevor. And don't think I won't be having a talk with Trevor and his parents, too."

"Thanks."

Evie straightened her shoulders and went to wait for Javan out in the front office. She slipped into a muted-blue cloth-covered chair next to a bulletin board covered with papers: announcements about piano lessons and dance lessons, the schedule for the field day program, information about summer camps. Carolyn sat at her desk, talking to someone on the phone. Who knew what the woman thought of Evie? She probably considered her a horrible mother—unable to control her son. There was no way the other woman could understand how hard Evie tried with Javan. This was something she had to figure out on her own. One little breakthrough with Javan didn't mean he wouldn't shut her out again when they got home. What now? Was it appropriate to take a little boy for ice cream when he'd punched a classmate?

★ ★ ★ ★

Kendall preferred to have her conversations with her girlfriends face-to-face, while indulging in corn chips and guacamole. And here she sat, side by side by side by side with Rachel, Sonia, and Melissa, waiting for a Saturday-morning pedicure. The salon welcomed a constant flow of women of all ages—young girls accompanying their moms, teens, twenty-somethings, and on up to women who reminded her of Mina. A large-screen TV filled one wall, tuned to some action movie that added another layer of noise to the constant hum of voices and the ever-ringing phone.

Kendall should relax, but the overcrowded room, with massage chairs just inches from one another, made her feel a bit claustrophobic. "Exactly how are we supposed to decide anything sitting like ducks all in a row while we get pedicures?"

"Oh, stop complaining. We're all overdue for a little pampering." Rachel settled back in the oversized massage chair, closing her eyes as the water in the ceramic basin swirled around her feet.

Melissa, who sat in the chair farthest from Kendall, leaned forward. "Sonia's the one with all the details. Just let her do the talking. I'm going to sit back and enjoy this pedicure."

Why was she resisting the opportunity to unwind? Sure, they were here to talk about their summer trip. But having a chance to unwind while someone massaged her feet . . . Kendall needed to spoil herself for half an hour. Let someone take care of her, instead of being the one caring.

She readjusted her body in the padded chair, pushing away thoughts of all the other things she could be doing. This was not a waste of time. "So, what did you find out, Sonia?"

"One of Kevin's friends went to the Riviera Maya last year. It's on the coast of Mexico. Cozumel is right across the water. There are resorts up and down the coast with all-inclusive plans: airfare, hotel, meals. Even tips." Sonia paused as a nail tech sat in front of her on a low wheeled stool. She handed the woman a bottle of bright pink polish.

"Whoa." Kendall held up her hand as if blinded. "That's a crazy color."

Melissa showed off a bottle of vivid blue nail polish. "What do you think of this, Kendall? It's called 'Blue My Mind.'"

"You're kidding, right? I'll stick with this red." What was it again? Kendall turned over the bottle of polish and read the label: " 'I'm Not Really a Waitress.' "

"I decided on a classic French manicure." Rachel joined the conversation, not bothering to open her eyes as she tested the different massage buttons on the arm of the chair. "Who comes up with these names?"

"Now that we have that all settled, can we talk vacation?" Sonia attempted to restore order, even as the petite woman seated before her trimmed her toenails. "Does an all-inclusive deal sound good to you three?"

"Absolutely. The less we have to do once we get there, the better. I want to relax." Melissa looked half asleep where she sat.

"Is the last week of June still the best time for everyone?"

"I had Evie block me out of the schedule." Kendall turned the massage chair to "rolling massage," shifting so her lower back and shoulders got a good workout.

"And both my parents are coming to help with the twins." Melissa sighed. "My father has planned at least two trips to Toys 'R' Us with the boys. They will be thoroughly spoiled by the time I get back."

"I hope to have a lot of the wedding details settled by then." Rachel's voice always pitched a little higher when she said the word *wedding*. "Remember, this trip to Mexico is also going to be our weeklong bachelorette party."

"Oh, I haven't forgotten. I'll make sure to plan some fun things." Sonia made a few notes in her iPhone. "And who knows? We may have found your perfect dress by then."

Melissa sat up straighter as a technician prepared to start her pedicure. "Did your mom change her mind about that dress you tried on?"

"No. She still says it makes me look old."

"That dress doesn't make you look old, Rachel." Kendall moved so fast, water sloshed over the side of the foot basin. "You looked like an advertisement in a bridal magazine. Exquisite."

"I thought so, and you thought so . . . but there's no changing my mother's mind once she's made a decision about something."

"Do you know what kind of dress she wants you to wear?"

"One like hers, probably."

Sonia joined the conversation. "One like hers—or hers?"

"Oh, probably hers—but it would take forever to alter that dress. I'm taller than my mother. And it's not the style I want." Rachel pressed her fingers against her temples and rubbed in a circular motion. "I've waited for this day for so long. But how do I have what I want and what my mother wants?"

"Maybe you can't have both things." Kendall swished the water with her feet, careful to keep the liquid in the basin this time.

"That's what Tony says."

"Smart guy. Of course, we knew that. He proposed to you, didn't he?"

Kendall watched as a nail tech settled in front of her, placing a plastic bin of manicure tools beside her stool. "We'll go looking again. Maybe you'll find a dress you love even more than that other dress. Or maybe your mom will change her mind when she sees you wearing it a second time."

"All I know is, one of us is going to have to change."

"Speaking of change—Rachel, you're never going to believe who showed up in my office."

"Who?"

"Griffin Walker and his brother, Ian."

"Who?" Rachel scrunched her nose as she tried to match the name *Griffin Walker* with a mental image.

"Ian's the teenager who had an anaphylactic reaction during my birthday dinner, remember? Griffin's his older brother—and his guardian."

"I thought you told me the guy didn't want you to be his brother's doctor. What happened to the whole 'tomato, ta-mahto' thing between you two?"

"It's the craziest thing. The guy has a Jeep—"

"That's enough to make you like him."

Rachel's laugh interrupted Kendall's response. "Hush. Then his Jeep broke down on I-25 and I rescued him. And then he called and asked for help fixing the thing."

"What? Does Griffin Walker think you work for Triple A on the side?"

"I offered to help."

"You and Jeeps. Never understood the attraction." Melissa leaned forward, careful not to jostle the nail technician working on her feet. "Are you interested in this guy?"

"Nooo. I met his ex-wife."

Rachel buried her face in her hands, shaking her head. "Ken-dall, this is starting to sound like a soap opera—not that I watch those things."

"I know, I know. I'm just trying to be a friend to Ian. His parents died about five months ago."

"So that's why his older brother is his guardian."

Kendall nodded "Exactly."

"What about that other guy—what was his name?"

"Heath Parker."

Now they had both Sonia's and Melissa's attention. Sonia spoke first. "Girl, what is going on? We don't get together for a couple of weeks and suddenly guys are everywhere in your life."

"It's not like that at all. Griffin Walker is all about being a single guy—he told me as much." This time it was the memory of a handsome doctor causing her to relax back in the chair and close her eyes. "But Heath Parker? Well, all I can say is, stay tuned."

"There's potential?"

Kendall tried to ignore the excitement threaded through Melissa's question. No need to overreact.

"I hope so. As far as Griffin Walker is concerned, I'm nothing more than his brother's doctor. And that's fine with me. But Heath Parker? I'm interested to see where this relationship might go. And I haven't said that about any guy in a long time."

CHAPTER TEN

★ ★ ★ ★ ★

"Kendall, it's Griffin."

Kendall swiveled the chair in her office away from the roll-top desk cluttered with lab reports and patients' charts. Twelve fifteen—and the last patient of her regular Wednesday half day was a no-show. She'd been debating putting off doing her notes and going for a swim, but the thought of walking upstairs to grab her inhaler and change out of her work clothes into her bathing suit exhausted her. And then Evie had said Griffin was on the line. Why was the man calling again? The way he'd shut her out after the run-in with his ex on Saturday, she half ex-pected him to call and request that Ian's charts be transferred to another practice.

"Griffin."

"Um, I was wondering if you could help me out—"

Kendall decided to put the man out of his misery. "Jeep problems again? If you need a tool, come on over and get it."

"My Jeep's fine. I need help getting Ian's Jeep."

"You bought it?"

"Yes, but I didn't realize the dealership was closed from Sunday to Wednesday. And normally they close by five, but the owner said he's working late and if I can get there by six thirty, he'll wait for me. I checked with the guys here at work, but everyone else has plans. And I'd take Ian, but he has to work on some kind of group project for school. You game?"

Kendall stared out the window at the Colorado blue sky. No clouds. She squinted. Was that an Academy glider circling the Front Range?

Why would she want to spend any more time with Griffin Walker? He obviously considered her nothing but a good last resort. But what about her desire to help Ian? How could she avoid one brother and still help the other? And that was all Griffin was asking—for her to help him do something nice for his brother.

"Kendall, you there? I know this is last-minute, but if I have to put up with Ian asking about this Jeep one more night—"

Fine. She would do this for Ian.

"What time were you planning on doing this?"

"I get off close to five. If you could swing by and pick me up, that would be great. After we get to the dealership, you're free to go."

Griffin Walker didn't want her hanging around any longer than necessary. But then she was doing this for Ian—not to spend time with his going-to-be-single-forever older brother.

"Fine. That gives me time to do a few things. Read lab reports about people's immunoglobulin levels. Those sorts of things."

"Give me a flight plan any day."

"If I tried to read one of those, who knows where we'd end up."

She managed to shove all thoughts of Griffin out of her mind while she beat back the papers on her desk, went for a swim, and took Sully for an extra-long walk, all the while insisting that he not pull her arm out of the socket.

"Wanna go for a ride, boy?" She toed off her tennis shoes, hanging Sully's leash on the brass hook by the back door while the dog bounded around her. Kendall surveyed her outfit: khaki-colored linen-blend cargo pants and a white V-neck T-shirt paired with a yellow racer-back tank top. A quick run of a comb through her hair, a quick brush of her teeth, slip her feet into a casual pair of espadrilles, and she was ready to go. This was helping out a friend—and Ian was that friend. She proved it to herself by forgoing makeup. She stared at herself in the mirror, noting how fatigue painted dark circles under her eyes. Well . . . maybe a two minute makeup fix. Even Griffin deserved someone who didn't look as if she were anemic.

Twenty minutes later, she sat outside the Walkers' house, watching Griffin run down the driveway at the sound of her honking the CJ5's horn. The man certainly knew how to fill out black jeans and a black polo shirt, which only served to accent his graying hair. Not that he'd catch her looking at him. Griffin opened the door but stopped with one leg in the Jeep, one out, when he realized Sully lounged in the front seat. "You're bringing Sully?"

"Why not? He likes going for rides in the Jeep."

"I invited *you* to help me—not your dog."

"Love me, love my dog."

Kendall ignored Griffin's muttered comment that sounded as if he'd said, "Don't make me choose, woman. Don't make me choose."

As if there were any choosing going on.

Sully settled in between them, resting his long nose on Griffin's shoulder.

"Tell your dog to move." Every time Griffin tried to move the dog's head, Sully burrowed closer.

"He's happy. Let him be."

"Don't shed on me, dog."

"Goldendoodles don't shed. It's part of their charm." Kendall eased the CJ5 into the traffic on I-25. "Let's hope rush-hour traffic doesn't work against us."

"I called to say we were on our way. Thanks for helping me out. After we talked, I tried getting my friend Doug, but he wasn't available." Griffin stretched his legs out. "You really need to get a CJ7, Doc."

"Stop bad-mouthing my Jeep. I like my 5 and I'm not trading down." Before he could respond, she changed the subject. "How's Ian?"

"As good as can be expected."

"Do you think he's finally settling in?"

"Not like he has a choice."

Kendall weighed what to say next and went with the say-it-like-it-is policy. "You have a choice, Griffin."

"What do you mean?" She heard the bite in his tone, even as he continued to stare out the windshield at the long line of cars advancing up Monument Hill. "I'm stationed here. I can't move to make Ian happy."

"I'm not suggesting you move. But you can do whatever it takes to help him adjust, to like it here."

As she looked right to move over to pass a slow-moving truck in the left lane, Kendall saw Griffin tug at the thick gold chain hanging around his neck.

"I'm not sure being here is the best thing for Ian."

His words brought her up short. What did he mean?

Without thinking, Kendall reached over, placing her hand on Griffin's forearm. "Of course it is. Ian needs you. You're the only family he has."

"I am not cut out to be the guardian of a sixteen-year-old kid."

"Lots of men your age are fathers by now, Griffin." She had to shift gears, causing her to remove her hand from his arm—but not before she noticed that it was toned. Muscular. "Some of your buddies must have kids Ian's age. Ask them how to connect with Ian."

Silence stretched between them as taut as Sully's leash when she tried to restrain him from chasing a rabbit. When Kendall looked over at Griffin, he stared ahead, his lips thinned to a straight line. What had she said to irritate him?

"I'm a single guy, Doc." A rough edge graveled his words. "I don't hang around parents much, talking about the dos and the don'ts."

There he went again, erecting the barrier of singleness between them. Could he make it any clearer he had no interest in changing his status? "Single or not—and I get that your choice is *single*—you're still Ian's brother. He needs you. Your parents obviously wanted your brother to be with you if something happened to them."

"I wish I knew why." Griffin rubbed at the pressure between his brows with his thumb and index finger.

"Maybe you should stop asking why and start asking God how you're supposed to develop a relationship with Ian."

Griffin reached over and tugged a lock of hair lying against her neck. A quicksilver shiver raced up Kendall's neck.

"You've always got an answer, don't you?"

"I try to. Got me through residency."

"You always wear your hair short?"

"Hmm? Um, yeah. Pretty much my whole life." Kendall fingered the feathered ends, trying to stay focused on the highway and not be distracted by Griffin's perusal. He shifted in the seat and watched her as she drove. "Because of my asthma, I spent a lot of time in the hospital. If I wasn't in the hospital, I was at the doctor's office. It was easier to take care of if it was short. When I got older and went to medical school . . . well, long hair would have been a hassle."

"Good thing you look nice with short hair. Some women look like guys."

"Maybe that explains it."

"Explains what?"

"Why you thought I was a guy when you first met me."

Instead of laughing as she expected, in the dim light of the Jeep, Kendall just caught the grimace that marred Griffin's face.

"Sorry. Was never good at the compliments."

Griffin Walker was trying to compliment her?

"Oh, I don't believe that. I bet you've broken quite a few hearts in your days."

"Yeah. Yeah, I have."

Only the way he said it, Griffin didn't sound proud.

"After my wife and I divorced, I was all about women. And they certainly didn't seem to mind the attention. Or my no-strings-attached clause."

Kendall kept her eyes trained on the patch of highway illuminated by her headlights. This conversation was going unexpected places.

"I piled up a lot of regrets after my divorce. Most of them have names." Griffin shifted again in his seat so that he stared out the windshield instead of looking at Kendall. "Once I became a believer, I thought about contacting each of them. Saying I was sorry. Seemed like the least I could do."

"Or the most."

"So you think I should call all those women?"

"*All those women?* Like there's a list a mile long?" She held up her hand, shaking her head. "No, don't tell me. That's none of my business. And to answer your question, no, I don't think you should call them."

Silence filled the space between them. Kendall waited. What could she say? Griffin spoke first.

"Doesn't the Bible say if you've sinned against your brother—well, your sister—you should go and make amends?"

Kendall drove for a few moments, mulling over her answer. "Well, if I'm thinking of the verse you mean, it actually says to go to your brother—or sister—if he or she sins *against you.* It's talking about when another believer does something wrong to you—how you're supposed to handle that." She paused. "All of those things . . . those relationships with the other women, did they happen before you were a believer?"

"Yes. So?"

"So, you asked God to forgive you, right?"

"Yes." His sigh seemed pulled from the deepest recesses of his heart. "It seems like a million times."

"Well, forgiveness only takes one time. God says he separates us from our sins as far as the sunrise is from the sunset."

"Doug—my sponsor from when I was a cadet at the Academy—told me the same thing." Griffin turned to look at her as she stopped in the parking lot of the car dealership. "It's different talking this out with a woman."

She could only imagine. Kendall put the Jeep in park, turning so she could look at Griffin. She'd parked near one of the lights illuminating the lot, so the inside of the Jeep wasn't completely dark.

"God may give you a chance one day to talk to one of those women. To ask forgiveness face-to-face. But until then, consider it done. God has forgiven you. His forgiveness should be—*is*—enough."

Griffin seemed to consider her words.

"If you had been one of those women and I came and asked forgiveness, would you be able to forgive me, Kendall?"

"W-what?"

Griffin's intense gaze held hers. "If I had . . . hurt you, and came back today, and asked you to forgive me, would you?"

Kendall stared into Griffin's eyes that, even shrouded in the semi-darkness of the Jeep, seemed to beg for absolution.

She reached out, touched the side of his face, feeling the roughness of his jaw where it clenched beneath her fingertips. She tried to imagine loving Griffin and realized it wasn't so very hard to do. Imagine his hurting her and then coming back years later to ask forgiveness. As a believer, she had only one choice. As a woman . . . well, sometimes making the right choice warred with a broken heart and destroyed dreams.

"Yes, Griffin. I would forgive you. I would."

The air around them stilled. Filled with something unspoken. She wanted to move her hand, allow herself to explore the rugged outline of Griffin's brow, see if his salt-and-pepper hair was soft or coarse to her touch. But she didn't dare.

She searched his face, his eyes now closed, thankful to see the tension ease, the lines bracketing his mouth lessen. He heaved a sigh, as if a weight lifted off his shoulders.

"Thank you, Kendall. I had no idea how much I needed to hear those words." As he spoke, her fingers grazed the corner of his mouth.

Kendall willed herself to stay still, to not ruin this unguarded honesty between them by thinking it was more than a moment between friends. Unlikely friends at that. The hitch in her breath . . .

Ignore that.

"You're the first woman I've been able to talk to about . . . all of that." Griffin moved away. "Really, you're the first woman I've ever considered a friend."

Friend. Wow. This was like one of those awful scenes in a movie when the girl who was in love with the guy didn't realize he only saw her as a friend.

Not that she was in love with Griffin Walker. Not even close.

A few moments of good-for-the-soul confession didn't mean she felt anything more than friendship for the man who continued to talk the entire time she wrestled her emotions back into submission.

"I'd better get in there before the guy thinks I decided I didn't want that Jeep." Griffin stepped out of the CJ5 in one fluid movement, filling the interior of the Jeep with cool night air. "No need to wait for me, Doc. Thanks for your help."

★ ★ ★ ★ ★

What had prompted that bare-his-soul conversation with Kendall Haynes?

Griffin sat in his brother's new-to-him Jeep, watching the lights inside the dealership go off one by one. Calling Kendall to help him tonight was stupid enough—and then he talked about his past mistakes and needing forgiveness.

What was he doing, treating Kendall like some sort of female father-confessor? Thank God seeing the owner standing by the window of the dealership refocused him on reality. What else would he have confessed to her? And why?

His relationship with Ian survived on monosyllables. Had he been that noncommunicative as a teenager? He couldn't ask his mother that question. Tracey's complaints about how distant he was when they were married still echoed in his mind.

"You have nothing to say?" His wife's voice forced him to look at her, away from the papers he held. Separation papers.

"No."

"Of course not." Tracey grabbed the document from him, slamming it down on the breakfast table. "I tell you I want a divorce and you have nothing to say."

"What am I supposed to say? You've made up your mind."

"This whole marriage was a mistake from the moment I said 'I do.'" Tracey seemed determined to force him to fight. "Admit it."

"Being married to me never seemed to hold you back." There. He said something. It didn't change anything. Didn't eradicate all the months of silent separation punctuated by Tracey's tantrums and his attempts to appease her.

"Hey, I put my career on hold while you got your wings—"

"Don't go there." Griffin stared at the woman he once thought he loved. "You networked like crazy while I was in flight school—took advantage of those duty stations and got exactly what you wanted. You're the one who opted for back-to-back remote assignments."

"It was better than coming home to you every night—"

The slam of the door as Tracey walked out for the final time morphed into the sound of some driver honking his horn.

Griffin rubbed his hand over his face, wiping away the remnants of the memory. After the flameout of his marriage, he swore he'd never fail like that again. Why give some woman the power to wound him the way Tracey had?

The relationships with the other women satisfied only one desire—if that. Talking to Kendall tonight somehow helped him to grasp the reality of God's forgiveness in a way he hadn't before. But it didn't mean he wanted to fall in love again. Get married again. He liked Kendall Haynes . . . as a friend. And that's all she could ever be. If she knew everything about him, she'd never want anything more with him. And he didn't want anything more than friendship from her. And a casual friendship, at best.

By the time he got home, it was almost eight thirty. The darkened house indicated Ian was still out studying with his friends. Griffin parked out on the street, ran into the house, backed his Jeep out of the garage, and then pulled the new purchase into it. This was going to be a kick, surprising his little brother. He hadn't stopped talking about the Jeep Cherokee since they looked at it on Saturday. Griffin insisted he was thinking about it, trying to see if there was a better deal. Of course he hadn't thought about what he was going to do with it if—when—Ian went to live with the Jamisons.

He mulled over his options as he walked into the kitchen to look through the measly selection of leftovers in the fridge. A quick scan of the interior of the fridge revealed . . . nothing. He straightened, scratching the stubble along his jaw. Did he have time to call Mrs. Jamison again, see if she and her husband had come to a decision about Ian?

He jerked around when the front door opened and Ian walked into the house. His brother deposited his backpack on the couch and joined him in the kitchen.

"I'm starved. What's there to eat?" Ian moved past him and mimicked his movements of peering into the fridge.

"Nothing. Believe me, I just looked. You want to go drive through Good Times and grab a burger?"

Ian paused with the fridge door halfway open. "This late at night?"

"Why not? You got all your homework done, right?"

"Yeah."

"Well, let's go grab a burger then." He headed toward the garage. "Tell you what, you can drive."

Ian raced up to him. "You're gonna let me drive your Jeep?"

Oh, this was even more fun than he planned. "Yeah, I'm going to let you drive the Jeep." Griffin opened the door leading out to the garage. "That one."

His brother didn't scream like a girl—but it came pretty close. "My Jeep! You bought my Jeep!" The next minute Griffin was engulfed in a bear hug. "Oh man, oh man, oh man . . . thank you!"

Griffin managed to wrap his arms around his brother. Pat him on the back. Then he realized this was the first time he'd ever hugged Ian.

Not during any of his too-few visits home.

Not at their parents' funeral.

But standing in a semi-lit garage by a Jeep Cherokee.

About time.

CHAPTER ELEVEN

★ ★ ★ ★

*I*t would have been so much nicer to drive to dinner with Heath.

To the board meeting.

Kendall needed to keep reminding herself why she was here tonight. This was a meeting, not a dinner date. It would be her, Heath, and at least four other people discussing Heath's business plans. And she was here to listen more than to participate in the discussion.

Kendall stood outside the Craftwood Inn in Manitou Springs, the glow of the lighted script letters across the front of the building inviting her inside. Heath told her to call when she arrived, but she hated to pull him away from a meeting just because she was running late.

Navigating the stone steps up to the entrance of the historic building would be a little tricky in her heels. For once, she wished she'd worn flats. But the added inches of her shoes gave her a boost of confidence as she walked into the restaurant, allowing the maître d' to take her short jacket and lead her to Heath's table near the long wall of windows.

Breathe. Breathe.

She'd treat this like any other professional meeting. She had plenty of experience with those. No one needed to know she'd run upstairs after work, reapplied her makeup, and re-gelled her hair before slipping into a favorite cranberry-colored sheath. Simple, yet elegant.

Heath broke off in mid-sentence when he saw her, a smile curving his lips. As he stood and walked toward her, everyone at the table stopped talking and watched them.

"Kendall." Heath wrapped an arm around her waist and pulled her close, dropping a kiss on her cheek. She liked the feeling of being tucked up against him as they moved toward the group. He leaned closer and spoke low. "I've been watching the doorway, waiting for you to get here."

So much for maintaining a businesslike demeanor.

"I'm so sorry I'm late, Heath." She nodded to the others at the table, several of the men rising to their feet along with Heath. "Clinic ran late. An emergency with one of my elderly patients."

Murmurs of sympathy surrounded Kendall as she slipped into the circular-backed chair Heath held for her. "Please, don't let me interrupt your conversation."

"We were just talking sports . . . nothing important yet." Heath helped her slide her seat closer to the table covered with a white cloth. "Enjoying some appetizers. We ordered small plates of elk, antelope, and scallops."

Kendall accepted the menu the waiter handed her. "Well, the NFL draft is over, so I'm just waiting for the football season to start. But surely someone here is into baseball."

A few of the people sitting around the table called out their favorite teams. While conversation resumed around her, Kendall focused on the menu. After ordering a glass of iced tea and a seafood entrée of Durango Bass crusted in walnut and fennel, Kendall assessed the others. Several people looked to be her age, while two of the men looked to be easily fifteen years older. Heath took charge of the conversation.

"I'm certain many of you know Dr. Kendall Haynes, if not personally, then because of her stellar professional reputation in the community."

Kendall resisted the unprofessional urge to squirm.

"Kendall, let me introduce you to my team." He shifted, placing his arm around her shoulder, and began introducing people, going counterclockwise around the table. "Dr. Janice White is an ob-gyn with Springs Women's Clinic. Dr. Tom Clark is a neurologist in town. Tom and I enjoy a good game of handball, too. Then there's Frank Bennett, he's a retired air force colonel. He's on the board because of his business acumen and international experience. Don't know what I'd do without him. Same with Leslie Meyer. She's a lawyer here in the Springs. She's kept me sane during this process."

Kendall took the time to greet each person one by one, recognizing the two physicians by name. Everyone else was new to her. Four physicians—well, three, because she wasn't on the board. A businessman and a lawyer. There was some sort of joke waiting to be told there. Kendall looked forward to learning more about Heath's plans for his organization. She'd been surprised when he invited her to the combination dinner and board meeting. After insisting he welcomed her insights, he hadn't reissued his invitation to become a true member.

"I've explained to Kendall how I hope to improve health care for third-world countries, with an initial focus on Africa, since that's where I spent the last five years." Heath passed her a basket of rolls, encouraging her to indulge. "I'm eager to get past the planning stage and see the organization go from a dream to becoming a reality."

"I've been doing the research you requested, Heath, and I think your idea of becoming an NGO is the best option." Leslie tapped a long red fingernail on the black folder beside her plate.

"An NGO? Is that some new term for mission organizations?" As soon as she spoke, Kendall wished she'd sat quiet and listened. This wasn't her meeting. She needed to sit back and observe, not ask unneeded questions.

"No, *NGO* stands for 'non-governmental organization.'" Heath handed her a black paper folder identical to the ones everyone else at the table had. "At its core, the organization is grounded in the Christian principle of helping the poor. But securing government moneys enables me to do that all the better."

Leslie waited for Heath to finish his explanation before continuing. "There are so many countries that are closed to . . . um . . . religious groups. If we go more low-key on that aspect, then we have a better chance of having a wider reach to more countries."

That made sense. Many missionaries went into countries via tent-making ministries—working within a secular job providing opportunities to develop relationships with the people living around them.

Conversation stopped as the waiter arrived and served salad and soup. Heath moved closer to Kendall and whispered, "I'm so glad you're here. I could hardly concentrate because whenever anyone came in, I hoped it was you."

As he spoke, Heath rested his hand at the nape of her neck. Warmth radiated up her neck, scorching her face. He wasn't the only one struggling with being distracted.

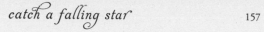

"I'm excited to be here. I can't wait to hear more about the organization."

"Business first, pleasure later."

Oh.

As Kendall ate her salad of spinach, blackberries, pear, hazelnuts, and French Brie, Tom discussed more details of the program. "I drew up some preliminary objectives as you requested, as well as working on an overall charter for the group. Have you come up with a name yet?"

Heath set aside his house salad. "I've been mulling over a few options. Too bad the World Health Organization is already taken." Laughter flowed around the table. "I like having the word *health* in the title. Maybe *benefits* or *access* or something else I haven't come up with."

Kendall tossed word combinations around in her head. "Something like International Health Access?"

"Something *exactly* like that." Heath reached down and clasped her hand underneath the table, squeezing it. "Maybe we should formally invite Dr. Haynes to join the board."

"No, no, I don't think so." Kendall waved away his suggestion. "I'm supposed to be listening. I shouldn't have said anything."

"Not at all." Tom gave her a nod of approval. "We welcome your input."

But when Kendall glanced around the table, Leslie's hard stare contradicted Tom's words. The woman looked anything but thrilled to have Kendall there.

Tom scanned a document beside his plate. "So, the primary objective is to improve the health standards for third-world countries."

"Yes, although I realize we need to craft that idea into a more compelling vision statement." Heath tossed a smile her way.

"Maybe I should brainstorm that with Kendall, too. She seems to have a way with words."

"And one of the ways you want to do that is to sell products made by women, specifically single mothers and widows."

"Yes. I meant to bring some samples tonight. Kendall let me ship the packages to her office, since I'm still in a hotel until I find a house here in the Springs." Heath flipped open his folder. "I apologize for leaving them back in my room. But page five of the documents I mailed each of you contains photographs. Baskets. Clay beads for bracelets and necklaces. That sort of thing."

"These are lovely." Kendall turned to page five in her folder and admired the color photos of several styles of handwoven baskets and vibrant multicolored beads fashioned into bracelets and necklaces. "Where do you think you'd sell these?"

Janice spoke up. "That's my department. I'm investigating a variety of options. Everything from craft shows to physicians' offices to churches. I have a friend who is involved with a mission organization who has had great success with this type of product."

Heath nodded his approval. "If Janice wasn't such a successful physician, she could have gone into business."

The woman almost preened under Heath's praise. "I believe in what you're doing, Heath, you know that."

Once again, the waiter arrived and began serving dinner. Kendall closed her eyes and inhaled the aroma of fennel mixed with the tangy cranberry chutney served with her meal. Conversation became more casual for a few moments, until Tom refocused on business.

"Since this is a board meeting, I'll keep moving things along." He shuffled through his stack of papers. "You also want to get moving on that supplement or herb—what did you call it,

Heath?—that you studied over in Africa. What's the financial potential for that?"

Heath paused for a few moments, then resumed peppering his elk. "Improving nutrition—absolutely part of the plan. But not on the agenda tonight. I forgot to mark out that part of the discussion, Tom. It's really too early to consider."

"But at the last meeting you seemed quite eager—"

"Yes, I am. But I'm tabling it for now. I'll get back to you on it."

Tom paused. Met Heath's eyes. Some unspoken communication seemed to flow between the two men—or was she imagining things? This was a board meeting, not some sort of scenario for medical intrigue. Kendall wanted to ask a question. Or excuse herself and go hide in the ladies' restroom so the two men could talk more openly. But all she could do was concentrate on her entrée.

"Heath, I did look into some commercial property, as you requested." Leslie moved her plate aside and placed a yellow manila folder on the table. "The good news is, commercial property is still a buyer's market here in the Springs."

"Great to hear. I'm debating how to combine this foundation with practicing medicine—or if I even do that." Heath focused on Leslie. "Why don't you fill in the board on what you found?"

An hour later, Heath and Kendall lingered at the restaurant after the rest of the group left, enjoying cappuccinos with just the right amount of steamed-milk foam on top.

Heath loosened his golden-yellow tie, releasing a soft groan as he patted his flat stomach. "I overate."

"Easy to do here." Kendall enjoyed the quietness of the restaurant after several hours of nonstop talking among the board members.

Heath tapped the empty dessert plate in front of him with his fork. "I should have skipped dessert. But cheesecake is always hard to say no to."

"Oh, well. Work out fifteen minutes longer tomorrow. That's my plan."

Good idea, Doctor." He surprised her by clasping her hand and lifting it to his lips, pressing a warm kiss against her skin. "Thank you."

Her heart rate skidded. Ah, a thank-you kiss on the back of the hand.

"I felt like the luckiest man in the room, to have you here."

"Heath, tonight was not about me."

"I know that. I mean, I wanted you to hear more about International Health Access. IHA—great name, Kendall." Heath continued to hold her hand. "But having you here was more of a distraction than I bargained for. What perfume are you wearing?"

Kendall shrugged. "Nothing."

"Nothing? Odd name for a perfume. But it's tantalizing." Heath traced a slow circle on her hand with his thumb.

"I mean, I don't wear perfume, Heath." His touch unsettled her, making it a challenge to think of tonight as a just a business meeting.

"You don't? Why not?"

"Occupational hazard. So many of my patients have allergies. Or asthma. I can't spend my whole day worrying about whether my perfume is going to bother someone. So I don't wear any perfume."

"So you're alluring all on your own."

"I wouldn't say that."

"I would, Dr. Haynes. I would." He lowered his voice. "Very alluring. I find it difficult to believe I haven't kissed you. Yet."

Kendall's breath caught in her throat, her eyes locking with Heath's. There was no mistaking the hint of desire in the blue depths. He wouldn't kiss her here, would he? In the middle of, well, really in the *corner* of the restaurant? Would she let him?

Heath's smile gentled her emotions. "Don't worry, beautiful lady. When I kiss you, I won't be worrying about a waiter walking by and bringing me the check."

When he kissed her . . .

Within a matter of minutes, Heath paid the check, retrieved Kendall's coat, and escorted her outside. They were the last ones to leave the restaurant, having lingered over their coffees and dessert. The air was cold and crisp, a brilliant moon glittering among the tree limbs above them decorated with flowers waiting to bud. The staircase leading down to her car was cast in shadow.

"I'm parked down below."

"Then I'll walk you to your car." Heath clasped her hand with his, pulling her to a stop with a gentle tug. "But first, there's only one way to end this night on a perfect note."

He turned her toward him, pulling her into his embrace. His arm around her back was strong, secure. He tilted her face up, his touch gentle, his eyes cloaked in the night.

"What a surprise you are, Kendall."

"A surprise?"

"Yes. I came back to the States, planning to concentrate on work . . ." His fingers tangled in her hair. "I didn't plan on falling in love."

His words caught her off guard. "Is that what this is, Heath?"

"I hope so. Don't you?"

His first kiss kept her from answering his question.

Kendall stilled as Heath cradled her face with both his hands, his mouth a tantalizing taste of warmth and temptation. He followed the first kiss with another one, even more potent than the first, so that she clasped the lapels of his coat to stay on balance.

A breeze. A rattle of tree limbs. Kendall pushed herself away, forcing herself to think. To act rationally. She was standing outside a restaurant—making out like a teenager with Heath Parker.

Enough.

"I-I think you need to walk me to my car."

Heath's chuckle reverberated against his chest. "All right. One of us needs to think clearly. Although I'd like nothing more than to kiss you again."

Kendall buried her face in his coat. "I'd like that, too." Had she just admitted that? Well, why not? Her response made it obvious. "But I still think you should just walk me to my car."

Heath pressed his lips against the corner of her ear. "And you surprise me again, Kendall. I shall walk you to your car. And look forward to kissing you again . . . sometime soon."

★ ★ ★ ★ ★

Heath's kisses lingered in Kendall's mind—on her lips—all the way home. The scent of his cologne had embedded itself in the fabric of her coat, and she turned the collar up and buried her nose in the material, recalling the feel of his embrace. Security. Something she hadn't felt in a long time.

And desire.

That, too.

She rubbed her cheek along the soft fabric, chewing on her bottom lip. Heath all but said he was falling in love with her. Her—Kendall Haynes. The girl-now-thirty-six-year-old-woman who spent most of her life waiting.

Her fingers worked the weave of the material. No, that wasn't right. She'd done things with her life. Pursued her dreams. Accomplished some, if not all of them. Her dream of having it all was mostly accomplished . . . but a woman couldn't put a ring on her own finger, couldn't force the "I do."

Although she'd considered it more than once.

But Kendall refused to settle.

And at least one man had been more than willing to let her know that marrying her would have been just that: settling. And then there were the Christian guys who played the faith card—who knew the right things to say, the right things to do—and then insisted that sleeping together somehow was right, even good. *Expected.* Everyone did it.

Well, everyone might be doing it.

But Kendall had managed not to tumble into bed with a guy. Her dream was to still be pure on her wedding night. Although Heath Parker would present some enticement to think otherwise. Surely if they talked things out like two mature adults, he would agree with her. Right?

Kendall pulled her car behind her combo office/home. She was being silly. Two kisses and she was worrying that Heath might want to sleep with her. Although those were some rock your-world kisses. She gripped the steering wheel and stared out into the night. If nothing else, he made it clear that, unlike Griffin Walker, he didn't see her as just a friend. A brief image of Leslie Meyer's glare broke through Kendall's thoughts. The woman disliked her—but why? Maybe she was interested in Heath? Not surprising.

Not her problem—unless Heath asked her to join the board. Then she'd maintain a professional demeanor and distance with the woman. And no matter what, she'd take her relationship with Heath slowly and make the right choices, trusting Heath. Trusting he wanted to make the right choices, too.

CHAPTER TWELVE

★ ★ ★ ★ ★

*G*riffin lay in his bed, forcing himself not to move. If he did nothing more than breathe . . . barely . . . then maybe the world would stay upright. Since three o'clock in the morning it was as if someone strapped him to a giant carnival Tilt-A-Whirl and spun him out of control. But if he waited . . . another minute or two . . . or ten, surely the vertigo would stop.

What time was it? Did he dare risk a look at the alarm clock on his bedside table? That would require turning his head to the left. And that much movement would give his room permission to pitch and roll as if he were on his own torturous journey to the Land of Oz.

Was Ian awake? Most days, the teen slept until either hunger or Griffin's insistent demands pulled him out of his bed. Of course, on a Saturday all bets were off. Maybe it was ten? Or eleven?

He had no idea.

The sheets and bedspread tangled around his legs and torso, his flannel pajama bottoms twisted around his legs. He tossed his T-shirt aside on his last trip to the bathroom—right before a bout of dry heaves.

No matter how much he fought vertigo—denied it, raged against it—it was an enemy he couldn't conquer. Eighteen months ago, the ailment tossed him out of the cockpit and to his knees. Doctors were no help, what with their "It should resolve over time" jargon. *Yeah, right.* Here he was, and yet another episode assaulted him in the middle of the night. The vertigo taunted him, receding, and then flaring up.

"Griffin?" His brother knocked at his bedroom door before opening it partway and poking his head inside. "You awake?"

Griffin hoped he could talk without moving his head. "Yeah . . . I'm up."

That hadn't been too bad. Just a little rocking of the USS *Vertigo.*

"Whoa. You look awful."

With his eyes still closed, Griffin heard Ian walk over to his bed. No need to push his luck by looking at his brother.

"You sick?"

"Uh, yeah. Just a bit."

"Is there anything I can do?"

He wanted to ask Ian if he had a magical cure for vertigo. Pixie dust, maybe. Or a genie in a bottle.

"Nope. I'm good."

"You look like a cadaver."

Even the weak chuckle that escaped tilted Griffin's world. "Since when have you seen a cadaver?"

"NCIS." From the sound of his voice, Ian still stood nearby. "You want something to drink? Mountain Dew? Coffee? I could probably figure out the coffeemaker."

Griffin risked running his hand over his face. "No coffee, unless you bring a bucket along with you for the mess I make after I drink it. How about a bottle of water?"

"Okay. Be right back."

His brother beat a hasty retreat, probably afraid Griffin would toss his cookies before Ian escaped. Not that Griffin had anything left in his stomach.

He needed to see if things had improved at all in the last half hour. He opened his eyes, thankful when the room stayed upright. Maybe the episode was finally abating. Next test was to turn his head to the left. Slowly. So far, so good. Now to raise his head off the pillow—well, really, his mattress. He'd thrown his pillows off the bed in a fit of frustration. One was in the corner, another behind his door.

With every inch that he raised his head, the feeling of pressure, of the room beginning to sway, increased. Griffin gritted his teeth. He hadn't experienced a full-blown episode in weeks—months—and now he was flat on his back again. And the medical board was meeting the end of May to review his case. How was he going to get reinstated to fly if they knew he still dealt with everything from mild dizziness to out-of-control vertigo?

The board would permanently disqualify him.

Time to sit up.

With one swift motion, Griffin grabbed a fistful of blankets, shoving them away so he could swing his legs over the bed and right himself.

And the world went end-over-end as if he'd programmed it to do a barrel roll.

He knew that, in reality, nothing moved. The dresser and chair stayed upright. The floor remained the floor, the ceiling the ceiling, rather than tumbling over and over as if someone flipped a switch and sent his room on a permanent spin. But reality or not, what he saw was a visual tornado of everything—the walls, the floor, the ceiling, the dresser—tumbling around him.

Big mistake.

Eyes squeezed shut against the nightmarish optical illusion, he heard Ian enter his room again.

Griffin sucked in a breath. "Help me up."

"Are you sure?"

"Help me up . . . or I'm puking right here."

His brother dropped the open bottle of water, dousing Griffin with a cold spray. Then he grabbed Griffin's forearms and pulled him to his feet, helping him stagger to the bathroom. Griffin gripped the side of the doorway, holding himself upright.

"I can take it from here—"

"Really?"

"Believe me, you don't wanna stay . . ."

He heard Ian retreat even as he stumbled across the cold tile floor and hit his knees in front of the toilet, his palms and knees slamming against the floor. Some things a guy had to deal with on his own. What was the kid going to do, hold his hand? Tracey hadn't even stayed by his side when they were married and he came down with the flu.

Minutes later, Griffin realized he had two choices. He could lie down on his bathroom floor until the vertigo ceased. Or he could combat-crawl back to his bed. Right now, hunkering down on the cold tile and asking Ian to cover him with a towel sounded like the best option.

He wasn't one to give in to self-pity. He believed in taking care of himself, not asking anyone else to help him. That approach had gotten him through most things, including four years at the Academy. After his divorce, he managed to convince everyone he was fine, happy to be single and free again, even as regret stalked him. And now dizziness—an invisible foe—forced him facedown on his bathroom floor. He'd ignored the symptoms. Tried to bluff his way through a medical exam after he stumbled and fell on the flight line after bringing his A-10 back to base. All his efforts got him was chained to a desk assignment at Schriever Air Force Base.

Ian nudging his leg pulled Griffin from his reverie. "I'm calling Dr. Kendall—"

"No, you aren't." Griffin pushed himself to a sitting position and then groaned as the bathroom whirled around him.

"Like there's anything you can do about it."

"Ian, don't call her." With his head between his knees, Griffin spoke to the floor.

No response. Wasn't there some position that wouldn't cause everything to spin? So his brother called Kendall. All right, then. She would ask a few questions. Tell Ian to make sure Griffin kept up on his fluids. Let the kid call the good doctor.

He didn't care.

★ ★ ★ ★ ★

"Where is he?" Kendall handed Sully's leash to Ian. Why she brought the dog, she didn't know. It wasn't like she needed a chaperone to check on Griffin. If nothing else, the dog would keep Ian occupied while she was with his brother.

"Last time I was upstairs, he was in the bathroom trying to crawl back to bed."

"Crawl back to . . ." Kendall dropped her leather satchel by her feet, then kicked off her black wedge flip-flops decorated with faux rhinestones. "How long has he been like this?"

"He seemed fine last night. We watched *The Italian Job* and grilled steaks. I got up a couple of hours ago and that's when I found out he was sick. Do you think it's the flu?"

"I won't know until I see him. Where's his room?"

Ian pointed up the stairs. "His bedroom is the back one. Don't look in my room."

She headed toward the stairs. "My brother's room was always a mess, too. Probably still is. Drove my mom crazy."

"Yeah. My mom feels . . . felt the same way. She always told me that shutting my door wasn't what she meant when she told me to clean my room."

Kendall wanted to go back and hug the teen, but right now she needed to take care of Griffin.

"What can I do, Dr. Kendall?" Ian stood by the couch, still wearing the baggy navy-blue sweatpants and T-shirt he probably slept in. Did he own any other kind of shirt?

"Take Sully for a quick walk around the block. He'll behave better if he's tired out. I'll come down and talk to you as soon as I figure everything out."

Walking down the hallway, she couldn't help but notice again how barren the townhome was. No pictures on the wall. A quick glance into Ian's room confirmed the teen's admission: Clothes tossed everywhere. Textbooks spilled from his backpack. A computer laptop sat on his desk, which was covered with papers and magazines.

Not her problem.

She came to Griffin's bedroom, the door half open. "Griffin? It's Kendall. You decent?"

She waited for a few seconds before Griffin answered her, his voice muffled. "No. Go away."

"Well, I'm a trained medical professional, so I don't care if you're decent or not. Ian's worried about you. And so am I. Ready or not, here I come."

She only hoped Griffin lied when he said he wasn't decent.

She settled into her *Dr. Kendall Haynes* mind-set and pushed open the door, stepping into Griffin's bedroom. Just as Spartan as the rest of the house. White-beige carpet. A king-sized bed covered with a tangle of white sheets and a striped comforter in various shades of brown. A dresser of the same dark wood as the headboard, with Griffin's watch, his wallet, and a few receipts tossed on top. Walls still painted white. Basic brown curtains covering the windows. A quick scan of the room showed it was . . . empty.

Empty?

No Griffin in the bed.

Where was he? What had Ian said? *He's crawling back to bed.* Uh-oh.

She stepped around the foot of the bed, ignoring the temptation to straighten the sheets, and found Griffin sprawled on the floor. And decent.

Well, mostly. A man without a shirt was no reason to blush. She was a big girl, after all, and a doctor. And Griffin Walker was one sick guy if he couldn't even get off the floor. But still . . . she'd never seen the man without a shirt.

And now she knew where his tattoo was.

She knelt beside him on the carpeted floor, wondering for half a second why the man would have a tattoo of a three-headed beast on his left shoulder blade. Just another piece to the puzzle of Griffin Walker. Then her fingertips touched his brow, slipping through his short-cropped hair. Softer than she imagined.

Focus, Kendall. You are a doctor examining a patient, not a woman in love.

And that was a crazy thought. She was most definitely not a woman in love—at least not with Griffin Walker. She was a family physician, and after that she was Griffin's *friend*.

Her fingers rested on his forehead. He didn't appear to have a temperature.

"Kendall . . ."

"Hey, Griffin."

His eyes remained closed, his lips barely moving. "Get out of my room."

"All in good time, sir." She pressed two fingers against the pulse beating in his neck.

"Not dead."

"I know that."

"Wish I was." He moved his head the barest of inches and grimaced.

"Do you have a migraine?" He never mentioned that as a problem before.

"Nope." He swallowed. Licked his lips, which looked dry and flaky.

"Do you have ear pain?" She kept her voice low.

"No."

"Neck pain?"

"No."

As she asked each question, Kendall probed gently around Griffin's head and neck.

"How about we get you to roll over on your back?"

"How about we don't." Griffin's hand snaked up and clamped around her wrist.

The man was sick, but he was strong.

Kendall decided to use her best *Dr. Kendall Haynes* voice. "Let go, Griffin. I'm trying to help you."

His grasp didn't weaken. "Then leave me alone."

"You are a typical guy when you're sick. Grumpy."

Silence.

"And no sense of humor, either." Kendall waited for a few seconds. The only sound in the room was Griffin's breathing mingling with her own. "Did you take something, Griffin? Drink something?"

A growl curled Griffin's lips and he opened his eyes halfway, trying to make eye contact with her—and failing. "You're kidding, right?"

"Look, if you won't tell me what's going on, I have to pursue all the possibilities." She placed her hand over his where he still gripped her wrist. His skin was cold to the touch. "And just because we're friends doesn't rule out you doing stupid things."

His eyes closed. "No drugs. No alcohol."

"Well then, assuming you didn't fall and break something— like your stubborn neck or thick skull—I suggest we get you up off the floor and back into bed."

"Only if you want me to throw up all over you."

"You wouldn't be the first person to do that." Kendall hoped her attempt at humor, weak as it was, would get both of them through this. "Too bad I didn't think to bring a change of clothes. I'll just have to borrow one of your T-shirts, since you are opting out of those today. Or maybe one of Ian's. It might fit me better."

She patted Griffin's shoulder in an encouraging let's-get-going-already way. The best place for him was safely tucked in bed.

"If I'm getting in bed, I'm getting in it by myself."

"Of course you are." Kendall couldn't resist another attempt at humor. "Did you think I was suggesting otherwise, Colonel Walker?"

At last—the merest of smiles quirked the corner of his mouth.

"Do you talk to all your patients like this?"

"Never. And you are not my patient. You are my most stubborn friend. I wouldn't take you on as a patient." She stood, resisting the urge to touch Griffin's face, his hair . . . trace the outline of his tattoo. "While you get yourself upright, I'll get the bed ready."

She turned her back and focused on straightening the jumble of sheets and blankets tossed all over the king-sized bed. Why oh why did Griffin Walker have to purchase such a large bed? Kendall had to stand on the bed frame to set everything to rights again. Now, where were his pillows? The man used pillows, right? She searched the room and saw one tossed behind the door.

The bed moved as Griffin grasped the mattress with both hands. She'd forced herself to ignore his guttural moan as he moved across the floor. The man wanted to do things for himself? So be it.

"I'm just going to get your pillows—"

"Leave 'em . . ." Griffin stood for a few seconds and then fell into bed. Another moan slipped past his clenched teeth.

"Griffin, what is going on? This isn't the flu or a migraine. Help me out here." Kendall covered him with a blanket, evaluating the pasty-white color of his face, trying to remain detached. Clinical. And she thought he looked bad when he was on the floor. She pushed his damp hair back from his forehead.

Griffin turned his face away. "Can I have some water? Ian threw the last bottle on me."

"I don't blame him." Kendall marched from the room, sorry she wasn't still wearing her shoes. Trying to stomp away in bare feet didn't have the same effect.

Downstairs, Ian sprawled on the floor in front of the TV, a sleeping Sully stretched out beside him. Griffin may not be much for spending money on furniture, but he'd splurged on a sixty-inch wall-mounted flat-screen.

Ian lifted his head up off his folded arms. "How is he?"

"He's sick, but you knew that." Kendall walked into the kitchen, which bore testament to the Walkers' nothing-but-the-basics lifestyle. Except for dirty dishes from their steak dinner last night, and a cereal box and a bowl and spoon from Ian's breakfast this morning, the sand-colored countertops and white appliances looked untouched. No photos stuck on the fridge with magnets. No pile of mail to be read. Nothing.

She opened the fridge, not surprised it was almost as empty as a display model at Lowe's. A six-pack of Mountain Dew. Several bottles of water. An almost-empty gallon of milk. Some lunch meat and some sliced Cheddar cheese. Half a loaf of bread. She could see a lone onion and green pepper residing in the crisper. The Walkers' favorite words for meals must be *to go.*

Ian came up behind her, Sully ambling beside him. Kendall grabbed a bottle of water, stepping aside as the teen reached in for a soda.

"How are you feeling, Ian?"

"Me? I'm fine. No problem." He popped the top, the soda fizzing. "Why?"

"Just trying to figure out if Griffin might have food poisoning." She tapped the unopened bottle of water against her leg, the cold seeping through the material of her pants. "What did y'all have for dinner again?"

"Griffin grilled steaks. Baked potatoes. We had Oreo ice cream for dessert."

"Hmmmm. Let me think on this some more." She patted Sully on the head and Ian on the back as she exited the kitchen. "Don't worry."

While she climbed the stairs to Griffin's room, Kendall searched her brain for clues to his illness.

Help me out here, God. Something's wrong and I can't leave Griffin with Ian when I don't know what it is. If he's not going to tell me, then I need you to help me figure it out.

She began running through possible diagnoses as she twisted the plastic top off the water bottle. When she walked back into Griffin's room, he was resting, eyes closed, pain cutting grooves in his forehead and at the corners of his mouth.

"Hey." She rested the palm of her hand on his forehead, hoping the coolness from the bottle transferred to his skin. "How you feeling?"

"Mostly dead."

"What? You're a *Princess Bride* fan, too? I may have to still be your friend." Kendall gave his shoulder a gentle nudge. "I've got your water. Ready to sit up?"

"No. But my mouth feels like somebody dragged it all the way to the top of Pikes Peak and back." Griffin opened his eyes, which were dulled to the color of her father's faded blue work shirt. Whatever was wrong with the man, he was exhausted.

As he struggled to sit, Kendall grabbed the covers that fell away from his shoulders, positioning them up high around his chest. A thick gold chain hung around his neck and fell to his mid-chest. Two white-gold wedding bands hung suspended from the chain. Now, what was the symbolism of that? First a tattoo of some kind of mysterious, multiheaded beast, and now wedding bands. The man prompted more questions—and no answers.

Focus, Kendall, focus. Be the doctor. Try to remember that Griffin Walker is not noticing you—and don't go noticing him. Except as a patient.

She held the water bottle out to him. "You need help with this?"

"No, as soon as the room stops spinning, I'm good."

As soon as the room stops spinning.

Vertigo.

Bingo.

When she locked eyes with Griffin, the blank look he gave her confirmed her suspicion. "So, is this your first bout of vertigo?"

As if defying her diagnosis, Griffin sat up and took a gulp of water. Grimaced, as the movement probably caused the room to rock and roll. "This is my first serious flare-up in weeks . . . yes."

"When were you first diagnosed?" Maybe if she played it nonchalant, he'd answer her questions.

"Eighteen months ago."

"That's why you're not flying."

Silence.

That would be a yes.

"Has it been getting better up until now?"

"I thought so." He tipped the bottle up and drank as if he were in a battle to best the vertigo. When the bottle was empty, he sat back, his face pale. "Do me a favor and grab me a T-shirt, please? Middle drawer."

Kendall wasn't surprised to discover Griffin folded his clothes with military precision. She selected the first T-shirt on top of the pile, something with a stitched logo. Was that a warthog? Shaking her head at the curious animals in Griffin Walker's life, she handed him the shirt.

"And no, I don't need help."

"I wasn't going to ask." She took the empty plastic bottle and tossed it in the wastebasket in the bathroom. Straightened the white cotton towels hanging on the rack. Learned what type of toothpaste and toothbrush Griffin Walker used. Counted to sixty.

"Okay, now I'm decent."

"I'm a doctor, remember. I've seen worse."

That didn't come out right. And there was nothing wrong with Griffin Walker's physique. It was obvious from the defined muscles in his arms and torso the man worked out.

She stood at the foot of his bed. "Do you want me to order a prescription for you? Something for the nausea? To help you sleep?"

"No."

"You are going to make an appointment with your doctor, right?"

"Wrong."

She stomped her foot. Where were her shoes when she needed them? "Oh, come on, Walker! You need to get looked at—"

"I've been checked out. By a flight doc at my prior station in Arizona. By an ENT. By I don't know how many doctors down at the School of Aerospace Medicine in Texas. They all agree I have vertigo. They all agree there's not much they can do for me, except run some tests that might make the vertigo worse. So, I'm grounded until the vertigo stops—or until a medical board clears me to return to normal flying status."

Griffin's words were clipped and he refused to make eye contact with her.

"Fine. Is there something I can do—"

"Obviously not."

Instead of angering her, his verbal stonewalling broke her heart. There was one thing she could do for him. "May I pray for you?"

Griffin looked up, his brow furrowed in pain—or surprise. "What?"

"May I pray for you?"

She knew he'd say no. The man was so private, so indepen-
dent. He wanted a friend, but one who stayed well outside the
emotional boundaries he set up. But her offer, motivated by
compassion, slipped past her common sense.

"Sure."

Kendall almost didn't hear Griffin's whispered response. Yes?
He said yes? She stepped around to the side of the bed again,
afraid he'd change his mind. Without asking, she slipped her
hand into his and rested her other hand on his shoulder before
closing her eyes.

"Dear God, thank you that your ears are open to our prayers.
Thank you that you love us, sometimes despite ourselves. I
bring my friend Griffin to your throne of grace because you
promise that we can come to you whenever we need mercy and
grace. Griffin's weary of all this vertigo—and this flare-up has
really thrown him for a loop." A soft giggle escaped her lips and
she just caught the sound of Griffin's weary chuckle. "Sorry,
God, that was a lousy pun. You know doctors don't know everything. You know how frustrating that is because we want to
help our patients when they're sick. So far the doctors haven't
helped Griffin. It's not about doctors, God. It's always about
you. You are Jehovah-Rapha, the God who heals. I ask you to
please heal Griffin of this vertigo. Amen."

As silence filled the room, Kendall continued to stand beside
Griffin's bed. She kept her eyes closed, her hand still wrapped
around Griffin's larger one. She wanted to keep praying . . . even
without words, she *was* still praying for him. For healing. For
comfort. For strength.

"Kendall—"

Her eyes flew open. From his position leaning against the
headboard, Griffin watched her. "Yes?"

"Thank you . . . for praying."

"Any better?"

"I'd love to say yes . . . but no. I need to lie down."

"Then lie down." She pulled the blankets up over his shoulders, smoothing them out. She resisted the urge to touch his face. His hair. Just to comfort him, of course. "You try to get some sleep. I'll take Ian with me and keep him busy—take him to lunch, make sure he's ready for school on Monday."

Griffin reached up and gripped her hand. "Thanks, friend."

"You're welcome, friend."

She stood watching him for a few brief seconds, willing the words she'd spoken to be true. Of course, she was more than thankful Griffin agreed to let her pray for him. And he *was* her friend. He was. It wasn't his fault that at times her wish-I-may heart longed for more.

Friendship with Griffin wasn't "less than." It should be enough. It *was* enough. Hadn't friendship been enough in times past with other guys? She wouldn't waste her time wishing for something else. She exited Griffin's bedroom, closing the door so he could rest in silence. She paused halfway downstairs. After all, there was Heath Parker. He had made it clear he was ready for more with her—ready to pursue romance with her. That he might even be falling in love with her. And who knew where that might lead?

Why was her heart tugging her toward the man determined to stay single?

She was being silly. Naive. Ungrateful. That's it, she was ungrateful. For so long, she wanted to have it all: career, marriage, kids. And then she became so focused on her career, so hurt by the one or two romantic rejections, she lost track of her hopes for marriage and family. She needed to realize God could very well be answering years and years of her prayers—through Heath. He was a believer. He wanted to help others, just as she did. He understood the demands of medicine. He respected her as a physician. And he certainly noticed that she was a woman, too.

Sure, Griffin Walker intrigued her. Maybe even tempted her.

But she knew the right guy when she saw him—and Heath Parker was that guy.

CHAPTER THIRTEEN

★ ★ ★ ★ ★

*G*riffin had known he would hate his job the moment he got his orders to transfer to Colorado Springs. He just didn't know how much.

Of course, he did the job. Went to the meetings. Read the emails. And at the end of every workday, he crossed another date off his desk calendar. Another twenty-four hours closer to the medical board. One less obstacle standing between him and flying.

He clicked the controller to the garage door, idling his Jeep until the door swung back and he could pull in next to Ian's Jeep Cherokee. Buying the vehicle had been a smart choice. Ian now drove himself to school. One less thing for Griffin to worry about.

Griffin grabbed the sack of groceries he purchased on his way home and headed into the house. Tonight his brother could choose the main course. "Hey, Ian. I'm home."

No response.

"We've got options tonight for dinner. You want steak or chicken?" He set the bag on the kitchen counter, tossing his keys next to it before walking through the house and standing at the foot of the stairs. He was no longer on a first-name basis with all the cashiers staffing the fast-food drive-throughs within a three-mile radius of the town house. Now he was all about grilling. Maybe he should take the time to teach his brother how to handle the gas grill.

"Ian? You up there?"

More silence.

Ian had to be home—his Jeep was in the garage. Had he fallen asleep doing homework?

Griffin bounded up the stairs to Ian's room. If he was asleep, he wouldn't be for much longer. Ian wasn't the only tired Walker brother. Griffin would show Ian how to start the grill, get him prepping the chicken, and then go change out of his uniform. With a quick rap on the door, Griffin leaned into Ian's room—and found him sitting on his bed, knees pulled up to his chest, arms crossed on top, a pair of stormy hazel eyes zeroing in on him like a laser.

"Didn't you hear me call you?"

"I heard." With the lower half of his face buried in his arms, Ian's words were muffled.

"If that was a yes, why didn't you answer?"

"Mrs. Jamison called."

"Don't you mean that Mac called?" Griffin started to back up. Time was wasting.

"No. *Mrs. Jamison* called to tell me that she and Mr. Jamison were looking forward to having me move back with them." His brother sat up straight, hurling the words across the room at him.

What? Griffin stood in the doorway, his mind scrambling for words. Every sentence he latched onto felt like an evasive maneuver.

"She forgot to store your phone number in her cell phone, so she decided it was easier to call me. She said you can call her back and finalize the plan." Ian recrossed his arms over his chest, never once looking away from Griffin.

"Ian, look—"

"When were you gonna tell *me* the plan, huh, Griffin?" Ian jumped off the bed and stood in the middle of the room. "When were you gonna tell me that you didn't want me here? When you handed me a plane ticket and drove me to the airport?"

"I hadn't made a final decision about this—"

"That's not what Mrs. Jamison said. She said you talked it all out. Me finishing up the school year here and then heading back to Panama City this summer. She said you told her I was having such a tough time here—"

"You are having a tough time—"

"I am not! I've got friends. I'm not flunking out. I'm sorry you have to feed me—but hey, other than that, I'm not that much of a bother. I didn't ask you to buy me the Jeep. And it wasn't your money anyway. I know Mom and Dad left me a trust fund."

"Stop it, okay? Just stop it." Griffin advanced into the room, resisting the urge to grab his brother by the shoulders and shake him. "I never said you were a bother."

"Then why did you ask Mrs. Jamison to take me?" His brother pushed past him. "I get it. I'm not your real brother. Just somebody your mom and dad felt sorry for."

"Ian—" Griffin heard his brother's footsteps thunder down the stairs. "Get back here so we can talk this out."

"I'm not staying where I'm not wanted."

The house vibrated with the sound of the front door opening and then slamming shut. Where was Ian going? Griffin stood at the top of the stairs. What should he do? Ian needed time to cool down. He would probably walk around the block a few times. It wasn't quite dark yet, but the temperature was sliding into the thirties. Ian only had on jeans, a T-shirt, and tennis shoes. He'd be back within fifteen—still angry.

When Griffin heard the rumble of the garage door opening, he dashed down the stairs, straight for the garage. But by the time he threw open the door, Ian was backing the Cherokee out of the garage, the headlights arcing across Griffin's face as his brother spun the Jeep around.

"Ian! Stop!"

He ran through the garage and down the driveway, only to see the red glow of the Cherokee's taillights as Ian gunned the motor and sped down the street. Griffin stood with his hands on his hips and debated his next move. Should he chase the kid down? Let him go? Where was he going? To Jeff's? Probably best to give his brother some space.

Returning to the house, Griffin stashed the packages of chicken and steak in the fridge. He'd postpone dinner until Ian came home. They would sit down, eat, and talk things out. Griffin slathered peanut butter and tart cherry preserves on two slices of whole wheat bread, chasing the sandwich down with a few chugs from the milk bottle. The microwave clock read seven fifteen. He'd give Ian an hour—an hour and a half, tops. Then he'd call his little brother and tell him it was time to come home.

★ ★ ★ ★ ★

"You know I have to get rid of you now, dog." Kendall scrubbed the already-damp towel across Sully's wet fur as the goldendoodle squirmed on the floor by the pool. "I told you if you ever got in my pool, I was done with you."

Sully whimpered, as if apologizing for interrupting her evening swim by jumping into the water—*right on top of her.* What had the dog been thinking? That she needed to be rescued?

"You better say you're sorry." She uncovered his face, staring into his sad eyes and shaking his soggy muzzle. "Now I've got to clean this thing."

Once she was satisfied the dog was mostly dry, Kendall wrapped herself in a towel and took the stairs to her loft. So much for a relaxing swim to take her mind off the fact that Heath stood her up tonight. Well, he hadn't stood her up. Not exactly. It's not as if she sat at the Elephant Bar and waited for him to show up. No, he'd been the gentleman she knew him to be, calling and telling her that he couldn't make their date and rescheduling for a week later. He tried for something sooner, but between another round of wedding dress shopping with Rachel and the annual conference of the Colorado Academy of Family Physicians, Kendall was booked solid.

"No sooner than that?" Heath's disappointment almost convinced her to force something into her schedule.

"I'm sorry, Heath. I don't have a free moment all week. Maybe I'll see you at church?"

"Absolutely. I'm so sorry about this, Kendall. I'll miss you."

She hung up, realizing he hadn't explained what had come up that caused him to cancel. Not that it mattered. She wasn't going to call the man back and ask, *So tell me, what's more important than our date?* Maybe something with the board? But if it was with his board, why didn't he include her?

Kendall ran her fingers through her moist hair. This was no time to overthink things. Heath needed to reschedule. Period. Moving on. And she had the rare commodity of a free evening. Now all she had to do was figure out how to spend the time. First things first. She refused to have the odor of wet golden-doodle permeate the night.

"Sully, go to your bed."

The dog slunk to his corner where she had pulled his dog bed, casting a look at her over his shoulder.

"Don't even look at me like that. This is your own fault. Get on your bed and stay there until you dry off."

Just to show him that she still loved him—and wasn't going to send him to the pound—she tossed him a dog treat on her way to her room to shower and change. The hot shower wasn't as invigorating as if she'd completed her swim, but it eased some of the tension of the workday from her shoulders and neck. She'd seen twenty patients today—and had the paperwork to prove it.

Fifteen minutes later, Kendall padded out to the kitchen in a comfortable pair of old jeans and a stretched-out gray sweater that had softened with age. She'd substitute whatever she found in her refrigerator for whatever Heath had planned for dinner tonight. And if that failed, she could go downstairs and raid the office fridge.

Now what?

Read a book on her Kindle? Watch something on Hulu? Call and check on Griffin and his vertigo?

Nope. She was not going to check on that man. He was a grown-up and if he needed something, he could call. Except Kendall knew he was too stubborn to call. His mind could be rolling like the Mind Eraser roller coaster at Elitch Park and he'd just sit there and take it. Or more like he'd lie on the floor, half dressed, and take it.

At least Ian was smart enough to call her when his brother had been reduced to crawling a few days ago. She never imagined seeing Griffin Walker—Mr. Strong and Silent—sprawled on the floor. Even flat on his face, the man was attractive, tattoo and all.

"And you are a wretched, wretched woman to even notice." Kendall muttered the admonition as she pulled the foil cover off a yogurt, scooped out a spoonful, and then stuffed it in her mouth.

Well, then, what about his tattoo? Why did the guy have a crazy tattoo of a gray three-headed beast on his right shoulder blade? Was it a dog? A wolf? People got tattoos because they meant something—well, usually. But what could Griffin's tattoo mean? She could always Google it, but that felt like she was stalking the guy. Maybe she would ask Griffin the next time she saw him. Friend-to-friend.

Sure. And right after that she'd ask him why he wore two wedding rings on that gold chain around his neck. They were his parents' rings, right? Surely they weren't the wedding bands from his first marriage.

Standing at the breakfast bar, she riffled through the papers piled on the counter. There was a yellow sticky note reminding her about the date to go look for bridesmaid dresses with Rachel. Wonderful. And it was stuck to an online dating application Sonia talked her into filling out months ago. How ironic. She scanned the questionnaire. Was she content? Was she humorous? Was she efficient? What was her background like? Was she good at resolving conflict? Was her faith important to her? Was she looking for a serious relationship?

Was she looking for a serious relationship?

Yes, yes, she was.

And she wasn't going to finish filling out an online dating questionnaire, was she? Hadn't she decided Heath was the obvious answer to her *Where is he, God?* question? Did she really think she'd find a better match by marking the appropriate boxes on this questionnaire? Griffin was perfect for her.

Wait. She meant *Heath.*

Heath was perfect for her.

Aaaargh.

Griffin-with-the-tattoo-and-the-I-used-to-be-a-bad-boy-but-now-I'm-not smile was a distraction.

Heath was perfect.

She just had to keep the two straight.

A quick staccato rapping on the back door to her loft interrupted her tearing the application in half, preparing to toss it in the trash can. She crossed the room, placing a hand on the doorknob, ensuring it was locked.

"Who is it?"

"It's me—Ian Walker." The boy's words were muted by the barrier of the door.

Ian? Was something wrong with Griffin again? Why hadn't Ian called?

She unlocked the door and yanked it open. Why was Ian at her house? It was after nine. His shoulders were hunched underneath his T-shirt, his hands balled into fists.

"Ian, are you okay? Is Griffin still sick?"

The boy's lower lip quivered, his eyes wide and red-rimmed. "Yeah, my brother's fine. But I-I . . ." He seemed unable to get the rest of the words past his lips.

"Ian, are you hurt?"

"No, but I wish I was."

What in the world?

"Ian, tell me what's going on right now."

"Dr. Kendall, I wrecked your Jeep."

★ ★ ★ ★ ★

CHAPTER FOURTEEN

*T*en thirty.

Griffin stared at the display on his cell phone. Where was his brother?

Patience gave way to anxiety an hour ago. When he tried to call Ian, his brother's cell phone rang—upstairs. Griffin found it lying on his brother's desk under a pile of homework papers. His call to Jeff led to a dead end when the other teen said Ian wasn't there—and that he hadn't talked to Ian all day.

Griffin could do nothing but wait for Ian to walk through the door and explain where he'd been. Now Griffin knew what his parents experienced every single time he decided to ignore curfew back when he'd been in high school. Then, it was no big deal to walk in an hour or two late. On this side of the experience, he understood why his mother paced the living room while his father waited to hold court in the family room.

Ten forty. He was done with waiting. Time for some kind of

action. Griffin shrugged back into his coat, grabbed his keys off the kitchen bar, and headed for his Jeep. If he had to drive up and down every street in Colorado Springs, so be it. He would track down his brother.

As he turned south on Academy, his cell phone rang. He clicked on his Bluetooth earpiece, praying he'd hear his brother's voice.

"Griffin Walker."

"Griffin, it's Kendall. I need to talk fast. Can you hear me?"

"Kendall? Why are you whispering?" This was not the time for the woman to play games. "Look, I can't talk now. I'm trying to find Ian—"

"I *know* that. Be quiet for a minute."

Did the woman just shush him? Then he heard her muffled voice, as if she'd covered the mouthpiece with her hand. "Swimsuit . . . go ahead down . . . in a minute."

What in the world was going on?

Kendall's voice came back on the line, still whispering. "Are you there?"

"Of course I'm here, but I'm about to hang up. "

"Don't hang up. Ian's here. He's been here for almost two hours."

With a quick yank on the steering wheel, Griffin pulled over to the side of the road, an overload of adrenaline chased with relief coursing through his body. "Why didn't you call me sooner?"

"Oh, good grief. Back down, will you? I'm on your side. I couldn't call you. I wanted your brother to *stay here.* If I'd even mentioned calling you, he would have bolted. So I've been playing Wii Sports Resort with him and letting him talk."

"I'm coming over."

"Stop. Will you listen to me first?"

"Only if you stop whispering."

"Oh, right. I don't have to do that anymore, do I?" The next time Kendall spoke she didn't sound like a CIA operative reporting in to headquarters. "Before you go ballistic on Ian, I want to tell you what happened. And while you drive over here, I want you to think about what you're going to say and what you're *not* going to say. Got it?"

The wind buffeted the soft sides of the CJ7. "What? Are you planning on scripting the conversation for me?"

"Don't get smart, Walker." He heard Kendall take a deep breath. "The first thing you need to know is that Ian wrecked my Jeep—"

"What?" Griffin's shout ricocheted off the Jeep's ceiling. Of all the things Kendall Haynes could have said, he hadn't expected to hear that his brother wrecked her Jeep. "Why did you let Ian drive your Jeep?"

"I didn't. My Jeep was parked behind my building, minding its own business. Stop interrupting and let me tell the story."

Griffin gripped the steering wheel. "Fine. Tell the story."

"Ian was driving too fast. When he came around the back of my building, he hit a patch of gravel and spun out—and into my Jeep. I've got some front fender damage. Ian's Cherokee is going to need a new radiator."

"Great. The kid's had the Jeep how long—"

"He's upset, Griffin. He wanted to talk to me—he said you're sending him back to Florida. No matter how much I tried to convince him that wasn't true, I couldn't."

Griffin ignored Kendall's unasked question. "Where's Ian now?"

"He's downstairs swimming in my endless pool—"

"Your what?"

"My endless pool. I've got a small indoor pool in the back area of my office. I use it to exercise. Oh, never mind. It doesn't matter."

"It's almost eleven. Why is Ian going for a swim?" Griffin pulled back onto the road, heading for Kendall's. "I know he didn't leave here with a pair of swim trunks."

"I usually have some swimsuits and trunks around the office—"

"Oh, really? What do you do, throw impromptu pool parties for your friends?"

"No. I let some of my patients use the pool, you idiot."

Griffin imagined Kendall stamping her foot in frustration. Rolling her eyes. That's one of the things they did best: annoy each other.

"I'm almost to your office."

"Don't come around the back. Ian will see you." Kendall's voice dropped to a whisper again. "I'll meet you at the front door of the clinic. Text me when you get here."

Kendall signed off without saying good-bye, leaving Griffin to wonder how many times the woman was going to save his neck. Wasn't the guy supposed to save the gal? At least that's how he heard it went in romance novels. Not that his relationship with Kendall was romantic. Friends is what they were, friends is what they'd stay.

★ ★ ★ ★ ★

Griffin came barreling up the front walk to her office like a soldier charging the beach on D-Day. Kendall had half a mind to keep the door locked until he calmed down, but barricading him outside the building would only upset him more.

As soon as he stood in front of the double glass doors, she pushed one open, grabbed his hand, and pulled him inside. Then she went on tiptoe, fisted the collar of his jacket in both hands, and forced him to stand still.

"Stop, Griffin."

"Are you crazy, woman? Let go of my coat. I need to talk to my brother."

Kendall hung on to Griffin's jean jacket, trusting his innate manners would not allow him to drag her down the hallway. "*Stop.* I need to say a few things."

He covered her hands with his, distracting her. She had the overwhelming urge to turn her hands over and clasp his hands to hers—to somehow connect with this man who infuriated her. Challenged her. And appealed to her. This close up, she could see the tiny scar on his chin. How did that happen? The intensity of his emotions simmered in the depths of his blue eyes.

Griffin spoke through clenched teeth. "Kendall? Are you just going to hang on my coat all night long?"

"If I have to. Are you going to listen to me?"

When he tried to cross his arms over his chest, Kendall took that as a yes. She eased her hands off his collar. Went down off her tiptoes. Took a step back.

The two of them squared off in the dimly lit hallway. Griffin spoke first. "What did you want to say?"

Kendall took another step backward, just for good measure. "Ian's upset."

"I know that."

"And not just about wrecking my Jeep." She waited, but Griffin stood silent. "He said you've asked another family to be his guardians."

By the way Griffin's shoulders stiffened, even as he continued to lock eyes with her, Kendall knew it was true. "Why?"

"He's unhappy here. All of his friends are back in Florida, where he grew up. Ian needs to be with people he knows. He should graduate next year with his classmates."

"He should be with his *family*. Obviously your parents wanted that or they wouldn't have made you his guardian in the event of their deaths."

"I can't offer Ian a family, Kendall."

Kendall paced toward him. "I can't believe you said that. Just because Ian's adopted—"

"I don't care that Ian's adopted. That's not what I meant. You should know me better than that by now."

"Then what do you mean?"

Griffin strode past her up the hallway, disappearing into the dark, then turned, and came back. "Look at me, Kendall." He raised his arms out from his body a few inches, feet planted wide apart. "I'm single. In the air force. Hoping to fly again as soon as the medical board okays it."

"Your point is?"

"Single. Military. Pilot. That is no kind of family for Ian. He deserves better."

"You won't always be—"

"Nothing's going to change, Kendall." Griffin's inflexible stance mirrored his words. "Nothing."

"What? You've been divorced, so no more marriage? Yes, I've heard you say that, but it's ridiculous, Griffin."

"I'm not discussing this with you."

Kendall caught his arm as he stalked off, as if she could stop six feet of angry from going anywhere. "What's the real reason you're doing this?" She shook his arm. "He's your brother. He needs you. Family sticks together when things go wrong."

He rounded on her. "You once told me to be the guy Ian needed. I'm not that guy, Kendall. I'm not that guy."

"You could be . . ."

"No, I can't be. I'm the guy who wrecked a plane and ruined his best friend's career."

"What?" She stepped back. What had Griffin just said? He wrecked a plane?

Kendall watched Griffin slump to the ground, his back pressed up against the wall in the middle of the darkened hallway. She knelt beside him, touched the rough denim covering his shoulder, then the side of his face, which was turned away from her.

"What did you say?"

"I'm the last guy who should be Ian's guardian." Griffin stared straight ahead, his eyes trained on the opposite wall. "The summer between my junior and senior years at the Academy, I went flying with my buddy David. We took a couple of girls we knew in the Springs. We were flying low, just for fun. I got careless." He covered his eyes with his hand, as if shielding himself from seeing the memory replaying in his mind. "I was the pilot . . . and I wasn't paying attention . . . showing off . . . I didn't notice the fuel switch was on LEFT, and the left tank ran out of gas. The engine quit and I switched the fuel over to both, but it was too late. We didn't have the altitude to restart the engine . . . so we crashed."

"Oh, Griffin, how awful for you   "

"How awful for me? I walked away from the crash with a broken collarbone. One of the girls broke her arm. David . . . he broke his back." Griffin shook his head, his eyes squeezed shut, his fingers kneading his forehead as if the movement could erase the memories.

Kendall risked pulling Griffin close, sitting beside him and daring to slip her arm through his. At first he resisted, but within seconds the tension left his body and he relaxed. Let her hold him. But what could she say?

"It was an accident—"

His words rasped across hers. *"It was my fault."*

Kendall pressed her lips together. She needed to be quiet. Be still. Not try to explain away Griffin's pain. He wanted a friend?

She'd be his friend—but not a Job's comforter who tossed easy answers into his open wound.

So she sat in her office hallway, embracing Griffin Walker. His knees were pulled up to his chest, but he allowed her to draw him against her, his head resting in the crook of her neck and shoulder, his hair soft against her skin. Neither of them spoke, but their breathing fell into a quiet rhythm together. Somehow Griffin moved, and the strength of his arms encircled her. With her arms still looped around his waist, she allowed herself to take pleasure in the warmth of his nearness as he leaned into her. The softness of his hair brushing against her jawline. The whisper of his breath warming her skin.

Sometimes people just needed comfort—a literal shoulder to lean on when they were hurting. She could be that for Griffin.

"Doc?"

The nickname caused a small ripple of laughter to course up her throat. "Yes?"

"You're driving me crazy."

That was the last thing she expected him to say.

"Hey, I'm being nice here." She turned so she could look in his eyes and realized he was serious. But not in the way she'd thought. His eyes glinted with something dangerous, a warning that she was trespassing.

He reached up and slid his hand across the base of her neck, his fingers grasping the short tendrils, tugging her toward him with just the slightest bit of force.

His next statement was a husky whisper. "This is a mistake."

"Of course it is." She matched her words to his, an even softer whisper.

Why did the man keep talking, keep watching her, even as he pulled her closer?

"I'm only going to kiss you one time."

"I never said I wanted you to kiss me."

"Kendall . . ."

He was so close his breath warmed her lips. A ghost of a kiss.

"What?"

"Stop talking."

Kendall's eyes closed the minute his lips covered hers, demanding a response. Within seconds he gentled his touch, grazing his fingertips across her jaw and then tracing the length of her throat, causing tingles to course up and down her spine. A low moan and he seemed to search for more, causing her to grasp his shoulders as he pulled her into his arms.

He might only be kissing her once . . . but he was being thorough. One kiss melded into another and another.

"What are you guys doing?" Ian's question echoed through the hallway.

Kendall froze. Pulled herself away from Griffin, thankful when he moved as if to shield her from his brother.

★ ★ ★ ★ ★

Griffin stood, stepping in front of Kendall. One of them should have a minute to regroup before having to deal with Ian. He found the off switch for his emotions, flipped it, and focused on his brother.

"I came to get you, Ian. I've been worried."

Ian wore a pair of baggy swim trunks decorated with a Hawaiian floral print, a towel draped across his thin shoulders. Water dripped from the hem of the bathing suit onto the floor.

Griffin pointed to the wet spot near Ian's feet. "You're getting the carpet wet."

Kendall moved to stand beside him. "It doesn't matter."

Ian's *What are you guys doing?* hung unanswered, an invisible barrier between them. It wasn't as if Griffin needed to spell it out for his brother. His words were the ultimate rhetorical question. And it wasn't as if he could explain why he kissed Kendall Haynes.

He kissed her because, God help him, he wanted to.

He found himself sitting in the hallway telling Kendall Haynes something he didn't even like to think about, much less share with anyone else. And instead of explaining away his mistake with platitudes and right answers, she wrapped her arms around him and sat with him.

Just let him be.

For the first time in all the months of battling vertigo, waking up day after day wondering if his world would tilt on its axis or not, he was able to be still. And being close enough to Kendall to hear her heart beat, Griffin couldn't deny how this strong, yet tender woman touched his heart.

Kendall walked toward Ian, pulling Griffin's thoughts back to the present.

"You probably want to get changed, Ian, so that you can head home with your brother." She looked back at Griffin. "Do you want to wait here or come with us?"

"I'll wait here."

"Fine. I'll show Ian where he can shower and then I'll head upstairs. The front door locks automatically. I'll, uh, talk with you both soon, I guess."

"Yeah."

She disappeared into the darkness of the hallway with his brother.

And that was that.

CHAPTER FIFTEEN

★ ★ ★ ★

Finally. The workday was over. Kendall could stop trying to evade thoughts of Griffin Walker's startling kisses while she focused on her patients.

Not that she was going to spend the evening thinking about kissing Griffin last night—or ever again. Because, as Griffin said, he was only kissing her once.

Kendall smoothed unscented lotion on her hands as she walked up to the front desk. After a long day of seeing patients, and washing and rewashing her hands, her skin itched so much she longed to scratch it raw. Maybe she should install a whole-house humidifier for the office/house complex.

"Evie, where did you put that third package that came in for Dr. Parker?"

Still facing away from her, Evie lifted a hand, stopping Kendall from repeating her question. As she got closer to the desk, Kendall realized her receptionist was counting out the cash drawer—a necessity for patients who preferred not to use credit cards or checks. Half an uneaten sandwich from Panera sat on a paper plate, and the tangy scent of two slices of dill pickle made Kendall's mouth water. Apparently Evie hadn't taken time for lunch today, either. She still couldn't figure out which were busier: Mondays after a weekend or Fridays going into the weekend.

Maybe she'd go grab a sandwich while she waited for Evie to finish her calculations. Thank God Shelby, one of her regular pharmaceutical reps, brought lunch in today.

"Good night, Doc." Liz, the medical assistant who worked late that night, waved as she left.

"Thanks for all the help with Kory. He's not crazy about immunizations."

"What kid is?" With a jangle of her car keys, the girl exited the building.

Kendall walked down the long hallway, stopping to turn off the light in one of the exam rooms. Evie hadn't shut down the office sound system yet, and Kendall hummed along with the instrumental piano music. Everyone in the office got a turn selecting the music. The only thing Kendall vetoed was heavy metal or lurid lyrics. This was a family practice and she didn't want irate parents complaining to her about the type of music they listened to in the waiting room.

Evie found her in the break room a few minutes later. Kendall had kicked off her brown leather clogs and sat at the round wooden table surrounded by four chairs. She'd scavenged a Sierra Turkey sandwich from the fridge and a can of North Carolina iced tea. The clock on the wall indicated it was five forty-five. The meal certainly counted as a late, late lunch.

"What did you need, Kendall?" Now that it was just the two of them, Evie relaxed and dropped the "Dr." title.

"I wanted to know where you put the box that came in for Dr. Parker."

"Oh, that. I can get it for you. Are you seeing him again to-night?"

"Very sly." Kendall tore off a piece of the sandwich and popped it in her mouth, savoring the tang of the chipotle mayo and red onions. "No and yes."

"What kind of answer is that?" Her receptionist stretched her arms over her head and yawned.

"Dr. Parker is seeing a couple of patients here after hours— some friends of his who are just back from the mission field and need a basic checkup. I think it's for health insurance." Kendall bit into the sandwich, realizing how hungry she was. She swallowed before continuing. "After that, he's going to come upstairs for some dessert."

"Uh-oh."

Kendall wadded up her napkin and tossed it at Evie. "Oh, don't be like that. I'm thirty-six years old, for goodness' sakes. I can take care of myself. We'll have some cake and then take Sully for a walk. My reputation is safe with Heath Parker."

"If you say so." Evie walked over to the compact kitchen area and surveyed the dirty dishes and silverware piled in the sink.

"You sound like my mother when I was sixteen." Actually, Evie sounded more like her mother talking to Bekah. Kendall's nonexistent love life in high school negated any reason for her mother to lecture her about the dos and don'ts of dating. Kendall retrieved another napkin from the basket on the table. "Believe me, Sully's so protective that if the man tried anything, the dog would be all over him."

She watched as Evie rinsed the collection of coffee mugs, plates, spoons, and forks in the sink and loaded the dishwasher, turning it on so everything would be clean in the morning.

"Don't worry about that, Evie. Logan and Javan are waiting for you. Get on home."

"It's no problem. My husband manages everything just fine without me. I'll finish this and then go get the package." Evie wiped down the small expanse of countertop. Straightened the coffeemaker. The wire basket of sugar and sweetener packets.

"Put the package on the counter of the MAs' desk so Dr. Parker will see it when he gets here." She watched Evie begin to rearrange the items in the fridge, opening Styrofoam containers and tossing food that didn't meet her still-good-enough-to-eat standard. "So, how are things going? Your adoption is almost final, isn't it?"

"We can sign the final papers in three months." Evie dumped a several-days-old salad into the trash.

"No problems with the birth father?"

"No. The lawyers posted the proper announcements in different papers and we've never heard anything." Evie organized the sodas in the fridge so that they lined up by flavor. "So the lawyer's not worried that he'll contest the adoption. We're fine there."

"And the mother relinquished her parental rights?"

"After her last DUI and her conviction."

"But?"

"But what?"

"Is there some other problem with the adoption?" Kendall watched Evie, who stayed facing away from her the entire time they talked. Her voice never changed from a monotone, almost as if the information had nothing to do with her. After a long pause, Evie shut the refrigerator door, turning to answer her question.

"I told Logan that I'm not sure I want to go through with adopting Javan."

Kendall couldn't have heard correctly. Her receptionist talked about adopting for years. She posted photos of Javan all over her desk.

"Why?"

"It's not working . . ." Evie covered her face with her hands so her words were stifled. "I'm not . . . the right mom for him. He's just so angry with me all the time."

Kendall crossed the room and wrapped her arms around her receptionist. "What are you saying? Of course you're the right mom for Javan. He's been with you almost two years. You love him like he's your own son."

Evie's shoulders shook. Once. Twice. Then she sniffed. Rubbed her hands across her face. "I'm learning loving somebody isn't enough sometimes, Kendall. Every time I think I make headway with Javan, something happens—or nothing happens—and he rejects me again."

Kendall's words of reassurance remained unspoken. Was loving someone, despite his rejection, enough to make a relationship work? When it came to her failed romances, no. And how she felt about Griffin Walker—whatever it was she felt for the man—couldn't get past the barrier the man erected between them. Sure, he'd kissed her, but only after telling her that he had no intention of kissing her again. Figuring things out had to be different when it came to a mother loving a child.

"Javan loves Logan. He's fine when I'm here at work and it's just the two of them. But the minute I come home, Javan's awful. He hates me." Evie shook her head, whipping her long ponytail back and forth. "I never thought he'd hate me."

"But surely things will get better . . . Maybe if you see a family counselor?"

Oh, how Kendall wanted to mention how her faith comforted her when life broke her heart. But after working with

Evie for five years, she knew that talking about God meant being ready with an answer. And Evie wasn't asking any questions. Yet.

"Things are going from bad to worse—" Evie leaned into Kendall's embrace, her rigid stance relaxing, her whisper scraping across Kendall's heart. "I remember when I was a little girl, how I wanted ballet lessons for my tenth birthday. I sat by my bedroom window every night for weeks, wishing upon stars. I'd pick one star, then another, then another. 'Wish I may, wish I might,' you know? One night, I saw this yellow light streak across the sky. I thought it was a sign . . . a yes."

"What happened?"

"No dance lessons." A bite of regret tainted Evie's laugh. "It was a silly idea. With five kids and my papá's job barely keeping food on the table, my parents couldn't afford dance lessons for me. When I told my mamá what I'd seen, she explained it was a falling star. I stopped making wishes after that. It was foolish of me to think I could ever be a ballet dancer. And then all those years . . . trying to have a baby . . . and failing. When Javan came along, I started hoping again. But being a mamá is not in the stars for me either. I've tried to force it."

Musical notes from Evie's cell phone interrupted her. She pulled it from her scrub pant pocket, taking a step away from Kendall.

"Yes? Yes, I'm done at work. I'm just running a bit late. There's no need to be so short with me, Logan. I work outside the home, remember? Do you need me to pick up anything? Fine. I'm leaving now."

Facing Kendall again, she tucked the phone away, shrugging. A smile wobbled on her lips. "Logan, wondering where I was. I-I'll go grab the package."

"If you ever want to talk about things . . . about Javan—"

"It'll be fine, Kendall. We'll figure it out. Adoption might not be the right thing for us."

★ ★ ★ ★ ★

Kendall checked the cinnamon streusel Bundt cake in the oven. A blast of hot air wafted from the oven across her face as she bent to test the cake with a toothpick. Almost done, but not quite. And so far she hadn't burned it. She fared better in a chemistry lab than in a kitchen, but Rachel's recipe was fool-proof—or so she'd said. Kendall thought something homemade would be nicer than a pre-packaged dessert. And she might as well admit that, yes, she wanted to impress Heath.

Evie's words still lingered in Kendall's mind. Her receptionist was more than an employee, she was a friend. Not a let's-go-have-some-Guac-Live kind of friend, but they still talked about personal things. Sometimes. Then there were the days the office was so busy they barely had time to say hello to each other. But one thing Kendall knew for certain: Evie ached to be a mom. For the past year, she kept everyone in the office regularly up-dated about Javan's adoption. The situation couldn't be so bad that she'd back out now.

Sully circled her legs, whining and nudging her toward the door.

"Sorry, Sully. We're not going for a walk now."

She noted the time on the oven clock. Just after eight. Hmm. Heath should be done by now. He said he had two quick physi-cals to do for his friends and then he looked forward to spend-ing time with her. Warmth tingled across her neck and face when she remembered the kiss that accompanied his words. The man certainly knew how to say hello—and to let her know he'd missed seeing her.

But, as she told Evie, she was old enough to take care of herself. She could resist temptation in the form of Heath Parker. Not that she had a whole lot of experience resisting temptation. The last few years had been more about work than romance. And growing up? She didn't even need to try to maintain her reputation—much less her purity. After the embarrassment at her homecoming dance, no guy wanted to ask her out.

She wandered back to her bedroom, all the way to the farthest corner of her walk-in closet. Hidden behind the few fancier dresses she owned—bought out of necessity for residency celebrations that she attended solo—was her first-ever little black dress. Truth was, she could probably still fit into it. Some women would be proud to say they wore the same size they had in high school. But really, what woman wanted to be in her thirties and still shopping in the juniors' department?

Kendall pulled the covering off the dress, the thin film of plastic clinging to her hands, creating static in the dry air. She held the dress up against her body, turning to the right and to the left. After all these years, the tiny sparkles woven in the black material still glinted when she held it up to the light. Wearing this dress, with its thin spaghetti straps and feminine sweep of fabric just to her knees, had made her sixteen-year-old self feel so grown up, especially when she'd slipped on the pair of black three-inch heels.

"You look stunning, Ken." Her father stood behind her as she faced the mirror over her dresser, his hands on her shoulders. He leaned in and placed a kiss on her cheek.

Kendall closed her eyes, inhaling the scent of grease and oil and sweat from the auto repair shop that always clung to her father's clothes. "Thanks, Daddy."

"So, who's this boy that's picking you up? He didn't even come over and ask permission to take you to the dance."

Kendall positioned a silver bobby pin with a tiny floral rhinestone in her hair, hoping it would make her look more feminine, despite how short her cut was. "He's not my boyfriend. We're just going to homecoming. His name's Phillip and he's a junior, like me. You'll meet him when he comes to pick me up."

She stepped back, wishing she had a full-length mirror so she could see the overall effect of her hair, her dress, her shoes. Maybe when Phillip saw her tonight he would have the same look of approval in his eyes that her dad did. Maybe they would go from "just friends" to something more. He asked her to homecoming—that had to mean something.

Kendall discovered exactly what Phillip's invitation meant when he arrived at her house. They were double-dating with his best friend, Brian, and his girlfriend, Heather. From the minute she got into the car until she insisted Phillip bring her home early from the dance, she watched Heather flirt with both Brian—and Phillip. For a teenager, the girl certainly knew how to play one guy against the other.

At the high school gym, decorated in the school colors of white and green, Phillip danced with her one time, all the while watching Heather dance with Brian. Then he deserted her to go try to separate his best friend from his date.

Kendall retreated to the girls' bathroom—and that's where Heather found her. Heather wore her hair in long, loose curls over her shoulders. She opted for an icy blue dress that matched her eyes and shimmered against her long torso and legs. It was easy to forget Heather was the sophomore and Kendall was the junior.

"Having fun?" Heather leaned into the mirror, checking her makeup.

"Sure." Kendall could only hope the other girl couldn't tell she'd been crying.

"Well, you can thank me for arranging it for you."

"What do you mean? Phillip asked me to the dance." Although Kendall couldn't figure out why now.

"He asked you to the dance because I told him to."

"That's a mean thing to say." Kendall moved toward the exit, but Heather blocked the way.

"It's the truth. He likes me, but I'm dating his best friend—at least for now. So I told him if he came to homecoming with someone else we could still have a chance to dance together." The girl's arctic-blue eyes dismissed Kendall. "But just about everyone else was already asked to the dance, so he decided to ask you."

"You're lying." Kendall shoved past her, yanking the bathroom door open.

"Who is he dancing with? You or me?" Heather's taunt followed her out into the gymnasium.

The faint scent of cinnamon pulled Kendall from the memory. She had watched Phillip that night. He jockeyed for position with his best friend, dancing every dance he could with Brian's date. Kendall stood in the corner, wishing she were truly invisible instead of just feeling that way. She finally demanded that Brian take her home. When her father asked her why she was home before eleven, she told him she had a migraine. It was the only time she ever lied to him.

Kendall slipped the dress back behind the other dresses, hiding it from view. Why did she even keep it?

Exiting the closet, Kendall noticed the aroma of cinnamon grew stronger, tinged with the smell of something burning. Her cake!

An acrid billow of smoke rolled out of the oven when she opened it. Why oh why had she gotten lost back in high school? Turning off the oven, she slammed the door shut. Best to leave the ruined cake in there. Heath would have to settle for coffee.

Where was he? He should be finished with two physicals by now.

Was he having problems shutting down the computer system? Kendall slipped on a pair of teal ballet flats, deciding to go downstairs. Wait. He wasn't planning on accessing medical records. He said that he would do a simple history and physical, using paper documents. Although he expressed admiration for Kendall's electronic medical records system when he found her working on patient notes. Despite Kendall's assuring him the system was easy to work—even showing him the first few steps—Heath insisted plain old paper and pen were fine for him.

The lights in the office were dimmed, the area quiet. As she walked down the hallway toward one of the back exam rooms, she heard Heath's voice.

"Kupu has proven to be extremely helpful in building up immunity. I was very pleased by my preliminary tests and have no reservations about recommending that you use the minimum daily dosage." He stepped out of the room as he spoke with a middle-aged man and woman. Must be his friends who were just back from the mission field.

Seeing her, Heath stopped short, before his welcoming wide grin spread across his face. "Dr. Haynes. I didn't know you'd come back into your office."

Dr. Haynes? Well, he was seeing patients, after all. It was probably best to maintain a professional demeanor.

"Dr. Parker. I just wanted to make certain you had everything you needed." She held out her hand to the two other people waiting beside Heath. "Hello, I'm Dr. Kendall Haynes."

"And these are the Bensons. I kept them much too long tonight." He moved the couple toward the front of the office.

"Oh." Kendall stepped aside. "Sure. Well, the door will automatically lock behind them."

"Right. I remember you saying that." Heath tossed a grin over his shoulder. "Be right back. I'll walk them out."

Kendall watched Heath escort his friends to the front door. Well, that was a bit . . . abrupt. But then, it was later than she'd expected. And really, there was no reason for Kendall to be introduced to the Bensons. It wasn't like she'd meet them again.

After ensuring that the door was locked, Heath came back and enveloped her in a warm hug.

"I'm sorry I kept you waiting." He groaned. "You know how some people talk and talk and talk."

Kendall leaned back to look at Heath. "So you knew the Bensons on the mission field?"

"Yes. I knew them when I was over in Africa." Heath pulled her close, nuzzling her neck. "You smell delicious."

"Oh, that. Well . . ." Kendall bit her bottom lip. Time to confess. "I was hoping to invite you to share some coffee and cinnamon streusel Bundt cake after we took Sully for a walk."

"But?" He linked his fingers through hers as they walked up the stairs to her loft.

"I got sidetracked and the cake got, um, singed. Sorry. I can still offer you coffee."

"Coffee it is then." He paused outside her door. "I'm sorry things ran so long. I hate to keep a beautiful woman waiting. Wow. That sounds so clichéd."

"I don't mind a cliché every now and then."

He traced the outline of her face. "Believe me, Kendall, you are anything but typical. I am so glad I found you."

★ ★ ★ ★ ★

Memories of last evening lingered in Kendall's mind as she walked into the office the next morning. Being with Heath helped her shove memories of Griffin—and his impetuous kiss—out of her mind. And why not? With his charismatic personality and low-key sense of humor, Heath helped her relax while at the same time making her feel special. It wasn't until she'd kissed him good night and settled into bed that Griffin Walker invaded her thoughts. Then the lurking memory of his kiss refused to be ignored.

Why was she letting Griffin—a man who seemed to regret kissing her before it happened—distract her from Heath, the man who wasn't afraid to admit he cared about her? Kendall wasn't going to let Griffin's kiss disrupt her life—well, more than a few nights' sleep. Thoughts of Griffin Walker had derailed her long enough. She was tired of being the girl—the woman—no one wanted. And Heath's actions showed that, at least to him, she *wasn't* that woman. But why wasn't Heath the one invading her dreams at night? She needed to focus on everything right in her life. Her practice. Her patients. And all the possibilities with Heath.

Griffin was her friend. Nothing more. Because that was all he wanted—friendship. The kiss had been . . . what? Some sort of glitch on his emotional radar? Kendall should thank Ian for interrupting them. And Griffin said he was only going to kiss her one time, so she didn't have to wonder if he'd ever kiss her again. All she had to do was stop thinking about Griffin.

Just. Stop.

She'd keep telling herself that until it happened.

Kendall stood in the doorway leading into the Rocky Mountain Family Practice. Evie and Renee were already at their desks. Kendall couldn't help but notice that Evie looked as if she'd spent the entire night sitting up watching movies. Her wavy black hair was pulled back in a careless bun at the nape of her neck, and she'd forgone her normal makeup routine. That wasn't like her receptionist.

"Do you need anything?" Kendall placed a hand on Evie's shoulder.

"Hmmm? I'm fine. Long night." Evie focused on powering up her computer.

"Everyone at home doing well?"

"Now that I'm here, yes."

"Evie, about Javan—"

"I can't talk about it now, Dr. Kendall. Please." A sheen of tears caused Evie's eyes to glitter.

Kendall squeezed the woman's shoulder. "I'm sorry." How could she salvage this conversation? Put it back on more normal footing? "Would you check something out for me when you get a chance?"

"Sure. What do you need?" Evie pulled a notepad forward and picked up one of the bright-colored Sharpie pens she preferred to use.

"Dr. Parker was talking to the missionary couple he met with last night. He mentioned a supplement to them . . ." Kendall tried to remember the name. "I'm not sure what he called it. I think it was something with a *k*."

Kendall didn't miss how Evie stopped writing for a moment, seeming to almost want to ask her a question. "Have you heard of this supplement before, Evie?"

"Not directly, no."

"But?"

"Well, a couple of weeks ago, Dr. Parker came by to pick up the first two boxes he had shipped here. I found him talking to Peter Harrington's parents. He was saying how this supplement he knew of was supposedly so beneficial for kids with allergies and asthma."

"This same supplement?"

"I can't say for sure. I couldn't hear the name—it sounded like *cup of* or something like that."

"Odd." Not that anything was wrong . . . just odd that Heath would suggest a supplement to some of her patients without mentioning it to her first. "Anything else?"

"It's probably nothing—"

Kendall stepped closer, lowering her voice. "What, Evie?"

"You know how Dr. Parker stopped by earlier this week, looking for the third package? Paul told me that when he stepped out of an exam room, Dr. Parker went into the exam room." Evie fiddled with the pen in her hand. "He didn't realize it until he went back in to finish up his notes on the patient he'd just seen. Dr. Parker was sitting at the desk."

Kendall's mind scrambled to understand what Evie was telling her. "What did Heath . . . I mean, Dr. Parker say?"

"He was on his cell phone. He told Paul that he'd ducked into the room because it was empty and he'd gotten an unexpected overseas call."

"Well, that makes sense."

Didn't it?

"Dr. Parker apologized and left the room right away."

"And that's it?" Kendall ran her fingers through her hair, tousling the ends.

"As far as I know."

"I'm sure it's nothing. But do me a favor and call the Harringtons and get whatever information you can for me—starting with the name of the supplement. And then do some investigating on your own."

Evie reached for the phone on her desk. "Sure thing. I'll let you know what I find out."

CHAPTER SIXTEEN

★ ★ ★ ★

"That should just about do it, Ian."

Kendall stepped back, hands on her hips, checking the fender of her CJ5. Ian stood beside her, surveying his work. It was warm for the second week in May—a perfect day to be outside and smoothing out the dent on the Jeep. Sully lounged in the grassy area near the back door of the building, chewing on a bone.

"Did I do a good job, Dr. Kendall?" Anxiety threaded through Ian's voice.

They'd spent the morning removing the damaged front fender of her CJ5. Then she instructed Ian how to pound out the dent. The last step? Some touch-up paint. Her dad always told her to take pride in her work.

"Yep. It doesn't have to be cherry—that's car lingo for 'perfect.' But it looks great. As soon as I can manage a free weekend, I'm heading up into the mountains with this thing." Kendall told Ian to pick up the rubber mallet and the block of wood they'd used to bang out the dent while she grabbed her dad's dent puller.

"Do you off-road?"

"I did some—for a while. But it's a pricey hobby. You're always breaking something on a boulder. And, while I don't mind doing my own repairs on my Jeep, I don't like doing them on the side of a mountain."

"You're kidding, right?"

"Nope." She held open the door into the building, nodding for Ian to go ahead. "Come on, I'm ready for a break. It's hot for May. What happened to the typical 'Springtime in the Rockies' weather?"

"If it was snowing, we would have to do the repair in our garage." Ian waited while she unlocked the closet where she stored her tools.

"True." And the last thing she needed was to be hanging around Ian's house—and his older brother. Griffin had dropped Ian off earlier and left with a quick wave and barely a glance in her direction. "What time did Griffin say he'd be back?"

Ian checked his cell phone. "About now."

"Let's go wash up then. Do you want something to drink?"

"Got a Mountain Dew?"

"Funny thing—I just happen to have a six-pack."

As Ian sat beside Sully and chugged down the soda, Kendall placed a bowl of pretzels in front of him. "These are for Ian—not you, Sully." She shoved the dog's face away from the food. "So, what's the latest on you staying in Colorado?"

"I'm not." Ian stared out the floor-to-ceiling windows showcasing the Front Range. Even with it being the second week in May—and warm—snow still covered the Peak with a scattered pattern of white.

"Griffin didn't change his mind?" Kendall sat beside him, drawing her legs up underneath her.

"Wouldn't matter if he did. I want to go to the Jamisons'."

"Really?"

"Yep. It's no big deal." Ian grabbed a handful of pretzels. "I'm used to moving around. I did that a lot before I came to live with Mom and Dad."

"How old were you when that happened?"

"Four—that's when I first came to them as a foster kid. They adopted me a couple of years later."

"Were you in the foster care system before the Walkers adopted you?"

Ian drained the bottle of soda before answering. "On and off. Sometimes I was with my mom. Most of the time, I wasn't. You get used to it."

"I bet you loved becoming part of the Walkers' family."

"Not at first."

"What do you mean? Weren't you glad to have a mom and dad?" Kendall watched the younger Walker brother, trying to imagine what his life had been like.

"I didn't trust anybody by that time. My mom? She'd be there—and then she was gone. I don't know who my dad is, but I had a lot of 'uncles.'" Ian used his fingers to make quote marks in the air. "I didn't believe the Walkers—Mom and Dad— would keep me. The first year I stayed with them, I slept in my clothes and kept my suitcase packed."

"Oh, Ian . . ."

"Yeah, I made them miserable—especially Mom." He sniffed, wiping at his nose with the back of his hand. "But she told me she could love me longer than I could hate her. And she was right."

Kendall touched Ian's shoulder. "I had no idea. You must miss them both so much . . ."

"Yeah. But I thought . . . well, Griffin was there and I thought . . . but it was stupid."

Why couldn't Griffin see how much his brother needed him? How much Ian wanted a relationship with him? At sixteen, Ian belonged in a family just as much as someone like Javan did.

Javan.

Why hadn't she thought of him and Ian before?

She leaned toward Ian. "Would you do something for me?"

"Sure thing, Dr. Kendall. You want me to walk Sully?" Ian started to get up from the couch, all ready to take the dog outside.

"No, not that. Although you can take him for a run in a minute if you want to." Kendall paused, debating on how to present the still-new idea. "I have a friend who is adopting a little boy. His name is Javan and he's angry—acting out a lot. Kind of like you said you did with your mom. My friend is thinking about stopping the adoption. Would you be willing to talk to her, tell her your story?"

"Sure . . . if you think it would help."

"I do. I absolutely do, Ian."

Now all she had to do was figure out a way to get Ian and Evie together.

★ ★ ★ ★ ★

So much for a fast getaway.

Griffin managed to avoid talking to Kendall earlier this morning when he dropped Ian off to work on her Jeep. But there was no sign of either of them when he drove around the back of her building a few minutes ago. Just the newly repaired Jeep, displaying Kendall's and his brother's workmanship. He could call Ian on his cell and have him come downstairs, but that was rude. He wanted to keep his distance from Kendall Haynes—without being a complete jerk.

Then again, kissing her in the hallway the other night—what was that? Beyond stupid. The memory of her tenderness, the comfort he found in her arms, intertwined with the passion that ignited between them the second their lips touched—all of that lingered with him. He wasn't embarrassed when Ian discovered them; he was relieved. Without Ian's appearance he would have kept right on kissing Kendall Haynes until one of them said stop.

With a groan, Griffin hauled himself out of the Jeep. Surely he had the guts to go knock on Kendall's door and get his brother. Say hello. Good-bye. Leave. And restrict seeing the woman to when Ian had a doctor's appointment.

Climbing the stairs to the loft, he gave two swift raps on the door.

"The door's unlocked, Ian—"

Griffin watched Kendall stiffen when she saw him standing outside her loft.

"I'm here to get Ian."

"He's not here. He took Sully for a run." She tucked her hands in the back pockets of her jeans that were torn at the knees. "Do you want to come in and wait for him?"

Did he want to come in? No.

"Sure." He jammed his hands into the pockets of his jean jacket, striding past her. "The Jeep looks good."

"Yep. Ian's a quick learner. How's his Cherokee?"

Griffin watched her perch on the arm of her couch, her bare feet swinging a few inches from the floor. "I told him that we didn't work on his Jeep until yours was fixed. Seemed only fair."

"He said you're still sending him back to Florida."

The woman shot straight.

"Yes. As soon as school gets out."

"Griffin, I was just talking to your brother. If you heard how badly he wants a family—how much he wants to get to know you—"

"Kendall. Stop." Why couldn't she let this go? "There are too many years between me and my brother. And he needs to be with a real family."

"You are his real family now, Griffin."

"A single guy does not constitute a family. And that's all I'm ever going to be."

"Why? Because your sins are so much worse than everyone else's? Because you think God operates on some sort of one-strike-and-you're-out system? Why don't you ask God how wide and deep his grace is, Griffin? Why don't you see what he has waiting for you, rather than deciding that yourself?"

"Enough, Kendall. We've talked about this—"

Kendall gripped the arm of the couch. "I'm sorry your first marriage ended in divorce, but that doesn't mean you have to stay single forever. You've made it clear that, despite kissing me the other night, you're not interested in me—" She was veering into no-man's-land again. "—but surely you'll find someone—"

"Kendall, believe me, if you knew everything about me, you wouldn't want to be involved with me."

His words brought her off the couch.

"Really? You're pulling the melodramatic if-you-knew-all-about-me line?" She stood with one hand on her hip, the other pointed straight at him. "We're adults, Griffin, not teenagers in some movie about puppy love."

"Being older means we've had longer to make mistakes."

"Enough already. I had no idea you could be such a drama king, Griffin. The reality is you like your life the way it is."

"You're wrong." Griffin closed the remaining space that

separated them until he was mere inches from her. "I can't have kids, Kendall."

There. He said it.

"You can't . . ."

". . . have kids." Griffin forced himself to continue looking into Kendall's slate-gray eyes as he finished the sentence for her. He said it once, so why was it so hard to say it again?

"Is there a medical problem . . . maybe there's something you could—"

Why wasn't he surprised when she switched on her doctor-brain and began asking questions, trying to fix his problem?

"I had a vasectomy fourteen years ago. That's a pretty final no to the whole can-you-have-kids question."

He watched her eyes widen, knowing this confession hit her harder than his hallway confession about crashing a plane a few nights ago. This was personal . . . intimate . . . a choice that weighed down his past, present, and future.

"My ex-wife insisted she didn't want kids. Ever." A snort of laughter blew past his lips. "Ironic, isn't it? With three kids, the woman looks like a finalist for the Mother of the Year award. Twins, even. Our marriage struggled almost from the minute we walked out of the Academy chapel. When she said, 'No kids,' I agreed with her. What did I know? I was twenty-four. I barely knew myself. I certainly didn't know my wife. We lived apart more than we lived together. I thought if I agreed to have a vasectomy, it would help save our marriage. At least I could stop one of the arguments."

Griffin closed his eyes, blocking out the barrage of questions in Kendall's eyes. "Tracey left six months later. The divorce was final within a year. And there was one advantage to my decision. I didn't have to worry about my choices once I was single, ya know?"

When he looked at Kendall again, she watched him, her hand at her throat as if his words stole her breath away. She worried her bottom lip with her teeth. If only he could stop talking and find comfort in Kendall's arms—the kind of comfort that would ease the ache of his confession.

"Griffin, you know vasectomies can be reversed—"

"It's done, Kendall. Don't you get it? I made a choice, I live with the choice. And since I've become a believer, I'm learning to live with the consequences of my choices."

"What? Like some sort of penance?"

"Some of us are meant to be single. I may be new in my faith, but even I've learned that." He raked his fingers through his hair. "Look, I want you to understand why I can't . . . can't do whatever this is between us. I know you're all about marriage and family. You're a *family* physician. Your subspecialty means you almost trip over kids when you walk into your practice."

"There is nothing between us, Griffin. You won't let there be—"

The shrill ping of Kendall's iPhone cut off her words. Griffin stood silent as she retrieved her cell from her satchel.

"Dr. Haynes."

Kendall listened to whoever was on the other end of the phone, tilting her head to the side as if struggling to understand. "Yes, he's my patient. Why is he in the ER?"

It was easy to see their conversation—his foolhardy admission—was over. He would wait for Ian in his car. Tell him to take Sully upstairs and then get back home. As he reached the door, Kendall called out to him.

"Griffin, wait. I have to leave. One of my kids is in the ER. Can you stay here until Ian and Sully get back? Just lock the door." She slipped into a pair of worn-out tennis shoes and slung her purse over her shoulder. "Sully will be fine."

"No problem."

"Thanks. I've gotta go." She hesitated for a second, as if debating whether to say something. "Thanks."

★ ★ ★ ★ ★

As she backed the Jeep out of its parking space, Kendall waited to be connected with the ER physician again.

"Dr. Alvarado."

"This is Dr. Haynes. I'm trying to get some information about my patient, Nicholas Wells. I was told he's in the ER and that you're taking care of him."

"Yes, his mom brought him about an hour ago now because Nicholas was becoming lethargic, light-headed, and said he was seeing spots. She said he hadn't been eating much the last few days and then today he started throwing up."

Kendall took the fastest route to Memorial Hospital, trying to concentrate on the conversation as well as the traffic. "I've seen a viral intestinal illness going around."

"At first we thought he might have that, or maybe a migraine. But his pulse is about thirty-five and he is in intermittent third-degree heart block."

"What?" Kendall gripped the steering wheel, forcing herself to stay focused on the traffic even as she tried to comprehend the doctor's information.

Dr. Alvarado continued presenting the case. "When we asked his mother about Nicholas's history, she told us about his allergies and asthma, but denied any history of cardiac disorders. In addition to his regular inhalers and antihistamine, she mentioned they had continued to give him the new supplement she'd gotten from your office."

"I never gave him a new supplement. Do you know the name of it?"

"The mom brought the container in with her. It's labeled Kupu."

Kendall's hand shook as she shifted gears. Was this Heath's elusive "supplement"—the one Evie was researching? Why was Nicholas taking it?

"Dr. Haynes?"

"I'm here." She slammed the brakes as the light in front of her turned red.

"Can you tell us anything about this?"

"I-I can't. I didn't prescribe it. But I can get in contact with someone who knows about it."

"Because this is an unknown substance, we're sending this off for toxicology testing."

"I'll be there in ten minutes. I can probably get information about it long before the tox report is back. Please tell the family I'm on my way."

"Will do."

Kendall turned left at the next intersection and then audio-dialed Heath Parker. Even as she mentally rehearsed her questions, his voice mail came on, directing her to leave a message.

"Heath, this is Kendall. Call me as soon as you get this message. I'm on my way to Memorial. One of my patients is there. He's having a reaction to some supplement you recommended to his parents." A million questions swirled through her brain. "What is going on? Call me."

Her thoughts focused on Nicholas. Eleven-year-old boy. Vomiting. Slow heart rate. Seeing spots. And some kind of supplement?

Wait a minute.

She voice-dialed the Memorial ER.

"This is Dr. Haynes. I need to speak to Dr. Alvarado again."

"He can't come to the phone. Your patient's heart rate has slowed even more and Dr. Alvarado's having to sedate him to start an external pacemaker on him."

The nurse's announcement left Kendall speechless. She needed to get to the ER. Now. "Tell Dr. Alvarado to order a digitalis and potassium level, if he hasn't already. I'll be there in five."

CHAPTER SEVENTEEN

★ ★ ★ ★

Kendall shifted in the padded metal chair positioned near the circular wood table. Normally when she entered one of the small rooms just off the hospital ER, she was in a position of authority—the one providing answers to a family's questions. Now she waited for a police officer to come in and ask her questions. She had plenty of time to stare at the walls, a neutral tone of yellow. Nothing too bright. The framed pastoral prints were selected . . . why? To create a sense of calm for the families who entered this room, sat at this table, and stared all sorts of this-can't-be-happening news in the face?

At least Nicholas was stable. He was still sedated, but the external pacemaker had raised his heart rate to a near-normal level and his blood pressure had improved. Despite Kendall's insisting she didn't know anything about Kupu, Dr. Alvarado seemed ready to lay all the blame for the child's problems on Kendall's shoulders. She was thankful Jim and Jean Wells trusted her.

Thank God they had a long-standing relationship that would get them through this. They knew she loved Nicholas and cared about his health.

She scanned her iPhone again. Still no return call from Heath. No text message. This, despite the fact that she'd texted and called him dozens of times in the past hour and a half. He'd call any minute now. He had to. Heath Parker was the only one with any answers.

Kendall jerked at the sound of the door opening. It didn't help that she was about to talk with a police officer looking like anything but a professional. She still wore the torn and stained jeans and an oversized COLORADO AVALANCHE T-shirt, with the collar torn out. Her go-to summer ensemble whenever she worked on her CJ5.

No matter what she looked like, she was a competent physician. She hadn't given Nicholas this "Kupu"-whatever-it-was. And she hadn't known what Heath was doing. How many of Kendall's patients had the man talked to? Evie mentioned only the Harringtons. Now the Wellses. She watched the policewoman enter the room, nod in her direction. This wasn't an interrogation. The police were merely gathering facts.

"You're Dr. Kendall Haynes, correct?" The officer sat across from Kendall, opening a small notepad. Her dark hair was pulled back from her face into a tight ponytail, her gray uniform shirt starched stiff. There was no hint of warmth in the woman's dark eyes.

Not that Kendall expected a pleasant so-nice-to-meet-you chat.

"Yes, I'm Nicholas Wells's family physician. I apologize for my clothes. I was working on—"

"How long have you been his physician?"

Okay, then. Let's get right to it.

"Since they moved to the Springs. I think that was about five years ago. I'd have to see his records to verify that."

"No need for that now. And Dr. Heath Parker—he's been with your practice for how long?"

"Dr. Parker isn't with my practice."

The police officer tapped the notepad with her pen. "Then why is he giving medication to your patients?"

"I have no idea." Kendall forced herself to unclench her fists. These were simple questions with simple answers. "But I am very interested in finding out the answer to that question."

"So you're saying you didn't know Dr. Parker recommended this supplement to your patient?"

"Absolutely not."

"You didn't know he'd given your patient a course of the supplement?"

"No." Kendall's cell phone buzzed. "May I check this, please? It may be Dr. Parker. I've been trying to reach him—"

The officer nodded, sitting back and waiting. But a quick glance at her phone proved it was only her sister Bekah calling. Well, Bekah would just have to wait.

"I-I'm sorry. That was a personal call. Nothing important. What's next?"

"Dr. Haynes, can you tell us anything about—" The officer glanced at her notepad. "—Kupu?"

"I wish I could. I've only heard Dr. Parker refer to some kind of herbal treatment he came across in Africa."

"When was this?"

Kendall paused. Her answer would sound like she was somehow involved with Heath and his future plans. But she wasn't. And she couldn't hide things.

"Dr. Parker invited me to attend a dinner meeting with his board one evening several weeks ago."

"I see. So you're part of his board, but you don't know anything about this drug?"

"No. I'm not on the board. My relationship with Dr. Parker is purely personal. We're dating . . ." There was nothing wrong with admitting she was dating Heath, was there?

"And you've dated for how long?"

"A month or so."

"I see."

Kendall would love to ask the officer just what she "saw." Then again, did she really want to know?

"Can you explain to me why Dr. Parker told Mr. and Mrs. Wells they could reach him either on his cell or at your office if they had any questions?"

Kendall stood. This conversation was starting to sound like a cross-examination. "Officer, I am not on the witness stand. I've done nothing wrong." She forced herself to take a deep breath, to try to sound less defensive. No need to arouse suspicion by getting up in the officer's grill. "I've told you everything I know. And honestly, right now I'm here as a physician who is trying to take care of her patient. I assure you, I'm more interested in finding out the answers to all these questions than you are. If you'll excuse me, I need to go check on Nicholas."

The officer also stood, blocking the exit. "Just one more thing, Dr. Kendall."

"Yes?"

"If you do talk with Dr. Parker, advise him to contact me as soon as possible. I have some questions for him to answer, too."

Kendall escaped into the controlled chaos of the ER. She straightened the badge positioned on the nonexistent collar of her shirt and walked to the nurses' station. She should have taken the time to change into scrubs. "How is Nicholas doing?"

The nurse pulled his chart, glancing at it for a quick update.

"He's resting. He's still sedated. We're in the process of admitting him to the pediatric ICU."

"Okay, thanks." The odor from the wilted flowers sitting in the glass vase on the desktop caused Kendall to take a step back. "Are his parents with him?"

"I believe so. Although his mother mentioned going to get some items so that she could stay overnight with him."

"Thanks again. I'm going to check in on him before I leave."

Kendall walked toward the curtained-off area that provided the Wells family some privacy. The ER was busy on a Saturday, with techs and nurses and physicians moving back and forth between bays. Telephones rang nonstop. From behind one curtain, a small child wailed.

"Knock knock." Kendall slid back the curtain just a few inches. "May I come in?"

She waited for Nicholas's parents to wave her in before stepping over beside the gurney where their son lay sleeping. With his heart rate up, his color had improved. Beneath the blanket, his chest muscles twitched in response to the external pacemaker. Kendall touched his forehead, watching the monitors beside his bed to get a reading on his heart rate and blood pressure.

"Well, he's looking better." She couldn't hold back the audible sigh of relief. "I think we'll see marked improvement from here on out."

"The ER doctor says Nicholas is going to the ICU." Even as she spoke to Kendall, Mrs. Wells never took her eyes off her son.

"He needs to be there until he's stable enough to be off all this technology." Kendall reached over and squeezed the woman's hand. "I know this was so frightening for both of you. I'm sorry this happened."

"Dr. Parker told us the Kupu would help build up Nicholas's immune system—" Mr. Wells gripped the metal rail that ran alongside Nicholas's bed.

"When did Dr. Parker talk with you about the, um, supplement?"

"A few weeks ago, wasn't it?" Mrs. Wells looked at her husband for confirmation. "He called us. He seemed so concerned about helping Nicholas get healthier."

"He called you?"

"Yes. We assumed you gave him our phone number." Mrs. Wells twisted her hands together in her lap. "He identified himself as a colleague of yours. Told us how you both cared about building up patients' immune systems—"

Mr. Wells stared at his son. "And now he's in the hospital . . . When I get the chance to talk to that guy . . ."

Only after she had a chance to talk with him first. And found out how he gained access to her patients' phone numbers.

"What did Dr. Parker say to you about the supplement?"

"I don't recall, exactly. He said it was new . . . that he'd be willing to let us try the first round free of charge." Mrs. Wells shook her head, as if trying to make sense of what happened. "I thought that was nice. He overnighted us the first bottle."

"Do you have the bottle with you? Can I see it?"

"We gave it to the ER doctor." Mr. Wells looked at his wife, who confirmed his statement with a quick nod. "I think he gave it to the police."

Of course he did. So the police could investigate the medication. And Heath Parker. And her.

★ ★ ★ ★ ★

She had a plan. She would stay calm—at least until Heath Parker showed up. Then all bets were off.

Kendall scoped out the lobby of the Antlers Hotel, where Heath was staying until he found a permanent home. The warm light from the modern chandeliers ought to soothe her spirit. The stone fireplace surrounded by leather chairs invited her to sit and relax. But at this point, Kendall doubted if she'd ever get the adrenaline coursing through her veins out of her system.

Of course, she'd never been to Heath's hotel room. He always picked her up at her loft, or she met him at church, or at the restaurant, like the time she met him for dinner with his alleged board. Kendall wasn't sure what Heath Parker was up to anymore, so she had no idea what those people were doing.

When she left the hospital and went home, she still believed Heath would call her. But by the time eight o'clock rolled around, she gave up hope. Maybe her "Call me right away. We need to talk about Nicholas Wells's being admitted to Memorial's pediatric ICU thanks to your so-called supplement" message scared him off.

Fine. If Heath wasn't going to call her, she'd find him. Kendall dumped her ratty jeans and short-sleeved shirt into the clothes hamper, showered, and then selected a pair of black dress pants and a black dress blouse, paired with wedge-heeled shoes. Not that she cared what she wore to confront the man. But she wanted to be able to look in Dr. Parker's eyes—or as close as possible.

She approached the receptionist, hoping she had the appropriate I'm-here-to-meet-someone persona. "Hello, I'm a friend of Dr. Heath Parker. Would you please ring his room and let him know I'm here to see him?"

The young woman's blue eyes, made up à la Cleopatra, widened, but she only said, "One moment, please" before calling his room.

Satisfaction, at last.

Short-lived satisfaction.

"I'm sorry, but Dr. Parker isn't answering his phone. May I take a message for him?"

"No, thank you. I'll wait in the lobby."

Kendall chose a chair facing the lobby's glass doors. *Is this what it feels like to be on a stakeout?* She always thought it would be more . . . thrilling. Right now exhaustion warred with frustration—and the two were at a stalemate.

The battle continued with every glance at her iPhone. Within thirty minutes, she paced the sand-colored marble floors of the lobby, aware that the receptionist watched her movements. What could she do, order her to leave? Demand she sit down? An hour later, Kendall changed her walking tour and paced the carpeted hallway to the left of the main lobby. She debated calling Rachel or one of her other friends to vent, but she needed all her attention focused on what she was going to say when Heath finally showed up. She only hoped he made an appearance sometime before breakfast tomorrow.

Just before midnight, Kendall heard Heath's voice coupled with a woman's sultry laugh.

Interesting. Not that she was here to ask about *her*. They'd never used the word *exclusive*. Shame on her for assuming that's what the man meant with all his talk of falling in love. Well, shame on her for a lot of things, apparently.

Kendall stood, positioning herself in the middle of the lobby so that Heath and whoever he was with couldn't miss her. Out of the corner of her eye, she couldn't help but notice that the receptionist leaned on the desk, ready to watch the showdown.

The man walked into the lobby, his arm around Leslie

what's-her-name's waist, his jacket draped over her shoulders. No wonder the woman was cold. Her dress skimmed her thighs. And what was that old-fashioned saying about "displaying your goods in the shop window"? Appropriate.

"Heath."

Kendall's voice sliced through their laughter. Heath looked away from Miss-Forgot-to-Wear-a-Complete-Dress. Stopped. A smile of satisfaction curved Leslie's lips when she caught sight of Kendall. Caught in the act—and proud of it.

"Let's skip the what-are-you-doing-here question. I've called you all day about my patient being hospitalized. He used your *supplement*—and I use that word loosely—and had a life-threatening reaction."

"I'm sorry to hear your patient is sick, Kendall." Heath leaned in and whispered something to Leslie. Patted her tush as she headed for the elevator. "Why does that concern me?"

"He had a reaction to something *you* gave him, Heath."

"So he—or rather, his parents say." Heath didn't even bother to look at her, preferring to watch Leslie as she stood by the elevator, waiting for the doors to open.

"Are you suggesting that supplement is harmless?"

"I'm saying that previous tests on Kupu have shown no serious side effects."

Kendall paced closer, grabbing his arm to force his attention back to her. "Heath, what were you thinking, giving a supplement to my patients without consulting me first?"

"We're not partners, Kendall. I don't need to consult you."

"You talked with my patients. In my office."

"It was nothing more than a friendly conversation. A suggestion." Heath loosened his green-and-blue-striped tie. Yawned. As if the conversation bored him. "They were free to try the supplement or not."

"Do you realize the police questioned me? That you've impli-cated me in I don't know what?"

"We've talked about how important nutrition and supple-ments are for kids with asthma and allergies. You've agreed with me about the importance of building up patients' immunities." He looked her up and down. Smirked. "And you did attend a board meeting . . ."

His words and actions clicked in place like the pieces of a puzzle. Heath Parker wasn't pursuing her for love and marriage and a family. He was setting her up . . . using her as a front for his . . . whatever this was . . . illegal supplement.

Kendall struggled to keep her voice low. "You tabled the discussion the night I came to dinner. I had no idea you were giving it to people—"

"It's the only way to test the efficacy of the medicine. You're a doctor, you know that."

"That's what the FDA is for, Heath."

"I am not wasting the time and money of the FDA. Red tape. I've seen the benefits of this day-to-day on the mission field. If I can do my own tests, develop my own data, compile the research—"

Kendall pressed her fingers against her temples. "Do you real-ize what you've done? How you've put me at risk?"

"The ends always justify the means, dear Kendall. I had the supplement. You had the population base I needed. And the reputation."

"Are you saying that more of my patients are taking this drug?"

"Of course. It's the only way to get adequate results."

Kendall didn't know how it happened. One minute she was trying to unravel all the information Heath Parker dumped on her while trying to figure out how he'd gotten access to her patient records. The next minute she slapped him. *Hard.* Her palm and fingers stung, but from the red outline of her fingers on his face, Heath's skin throbbed, too.

"Wha—?" Heath stumbled back. Kendall knew she had his attention—that she'd rocked him out of his complacency.

"I want every single name, do you understand me? Every. Single. Name. Get them to me by tomorrow morning. You'll be hearing from my lawyer." Kendall advanced on him again, poking her finger in his chest. "You may think you can mess with me, Parker, but you won't hurt my kids."

★ ★ ★ ★ ★

"Come here, Sully."

Kendall patted the foot of her bed, inviting the dog to climb up next to her. He only needed to be asked once. Invitations to sleep with her were rare. Sully plopped his front paws on the patterned comforter and then wiggled his way on top of the mattress, finally positioning himself in the center of the bed.

Kendall didn't care. She wrapped her arms around the dog's furry neck, pulling him close.

"What happened to 'older is wiser,' huh?" Kendall lay back against the pile of pillows, pulling the dog with her so that he stretched out alongside her. "I'm on the wrong side of thirty-five and getting played like I was in high school. Only this hurts worse."

Except she wasn't going to cry over Heath Parker. After homecoming, she cried for weeks over Phillip—not that anyone ever knew it. She came home from the dance, stuck her dress in the back of her closet, and resorted to hiding out in the garage with her dad. But at night, as the other girl's words replayed in her head, she muffled sobs with her pillow.

And the other resident—the one who'd showed up for their *first* date and announced he realized they weren't right for each other? Yeah, there'd been tears then, too. But not for as long. And that time she threw herself into her residency. Her patients. Her purpose.

"How did I not see it? Am I that desperate?"

Was she? Sully wasn't answering, so it was up to her. Desperate or not, reality slapped her in the face: She was thirty-six. And alone. She thought she'd been picked. At last, someone thought she was enough.

Oh, yeah. She'd been picked, all right. Heath Parker chose her to take the fall for his drug scam. Well, she wasn't going down without a fight. Why she threatened him with her "lawyer," she couldn't figure out. She had an accountant, not a lawyer. So far, the investigation wasn't about her. If she needed a lawyer, she'd get one—someone who could make sure Heath Parker never hurt another kid again, and could wipe the smug grin off his face at the same time. There was one thing she could do: report him to the state medical board. Was he even licensed to practice in Colorado? She'd assumed too much about Heath Parker.

She knew she wasn't the one really hurt in all this. She needed to remember Nicholas. He was the one spending the night in the hospital, not her. Kendall rubbed the heels of her palms against her eyes, wishing the tears would come and wash away the ache.

There was no need for her to have any tests run. She'd get over having her heart broken.

Not that Heath Parker broke her heart.

But Griffin Walker had.

No, no . . . this was not the time to think about Griffin Walker—Mr. Do-Not-Cross-This-Line. Heath Parker was all charisma and charm. Griffin Walker could audition for a reality show about bachelors *not* looking for true love.

And Kendall had to fall in love with him?

Yes, yes, she did. The man threw up roadblock after emotional roadblock, and Kendall's heart vaulted over every single one.

What was wrong with her? Was she so "less than" that no man would ever want to marry her? It sure looked that way. No matter how she tried, her longed-for golden ring—career, marriage, family—would always be right beyond her grasp.

She was the one who skewed the grading curve in her college classes. The "gunner" in medical school. Always aiming for the top grades, the top 1 percent. And she always achieved success.

Excelled.

Won.

"But I'm the loser tonight, Sully." Kendall hugged the dog tighter as he licked her face. "Rejected. Played. Wow. Can it get any worse? Don't answer that."

CHAPTER EIGHTEEN

★ ★ ★ ★

Colorado Springs just wasn't big enough for Griffin and his ex-wife. He hadn't been skulking around town holding his breath, hoping not to run into her again—not really. But the what-if of meeting Tracey lurked in the back of his mind ever since he'd seen her at the restaurant.

And now here she was, entering the lobby of the Y as he dragged his sweaty body out of the gym. He knew he should have skipped the workout when Doug bailed on him. But no. He had to stay the course, ignore the vertigo dancing an off-kilter jig in his head, and push himself through a Spin class led by a fitness sadist.

"Well, this is a surprise." Tracey stopped walking, pulling Griffin up short. "I had no idea you worked out here."

The fact was, the woman knew nothing about him, not after a dozen years of silence. Any intel she had about him was all hearsay, passed through the infamous cadet alumni grapevine.

"Tracey." Griffin shifted his canvas workout bag to his other hand, scanning the area behind her. Where were her replacement husband and too-cute-to-be-true kids to complete the happy family his ex had created?

"Just me today. Todd didn't feel like working out, so I left him home on dad-duty with the trio. We're still getting settled in—we bought a house in the Briargate area."

"Congratulations." At least God hadn't been so cruel to have them set up "Home Sweet Home" in his neighborhood.

Griffin couldn't resist assessing the woman he'd been married to for six years. She'd changed—but then, twelve years would change anyone. He had to admit she still looked good. She wore her medium length auburn hair down, skimming her shoulders. Back when they were married she kept it pulled back and pinned up—easier to deal with. There were fine lines around her eyes, but they didn't detract from Tracey's classic beauty. He'd always liked how her moss-green eyes revealed her moods—until Tracey settled into one unshakable emotion: resentment.

"We've both gotten older." Tracey touched the side of her face as if uncomfortable under his scrutiny. "Older looks good on you—it usually does on a man. I like the gray in your hair."

"Thanks. You . . . look good, too, Tracey." From her coordinated outfit of sleek black yoga pants with a matching black-and-lime-green top paired with trendy tennis shoes, she still approached shopping as an art form.

"Oh, just tell me that I look exhausted and get it done with." She sighed as she ran her fingers through her hair, tossing it back as if being tired was no big deal. "I have three young kids. I'm always worn out."

Griffin tried to think of an appropriate response. Something like *You don't look that bad.* Having a conversation after years of silence wasn't all that simple. And really, what did they have to say to each other? He'd made his choices and she'd made hers—even if her overflowing life looked nothing like the "No Kids Allowed" one she'd demanded from him.

"I was surprised to hear you were flying a desk, Griff. Being a pilot is your life. What happened?"

Now she was interested in his career?

"Nothing that won't be cleared up in a few weeks."

"You get in trouble?"

"No." He could continue to evade her questions or put a stop to her curiosity. "I . . . had some problems with vertigo. I'm better now. I expect the medical board to reinstate me to flying status again."

"I hope so. You're one of the best pilots around."

Imagine that—a compliment from Tracey. Not that it mattered to him. Let the woman think what she wanted about him. They'd had their chance at a relationship and botched it. Then she'd left him reeling with the repercussions of a decision he couldn't undo.

"I didn't get a chance to ask the other day—how are your parents? I think it's great they let Ian come visit you."

And just like that, Tracey crashed into his personal life.

"Ian's not visiting me, Tracey—he lives with me. I'm his guardian now because our parents were killed five months ago."

"I'm sorry—"

Griffin took a step back. "Enough, Tracey. I'm not going to stand around and discuss my life with you just because you decided to move back to the Springs. We didn't talk for years. And you know what? I'm good with that."

"Griff—" Tracey took a step back, too.

"You walked out on me after demanding I give up any chance of having a family to try and make our marriage work.

And now here you are—and you've got it all. And I'm still stuck with the consequences of the choice I made years ago to keep you happy."

Finally he'd had the chance to speak out loud all the imaginary, one-sided conversations he'd had with Tracey through the years. But as his words died down, Griffin realized the entire lobby area of the Y had stilled. People watched him as he lit into his ex-wife, who stood staring at him, offering no defense.

Great. Just great.

"I'm outta here." He exited the lobby, almost running to where his Jeep waited in the parking lot. Maybe he should go back and apologize for what he said. But the truth was, if he found himself face-to-face with Tracey again, more resentment would spew out of him.

He started the Jeep, jammed the stick shift into reverse, and tore out of the lot, not sure where he was headed. He couldn't outrun his past, and his future looked bleak.

★ ★ ★ ★ ★

"Thanks, Warren, I really appreciate this."

Griffin's old Academy classmate walked beside him on the flight line of the local airport, leading him to where his Cessna 172 was parked. "I'm just sorry you can't take her up."

Griffin scanned the various planes standing at rest. "Yeah, well, I'll wait until I'm cleared to fly and then I'll come back and celebrate with a night flight."

"All right." Warren patted the side of the plane and then moved out of Griffin's way, shielding his eyes from the sun that was setting behind Pikes Peak, tingeing the sky yellow and orange. "You need anything?"

"Nope. I'm good."

"Fine. Just give me a wave when you're done. I'll be over working on my buddy's plane in the hangar."

Griffin waited until Warren walked off before hauling himself up into the cockpit of the Cessna. He settled behind the dual controls, surveying the view of the Rocky Mountains outside the windshield.

If only he could perform a preflight check and then take her up. Escaping into the blue sky was always the best way to clear his head. But he hadn't broken the boundary of his "Do Not Fly" status in almost two years—and he wasn't going to let his tirade with Tracey cause him to do anything else stupid today.

He shifted in the seat, his workout T-shirt and gym shorts still damp with perspiration. He should have gone home and changed first, but after his one-man showdown, his only thought was to get somewhere—anywhere—to think. And this was where he'd always done his best thinking: in a plane.

Griffin closed his eyes, inhaling the familiar scent of asphalt and gasoline as he mentally rehearsed the preflight checklists.

Exterior first: struts, tires, brakes, elevator, ailerons, flaps, rudder, engine, and oil. Interior checks: radios, navigation, master switch—on. Fuel switch to ON and start the engine. Then taxi to the active runway for takeoff. He mentally scrolled through the radio calls and frequencies: ATIS, clearance, ground control, and, finally, tower for takeoff clearance. He could almost taste the freedom waiting for him as he visualized flying above the vista of the Front Range, leaving the weight of his responsibilities back on the ground.

What if the medical board didn't clear him to fly again?

God, you wouldn't do that to me, would you? I'm a pilot. It's what I do. It's who I am.

Didn't God promise to give him the desires of his heart? All he'd ever wanted was to fly . . . surely his vertigo-induced hiatus was almost over.

But what about his desire to have children?

God could certainly work miracles, but he wasn't going to nullify Griffin's stupidity.

Griffin watched a plane taxi down the runway, gaining speed as its wheels lifted off the ground and it soared off toward the horizon.

He hadn't realized how angry he was at Tracey until she showed up again, living the life he never would. Why had he ever let her talk him into having a vasectomy? Why hadn't he stood his ground, insisted they wait, think things out?

Acquiescing hadn't saved his marriage.

And it cost him any hope of becoming a father.

And now it cost him any chance of a future with Kendall because she deserved it all: A husband. Children.

And the reality was, as much as he wanted to blame Tracey, he had only himself to blame.

The fact hit him with the force of unexpected turbulence.

No one made him sign the permission papers for the vasectomy—he did that all by himself. As much as he wanted to say that his ex-wife "forced" him, Griffin was an adult at the time. Yes, he'd made an immature decision out of desperation. But it was his choice—and now he had to man up and live with the consequences.

And after twelve years, he needed to stop blaming Tracey. More than that, he needed to forgive her for walking out on him. Maybe he had worked harder than she had to save their marriage. Maybe not. But he had to stop holding her responsible for their divorce.

God, where did he go from here?

No marriage.

No children.

And maybe . . . no flying.

He had to stop saying he couldn't live on a permanent "Do Not Fly" status. It was time to ask God how. How did he forgive Tracey? How did he accept the reality of his future—especially if he was grounded?

"I can't do this—any of this—without you, God."

The words he spoke hung in the air. The truth settled on his shoulders and Griffin shifted under the weight. Let it settle there. There was no getting away from it. Maybe by the time he stepped out of the plane, he'd be a little closer to accepting his limitations—and God's strength.

★ ★ ★ ★

Where was everyone else?

Evie parked her SUV behind the Rocky Mountain Family Practice in the near-empty lot. Besides her car, there was Kendall's red Jeep—but who drove the rust-colored Jeep Cherokee? Had Kendall convinced someone else in the practice to purchase a Jeep? There was no way Paul would trade in his Harley.

Today was Monday, right? Yes, because the echo of Javan's weekend standoff followed her all the way to work. Evie gathered up her cross-body purse and the two boxes of Krispy Kreme doughnuts she'd purchased to share with the rest of the staff during their early-morning meeting. At this point it looked as if she and Kendall—and some mystery Jeep lover—would split two dozen doughnuts.

Balancing the boxes against her body, she pulled open the back door to the clinic. "Dr. Kendall?"

"In the break room, Evie."

At least Kendall was here for the 7 AM meeting. Where was everyone else?

When she entered the break room, her boss stood at the kitchen counter, pouring coffee into her favorite mug labeled with the words MED SCHOOL: IT BEATS A REAL JOB. At the circular table covered with a blue-and-white-checked plastic tablecloth sat . . . Ian Walker?

"Good morning, Evie." Kendall raised the pot of coffee. "Want some?"

"Good morning, Dr. Kendall." Evie deposited the boxes onto the table, lifting the lid to display the assortment of pastries. "And good morning, Ian. I didn't know we'd brought you on staff. Help yourself."

"Morning, Mrs. Gardner." He eyed the doughnuts and then looked at Kendall. "Is it okay if I have one?"

"Evie said it was. Go ahead."

While Evie sweetened her cup of coffee, Ian selected a glazed doughnut and a strawberry-filled one dusted with powdered sugar.

Evie moved a pile of napkins onto the table. "So, where is everyone else?"

"This is it for today. You, me, Ian. I told the rest of the staff to come in at the regular time." Kendall pulled a carton of milk from the fridge and poured Ian a glass.

"Really?"

What was her boss up to? Did Kendall want her to talk to Ian about something?

"I'll let Ian explain."

The teen swallowed a bite of doughnut, white powder gathering at the corner of his mouth. "Well, uh, Dr. Kendall and I were talking about how my parents adopted me. And she mentioned how you're adopting a little boy . . . uh, I can't remember his name."

"Javan." Evie gripped the coffee mug with both hands, warmth seeping through the ceramic sides.

"Javan. Yeah. Cool name." Ian finished his first doughnut and took a gulp of milk. "Anyway, I told Dr. Kendall how I gave my mom and dad a lot of trouble when they first adopted me. That's when she asked if I would talk with you."

Evie couldn't stop herself from looking at Ian. Adopted. Well, that explained why Ian, with his slender build, straight brown hair, and hazel eyes, looked nothing like Griffin Walker. She just assumed one brother looked like their father and the other brother looked like their mother.

"So, what do you want to know?" Ian finished off half the second doughnut in one bite.

What did she want to know? She thought this morning was going to be a staff meeting, not a chance to ask Ian Walker questions about being adopted. Did he think she carried around a list of questions to ask adopted kids?

Kendall stepped into the quietness that stretched between the trio. "Ian, you told me that you weren't very happy when your parents first adopted you. Why?"

"I was four when the Walkers became my foster parents—six when they adopted me. Things were bad with my birth mom. She was addicted to meth. The authorities finally took me away from her for good when she left me home by myself for a whole weekend."

"Oh, Ian. How horrible." Kendall's words mirrored Evie's thoughts.

"It wasn't the first time she left me home alone." Ian shrugged his shoulders. "Just the longest. I think one of the neighbors figured it out somehow and called the police because they showed up Sunday night and took me away."

"You were probably glad to get somewhere safe, huh?" Kendall nudged the box of doughnuts toward the teen.

"Here's the weird thing. I wanted to go back home with my mom. I kept waiting and waiting and waiting for my mom to come get me." Ian stared at the table, ignoring the doughnuts. "But she never did."

"But the Walkers—they were nice to you, weren't they? They loved you, right?"

"Oh, they were great. Dad taught me how to play baseball. How to throw a football. It was so cool to finally have a dad. I never liked my mom's boyfriends." Ian stared at the wall across the room. "And Mom made all my favorite meals. Macaroni and cheese. Spaghetti. Sloppy Joes. She tried to read to me at night, but I wouldn't let her. She didn't care that I slept in my clothes, on top of the blankets. Every morning, I woke up, covered with a blanket. I knew she did that 'cause I woke up one time when she was doing it."

Kendall crossed the room to refill her coffee mug. "Why were you so mad at your mom—and not your dad?"

"For the longest time, I couldn't tell you why. She'd be so nice—and I would slam doors in her face. I'd let Dad kiss me good night, but not her. I'd call him Dad and her Mrs. Walker."

"What changed?"

"One night after Dad put me to bed, I got up to get a drink of water. I guess this was about a year after I went to live with them. And I heard Mom and Dad talking. Mom was crying. And Dad was praying. He said something like, 'God, help us love Ian no matter what he says. No matter what he does. Just like you love us.'"

"And that changed everything?"

"Nope. The next day, I told Mom I hated her. Screamed at the top of my lungs. She walked over and knelt down right in front of me and whispered, 'I am going to love you longer than you can hate me, Ian. I know your birth mom left you. But I'm your second mom—and I promise you I will never, ever stop loving you. I am not going anywhere.'"

Ian swiped at his eyes with the back of his hand. "I wasn't mad at my second mom, Mrs. Gardner. I was mad at my birth mom. And I couldn't tell her—so I took it out on my second mom. Does that make sense?"

It was difficult to see Ian through the haze caused by the tears in her eyes. Evie cleared her throat. "Yes."

Yes, it makes sense. Does it make what Javan does hurt less? No.

"All I can figure is maybe Javan's doing the same thing to you. If he is, don't quit on him. He needs you. Every little boy needs a mom—and he's already lost one."

Kendall reached across the table and touched her hand. "I know you weren't expecting Ian here this morning, Evie. And I apologize for the surprise tactic. After the last time we talked, well, I was afraid you'd resist my suggestion to meet with Ian. But I thought maybe Ian could help you see it from his side— and from Javan's side."

"I appreciate this, Dr. Kendall. And you, too, Ian. I know that no teenager wants to get up this early in the morning. And you didn't even know there'd be doughnuts." Evie turned the half-empty mug of coffee around in her hands, staring into the black liquid. "Anyway . . . thanks for talking with me."

The sound of the back door opening brought Evie to her feet. "Sounds like somebody else is here. And I need to get up front and get ready for patients."

Kendall stood. "Evie, do you want to—"

"We can talk more later, Dr. Kendall. I don't want to keep your patients waiting."

CHAPTER NINETEEN

★ ★ ★ ★

*G*riffin handed Doug the cold bottle of Coke he requested, watching as the older man peered into the bowels of his Jeep.

"How long we been working on this thing, Griffin?"

"Three, maybe four hours." Griffin wiped his forearm across his brow, wicking away the sweat with the sleeve of his cotton shirt. He walked to the front of the garage to get a better look at the mountains to the west. The sun was dipping below the Front Range, which meant the air would cool off—and so would the garage.

"Thought you said this was a quick fix."

"It should have been." He gulped down half a bottle of water before continuing. "Then again, it never is with my Jeep. I just remind myself that Jeeps are built, not bought."

"You forgot to mention that when you invited me over to help you work on the beast." Doug walked outside the garage and stood in the driveway. Griffin followed him, drawn by the light breeze that cooled off his body.

"And scare you off?"

Doug's chuckle acknowledged Griffin's wisdom. "You know Jan expects us for dinner sometime tonight, right?"

"We'll make it. Ian and I may have to hitch a ride, though."

"So is Ian saying much about going back to Florida?"

Griffin drained the last of the water from the bottle, twisting the cap back on top. "Nope."

"You're both good with the decision?"

"Yep." Griffin walked back into the garage, tossing the empty bottle toward the recycle bin. Missed. "It's the best thing for Ian."

"Even though you're not flying—" Doug followed him and leaned both hands on the front fender of the CJ7.

"Flying or not, my parents made a mistake when they appointed me as Ian's guardian." Griffin began organizing the tools in his tool chest. "My brother almost died when he was with me."

"Afraid you'll make mistakes, huh?"

"I already have." Griffin clenched his fist around a wrench. "I can't do it, Doug. There's too much at stake."

He was surprised when his friend didn't argue with him. Instead, Doug lowered the hood, the metallic clang sounding through the garage.

"Why don't you get rid of this old clunker, Griffin?"

"What are you talking about?"

Doug thumped the fender with his fist. "It's nothing but a pain, you told me that more than once while we worked on it today. You said it breaks down all the time. Said you couldn't begin to imagine how much money and how many hours you've poured into this Jeep. What was one of those sayings you Jeep owners are so fond of? *Jeep* means 'Just Empty Every Pocket'?"

"I wouldn't think of selling this Jeep."

"Why not? Sell it for parts. Buy something newer—an SUV, maybe. Or a truck. No more hassles, no more wasting your weekends trying to fix it—"

"Sell it for parts? Are you kidding me? This is my Jeep." Griffin scanned the CJ7, memories of different road trips clicking through his mind in fast-forward. "I've invested time and money in this Jeep. I have no intention of getting rid of it— even if it is a hassle."

"And that's how God feels about you, Griffin." Doug stood, raising his soda in a salute to Griffin.

"What? We're talking about Jeeps—not me and God."

"You may have been talking about Jeeps, son. I was talking about Jeeps, you, and God." Doug came over and slung his arm across Griffin's shoulders. "Come on. Walk with your old sponsor-turned-friend. It's too nice a day to spend all of it in the garage."

The two men walked in silence for half a block. Griffin watched a neighbor mow his lawn, the scent of fresh-cut grass reminding him of his own neglected lawn. Two teen boys on skateboards whizzed by, their laughter floating back to Griffin. Did Ian like to skateboard?

"So, God and Jeeps." Doug bent down and picked up a stick, tapping it against his leg.

"Go on."

"You love your Jeep—even though it's left you stranded on the road more than once. Costs you good money. Takes your time. I even heard you say it 'wastes' your time."

"I didn't mean that—"

"I know you didn't. I'm just quoting you." Doug tossed the stick in the air. Caught it. "The point is, you're keeping the Jeep—imperfections and all."

"Right."

"Have you ever considered that God loves you even more than you love your Jeep?"

"Well, sure. I know that."

Doug waved away the comment. "No, I don't think you do. You think God will love you if you don't waste his time. God's invested in you, Griffin. He's sticking with you for the long haul. It's not based on performance."

The two men came to the end of the street. Paused.

"Which way do we go?" Doug looked right and left.

"You tell me. I have a feeling you're going to anyway."

"Ah, I think we're talking about two completely different things." He turned left. "You stumbled into your relationship with God because you realized you were broken, Griffin. Don't change the rules of engagement now. God redeems broken people and loves them in their brokenness."

Was that what he'd done? Changed the rules?

"What kind of life am I offering Ian? I'm so new at being a believer that I can still feel all my mistakes breathing down my neck. One of my biggest mistakes just moved to the Springs."

When Doug's eyebrows furrowed together over his eyes, asking "What are you talking about?" Griffin almost laughed. *Almost.*

"My ex-wife, her husband, and their three kids moved here. And the other day at the gym I told her exactly how I felt about our mess of a marriage."

"Some unresolved issues there?"

"You could say that." Griffin unclenched his hands, realizing he'd balled them into fists. "If I can't handle my past, how am I supposed to make sure Ian's ready for his future?"

"Was your family perfect growing up, Griffin? Wait, I can answer that for you. No—because you were in it." Doug's laughter invited Griffin to join in. "Your mom and dad never expected you to be a perfect brother for Ian, either. I can assure you that they weren't perfect parents. Your parents obviously wanted Ian to be with family if something happened to them. And you, my friend, are it."

Griffin wasn't trying to deny that Ian and he were family. But the scene from On the Border played through his mind again.

"Ian was safer with them than he is with me."

"It's not about Ian being safe." Doug's words slammed up against Griffin's protest. "Ian is safe because God is watching over him, wherever he is. If Ian had died that night in the restaurant, it would have been because somehow that was according to God's will, Griffin—not because you were a horrible brother."

Tears stung his eyes. Griffin blinked, wishing he'd thought to grab a pair of sunglasses.

"What kind of person doesn't take the time to get to know his younger brother?"

"No more looking in the rearview mirror, Griffin. You have today. And tomorrow." Doug stepped in front of Griffin so that he had to stop walking. The older man placed his hands on Griffin's shoulders. Gave him a quick shake. "And as many tomorrows as God gives you and Ian. The question is: Will you choose to accept the opportunity you've been given to be the brother Ian needs?"

★ ★ ★ ★ ★

"Do you have a minute, Ian?"

Griffin stood in his brother's doorway, surveying the teen's attempts to pack. He wasn't leaving for another two weeks, but Ian was determined to be ready to go. Dresser drawers were half open, a pile of jeans on the floor next to a towering stack of T-shirts. How many T-shirts did his brother own? Ian's underwear drawer was a jumble of whites, bearing testimony to his reluctance to match socks.

"I'm kinda busy." Ian dumped his backpack out on his bed, notebooks, pens, and loose papers cascading onto the maroon comforter.

"I see that." Griffin stepped inside the room, realizing that in all the months Ian lived in his townhome, he'd come in his brother's bedroom only half a dozen times. "I need to talk to you."

"Go ahead. I'm listening." His brother sat on his bed and began sorting through papers.

Griffin moved the textbooks and empty backpack to the back edge of the bed, sitting down near his brother. Ian stopped shuffling through papers and looked at him, his hazel eyes wide.

"What's up? I already said steak was fine for dinner. Or order pizza. Whatever."

"This isn't about dinner." Griffin slipped his hand into his jeans pocket, wrapping his fingers around the lengths of gold chain hidden there.

Except for the clutter, Ian's room looked like the rest of the house. The walls were bare, the last rays of the sun slanting through his window onto bland beige walls. He had a dark pine bed, a dresser, a desk—all brought from their parents' home. Somewhere in the boxes Griffin stored back in Florida were Ian's personal belongings: books, photos, awards, trophies. Photos of Mom and Dad. Why didn't Griffin think those things would be important to his brother?

Because he wasn't thinking of anyone but himself.

"I, um, have something to tell you and something to ask you." Griffin shifted on the bed, some sort of lump pressing

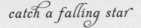

against his thigh. He reached underneath the comforter and pulled out Ian's pajama bottoms. "Wow. How long have these been lost in your bed?"

"Only since last night." Ian grabbed them, tossing them in the corner.

So much for comic relief.

Griffin cleared his throat. Tightened his fingers around the chains again as he whispered a silent prayer for help. "Ian, I want to tell you that I'm sorry."

His brother resumed sorting papers. Griffin could only hope he was listening.

"I've been wrong . . . about a lot of things. I thought Mom and Dad made a big mistake, making me your guardian. The truth is, I didn't want to do it."

"Tell me about it."

"It had nothing to do with you—and everything to do with me."

"Right."

"Ian." Griffin covered his brother's hand with his own, but Ian jerked away. "I mean it. The problems we've had? They were my fault. I hadn't been any kind of brother to you before Mom and Dad died. I was afraid to be your brother—your guardian—afterward."

Ian bolted off the bed, scattering papers onto the floor.

"How could you be my brother? I hardly ever saw you. You came home what—three, four times before the accident?"

"I know. I'm sorry—" Griffin stood but left space between him and Ian.

"Sorry. You're sorry." Ian turned on him, his words stonewalling Griffin's apology. "I was so excited about being part of a family. Mom and Dad talked about you all the time. And I thought I was gonna get a brother, ya know? I got nothing from you. Nothing. And now Mom and Dad are gone . . . I'm stuck with you."

Griffin stared at his brother, finally coming face-to-face with the consequences of his actions. Ian clenched and unclenched his fist, as if he'd like to take a swing at him. Griffin deserved it—and more. Everything Ian said was right. He couldn't change what he'd done in the past, but he refused to back down from the future.

"I did it all wrong. I was out of the house, busy with my air force career. I figured you didn't care. I was the one who didn't care enough. And then Tracey and I got divorced and things got even more messed up. I'm not making excuses for what I did, Ian. I'm trying to explain who I was back then."

"You're no different now."

"I am. Back then, I didn't believe in God. I know you haven't seen any difference because I've been so focused on getting back in the cockpit. I know you don't believe this. Why should you? But I am sorry."

Was his brother hearing anything he said?

"After Mom and Dad died, we should have talked. About how we were feeling. About missing them. About how things were going to work now that we were the Walker family. And it's my fault we didn't."

Griffin paused to see if anything he said made a difference to his brother. So far, no. "I was so caught up in my own problems—the vertigo, whether the medical board would let me fly again or not—I didn't think about you. I'm sorry. Really."

Why wouldn't his brother look at him? Ian remained as stiff as a new recruit standing at attention, except his shoulders were hunched, his face turned away. So far Griffin might just as well be talking to himself. Maybe he'd waited too long to try to repair the damage he'd caused by sending Ian back to Florida. But he had promised Doug—and God—he was going to have this conversation with his brother. He would finish it.

"Okay. That's what I wanted to tell you. I wanted to ask you, well, two things. Would you please forgive me for being such a lousy big brother?"

No response.

"And would you give me another chance?"

For just a moment, Ian's eyes locked with his.

"I know you're supposed to go to the Jamisons'. But I'm asking you to please give me another chance to do things right. Stay here. I won't do things perfectly, but I think if we work together, we can figure out how to be a family."

His words seemed to make no difference to his brother.

Griffin pulled the chains from his pocket. "Just one more thing. I've been wearing Mom's and Dad's wedding bands around my neck since the day I got back from their funeral. I realized today that's not right. There are two Walker sons—two brothers. So I bought another chain and put Dad's band on one and Mom's band on another. I want you to choose whatever one you want to wear. I'll wear the other one."

Ian took half a step forward. "Do I only get to wear one if I stay?"

"Whatever you decide, one of these chains is yours, Ian. You're a Walker. You're my brother. Two rings. Two brothers. I think Mom and Dad would want it that way."

Ian's response came out in a choked whisper. "Mom's. I'd like Mom's."

"Mom's it is then." Griffin pressed the chain suspending the ring into his brother's hand, folding Ian's fingers closed over it. A second later, a warm tear splashed onto his hand. Then another.

His brother launched into his chest, knocking Griffin back

against the edge of the bed. But he wrapped his arms around Ian and held on to his brother as he buried his face in Griffin's shoulder, a sob tearing from his throat.

★ ★ ★ ★

The vibration of Griffin's cell dragged him out of the depths of sleep. He half opened his eyes, realizing he was sprawled on the couch, the TV droning on and on.

What time was it?

When his phone buzzed again, Griffin reached out and patted the floor, searching for the iPhone. *There.* He pressed it against the side of his face, which was still adhered to the couch.

"Griffin . . . Walker."

"Mr. Walker?" Some girl's voice zipped across the line.

Griffin wiped a hand across his face. "Yes. This is Griffin Walker."

"This is Tara. I'm a friend of Ian's—your brother's . . . He's in trouble—"

"What?" Griffin pushed off the couch, switching the phone to his other hand. "What's wrong? Where is he?"

"He's having trouble breathing . . . I'm not sure what to do . . . Can you come get him?"

Griffin could now hear fear stretching the girl's voice tight.

"Put Ian on the phone."

"He doesn't know I called you. I'm scared . . . can you come get him?"

Griffin searched the kitchen counter for his keys, his wallet. "How bad is he?"

"He can hardly talk. He told me not to call you, but I don't know what else to do."

"Call nine-one-one. Does Ian have his inhaler or his EpiPen?"

"I dunno—" Now it sounded as if the girl was crying.

"If he does, have him use them. But hang up and call nine-one-one right now." Griffin ran toward his Jeep. "Wait! Where are you?"

He slid into his Jeep as the girl told him the address. "I'll be there in fifteen. If the EMTs get there and take Ian to the ER, call me back. Got it?"

"Yessir."

Backing out of the garage, Griffin checked the time. Nine forty-five. Ian asked to go watch a movie with friends. Griffin said yes, figuring he needed some downtime after their talk. That was almost three hours ago. Why would his brother be having trouble breathing?

★ ★ ★ ★ ★

Griffin thought he'd be relieved to beat the ambulance to the hospital. But watching the EMTs wheel Ian in on a gurney about took him out at the knees. The back of the gurney was set upright so that Ian couldn't lie back. An oxygen mask covered his brother's pale face, a light mist escaping from the sides before evaporating beneath the teen's eyes. Even with his eyes wide open, Ian seemed disoriented as his shoulders rose and fell in his efforts to breathe.

"We gave him a neb treatment on the way in per protocol." The EMT pushing the gurney updated the nurse who met them at the ER entrance. "And a shot of terbutaline. His pulse ox is eighty-two . . ."

"That's my brother—" Griffin's attempt to follow Ian back into the emergency room failed when a nurse blocked his way.

"Fine, Mr. Walker. Wait here, please."

"I'm his guardian. I want to go back with him." Griffin heard the automatic hiss of the doors as they closed, blocking his view.

"We'll let the staff get your brother settled. Then we'll see about you going back." The woman who was even shorter than Kendall, stood her ground and maneuvered him back to the waiting room.

Instead of sitting, Griffin walked to a corner of the waiting room and pulled his phone from his jean pocket. He should call Kendall. She could get him back there with Ian.

No. He wasn't going to pull any favors from Kendall Haynes.

But she was Ian's physician. She'd want to know what was going on. Just because he and Kendall had a falling-out didn't mean he shouldn't do the right thing by Ian. He tapped the phone against the palm of his hand and then walked over to the nurse behind the desk.

"Excuse me."

She didn't even look at him. "Mr. Walker, I told you that I'd come and get you once your brother was settled."

"I understand that." Right now this woman ruled over him. "I just need some advice. Dr. Haynes, Kendall Haynes, is my brother's family doctor. Should I call her and let her know that Ian's here?"

An arched eyebrow conveyed the nurse's opinion of him calling Kendall. "Let us handle the medical side of things. I am sure the ER physician will contact Dr. Haynes if that is necessary."

Griffin knew the conversation was over when the woman turned her back on him. He paced a slow circle around the room.

He hated hospitals.

Yes, people often assumed it was because he was a pilot. And there was that. How flight surgeons—and now the medical board—had the power to rip flying away from him. But the distant wail of sirens coming closer, the muted sounds of voices, the underlying hiss and ping of medical machinery whenever the automatic doors swung open, always pulled him back to visiting David after Griffin's cockiness caused him to crash a plane.

Griffin stood just inside the doorway, hands crammed into the back pockets of his jeans. Part of him hoped David was asleep. Would stay asleep. Then he could slip away. Avoid this conversation.

The air-conditioned climate of the Academy Hospital blocked out the warmth of the Colorado August afternoon. Through the window of David's room, Griffin could see dark clouds rolling in over the mountains, sure signs of the typical summer afternoon thunderstorms.

"Griffin." David's eyes opened, but even a nap couldn't erase the weariness, the pain lining his mouth.

Griffin walked into the room, the odor of antiseptic overpowering him. Get-well cards were taped to the wall opposite the bed. A bunch of multicolored balloons were tied to one of the arms of the white plastic hospital chairs in the corner. Griffin forced himself to make eye contact with his friend. If he stayed focused on David's eyes, he wouldn't notice the body brace . . . the Velcro . . . the straps . . . covering David's body.

Not much, anyway.

"How are you feeling today?"

"About the same, Griff. You?"

"Me? I'm fine. The docs say my collarbone will heal fast—in about six weeks."

A lot faster than David's broken back would heal.

"Great." David cleared his throat and then gave Griffin one of his familiar too-wide grins. "I'm doing rehab. It's a cinch—not even close to being as tough as Hell Week."

"No doubt. After surviving that, we can get through anything, right?"

David's reckless laugh seemed to dare anything to stop him. "Absolutely. Although the food back at Mitchell Hall beats the stuff here. And nobody back there threatens you with an enema—"

"*Dude—really? That's gross.*"

"*They tell me it'll be three months before they figure out if I'm commissionable or not. But I'll be walking across the stage in May to get my diploma with the rest of the class.*"

"*No doubt. Did they give you any limitations on what kind of plane you can fly?*"

"*They said if everything heals perfectly and I don't need a spinal fusion, that I'll be able to get in the cockpit.*"

Griffin stood beside the bed, one hand gripping the metal railing. "About the accident . . . I wanted to say . . . I knew better."

"*Hey, Griff. We both knew better. I shoulda had my seat belt on.*"

"*But I was the pilot . . . I was in charge.*"

"*Buddy, I'm not gonna let you take this all on yourself. It's gonna be okay. You'll see.*"

But it hadn't been.

David had *graduated from the Academy with his classmates. But while Griffin walked across the stage, David maneuvered his way across the stage in a wheelchair. Griffin forced himself to watch his friend, who ignored the standing ovation, knowing the only thing waiting for his friend was more surgery.*

He never called David after graduation, despite promises to keep in touch. What was there to say? He knew he ruined his friend's future—destroyed his dreams of being a pilot because the crash caused permanent nerve damage to his legs. There weren't enough words to cover that kind of mistake.

Movement off to the side caught Griffin's attention. Was it the nurse coming to get him so he could go be with Ian? He watched as she spoke to a woman waiting nearby, resting her hand on the woman's shoulder. *Looks like I'm in a holding pattern.*

CHAPTER TWENTY

★ ★ ★ ★

"Kendall, you need to get out front." Evie's words were high. Tight. "Now."

Kendall turned, slipping her arm through the sleeve of her white lab coat. "Is my first patient here already? I'm not late. Even doctors deserve to eat lunch every once in a while." She patted her pocket to ensure her stethoscope was there.

"He's here, but he's going to have to wait." Evie stepped into the office, shutting the door behind her.

"Why are you telling me to hurry up, then coming in here and shutting the door? Let's go." Kendall sidestepped the receptionist, but Evie blocked her from exiting.

"The police are here."

"What?"

"The police. And a dog. A drug-sniffing dog, Kendall."

Kendall yanked the door open, moving down the hallway. "What did they say?"

"They have a search warrant."

Kendall stopped, pressing her hands over her face. Inhaled. Exhaled. "Dear God, help me know what to do."

"They have a *warrant*, Kendall. They can search the place whether you want them to or not."

Right. She knew that. She couldn't bar the door to the back exam room area and tell them to leave.

She stood halfway to the front desk, trying to process what to do next. "How many patients are in the waiting room?"

"Three—four maybe." Evie waited for instructions, ignoring the ringing of the telephone.

"Let me think . . . let me think . . . Have Renee start calling patients and canceling appointments for the rest of the afternoon. Move them to tomorrow." *We will be open tomorrow, right?* She could only deal with what was happening right now. "I'll go talk to the police. You deal with the patients. It's apparent I won't be seeing anyone today." Why hadn't she taken the time to track down a lawyer? But she'd never imagined the police searching her office. "After the patients leave, try to reach Sonia. Her sister, Myrna, is a lawyer. Maybe she can give me some advice."

"Got it."

As her receptionist moved away, Kendall reached out and grasped her arm. "Wait, Evie."

"What else?"

Kendall held out her hand. "Pray with me? Please?"

She saw the woman hesitate. Knew she'd made her uncomfortable. "You don't have to say anything. I-I just need a hand to hold on to, you know? A friend . . ."

"Sure. I can do that part. Be your friend. You pray. I'll hold your hand."

Kendall grabbed Evie's hand. On second thought, she clasped

both of the woman's hands. "Dear God, help. Please. I know you haven't lost track of me today . . . you promise to never leave me or forsake me . . . but, God " Kendall sucked in a deep breath. "—there are police waiting to search my practice. Please protect me. Us. The patients. *Please*. Amen."

She squeezed Evie's hands. "Thanks. Okay here we go."

When she walked into the waiting area, the sight of two uniformed officers—a man and a woman—still surprised her. The man stood back, maintaining a firm grip on a leash attached to a German shepherd. A big dog that looked as if it was the one in charge.

"Good afternoon. I'm Dr. Haynes. What can I do for you, Officers?" Kendall decided it was best to keep some distance between her and the dog, so she didn't offer to shake hands.

"I'm Officer Walters. We have a warrant to search your office, Dr. Haynes." The woman, who was as all-business as the officer she'd talked to at the hospital, held out a document.

Kendall took it, unfolded the paper, and skimmed over it. Out of the corner of her eye she saw Evie talking with the patients sitting in the waiting room. "Could we discuss this in my office?"

"That's fine. But you do understand that we have a warrant—"

"My office is right back here." Kendall opened the door, hoping to forestall that announcement a third time. "Would you like something to drink?"

Or a bowl of water for your dog?

The officers followed her into the break room. "We're here on business, ma'am. The sooner we conduct our search, the sooner we leave."

"If I read this correctly, you're searching for illegal drugs?"

"Yes—we're trying to discover what may have caused Nicholas Wells's illness and subsequent hospitalization last weekend.

The report showed traces of cocaine and a significant amount of digitalis. The district attorney decided this was enough to launch an investigation."

"But I didn't—"

"You've not been named as a suspect at this time, Dr. Haynes. We're only here to conduct a search. Not discuss the case."

And it probably looked as if she was stalling. Guilty. Did they think her staff was hiding the evidence?

"Fine. I have nothing to hide."

Did all the criminals say that?

Kendall opened the break room door. "Go right ahead— wait. I had one patient in an exam room. Let me make certain he's gone."

A quick check proved that the medical assistants had dealt with the patients already there—assuring them that they would be called later tonight about follow-up appointments—and were calling the others due at the office later today. She could always have her nurse practitioner see anyone who couldn't wait later this evening. Evie was printing up a CLOSED FOR AN EMER- GENCY sign to post on the front doors. When Evie came running back down the hall, Kendall braced for more bad news. But what could be worse than having a large dog sniffing through her exam rooms while another officer rummaged through her prescription medicine cabinet?

Evie stopped in front of her, trying to catch her breath. "Re- porter."

"What?"

"There's a reporter from one of the news stations out front. I saw him getting out of his truck. He has a camera crew and everything."

"You're joking. Please, be joking." Kendall slumped against the wall.

"What do I do?"

Avoidance sounded wonderful. Run out the back entrance and go lock herself in her loft. She had enough food to last her a few days. And she could walk Sully in the middle of the night . . .

"Kendall?" Evie watched her.

"I'll talk to him."

"What are you going to say?"

"I have no idea."

She met the reporter as he came up the front walk to her office. Wind gusted around them, tugging at the man's windbreaker and red power tie. Kendall did a double take. Was he wearing . . . makeup?

"May I help you? Maybe find you an important story to cover?" Kendall would not allow the guy in her building to film the search. That's all she needed splashed all over the evening news.

"I'm looking for Dr. Kendall Haynes."

"I'm Dr. Haynes."

The man gave a snort of laughter. "Really? You look like you could be a medical student."

"I would invite you in and show you my medical school diploma, but I'm rather busy right now. Will you excuse me?" She opened the door to slip back inside.

"Ah, ah, ah, Dr. Haynes. I wanted to ask you a few questions." The man stepped in front of her, motioning the cameraman to move around.

Kendall crossed her arms over her chest, wishing she had on a pair of her heels, so she could stand a little taller during this face-off.

"Dr. Haynes, would you like to tell us how your patient is doing—the one who was hospitalized this past weekend because he took an illegal drug?"

"I don't discuss my patients. With anyone."

"But it is true that one of your patients was admitted to the hospital last Saturday because he'd taken some sort of illegal drug that he'd been given here?"

That wasn't a question. That was a statement—presuming her guilty.

"No comment."

"I couldn't help noticing the police car." Again, he motioned for the cameraman to pan the parking lot. "What are they searching for?"

"No comment."

"What's your relationship with Dr. Heath Parker, Dr. Haynes? An anonymous source said you and he were involved—until he broke it off. Is this your attempt to get back at him? Ruin his reputation?"

Kendall resisted the urge to knock the microphone out of the reporter's hand. "This non-interview is over. Good afternoon."

"But Dr. Haynes—"

Kendall enjoyed how the sound of the man's voice disappeared when she stepped back into the safety of the building. Then she remembered that a trained drug enforcement dog was sniffing around her office. Who was worse? The reporter or the dog?

★ ★ ★ ★ ★

Griffin sat beside Ian's hospital bed, thankful his brother slept. Now Ian lay curled up on his side, protected by the raised metal railings. His long hair was matted with sweat, and a nasal cannula fitted into his nostrils so that he still received oxygen. The kid had passed a rough night, between the breathing treatments, the chest X-rays—and Griffin reading him the riot act.

Maybe he should have saved that part for today.

But what was he supposed to do when Ian's friend, Tara, showed up at the ER to check on him? And then confessed that a group of teens had been smoking hookahs in her basement? Did his brother have no sense at all? Hookahs—with a chaser of nicotine for added fun.

Doug stopped by earlier that morning and prayed with him. Told him to not be so hard on himself.

Roger that.

Ian almost died on his watch—again.

Griffin pushed back, positioning the lounge chair so that it stretched out. The bedside monitor continued to emit a low beeping sound as it tracked Ian's pulse. He tugged the chain out from beneath his shirt, fisting his father's wedding band. If his parents were here . . . well, if his parents were here, Ian wouldn't be. And he wouldn't be in the hospital. He'd still be happy. Still have his family.

God, what were you thinking? Ian needed Mom and Dad. The kid's only sixteen . . . every boy needs his parents when he's sixteen.

But not at thirty-eight?

Griffin froze.

Where had that thought come from?

And no, he didn't need his parents like Ian still did . . . but he missed them . . . he wished he could call his father, ask for advice, hear him say, "You'll figure this out, son. I'm proud of you."

His father wouldn't be proud of him for some of the things he'd done.

But his dad loved him anyway.

And that was the more important thing. If he had to pick between his father being proud of him or loving him . . . he would choose his father's love. Because pride was based on performance. And love, well, love wasn't. Not from his dad anyway.

Here's the thing, Griffin. You're my son. Nothing can change that. I love you because you're mine. You don't have to do anything or be anyone to earn my love. It's yours.

The door to Ian's room opened, dissipating the sound of Griffin's father's voice.

Or was that God's voice?

As Griffin sat up, Kendall Haynes paused in the doorway.

"Kendall—"

"Griffin. Hi." She eased the door shut, muffling the clatter of a meal cart going by. She walked over to Ian, who continued to sleep. "I came to check on Ian."

"How did you know he was here?" Griffin walked to the foot of Ian's bed, watching as Kendall assessed his brother without waking him.

"I was checking on another patient. Someone asked if I was here to check on Ian Walker." Kendall walked around the foot of the bed, coming to stand next to Griffin, close enough for him to see the dark circles shadowing her eyes. "I told them no, because as far as I knew, your brother wasn't in the hospital."

"Can we talk about this out in the hallway?"

"Sure."

He followed Kendall back out of Ian's room, surprised at the immediate onslaught of noise. The shrill ring of a phone at the nurses' station. A muted conversation between a physician and a man and a woman standing outside the room just down from Ian's. The metallic sound of wheels rolling along the floor.

"Did it occur to you that I might want to know about Ian?" Kendall faced him, not wasting any time before launching an attack.

"Yes."

"And you didn't call because—?"

"Because the ER nurse said they'd call if you needed to be contacted."

"Thanks for that, Griffin." Kendall looked away, a sigh escaping through her pursed lips. "You couldn't have shoved me out of your life and slammed the door in my face any more effectively than that."

"Listen, I—"

"No, you listen. If you don't want to be friends, then . . . fine." There was the slightest pause, almost undetectable. "But I am still Ian's doctor until he leaves and I will always be *his* friend. Have you ever had a friend in the hospital? Wouldn't you want a call?"

His apology died in his throat.

She exhaled on a soft shudder, her fingers twisting her short hair into disarray. "I'll just go look at Ian's chart. Ask the nurses how he's doing. Let him know I stopped by, please."

"Do you want to talk to him?"

"No. He's exhausted after the night he had. I'll call him later, once he's home. I've got his cell number."

He wanted to say something. Find a reason to keep her here. But she was here only as Ian's doctor. And Ian's friend. Nothing more. "Thank you for checking in on Ian."

"You're welcome."

He waited for her to toss out another comment. Something to keep the conversation going. But Kendall took a few steps backward, then turned and made her way to the nurses' station.

He cleared his throat, as if to test it. Should he call her back? No.

CHAPTER TWENTY-ONE

★ ★ ★ ★

*S*he was not up for this.

Evie looked at Javan through the rearview mirror. He sat in his car seat, staring out the window as if the cars lining the parking lot were the most interesting sight in his six-year-old world. She should have left him home with Logan, deadline or no deadline.

"Come on, Evie. I need to make this conference call. Take Javan with you to the grocery store."

"He'll throw a fit."

"No, he won't. Help me out here, babe."

"I'll do it—but I know he'll hate every minute he's with me."

And so far, her prediction was coming true. Well, no tantrum yet. Instead, Javan ignored her. Bottom lip pushed out. Eyes focused on his tennis shoes. Shoving her hands away when she tried to buckle him into his car seat.

This would be a fun, fun trip to the grocery store.

As they entered the store, Evie muscled a cart from the long row waiting by the front doors. Did some employee jam carts together and then time customers to see how long it took them to get a cart separated from the gridlock?

"Come on, Javan. Time to get in."

"No. I wanna walk." Javan marched off, his stout legs stomping out the rhythm of his resentment.

Great. They'd be here forever. "Mamá wants you to ride in the cart, okay? You can watch my purse."

Javan never even looked back.

Score: Javan 1. Her 0.

Evie pushed the cart, catching up with Javan before he bypassed the produce section.

"We're going to get some fruit first, Javan. Turn right, niñito." She held her breath, letting it out in a relieved exhale when the little boy obeyed her. She double-stepped to keep up with him. "You want some apples?"

"Red ones."

"Red ones it is, then. Want to put them in the bag?" Evie pulled a plastic bag off the rack. "How about six? Can you count six?"

"Sure."

One by one, Javan dropped six apples into the bag. They moved from there to choose a bunch of bananas and some oranges.

"I wanna get cereal now."

"Cereal is all the way at the back of the store. I still need to get some salad stuff. We'll get that later."

"But I'm all out of Kix."

"I promise, we'll get some. It's on the list." Evie tapped her forehead and then moved the cart toward the bins of lettuce. "Come on this way with Mamá."

She gathered the different items for a green salad: romaine lettuce, red and yellow peppers, cucumber, red onion. Spying a container of sunflower seeds, she moved farther along to get that, too. What had she forgotten? Mushrooms. Logan always liked mushrooms in a salad. She turned back around . . . and realized Javan wasn't standing nearby.

"Javan?" She looked toward the grocery cart. Maybe he was in front of—no. From left to right, she scanned the produce section of the store. Where was he? "Javan?"

She took a few steps to the right. Stopped. Which way should she go. Right? Left? Stay here? Surely Javan couldn't have gone far.

"Javan?" This time she raised her voice a bit, in case he'd wandered an aisle over. A woman with short-cropped gray hair over by the pineapples made eye contact with her. "I'm looking for my son. He's six. Have you seen a little boy with curly black hair?"

The woman shook her head, her mouth curving in a sympathetic smile as she moved closer. "What is he wearing?"

What was Javan wearing? Evie closed her eyes. Tried to remember. "Jeans. A . . . an Iron Man shirt. My husband loves Iron Man. Tennis shoes—with Velcro. His name is Javan."

Why was she standing here talking to this woman? She had to find her son. She dashed over to the next aisle of the produce section. "Javan! Come here right now!"

Nothing. What should she do? Get a manager? Keep looking?

A touch on her shoulder caused Evie to whirl around.

"Ma'am, do you need some help?" A man wearing a black shirt and blue work apron stood next to the woman Evie talked to moments earlier.

"I've lost my son."

How could she have lost Javan?

"What's his name?"

"Javan." Evie described what the little boy was wearing. Again.

"Why don't you come to the front and we'll make an announcement—"

"No. No. I have to go look for my son—"

"We'll find him. If you're up front, we can bring him to you."

"I've got to find him."

Ignoring the employee's repeated request, Evie sprinted down the main aisle. She couldn't wait for someone else to find her son. As she passed each new aisle to her right, she paused, looked, hoping to see a little boy looking for his mamá. Looking for her.

"Help me, help me, help me . . ." Her words came out in short, whispered gasps.

Who was she talking to?

For the first time in her life, Evie wished she believed in God. Wished she could pray. Ask for help. Ask God to protect Javan. To find him. But she didn't believe in God. She had to do this herself.

"Javan!" She came to the end of the store aisles.

Nothing.

What to do now?

A man's voice sounded over the store intercom: "We have a Code Adam. A lost six-year-old boy with curly black hair wearing an Iron Man T-shirt, jeans, and tennis shoes."

Had someone taken her son? Grabbed him, dragged him from the store . . . she covered her face with trembling hands. She had to call Logan. He would know what to do. Panic roiled inside her, tumbling her thoughts around so fast she didn't know what to do. Find Javan. That's what mamás do—they keep looking until they find their little boys.

She turned left, running down the first aisle, not caring that she knocked into carts and caused other customers to step out of the way.

"Javan!"

The next aisle. Turn right. Run.

The next aisle. Turn right.

And there . . . there was Javan, his arms filled with three boxes of Kix, talking to an employee.

Evie didn't stop running until she dropped to her knees in front of Javan, the floor hard and cold. With a sob, she wrapped her arms around the little boy, crushing him to her, cereal boxes and all. Her tears wet his curls, her laughter and sobs mingled together in a melody of fear and relief.

"Where were you, niñito?"

"I wanted to get the cereal all by myself." Javan's voice quivered. "But I couldn't remember where the cart was. I couldn't find you."

Evie rocked him back and forth. "I found you, Javan. I found you."

"I'm glad. These boxes were heavy, Mamá."

Evie's breath stilled. Had he . . . ? Yes, Javan called her "Mamá."

Somehow, when she almost lost Javan, he found his way to her.

★ ★ ★ ★ ★

"You going to watch him sleep all night?" Logan's husky whisper caused Evie to turn her head so she could see him silhouetted against the hallway light.

"Maybe."

"I'd like some time with you, too, you know. What's a guy gotta do to get his wife's attention these days?"

"Just ask." Even as she answered her husband's question, her gaze returned to Javan. His Iron Man pajama bottoms were bunched up around his legs, the top twisted around his tummy. The scent of baby shampoo lured Evie close enough to plant a kiss on the soft curve of the little boy's cheek. With every inhale and exhale, Javan gave a soft, six-year-old snore.

"Come to bed with me, Mrs. Gardner?"

Evie rose to her feet, tiptoeing over to her husband and wrapping her arms around his waist. "You don't have to ask twice, Mr. Gardner."

Together, they walked down the hallway to their bedroom, switching off the hall light as they entered their room. Evie bit back a smile when Logan locked the bedroom door behind them. They learned the hard way that Javan thought nothing of opening a door without knocking.

She slipped underneath the soft cream-colored sheets, a sigh escaping her lips as she rested her head on Logan's broad chest. If she stayed still—quiet—she could hear the sound of her husband's strong heartbeat.

"You all right after today?" Logan's arm curled around her shoulders.

"Yes."

"After Javan got lost, I thought you'd be wired for sound—all strung out." His voice rumbled low in his chest as his fingers trailed through her hair.

"Believe me, I'm still on adrenaline overload. But I'm happy, too."

"Happy? You want to explain that to me?"

"Javan called me 'Mamá.' When I found him . . . he called me 'Mamá.'" She rolled onto her side, leaning on her elbow so she could look at her husband. "I can't say losing Javan was worth it . . . but Logan, the minute Javan said that, I could breathe again."

Logan tucked a long strand of hair behind her ear. "Why is the word so important?"

"You know my past . . . what happened when I was fifteen. Getting pregnant. Losing the baby—" The hot sting of unshed tears burned the back of Evie's throat.

"I told you, that doesn't matter to me, Evie."

"But it matters to me." Evie swallowed the salty taste of regret. "All these years staring at negative pregnancy tests. I started thinking maybe I'm not meant to be a mom."

"That's not how things work."

"It certainly seems as though Fate is trying to tell me something."

"So, Javan calling you 'Mamá' changes everything?"

"That and a conversation I had with one of Dr. Kendall's patients. I didn't tell you about that."

"You talk to all of Dr. Kendall's patients—" As if realizing this conversation was going on for longer than he anticipated, Logan repositioned his pillow and sat up, pulling her over so she rested against him again.

For a moment, Evie allowed herself to relax in the shelter of her husband's arms—the one place she felt safe.

"So who was this patient and what did you talk about?"

"His name is Ian. He's sixteen and he was adopted. He told me how he gave his adopted mom a lot of trouble at first and how she told him that she could love him longer than he could hate her." Evie clasped Logan's hand, weaving their fingers together. "He told me not to give up on Javan because he's already had one mom abandon him."

"Smart kid."

"I know."

"So does this mean you still want to adopt Javan?"

"Yes. I know it'll still be hard. And I may get discouraged again. But with you helping me, I know we can do this." Evie paused. "Dr. Kendall says she's praying for us, too. She knows I don't believe in God, but she still prays for me. I don't know why, but the thought of her praying for us . . ."

"It can't hurt."

"I know. And sometimes it feels like it helps."

★ ★ ★ ★ ★

Kendall expected an email. A phone call.

But she hadn't expected her sister, Bekah, to show up on her doorstep, unannounced.

"What are you doing here?" Kendall stood in her doorway, trying not to compare herself with her sister. Again.

But how could she not? Bekah wore her casual chic outfit as if she'd trademarked it. Skinny jeans paired with a fashionable pair of leather gladiator sandals, a sleek white top peeking out from underneath her pink jean jacket, with a fringed scarf decorated with rainbow-colored tiles flung around her neck as an afterthought. Her long black hair cascaded around her face, made up to accentuate her fawn-shaped eyes.

"Did I get you out of the shower or something? It is after ten." Bekah scanned Kendall's towel-wrapped body, wrinkling her nose at her sister's wet hair.

"No. I just finished swimming. Glad you knocked when you did. I was heading for the shower. Wouldn't have heard you."

Too bad she'd been perusing the news on her computer, hoping against hope that she no longer made the local news. At last, Heath Parker's name was getting more press than she was.

Sully scuffled around Kendall's bare feet, trying to see who was at the door.

"So . . . you probably want to come in. Let me get Sully settled." She grabbed the dog's collar and backed up, pulling the door open with her other hand. "Come on in."

Leaving her sister standing just inside the door, Kendall dragged Sully to her bedroom. While there, she took the time to slip out of her wet suit, towel off, and change into dry clothes. Jeans. A fuchsia-banded wrap top. A pair of white sandals. Nothing as fashionable as Bekah. Then she finger-combed her hair. Sully resisted being locked in her bedroom. But she couldn't handle her disobedient dog and her sister at the same time.

"Be quiet. I'll give you three dog treats if you be quiet. And a long walk . . . we'll both need it."

As she advanced down the hall to the living space, she breathed a short prayer. "Give me wisdom, God. Peace. The right words."

Kendall wasn't stupid—she knew what her sister wanted.

"So, Beks, I don't recall you mentioning a visit." Kendall went to the compact but efficient kitchen and began prepping her coffee machine. "Would you like some coffee?"

"Sounds good." Bekah followed her, leaning against the archway. "Ryan had a business trip and I decided to tag along. See the sights. Drop in on my big sister."

"Really?"

"Oh, don't worry. We're staying in separate rooms." Bekah rolled her eyes. "Not. But what Mom doesn't know . . ."

Please. She did not need to know the details of her sister's relationship.

"So, how are you doing?" Kendall filled the automatic coffee-maker with water and then flipped the switch on the machine before opening the see-through glass cabinet door and removing two pottery mugs.

"Good. Classes are winding down. I'll be so glad for the summer break. It's hard to focus on planning the wedding while I'm taking classes."

Kendall set the mugs on the small wooden table, adding a couple of teaspoons and a pair of cloth napkins. "So, has Ryan proposed?"

"Do you see a ring on my finger, Kendall?" Bekah lifted her left hand, waggling her slender fingers.

Kendall looked over her shoulder. No. No ring.

"That's why I'm here. I wanted to see if you'd come to your senses about giving me Mina's ring."

Well, there was nothing like getting right to the point. No need to wait for coffee. Or to pretend she wanted to spend time with Kendall.

"Ryan and I want to have a November wedding. But he can't propose without a ring—Mina's ring."

Kendall faced her sister, leaning her hip against the counter. "We've talked about this before, Beks. You *want* Mina's ring. You don't need it. Surely Ryan can afford to buy you a ring."

"Doesn't tradition mean anything to you, Kendall? Mina would never have left the ring to you except that you were always her favorite—always Dad's favorite."

"What do you know about my relationship with Mina? Or my relationship with Dad—"

"At least you had a relationship with them." Bekah flung the words across the room. "I don't even remember Mina. And Dad died when I was eight. You had ten more years with him than I did, Kendall. *Ten.* And he was always watching out for you, being so careful of you because of your asthma. Sometimes I lay awake in bed at night and wondered why you had asthma, and I didn't. I mean, how was I supposed to get Dad's attention?"

Kendall could only hope her mouth wasn't hanging open. Bekah *envied* her because she grew up struggling with asthma? As if days spent in the hospital were trips to Disneyland? As if not being able to go out for soccer or softball or even sing in the choir made for wonderful school memories? As if Kendall would have chosen to spend all those weekends in the garage with her dad instead of going out on dates?

Well . . . she would never give up those hours with her father. Back then there had been times when she wished the phone would ring. Wished she could erase the memory of the homecoming dance fiasco. But she tucked the memories of conversations with her dad, his laugh, his approving "Good job, Ken-girl" in her heart.

The sound of Bekah's shoes tapping against the cement floor jerked Kendall back to the present. Her sister grabbed a mug from the table and went to pour herself a cup of coffee. Apparently any heart-to-heart conversation was over.

"Kendall, stop being so stubborn. That ring is just sitting in the box somewhere—probably among your socks or underwear. Do you remember how old you are? That you've been all about your career for years?"

"Just because I'm not married now doesn't mean I won't get married—"

"We're not kids anymore, Kendall. Wishing doesn't make things so." Bekah found the sugar bowl and dumped a heaping spoonful of sugar into her coffee. "The reality is, I'm getting married. You're not. And that's the way it will probably stay. Me married. You single."

It didn't help that Kendall had stared down the reality for the last few days. It hadn't budged. She was single. And probably would stay single. Heath had played her. And Griffin . . . well, Griffin didn't love her. He liked her enough to confide in her. To kiss her senseless. But he didn't want to risk his heart with her. The two men's actions pummeled her heart. Would she curl up in a ball and die? No. But she didn't know when she would be ready to trust a man again.

If ever.

Kendall straightened her shoulders. "You're right, Bekah."

"I told Ryan that you're being—I . . . I am?" Her sister, who was ready to continue fighting for Mina's ring, stumbled into stunned silence.

"Yes. You are." Kendall flexed her hands. Open. Shut. Open. "Wait here."

As she exited the kitchen, she willed herself to stay focused. She wasn't doing this for real, was she? No, she wasn't.

Any minute now, she'd turn around. Go back to the kitchen. Tell Bekah she was happy for her, really she was, but she wouldn't, *couldn't*, give her Mina's ring. Kendall counted her steps to her room. She opened the door, ignoring Sully lounging on her bed with an *Uh-oh, you caught me* look on his furry face. She went to her dresser—not her underwear drawer—and retrieved the jeweler's box from where it sat among a pile of necklaces and bracelets. Sitting on her bed, she cupped the box in the palm of her hand.

She didn't need to flip back the lid. She had memorized the details of the ring. Every swirl and curve of the filigree design. The way the depths of the ruby glowed warm with promise when exposed to sunlight. How the white-gold band was worn, marked by the passage of time, as if carrying the memories of each day it had been on her Mina's hand.

She covered the box with her other hand, holding it close to her heart. Giving the ring to Bekah felt like she was breaking a promise . . . a promise she made to herself years and years ago. She'd done her best to be something, be someone valuable. Someone worth marrying.

And she was.

The truth stole her breath away.

Heath used her—but that didn't mean she didn't deserve a real relationship.

Griffin didn't love her . . . enough—but that didn't mean she wasn't worth loving.

She needed the right perspective on all those fairy tales Mina used to read to her. She needed the truth.

What if the prince had never shown up to rescue the princess from the castle, to release her from the spell?

The princess would have still been a princess.

She would have still been worth rescuing.

It wasn't the prince who made the princess valuable.

It was *who she was all along.*

For the first time in years, she remembered what Mina always said when she finished reading a fairy tale.

"You can live a fairy tale, too."

"How, Mina?"

"Listen to this Bible verse and tell me if it doesn't sound just like a fairy tale: 'For he rescued us from the domain of darkness and transferred us into the kingdom of his beloved Son.'"

"It does. It does."

"The wonderful thing is, Kendall, this story is true. For you. For me."

She'd already been chosen—already been worth rescuing. All Kendall had to decide was whom she was going to believe: the writer of a fairy tale? Or her Creator?

Kendall pressed a kiss to the faded velvet covering the jeweler's box.

Time to let go of trying to write her own life story. Time to embrace the life she'd been given. No, the life she'd made for herself. The life she'd been blessed with.

Time to let go of Mina's ring.

When she walked back out to the living room, Bekah faced away from her, looking out the windows at Pikes Peak.

"I thought you were crazy to combine your loft with your office." Bekah spoke over her shoulder.

"O-kay." Kendall waited, not sure how to respond.

"But I have to admit, this view is spectacular. And I love how open everything is."

"Thanks." She came and stood next to her sister. Offered her the box. "Here you go."

Bekah gasped. Bounced on her feet so that Kendall reached over and removed the mug from her sister's hands and replaced it with the jeweler's box.

She watched as her sister opened the box and did a happy jig in a circle. "Oh . . . oh . . . oh. It's as beautiful as I remember."

Kendall held the mug up high in the air as Bekah leaned in for a hug. "Hot coffee, remember?"

"Oh, right." Bekah giggled, stepped back, and then slipped the ring on her finger.

That hurt a little.

"Look. Isn't it perfect?" Bekah held her hand up for Kendall to admire.

Kendall swallowed the lump forming in her throat. No tears. Not now. "Yes. It's perfect for you."

"Ryan told me that you'd never give up the ring. But I told him I'd be able to convince you." Bekah twisted her hand back and forth. "I can't wait to show him."

"Well, why wait? You two should celebrate. Maybe start planning the wedding."

Within ten minutes, Bekah was gone. Mission accomplished.

Kendall walked back to her room, letting Sully out. She walked over to the bookcase, looking at the shelf filled with the fairy tales.

Maybe it was time to do something with those, too.

CHAPTER TWENTY-TWO

★ ★ ★ ★

"It's not official, but it might as well be."

Griffin sat across from Doug, testing the words as he said them out loud. "The flight surgeon who examined me said, and I quote, 'Don't plan on flying anytime soon.'"

He'd spent the last week back at the School of Aerospace Medicine in Texas having another medical evaluation. When the physician asked if he was still experiencing vertigo, he answered honestly—knowing how saying yes would affect the medical board's decision. He was tempted to call Kendall, talk it all out with the only doctor he ever considered a friend.

Or did he just want to hear her voice again? Recapture the comfort he'd felt when she held him after he told her about the plane crash?

He didn't try to figure out the real reason why he stared at his phone, debating whether to call Kendall Haynes or not. Because, in the end, he tucked the phone away, along with that desire.

Once he got back to Colorado, he drove straight from the airport to his former sponsor's house without bothering to call. With Ian back in Florida with the Jamisons, there was no reason to go home. No one to go home to. Griffin now sat outside on Doug's back deck, a glass of fresh-squeezed lemonade chilling his hand. If he wasn't facing the end of his career, he would have enjoyed the view of Doug's xeriscaped backyard, light on the grass and heavy on rocks and gravel and plants that didn't require a lot of water.

"So. How are you feeling?" Doug settled into the bright yellow Adirondack chair next to him, placing a plate of sliced watermelon on the matching wooden table between the two chairs. "Relieved to finally know where you stand?"

Relieved?

"I'm resigned. I'll do this assignment and retire. Figure out what I do after that." Griffin tasted the lemonade, the sweet-sour tang reminiscent of his life—although right now his future had most definitely soured.

"Might as well say what you're thinking. God knows. Care to share with me?"

"Why did God say no to this? I'm a pilot. It's all I've trained for—all I've done." Griffin stood and walked across the deck, turning to lean against the wooden railing and look at his friend. "This decision—my still having vertigo—doesn't make sense."

"Have you ever considered God was using the vertigo to get your attention, maybe even to redirect your life?"

"It's vertigo—not some sort of sign-toting angel."

"Agreed. But God can use anything—even vertigo—to get your attention."

Griffin considered this. "I'm listening."

"I agree with you that it doesn't make sense that you're not flying—and that you may not fly again. But you've done every-thing you can to stay in the cockpit, including hide the vertigo in the first place." Doug stood and came to stand next to him. "For some reason God closed the door on flying. The question is, are you willing to look around and see what door is open?"

"I hate to think that the job at Schriever is all there is. This is quite a trade-down."

"It's a job. Be thankful for that. I have a good friend who's been out of work for five years."

"When you put it that way, I guess there is something worse than not flying." He drained his lemonade, handing Doug his glass. "Thanks for listening. Again. I think I'm going to go for a drive. Think some things out."

"Sounds good."

Griffin climbed into his Jeep—and sat. He still didn't want to go back to the empty town house. The idea of calling Kendall crossed his mind again. Maybe she'd want to go four-wheeling?

Right.

He told her there couldn't be anything between them. And she no doubt believed him. There was no way Kendall knew how often he thought about her.

The afternoon stretched before him. Empty. If Ian were here . . . but he'd been in Florida for ten days. And Griffin was man enough to admit he missed his brother.

The sun beat down on his shoulders as he pointed the Jeep toward the Air Force Academy. Since being assigned to Schrie-ver, he hadn't gone to the Academy, not even to buy groceries at the commissary. It was easier to shop at the nearest grocery store. He hadn't been back since . . . well, graduation. Never made time for any of his class reunions.

Twenty minutes later, after a leisurely drive up winding two-lane roads on the western edge of the Air Force Academy, Griffin pulled into the parking lot near Harmon Hall, where the superintendent's offices were located. Pocketing his keys, he strolled onto the plaza area, noting the long lines of marble stones, replicating the strips down on the cadet terrazzo below. Memories flashed through his brain: walking the terrazzo to classes and meals as a doolie—a freshman—and being limited to traveling along the one-person-wide white marble strips that divided the area into twenty-eight-foot squares flashed through his brain.

Tourists milled around the plaza, stopping to look at the different memorials. Sculptures of different planes, of eagles in mid-flight, even a life-sized sculpture of General Harmon, the first Academy superintendent. A breeze swept over him, reminding him of walking to classes in all sorts of weather. Rain. Snow. High winds.

Griffin stood, training his eyes on the Cadet Chapel towering above him, the seventeen aluminum and glass spires pointing upward against the brilliant blue Colorado sky reminiscent of the outline of jets. He never attended services at the chapel as a cadet. The only times he entered the doors were for his wedding rehearsal and the actual thirty-minute ceremony.

He and Tracey graduated one day. Married the next.

Graduate. Get married. Go to flight school. He shoved the failure of his marriage and the consequences of his choices behind him, in the same place he put memories of David and the plane accident. And kept moving forward.

And somehow until the vertigo brought him to his knees, Griffin convinced himself he was living his dreams.

He lied to himself.

Griffin walked over to the low stone wall surrounding the plaza, leaning on it so he could look down on the terrazzo twenty feet below. And now, here he was, back where all those dreams started. And what did he have to show for it?

Nothing.

Really, God? I've got nothing?

Yes, his marriage failed—but he had tried to make it work, even sacrificing being a father.

Yes, he was still on nonflying status. But he had lots of great assignments and experiences that most people never dreamed about.

Yes, his parents were gone. But he knew they loved him—and that they trusted him with Ian.

He assumed he would always be a pilot. Once a pilot, always a pilot. And when he allowed God into his life, he assumed that was God's plan for his life, too. But maybe it wasn't about the job. Maybe it was about relationships. And God had to take the job out of the way to get Griffin to realize that.

Was God trying to get past all the stuff that Griffin thought made him "worthy" so he would realize God wasn't condemning him—or even accepting him—for who he had been in the past?

What was that verse he'd scrawled inside the flap of his Bible? *While we were still sinners, Christ died for us.*

God loved him when he was making all those wrong choices—and God would still love him if he made a wrong choice now. But even more important, Griffin needed to see where God was leading him now.

Which brought him back to his brother.

Yes, in the past, he had made no attempt to get to know Ian.

Yes, Ian was twenty-two years younger than he was.

But they were brothers. And, with God's help, they could be family.

God, what's the right thing to do? For me? For Ian? I asked him to stay—and he still left.

He could always ask Ian to come home again. But first he had to think of a way to get his brother talking to him. So far, every one of his phone calls to Ian had been ignored, rolling over to voice mail. Calling wasn't going to cut it.

Griffin pulled his keys from his pant pocket as he headed back to his Jeep. He raised his hand, noticing one particular key. His brother may not want to talk with him—but Griffin did have something Ian wanted.

His Jeep Cherokee.

CHAPTER TWENTY-THREE

★ ★ ★ ★ ★

Griffin was either making a fool of himself or he was finally going to convince Ian that he wanted a real relationship with him.

Either way, Ian would have his Jeep.

Griffin waited on the Jamisons' wraparound front porch, the air thick with Florida humidity and the scent of Mrs. Jamison's hanging flower baskets, bright splashes of color at evenly spaced intervals along the length of the porch. His body ached from the two-day, sixteen-hundred-mile car trip. Once he talked with Ian, he needed a shower to wash the grime from his body before snagging some sleep and then figuring out his flight home.

The front door opened, and his brother joined him on the porch.

"Griffin? What are you doing here?"

"Hey, Ian." Griffin dared to wrap his arms around his brother in a quick hug. "Pardon the road funk. I've been driving since Wednesday afternoon."

Ian pushed him away with a groan. "No kidding. And you were always telling me to shower."

"All in good time." He gave Ian a quick once-over. "You look good."

His brother shoved his hands in his pockets, bare feet sticking out from his jeans, a green tank top hanging on his thin frame. Had he gotten taller?

"So what's going on, Griffin? Everything okay?"

"Well, yes and no. I'm probably going to still be inactive as far as flying goes."

"That's tough."

"Yeah, well, the air force doesn't really want a guy with vertigo handling their A-10s, ya know?" Griffin shrugged. "But that's not why I'm here."

"I didn't think so."

"I want to ask you to come home." He rushed ahead, stopping Ian from responding. "Hear me out, please. We're family, Ian. And Mom and Dad wanted us together—but even more than that, I want a chance to get to know you. To really be your brother. And I want to do it right this time. We can get whatever you want out of storage—furniture, pictures—and haul it back to Colorado. I'm tired of living in an empty house."

Ian stepped back, folding his arms, not a sign of enthusiasm on his face. "Why are you doing this now, Griffin?"

"Because I've finally got my head on straight. And I can see how wrong I've been. And because I miss you, Ian." He had to do one thing before his brother answered him. "I did come to Florida for one other reason."

"What?"

"You forgot something." Griffin pulled the key to the Jeep

Cherokee from his pocket and dangled it before his brother. "You forgot this."

Now he had his brother's attention. Griffin stepped past Ian and pointed down the street. "It goes to that."

When he saw his Jeep, Ian let out a whoop that brought Mac and his two sisters—*what were their names?*—out on the front porch. By that time, Ian was off the porch and running across the lawn.

Mac watched his friend climb into the front seat of the Jeep, a huge grin spreading across his face. "You're here to take him back to Colorado, aren't you?"

"If I can convince him to come home with me."

"You won't have to convince him. He talks about you all the time, Mr. Walker."

"He does?"

"Yeah. He even says he might want to be an air force pilot like you." Mac moved away. "Good talking with you. I want to go get a look at this cool Jeep. See if your brother will let me drive it."

"Good luck with that."

Griffin stood on the porch and watched Mac badger Ian about driving the Cherokee. So far it looked as if the answer was no.

"I wondered how long it would take you to get out here." Mrs. Jamison stood beside him, offering him a glass of iced tea, probably sweetened as only real Southerners could make it. In a pair of capris and a casual cotton top, she reminded him of his mom.

"What do you mean?"

"When I called back to say we'd take Ian, I wasn't completely honest with you." The woman smiled as she listened to the two boys laugh together. "My husband and I prayed about your request, just as you asked us to do. And I got a clear answer. We were to take Ian—but only until you realized Ian was supposed to be with you. Permanently."

"Huh."

"God didn't tell me how long that would take. But let me put it this way: I haven't enrolled Ian in school for the fall."

"You're a wise woman, Mrs. Jamison."

"My husband says the same thing, Griffin." She gave him a slow wink, her eyes brimming with laughter. "I'm wise enough not to disagree with him, either."

★ ★ ★ ★ ★

Had he ever felt this tired—and this happy at the same time?

Griffin walked into his townhome, dropping his olive-green helmet bag onto the floor right inside the door. He'd deal with unpacking later. Right now, he wanted to crawl into bed and forget about the past four days. A road trip. Thirty-six hours with Ian, planning his return home. A flight back into the Springs and then a taxi ride home.

And in two weeks, he'd be flying back out to Florida, loading up a U-Haul with whatever Ian wanted out of storage, and making one fast trip back to Colorado. But with Mac and his dad helping drive, they'd manage it in a long weekend.

To fill the silence in the house, Griffin grabbed the remote and turned on the TV. The local news anchor appeared on the screen.

"Coming up, the latest on the investigation involving two local physicians, Dr. Kendall Haynes and Dr. Heath Parker. One cleared. One charged. More when we come back."

What? That Dr. Kendall Haynes can't be my Kendall Haynes. Who's been charged? With what? Who's been cleared?

Griffin sat and waited for the news to restart, barely hearing the ads for local car dealerships and the upcoming Sky Sox double-header. When the news team reappeared, he turned up the volume and leaned forward.

"Here's the latest on the story we first reported to you two weeks ago. Dr. Kendall Haynes, a local family physician and allergy/asthma specialist, has been cleared of all allegations related to the alleged poisoning of one of her pediatric patients that caused a life-threatening reaction."

Griffin watched as a professional-looking photo of Kendall flashed across the screen.

"Our investigation has shown that Dr. Heath Parker, an infectious disease specialist who recently moved to Colorado Springs after five years in Africa, is being charged with providing a dangerous substance to a minor, nearly causing his death. Police believe Dr. Parker accessed Dr. Haynes's medical records to obtain patients' names and contact information to recruit them as unknowing test subjects for an unapproved imported supplement purported to improve immunities."

The scene on the TV flashed to a video clip of a man identified as Dr. Heath Parker, brushing past a reporter trying to ask him questions.

"According to the police report, the supplement is being investigated for possible traces of cocaine and digitalis, a drug used to treat certain heart diseases, but found naturally in the foxglove plant. We will keep you updated on this story. In other news—"

Griffin muted the TV and threw the remote on the couch, going to retrieve his phone off the counter. He dialed Kendall, not even taking time to think about what he was going to say to her.

She answered on the second ring. "Dr. Haynes here."

"Kendall, it's Griffin."

Silence.

"Are you all right?"

"In regards to what?"

"I've been out of town. I just turned on the TV and heard about some investigation—"

"Oh. That. That's old news, Griffin. Why are you calling?"

"I was concerned . . . I've thought about you a lot these past couple of weeks . . . thought about calling you, but I didn't—"

"I see. Thanks for that. And you're calling now because . . . ?"

Why was he calling now? Because he hadn't stopped to think. Not that he could tell Kendall that.

"Wouldn't you call a friend if you thought they were in trouble?"

"Don't play the 'friend' card, Walker. The way you left it between us, there wasn't much of a friendship."

"About that. Kendall—"

"Look, I really need to take Sully for a walk."

Ouch. She might as well have told him she needed to wash her hair.

"I'll call you later then?"

"Sure, Griffin. Whatever."

"So in about an hour?"

"What?"

"I'll call you back in about an hour."

"Um, no, that's not good for me."

Griffin paced the length of the living room. "So when is a good time to talk?"

"How about I call you back when it's a good time for me to talk to you?"

"Look, Kendall, I wanted to tell you that I'm sorry. And that Ian's coming back and—"

"I've got to go, Griffin."

"Okay. Call me?"

"Bye."

★ ★ ★ ★

CHAPTER TWENTY-FOUR

*M*aybe one day, Griffin would no longer think of a doctor's office as enemy territory.

"Dr. Haynes will be with you soon, Colonel Walker." Liz stood in the doorway to the exam room, one hand resting on the doorknob, one hand holding a blood pressure cuff. "Are you certain you don't want me to check you in? Take your vitals?"

"I'm good. I just need to talk with Dr. Haynes."

As the medical assistant abandoned him, Griffin could only hope Kendall would listen to him.

Instead of sitting down, he paced the tight confines of the room, skirting the exam table. On one wall hung a mountain scene, golden aspens dotting the landscape as if someone had tossed handfuls of gold coins across the slopes. On the opposite wall several framed certificates declared Kendall Haynes an outstanding resident three years in a row. The woman didn't lack for awards.

Griffin froze as the door opened behind him with a soft click. Caught.

"We didn't have a chance to talk when you arrived, Colonel Walker—"

But not by Kendall. Her receptionist, Evie, entered the room.

"Please, call me Griffin." Griffin twisted his neck left then right, trying to shift the invisible weight knotting his shoulders and neck.

The woman's smile lit up her dark brown eyes. "Griffin it is. I wanted to let you know that Kendall doesn't know you're here."

"How did you pull that off?"

"I put a false name in the schedule. She thinks you're a new patient—that's why you have forty-five minutes. And why you're scheduled at the end of the day." Her gaze seemed to weigh his character, estimating his ability to pull this off. "I hope you realize my job is riding on your conversation with my boss."

"Your job. My future. There's a lot at stake."

Was the room getting smaller? Maybe the medical assistant should check his blood pressure.

"I need to get back up front." Evie gave him a thumbs-up and another grin. "I'm rooting for you."

"Sure you are. You don't want to lose your job."

"I want Dr. Kendall to be happy." Evie paused as she left the room. "You are going to make her happy, right?"

"That's the plan. Here's hoping your boss goes along with it."

Left alone again, Griffin sat in a cloth chair positioned across from the door. Stood and walked a slow, small semi-circle around the room, which took all of ten seconds. Sat again.

He'd waited three days for Kendall to call him—and realized she probably never would. Which meant going behind enemy lines to convince her that he was her friend—a friend who'd fallen in love with her.

Relax, Walker, relax. You're not here for a physical.

True, but doctors and flight surgeons wielded too much power over his future. Did he fly? Didn't he fly? Final answer, thanks to the medical board: He didn't. And today yet another physician would determine his future. He would lay his heart on the line for Dr. Kendall Haynes and let her decide what happened next.

Griffin wrapped his fingers around the gold chain hanging around his neck, his father's wedding band hidden against his heart beneath his blue polo shirt.

God, help me do this right. Help me tell Kendall how I feel. Don't let her kick me out of her office. Don't let her fire Evie . . .

He stopped mid-prayer as the door swung open halfway. Kendall spoke to someone standing outside.

"I'm going to see Mr. Smith—"

Mr. Smith? That's the best Evie could come up with?

"—but let me know if you get those lab reports back on Lily."

Griffin stood as Kendall walked into the room, releasing the gold chain, prayer unfinished. Her usual white lab coat with the Rocky Mountain Family Practice logo covered a casual dark dress. She held out her hand to greet him.

"I'm Dr. Kendall . . . *Griffin?*"

He hadn't realized how much he missed her until only a few feet separated them. Her eyes widened, searching his face as if trying to make sure she wasn't seeing things. A thin band of dark purple ribbon adorned her short-cropped hair. He knew he needed to take things slow—talk first in the hopes of earning the right to kiss her later. But all Griffin wanted to do was bridge the space separating them and pull her into his arms.

"Kendall."

Her name came out sounding husky, as if he had a cold. He cleared his throat, knowing he needed to talk fast or she would think he conned his way into an appointment so he could get a medical checkup.

"What are you doing here? Where's Mr. Smith?" Kendall peered around him as if expecting to find someone else lurking behind the exam table.

"I'm Mr. Smith."

"No, you're not." She looked at the clipboard that held the papers for Mr. Smith. Looked back at him. "What's going on?"

Griffin approached her, surprised when Kendall took a step back.

"You didn't call me back. And I needed to see you." He took another step toward her.

"Why?" She stepped back again.

"To clear things up." Step forward.

"Why?" Step back.

"Because I made a mistake." Step forward.

"What?" Step back—right into the closed door.

Fine. Now they could stop the evasive maneuvers and talk things out. Griffin took another step toward Kendall and reached around her to lock the door.

"What are you doing?" Kendall grabbed his hand. "This is my office. And you aren't able to lock the door."

So much for blocking her exit. "Fine. Evie knows you're in here. She also knows why I'm here. And I know I have a forty-five-minute appointment. Which gives us plenty of time to talk."

Only now he talked to the top of Kendall's head because she refused to look at him. Instead, she stared straight ahead, right at mid-chest.

"I am going to dock her pay."

They stood so close to each other, Kendall's words were muffled against him.

"She was afraid you were going to fire her."

"I just might do that." She pushed against his chest. "Back off, Walker, you're crowding me."

Griffin took both her hands, holding them near his heart. "Kendall, hear me out."

She refused to look at him. So close and yet so far away. He was going down fast.

When he knelt in front of her, a small gasp escaped Kendall's lips. "What are you doing?"

"I need to say some things, and I want to look you in the eye when I say them."

Pulling her hands away from his, she tugged at his shoulders, "Stand up, Griffin. This is ridiculous."

"Not until I say what I came here to say." Griffin never imagined himself kneeling at this woman's feet, but he'd stay there all day if he had to. He gathered her hands in his again. "Kendall Haynes, the first time we met, you rescued my brother. I didn't know you were going to rescue me. I didn't know how much I need you in my life. Falling in love with you was so unexpected. I don't even like doctors." That admission won him a small smile. "Until you. You challenge me with your strength. You heal me with your gentleness. You made me believe in me again . . . in the possibility of love again."

Kendall's eyes searched his face. "Why are you saying all this now?"

"I realized how much I love you. How much I need you. Life without you is . . . wrong."

He wasn't sure how Kendall would react to what he said next, but he had to finish what he started.

"Kendall, I know we have things to figure out. Ian's coming back to live with me. The fact that I can't have children hasn't changed—"

One minute he was talking, his words tumbling over one another in a rush to get past all the reasons Kendall shouldn't marry him. The next minute she leaned down, her fingers tightening against his, and whispered, "Stop talking."

★ ★ ★ ★ ★

Why was Mr. Strong and Silent a talker all of a sudden?

Enough words already. The man was driving her crazy.

It didn't take a doctor to diagnose how Griffin's heart rate increased when she lowered her lips to his. Kissing Griffin Walker was a heady mixture of controlled passion and the comfort of finding safety after too many nights alone.

Kendall missed him even more than she realized. The way his strength steadied her as he wrapped his arms around her and pulled her close against his chest. The way his love knocked her off balance even as it grounded her. This was where she was meant to be: loving Griffin Walker.

He ended the kiss only to press warm lips against the pulse beating just below her ear, then rested his head in the hollow of her neck. She stood in his embrace, eyes closed, overwhelmed by the reality that Griffin had come back. For her.

"Hey, Doc—" His voice rumbled against her ear. Low. Husky.

"Yes, Mr. Smith?" She couldn't keep the hint of laughter out of her voice.

"I love you."

"I love you, too." Oh, the freedom to say those words.

"And I want to marry you." He held her closer, if that was even possible.

"If that's a question, my answer is yes."

He pulled away from her, just enough so that he could look at her. "Before you answer me, think about what you're agreeing to, Kendall. I can't have kids."

"I know that."

"It's not that I don't want kids. I do. We can—"

"You're ruining the mood here, Walker." She placed her hands on either side of his face. "Focus. Proposal."

"I just want to make sure you know what you're getting when you say yes."

"I do know. I'm getting you. And Ian, of course. And whatever else God has planned for us. And he promises that his plans for us are good."

A knock on the door interrupted their conversation.

"Dr. Kendall?"

Kendall buried her face in Griffin's shoulder with a groan. "That's Renee. It's probably about the labs . . ."

Griffin refused to release her. "Tell her to come back. Tell her you're giving me a thorough physical."

"Don't be ridiculous." Just the thought made her knees go weak. "By now Evie's told everyone just who 'Mr. Smith' is."

"Fine. Then tell her that I haven't finished kissing you yet."

"That's enough, Griffin." Kendall slipped out of his arms, sidestepping his attempt to kiss her again. She motioned to the chair across the room. "Go sit over there. Behave."

Kendall straightened the collar of her lab coat before opening the exam room door. The sight of her entire staff waiting for her brought her up short.

"Do you have the results I was waiting for?"

"Yes. Paul handled them." Renee tried to conceal a smile—and failed. "Do you need any help with Mr. Smith?"

"No, no. I can take care of Mr. Smith myself."

Evie stood at the back of the group, biting her bottom lip. "Am I fired?"

"I'm not certain what I'm going to do about this—and your part in it, Evie." She paused half a second before giving her receptionist a slow wink. "I just may give you a raise."

From behind her, Griffin came, took her hand, and pulled her back into the office. Before shutting the door, he said, "I'm going to insist she give you a raise, Evie. A good one."

★ ★ ★ ★ ★

A star-filled sky. Griffin Walker. And an after-dinner drive in his Jeep up Gold Camp Road.

Romance came wrapped in all sorts of unexpected packages.

Dinner? Sharing barbecued ribs at Griffin's favorite restaurant. This, despite jet lag tugging at her eyelids, insisting she give into her body's demands for sleep after a nonstop, week-long celebration with Rachel, Sonia, and Melissa. Who knew the women had no intention of sleeping while they were in Mexico? Instead, the trio interrupted every single Skype session with Griffin, dragging her off to parasail or snorkel or hike to some ancient ruin.

Tonight's after-dinner activity? Stargazing while wrapped in Griffin's arms as they stood in his Jeep, taking advantage of the fact that he'd removed the soft top. The entire expanse of the sky stretched over their heads.

"You comfortable?" Griffin snuggled her up closer to his body, careful to keep them balanced as they stood on the backseat.

Kendall leaned against him, her head resting against his chest. Inhaled the heady mixture of the crisp night air and Griffin's appealing clean scent of soap. She'd have to make sure to find out his preferred brand and stock up on it. "Couldn't be better."

"I missed you." He rested his chin on the top of her head.

"So you said—every time we Skyped." She turned and kissed his scruffy jaw—just because she could. And because she wanted to. "Speaking of Skyping, the girls interrupted us right when you were going to tell me the significance of your tattoo."

"Really? My tattoo?"

"I'm curious." Kendall settled back in his arms. "I want to know why the man I love would get some kind of freaky-looking wolf-dog-beast-thing tattooed on his back."

"It's not that big a deal."

"Then tell me."

Griffin exhaled a sigh. "Since it's so important to you. The tattoo is of my Academy cadet squadron's emblem. We were Third Squadron, called Cerberus Three. In Greek mythology, Cerberus was a three-headed dog that guarded the gates of the underworld."

"And you got this tattoo because—?"

"Some of my friends and I decided to celebrate 'Hundreds Night'—that's when we have one hundred nights before graduation—by getting the tattoo. End of story. Satisfied?"

"One more question."

"Mmm-hmm?"

She tilted her head to try and make eye contact with him. "You planning on getting any more tattoos?"

"Nope. I'm good." He brushed a soft kiss across her lips. "You know, this is one of the few times we've been together in my Jeep that it hasn't broken down."

"Thanks to my mechanical skills."

After Griffin's chuckle faded, they stood in silence for a few moments, the shadows of the night sealing their embrace. An owl hooted somewhere in the distance as an invisible breeze rustled the nearby evergreen branches.

"Look at that!"

Griffin pointed to an arcing point of light streaking across the night sky. Before it disappeared, he reached up his hand, closing his fingers as if he'd grabbed hold of something.

"Got it."

She could hear his smile as he held his closed hand up in front of them. "Got *what?*"

"A falling star." With his left hand, he turned her left hand over, prompting her to hold her hand open, palm up. Then he placed his fist in the palm of her hand, before taking her other hand and covering them both with his left hand.

"When I was a little boy, my dad told me that if you catch a falling star before it disappears, it's yours to keep." He leaned close so he could whisper in her ear. "I'll share it with you."

His words brought tears to her eyes even as laughter spilled over her lips. "Griffin—"

"You want to see what a falling star looks like?"

Griffin moved her top hand away from his and then un-folded his fingers. In the darkness, she could see the outline of a ring on the palm of his hand.

"Griff—"

It was as if Griffin had reached up and plucked the jewel from the stars strewn across the cobalt-blue sky and somehow formed it into a ring. If she touched it, would it disappear?

"This is the magic of catching a falling star." Griffin's words, spoken low, served only to deepen the feeling of an enchanted moment for just the two of them. He slipped the ring, warm from being held in his hand, onto her finger. "It can turn into a dream come true. This was my mother's engagement ring. I remember how she said that when my father put it on her finger she found something better than a fairy tale."

The ring was a mere outline of a band and the glint of a jewel.

"My mom was a woman of strength and gentleness—like you." Griffin lifted her hand and placed a warm kiss where his offering rested. "It's an emerald, surrounded by diamonds."

"I'm sure it's exquisite—and I'll treasure it because it was your mother's ring."

"I can't do this properly and kneel, since we're in the Jeep. But Kendall, I couldn't be more serious. Will you—"

"Yes."

"I didn't finish."

"My answer is still yes. Now stop talking."

"You always gonna be this bossy?"

"Only when I need to be."

Kendall turned in his arms, her hands sliding across the soft material of his cotton shirt, and then holding on as his kiss overwhelmed her. His tenderness left her completely undone—an intoxicating mixture of wanting the kiss to last forever and needing to pull away to catch her breath. Loving Griffin Walker would always be a dizzying adventure of falling in love, following where God led them . . . and believing, no matter what, that they were each other's oh-so-unexpected dream come true.

ACKNOWLEDGMENTS

★ ★ ★ ★

My husband, Rob: Thank you for never once asking, "Why don't you cook anymore?" And thank you for being an amazing brainstorming partner. You're really good at helping me think out loud, you know? And thanks, too, for answering all my medical questions—the fictional ones for the book, I mean.

My kiddos, including my daughter- and sons-in-love: Thank you for accepting that your mom is a writer, which means y'all cook dinner when I don't. And thanks for cheering me on. It's a wonderful thing for a mom to embrace the support of her children.

Rachel Hauck, aka "Mentor Mine": There came a time during the writing of *Catch a Falling Star* when I said you were either going to make me a better writer—or you were going to kill me in the trying. Well, I'm still alive. Thank you for pushing me past myself. I treasured every email, every Facebook comment, every phone call—and especially the times we Skyped! Let's do it again, shall we?

Susan May Warren: Thank you for locking the doors when I thought about abandoning the Dark Side of the writing road and escaping back to the familiarity of nonfiction. Whenever I doubt myself, I hear your voice in my head saying, "You can write fiction, Beth." Your encouragement keeps me going when I want to quit.

The My Book Therapy Core Team (Alena, Edie, Lisa, Melissa, Michelle, Reba): Every writer needs a "safety net"—the people who talk her off the ledge when she feels like jumping. Each one of you represents a strand of "safety" for me.

My "Spiritual Ground Support" (Barbara, Shari, and Sonia): Thanks for praying for me as I wrote *CAFS*. Being able to send the three of you emails saying, "Here's what I need this week . . ." made such a difference for me. You gave me hope—and laughter, too. Lots of laughter.

Angela Gainer: A conversation with you was the catalyst for *Catch a Falling Star*. Thank you for being my friend . . . and for sparking this story idea.

Sonia Meeter, my "Preferred Reader": Thank you for being my first set of eyes on this story—for letting me know when it worked, and when it didn't. Without your insights I wouldn't have been able to write Evie's part of the story.

Rachelle Gardner: You've taught me that an agent is an invaluable resource of professional, advisor, mentor, and friend. When someone asks who represents me, I am always proud—and oh so grateful—to say you.

Holly Halverson: I went into edits of *CAFS* with confidence, knowing you were on the team.

The team at Howard Books (Beth Adams, Jessica Wong, Bruce Gore, and Laura Jorstad): Thank you for continuing to support my dream—and always answering my questions! I love telling people I'm a Howard Books author.

Doug Moore: I wanted a Jeep guy and a Jeep gal for this book—but what did I know about Jeeps? *Nothing.* Thanks for answering all my Jeep questions. Any mistakes in the manuscript are mine and mine alone. And, yeah, now I want a Jeep.

Warren Priddy: Years ago you crashed through my preconceived notions about pilots and showed me how a man of faith can also fly jets. Thanks to you and Francie for helping me make Griffin Walker come to life on the page.

★ ★ ★ ★ ★

catch a falling star

Beneath her smart, sassy exterior, Dr. Kendall Haynes is wrestling with the reality that life isn't turning out exactly like she imagined. But she's not the only one facing off with this unpleasant truth. A "chance" encounter with Griffin and Ian Walker on her thirty-sixth birthday leads her down an unexpected path that slowly unearths the tenderness of her heart. *Catch a Falling Star* is a story about hope in the midst of despair, honesty in the midst of pain, and courage in the midst of uncertain odds.

DISCUSSION QUESTIONS

1. What did you enjoy most about *Catch a Falling Star*? Did you predict the ending?

2. As the novel opens, Kendall Haynes is celebrating her thirty-sixth birthday. What words would you use to describe Kendall in these opening scenes? If you would have met her at the restaurant where she was celebrating with friends, do you think you would have liked her? Why or why not?

3. How would you describe the relationship between Griffin and Ian Walker when we first meet them in the novel? What are some of the changes in their relationship by the end of the story?

4. One of the themes of the book is the way various people respond to disappointment and unexpected circumstances in their lives. Which character's response most closely resembles yours? How would you describe their/your "MO" for dealing with life's pain?

5. Have you or someone you know been part of an adoption? Did Javan's reaction to Evie surprise you? What vulnerable desire was his anger seeking to protect?

6. How did you feel about Kendall's initial reaction to her sister's request to have the ruby ring their grandmother had given to Kendall? How did you feel when Kendall made her final decision about the ring? What would you have done? Why?

7. Another theme throughout the book is the relationship between siblings and how they navigate conflict. How would you describe the way Griffin and Ian handle conflict? What about Kendall and Bekah? Do you have siblings? How do you navigate conflict with each other (or with friends if you don't have siblings)?

8. Why does Kendall love her Jeep so much? Have you had a vehicle that you especially loved?

9. What was your initial impression of Heath Parker? How would you describe his fatal flaw?

10. How do you relate to God when you are disappointed or grieving?

11. When Kendall and her friends accompanied Rachel to look for her wedding dress, Rachel's mom shut down the process with her disapproval just as Rachel found the dress she loved. Do you relate to Rachel's fear of displeasing her mom? How do you respond in situations where you want something different from another person you respect or love? What is the difference between selfishness and self-respect?

12. What role does Doug play in Griffin's life? Do you think Griffin values their friendship? Describe. Do you have anyone like Doug in your life? What's it like for you when a friend challenges your way of thinking or attitude?

13. Have you ever had a "chance encounter" that, upon reflection, you saw as God's unexpected provision for you? How does this impact your openness to things that are not on your agenda, either for your day or your life?

14. Do you know anyone like Griffin who is the "strong and silent" type? As you got to know Griffin throughout the book, what other words would you use to describe him? What words or phrases would you like to be used to describe you?

15. How did you feel about the way the story ended?

ENHANCE YOUR BOOK CLUB

1. Read the Book of Ruth in the Old Testament. At your next book club, discuss the ways that each woman in the story responds to life not turning out exactly like they had planned or hoped. Which one do you identify with the most and why?

2. If you are married, invite a single person over for a meal this week and get to know them better. If you are single, invite a family over for a meal this week and get to know them better. Reflect on the question: "What gift does my current marital state provide as I seek to grow in my capacity to love God and others?"

3. Spend some time journaling about one way life has turned out differently than you imagined and the unexpected blessings and/or disappointment you have encountered as a result. At your next book club, discuss the ways you have wrestled with God and/or experienced His care for you.

4. Think about someone within your community who may struggle with discouragement about the current circumstances of their life. Write them a note expressing gratitude for one quality you appreciate about them.

AUTHOR Q&A

Having said that you would never write fiction, what was it like to complete your second novel?
The whole process of writing *Catch a Falling Star* was much faster than with *Wish You Were Here*, my debut novel. My first novel took three years to write; *Catch a Falling Star* was completed in four months. Why so quickly? Well, there was a deadline, of course. And I'd learned a lot in three years—all of which I applied to this story. I was excited to dive into Kendall's story because it had been perking in my brain for a year or more. She was more than ready to move to center stage.

What was your inspiration for writing Catch a Falling Star?
I knew that I wanted my heroine and hero to be older because I don't believe falling in love only happens in your twenties. And

then a conversation with my friend, Angela, became the catalyst for the entire story. I re-created part of that conversation in the chapter where Kendall and Rachel talk about being "single ladies of a certain age" while having dinner at a quaint mountain restaurant (which is real, by the way!).

Is there a character in the book that you most identify with?
Wow. Tough question. When Kendall's a bit snarky with Griffin? Um, I can be like that when I'm feeling the whole "I'm right, back down" attitude. I have learned that thinking "I'm right" is the wrong way to win an argument. I can tend to be black and white. But really, what I identified with the most was how Kendall, Griffin, and Evie each wrestled with the Story Question: What do you do when life doesn't go according to plan? Everyone faces that question. *Everyone.*

Which character was the most difficult to develop?
Evie. I knew that she wasn't a believer—and that she wasn't going to necessarily embrace the truth of God's grace by the end of the book. To me, that's real life. Sharing the truth doesn't mean that someone says, "Oh, of course! You're right! How did I not see that?!" And I wanted her story to be realistic and just as compelling as my main characters, without slowing the story down.

The experiences of singleness, adoption, and the loss of parents are prominent in the book. What led you to choose these as connection points among characters?
I write fiction—but I also write real life. So, I look at real life and then I laser in on what particular aspects of real life are going under the microscope for each novel. And those three were the ones that ended up in *Catch a Falling Star*. As far as the

topic of adoption, I've been watching a close friend walk that road for several years now. I've learned so much from her—the reality of adoption, how to walk life out in faith, choosing to love children unconditionally—and I wanted to weave that into this novel.

What do you say to someone who is living in a season of disappointment and grief about how life has turned out?
I've been there. Sometimes that season is of our own making—our choices cause the disappointment, the grief. Or sometimes others' actions hurt us and cause the grief. At one particularly tough time, I doubted God's trustworthiness. I didn't doubt the reality of God—just that I could trust him to take care of me. You know what? Doubting him didn't help me at all. By shutting God out of my life, I didn't have him to turn to when I struggled. And I didn't have him to turn to when I had reason to celebrate. But I learned a valuable lesson that transformed my relationship with God: The moment I turned back toward God, he embraced me. *Immediately.* I understand his lavish grace in such a tangible way. So, what would I say? God's in that season of disappointment and grief. You may give him the cold shoulder for a while, but he won't turn his back on you—or lose sight of you. And, truly, he will see you through it and somehow, someway, bring good out of it.

What was the hardest part of writing this story for you?
The beginning is always the hardest. I have a seed of an idea. Then I have to grow it up into an entire novel. Something with depth. With characters who are compelling. The "spark" is always exciting—but I have to ask God to breathe on it and ignite my writing into something so much more.

Did you decide on the title of Catch a Falling Star *before, during, or after you wrote the manuscript, and how did you decide on it?*
I tossed around titles while I fleshed out the story idea. By the time I sat down to write the novel, I had my title. Titles are key for me because they anchor me to my story.

Why did you pick Colorado Springs as the setting for this story?
I have to go back to my debut novel to answer that question. When I wrote *Wish You Were Here,* I had a lot to learn. (Nonfiction writer transitioning to fiction, remember?) So, I decided to set my book in Colorado because I knew that area. Easy, right? And then I decided that I love this area and it's a beautiful part of the country to live, so why not continue to use Colorado as the setting of my novels?

Do you own a Jeep?
I would like to own a Jeep. My husband's always talked about owning a Jeep. My youngest daughter now rides around town with me and points out "indoor" Jeeps versus "outdoor" Jeeps (hard tops versus soft tops). But, no, I don't own a Jeep. Yet.

Do you plan to write more fiction?
That's the plan. Yes. New characters keep showing up in my head with stories to be told.

What can we expect from you next?
Without giving too much away, I may move a bit north, possibly into Denver and Fort Collins and explore the whole "marry your best friend" mantra. And since I'm a twin, I'm mulling over a novel idea that involves twins.